PRAISE FOR
THE NOVELS OF RACHAEL HERRON

Splinters of Light

"An awesome book that grabs the reader by the heartstrings and wrings emotions from the soul in the form of tears as she expertly slices up the reality of life as seen through the eyes of a teenager, a mother, and a sister."

—Carolyn Brown, *New York Times* bestselling author of *Long, Hot Texas Summer*

"With this profoundly moving, compelling tale of a woman who is on the verge of losing everything, Rachael Herron will break your heart and then mend it again, leaving you stronger than before. Reading *Splinters of Light* is a bit like watching a trapeze artist dance nimbly across a high wire: You're left gasping in wonder at her grace and daring. And when the artist makes it safely to the other side, you cheer and want to see her do it all over again."

—Holly Robinson, author of *Beach Plum Island*

"Beautifully written and heartbreakingly real, *Splinters of Light* is a compelling examination of how the bonds between women—sisters, mothers, daughters—are tested by tragedy. The Glass family women will have you smiling in recognition and then grieving, laughing, and (consider yourself warned) sobbing along with them right up to the heartfelt ending."

—L. Alison Heller, author of *The Never Never Sisters*

continued . . .

Written by today's freshest new talents and selected by New American Library, NAL Accent novels touch on subjects close to a woman's heart, from friendship to family to finding our place in the world. The Conversation Guides included in each book are intended to enrich the individual reading experience, as well as encourage us to explore these topics together—because books, and life, are meant for sharing.

Visit us online at www.penguin.com.

"Rachael Herron has written a tenderly crafted story, compelling the reader to examine some difficult issues—single parenthood, family dynamics, and the heartbreaking realities of early-onset Alzheimer's—and handles each one with sensitivity and compassion. But the beauty of this novel lies in the strength and resilience of the love between two sisters. I closed the book and held it to my chest, full of gratitude."　　　　—Kimberly Brock, author of *The River Witch*

Pack Up the Moon

"Don't forget *Pack Up the Moon* when you're packing your bags— it's the perfect vacation or staycation read. It's filled with fiercely honest emotion, a celebration of the power of love to heal even the most broken of hearts."
　　　　—Susan Wiggs, #1 *New York Times* bestselling
author of *The Beekeeper's Ball*

"A superlative architect of story, Rachael Herron never steers away from wrenching events, and yet even moments of deepest despair are laced with threads of hope. . . . Herron is an inexhaustible champion of the healing power of love."
　　　　—Sophie Littlefield, national bestselling
author of *House of Glass*

"A heartbreaking story of loss and family that achieves an optimistic feel in the end. . . . The language [is] poetic and moving at many points."　　　　—*RT Book Reviews*

"An emotional roller coaster. . . . If you are in need of a heartfelt, highly emotional story, then look no further!"　—Dwell in Possibility

"The novel is remarkable in its poignancy and style. . . . Herron writes beautifully about the love between a parent and child. . . . *Pack Up the Moon* is a wonderful weekend read about love, loss, forgiveness, and family that leaves readers feeling grateful for their dear ones—and reaching for the tissues."　　　　—*The Gazette* (Montreal)

"A touching, emotional story based around really realistic characters who people can completely relate to. . . . It's beautiful and haunting and it's perfect."　　　　—Sunshine and Mountains Book Reviews & More

PRAISE FOR THE OTHER WORKS
OF RACHAEL HERRON

Also by Rachael Herron

Pack Up the Moon

Splinters
of *Light*

Rachael Herron

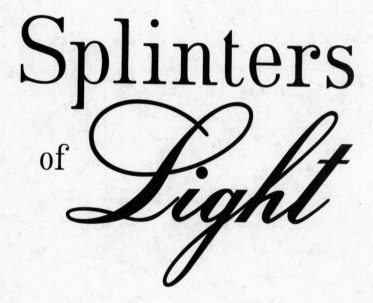

NAL
ACCENT

NAL Accent
Published by the Penguin Group
Penguin Group (USA) LLC, 375 Hudson Street,
New York, New York 10014

USA | Canada | UK | Ireland | Australia | New Zealand | India | South Africa | China
penguin.com
A Penguin Random House Company

First published by NAL Accent, an imprint of New American Library,
a division of Penguin Group (USA) LLC

First Printing, March 2015

ACCENT REGISTERED TRADEMARK—MARCA REGISTRADA

LIBRARY OF CONGRESS CATALOGING-IN-PUBLICATION DATA:
Herron, Rachael.
Splinters of light/Rachael Herron.
p. cm.
ISBN 978-0-451-46861-1 (softcover)
1. Twin sisters—Fiction.   2. Mothers and daughters—Fiction.
3. Domestic—Fiction.   I. Title.
PS3608.E7765S69 2015
813'.6—dc23   2014038529

PRINTED IN THE UNITED STATES OF AMERICA
1 3 5 7 9 10 8 6 4 2

Set in Bembo
Designed by Spring Hoteling

In honor of Alice Figueira, and the inspiring organization named for her, Alice's Embrace. And for Diane Lewis, who loved her mother like I loved mine.

Acknowledgments

While writing acknowledgments for any book, I'm always overwhelmed at how many people make a book. My deepest thanks go to my editor, Danielle Perez, for knowing what needed to be stripped away to make my characters truly come to life. Thanks as always to Susanna Einstein, one of my favorite people and the best agent in the world. I promise I'll try not to make you cry like that again. Thanks to Dana Kaye, for being the best publicist ever. I thank the crew at Zocalo, who keep me going with coffee and grins: Evelyn, Tom, Winnie, Cathy, Kat, Buddy, Ed, and everyone else. Thanks go to A. J. Larrieu, who knows her epigenetics from her heritability (any errors in science are mine alone). Thanks to one of my favorite firefighters, Lucas Hirst, who gave me lots of info I chose not to use, and thanks to my coworkers/friends at the firehouse, who, when I have to go do writing business, cover my shifts for me without complaining (within my earshot, anyway). Huge thanks to Rebecca Beeson, who endured many twin questions and is a beautiful writer herself. To Sophie Littlefield, thank you for propping me up so much during the writing of this book that I should probably build you a flying buttress or something. To Cari Luna, thank you for loving me even after I stole your rocks. To Lala Hulse, always, my love and gratitude for everything—I couldn't do any of this without you, not one single little bit. And to my sisters, Christy and Bethany Herron, who are and always will be my two best friends. You are the ones I will never let go.

Some days the rock I keep in my pocket feels like comfort. Other days it feels like a weapon.

—Cari Luna

The lesson:

memory, which once seemed impermeable, had always been
a muslin, spilling the self out like water, so that one became

a new species of naïf and martyr. And us, we're made a cabal
of medieval scholars speculating how many splinters of light

make up her diminishing core, how much we might harvest before
she disappears.

—from "Beasts" by Carmen Giménez Smith

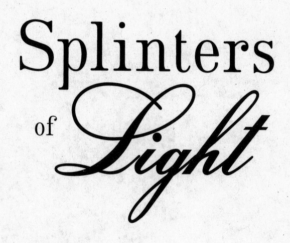

Splinters
of *Light*

Chapter One

EXCERPT,
**WHEN ELLIE WAS LITTLE:
OUR LIFE IN HOLIDAYS,**
PUBLISHED 2011 BY NORA GLASS

New Year's Eve

When Ellie was little, she and I changed all the rules. After my husband left, it was just me and my little girl (and my twin sister, but she's implied in everything I do). The cozy insularity of our little nuclear family became something to be feared overnight. Members of the PTA looked at me as if my husband's abandonment were something catching. If Paul had died, we would have received condolence calls, hamburger casseroles, and brownies made from scratch. But because he moved fifty miles east with Bettina the blond bookkeeper, because he started a new roofing company and a new family all at once, all we got were pitying looks in the school parking lot and small, halfhearted waves.

So we changed all the rules, starting with the hardest part: the holidays.

This is how we do New Year's Eve at my house. We don't go out. I'm scared of driving with all the drunks on the road after midnight, and besides, why would you start a New Year anywhere but in your own home, where you feel the safest, the most loved? (Once, when she was eight, Ellie begged to be allowed to spend New Year's Eve at her friend Samantha's house, but she didn't even make it till nine p.m. before calling me to come get her. "Lemon and honey, Mama," she said. "They don't do that here.")

We get to do whatever we want on New Year's Eve. There's so very little left of the year to damage that we figure if we spend the evening watching the entire *Die Hard* series, no one will mind. We eat what we want, too. Sick of holiday candy and chocolate by that point, we choose things at the grocery store like fancy pickles and ham poked with rosemary sprigs. We like ropes of salty black licorice that we get at a candy store on Tiburon Boulevard. The girls behind the counter always wince when we ask for half a pound, and once one of them admitted we were the only ones she'd ever sold it to. I make a sweet, fruity bread similar to German stollen that's supposed to be eaten for breakfast, but we eat it for dinner instead, sliced thinly, served cold, and slathered thickly with butter. I can eat six pieces before I start to feel sick, and Ellie, as small as she is, can pack away even more.

We also get to wear whatever we want. One year Ellie wore a blue two-piece bathing suit with a pink tutu. I wouldn't let her get too close to the fireplace for fear a spark would set her entire acrylic ensemble ablaze. When she got cold, she wrapped my black terry robe around her thin shoulders and trailed the length of it behind her like a vampire cloak.

In more recent years, we've taken to having a pajama party. New pajamas are de rigueur, carefully bought with the New Year in mind. Last year mine were dark blue, covered with grumpy-looking sheep wearing sweaters. Ellie's were green flannel with cowboys roping monkeys.

When the time grows near, we don't watch the prerecorded ball drop in New York. Even at a distance, it's too much of a party for us homebodies, my daughter and me. Instead, we keep an anxious eye on the clock, as if it might not get all the way to midnight if we don't watch it carefully. Both of us pretend no one else has slipped into the New Year yet. New Zealand hasn't already celebrated. New Yorkers aren't already in bed. In our snug home above Belvedere Cove, we are the first in the whole world to greet the early seconds of a newly minted year.

Then my Ellie goes to the front door and, with great solemnity, opens it to let the year inside. We make our tea, and *this* is the most important step.

It springs from a New Year's Eve when Ellie was sick with the flu, sicker than she'd ever been. She was four. Paul had left us a month before. I'd hoped Ellie would sleep through the night so I could cry alone on the couch at midnight as I watched happy couples kiss in Times Square.

But instead, she woke and came out of her room. She stumbled over the long feet of her favorite bunny-footed pajamas, coughing so hard she sounded like a dog barking.

I had a cooling cup of mint tea in front of me, and I had an idea.

I carried her onto the back porch, where, under a full moon, she picked a lemon off our tree. We squeezed the whole thing into the mug, and then I let her add a big spoonful of honey to it.

"Lemon," I said, "because the New Year might be a little sad, like a lemon is sour."

"Because of Papa?" Her eyes were wet with another coughing fit. They were Paul's eyes, so bright green it hurt to look at her sometimes. "Because he doesn't want to be with us?"

"With me, honey. You know he wants to be with you. Papa loves you." Paul, though, was too busy then soothing his very pregnant new wife to have any real time for his daughter, something that made me mad enough to spit acid in the direction of Modesto. "But we add honey because the year will be sweet, too."

She was asleep ten minutes after drinking the tea, her breathing easier in her chest. Mine was easier, too, knowing she hurt less.

I didn't think she'd remember it, but the next year, when she was five, she put on the same footed pajamas, even though they were by then too small, and tucked her body into her favorite corner of the couch. She looked up at me. "Lemon and honey?"

When my daughter kissed me at midnight that year, I missed my old life a tiny bit less than I had the previous New Year's. Paul was becoming more and more adept at dodging phone calls from his first daughter as he busied himself with his new family, but his leaving us meant I got this little girl all to myself. A girl with his blond eyebrows and my concern for wrongs to be righted. A little girl who liked to suck the rinds of our homegrown lemons (making faces all the while) as much as she liked to lick the honey spoon I handed her in the kitchen.

So this year, I wish you more honey than lemon. And I wish it for all your years to come.

Chapter Two

"I'm not wearing those," said Ellie. She remained where she was, lying flat on her back on her bed, her cell phone held above her face with a hand that floated, the phone seemingly weightless.

Nora said, "But these are the ones you asked for."

Ellie blew out her breath in a whoosh. "I was *kidding*."

How was Nora possibly supposed to know that? "I gave you the catalog a month ago and that's what you stuck your Post-it note on." Nora had thought the light pink pajamas with the ducklings had looked impossibly juvenile for her sixteen-year-old daughter, but she'd felt a warm glow as she'd clicked buy. It was proof that her little girl could still be just that—little. She'd even started a column: "Big Girls Still Like Footie PJs."

"I picked the ugliest pair of pajamas in the whole catalog and you thought I was serious," Ellie said. It wasn't a question.

The hurt was shallow—like a sharp jab under the nail—but it stung, nonetheless. "Okay, I'll wear them, then." They were almost the same size, a fact that surprised Nora every time Ellie raided her closet.

The phone jerked in her daughter's hand. Good. She'd gotten a reaction, at least.

"You can't."

"I could. Would you really mind that much?"

Ellie sat up, tucking the phone under her thigh. "Aunt Mariana is coming over."

"Yep."

"I bet *she* won't be wearing dumb baby pajamas."

Nora's twin, Mariana, still seemed cool to Ellie. Nora herself had lost the ability to be anything but pathetic to her daughter this year. No, that wasn't quite true, she acknowledged to herself. Ellie also thought her mother was naive, overly enthusiastic about too many things, and possibly stupid.

Nora refolded the pajama top and put it on top of Ellie's bureau. She used the cuff of her sleeve to rub off a water-glass ring. She'd have to take the Pledge to it later, when Ellie wasn't in the room to complain about the lemon smell.

"Mom." In Ellie's voice was the apology Nora had gotten used to not receiving in words. "You gotta see that's horrible. Right? You can see that?"

Nora stroked a flannel duck's head. "I guess if I'd stopped to really think about it, I would have been concerned about your choice." Instead, she'd been pleased that Ellie had taken a moment to choose anything at all. "I should have taken you to Macy's. Or Target. They have cute pajamas." Wanting to stop talking but unable to prevent her lips from moving, she said, "Want to go now? They're open till at least nine. We could make it and be back for—"

"No, thanks." The phone hovered above her daughter's head again. Ellie had hit sixteen years old like it was her job, like she was going to get a bonus from her boss if she could be the biggest pain in the ass possible. She didn't clean her room without threats of physical violence, and she had mastered the art of making Nora feel like something not even worth pulling off the bottom of a shoe.

"Have you played that game yet?"

"Which one?"

In trying to find her daughter a Christmas present she wouldn't hate, Nora had researched which multiplayer online games were most popular for Ellie's demographic. She'd used her Twitter account for the research since it was a safe bet Ellie never looked at her feed. Nora's followers, mostly longtime readers who were also parents and often single, had overwhelmed her with suggestions. *Queendom* seemed like a game Nora could get behind—with its feminist slant, women ruled the game's domain, and Ulra, the Dragon Queen, was both the ultimate monster and the creature players wanted to become.

"Uh-uh."

"Why not?"

Ellie raised her head and met Nora's eyes briefly. Then her head dropped back to the bedspread again. Her thumbs spun and danced over the phone's keyboard.

"Fine," said Nora. "I can see you're busy."

"It just seems like something *girls* would play."

Nora switched on the night-light—a tiny dark-haired fairy peeping out from behind the moon—even though Ellie hadn't slept with it on for at least three years. "You're a girl. In case you hadn't noticed." What Nora wanted was for Ellie to scoot sideways, offering her—even tacitly—a place to sit. A moment to talk.

"You know what I mean."

"It's a storytelling game. You get to narrate the action. And you're so good at writing—"

"No, I'm not. You always forget I'm not you."

Nora played her trump card. "And almost half of the players are male."

Ellie rolled to her side, newly interested. "Where did you read *that*?"

"Somewhere online, in all of my vast and far-reaching research into the game that you would like the most."

"How long did you spend doing that?"

Not long enough. "Days."

"Yeah?"

"Okay, at *least* two hours."

"Oooh." Ellie's tone was sarcastic, but Nora could tell she'd scored a point.

One measly point, racked up against Ellie's three million or so. It still felt good. "What *are* you going to wear tonight?"

"Isn't the whole point to wear whatever we want? I mean, that's what you wrote in that god-awful book."

A person could die of paper cuts, given enough blood loss. Nora had run every essay in *When Ellie Was Little* by her daughter before it was published, giving the then twelve-year-old Ellie ultimate say over what could and couldn't be published. She'd objected to one line that called her baby cheeks "pudgy," but the rest had stood. They never talked about the book, just like they didn't talk about Nora's lifestyles column for the *Sentinel*.

"Yes."

"Then I'm just wearing what I'm wearing now."

"Great." It was so *stupid* for Nora to want to argue with her. Of course it was fine if Ellie came downstairs in an antique Sonic Youth T-shirt and jeans.

"Great!" Ellie flopped back to the bedspread. Sometimes Nora thought what Ellie was best at was that backward dive. Forget the fact that she was in calculus, the only junior in the class, forget that she placed first in honors English—what Ellie could make a full-time job of was falling backward with a sigh so heavy it seemed likely to pull down the ceiling with her someday.

She didn't close Ellie's door behind her, but she heard the soft *thunk* of the door shutting before she reached the stairs.

Nora hated closed doors.

Chapter Three

A new tradition for New Year's Eve. An extra one.

That's what they needed.

Nora sat on the back porch with the plastic Michael's craft store bag at her side. It was balmy out, surprising for this time of year. Usually late December brought cold winds and thick fog to this section of the coast. Even as protected as the marina town of Tiburon was by the San Francisco Bay, it still got bitterly cold overnight sometimes, frost forming on the gnarled twists of hobbyist grapevines in backyards, ice coating the Mercedes and Land Rover windows.

That night, though, was warm enough for Nora sit outside with nothing more than Paul's old red flannel over her T-shirt. It was the best thing he'd left, besides his daughter, whom he wanted no part of, rat bastard. Nora looked down the hill and over the Smythes' new roof, past the Miller-Reids' redwood, which really needed trimming, down to the boats bobbing in the dark water. Most of them still bore their Christmas lights, a week old but still cheery. The boats looked tiny from the six-block distance, brightly lit toys left behind in a vast tub of black ink. The air smelled of pine and, faintly, of car exhaust.

From the bag, Nora took three fat white candles. The fake vanilla scent was almost strong enough to banish the smell of the trees. *Deodorizing the outdoors.* She took out the scraps of lace she'd bought, idly running the longest one through her fingers. What next? Instead of gluing the fabric to the candles, instead of perusing the magazines she'd brought outside with her for inspiring images to snip out with her paper scissors, she continued to stare into the night, seeing the inside of the doctor's office rather than the top of her back fence.

It should be more worrying, this staring habit of hers. It had been getting worse lately. A lot worse. That new inability to concentrate, something Nora had always excelled at, was the reason she'd gone to the doctor eight weeks before, the reason she'd done the first panel of blood work. She was forty-four. Too young to be starting menopause, but maybe she was hitting perimenopause. Maybe the doctor would give her supplements or instructions to go to acupuncture more often.

Then the office had called back, requesting more blood. Nora was pleased. They were taking it seriously. The next thing on her doctor's very thorough list was a neuropsychological test. It had been strangely exhilarating, doing silly tasks like drawing the face of a clock and explaining how the hands worked, demonstrating how to tie her left shoe. That was followed by another, shorter pen-and-pencil test during which they asked more seemingly random questions. Memory work. Then a PET scan of her brain, something that would measure the uptake of sugar, they said.

Nora had thought the doctor's overreaction was a good sign, solid proof that she had excellent insurance. But the week before, she'd begun to feel as if she were a scientific pincushion, someone they were just pushing for fun—*See how much blood she'll give us. Lay your bets on the table!* Maybe Nora was an experiment. She had consoled herself with the fact that she was probably good at it. She was acing their exams, whatever they were. She smiled when they jabbed her with needles that looked like straws, and she got to know the names of the phlebotomist's kids. He had two, Juan and Roberto. He was as white as sourdough, raised in the inland valley, but his wife was Latina, and she'd gotten to name the kids. She was pregnant again, this time with a girl, and she was going to let him name her. Nora told him with mock seriousness, *Nora's a good name. Sure,* he said, agreeing with her, but she could tell it wouldn't make the short list.

No one had diagnosed her with anything yet. She was getting older, that was all. Everyone had the same affliction, and at least she had her column in which to work it out. Whatever it was, she was sure she'd be able to milk it for both humor and a paycheck. She wasn't very worried. When her blood work came back, it didn't support a cancer diagnosis, and after she'd heard that, she'd relaxed. With any luck it would be something embarrassing. Her biggest reader response always came after her confessionals: *My daughter came as close to asking me for a divorce as she ever has. While sanitizing my Diva cup in boiling water, I let the pot go dry, and the cup caught on fire while Ellie was studying in the living room with three friends. If you've never smelled a burning menstrual cup, you've never lived, my friends. I had to shove cinnamon sticks up my nose while I aired out the place, and my daughter refused to talk to me until I promised never to say the word "menses" out loud ever again.* Her e-mail would blow up with shared mother-daughter humiliation stories.

Telling stories about getting older, being diagnosed with small strange ailments (corns, joint aches, vision degeneration), would just be good fodder. Memory lapses, the kind she'd been having lately, were more annoying than worrisome.

She blinked, unsure how long she'd been staring over the treetops.

With the marina lights still twinkling below, Nora took out

the tiny bottle of glue she'd bought at the craft store. It wasn't like she didn't have at least ten bottles of glue already in her craft room, but when she'd been at the store, she couldn't remember what kind she had. Mod Podge? Wood glue? Elmer's? Standing in the glue aisle, she couldn't even picture what her craft room looked like. Funny, really. Years ago she'd spent so much time setting up that space, which had been a wine cellar for the previous owners. She and Paul didn't drink much more than the wine they bought at the grocery store, and they'd laughed about a whole climate-controlled room just for alcohol. She'd rolled her fabric so that it fit in the wine bottle nooks. Her yarn fit in the round holes, perfectly—she could fit two, sometimes three skeins in each. She'd added two long wooden tables, an OttLite, and a space heater. Nora loved it down there, and so had Ellie before crafting had gotten embarrassing.

Before Nora couldn't remember what glue she had.

She'd bought a little bottle of Aleene's, just in case.

"Nora?"

She jumped, dropping the bottle of glue. It skidded away from her, off the side of the deck, and she heard it making tiny crashes as it rolled down the steep hill toward the Smythes' fence line.

Mariana said, "What are you doing out here?"

"I was . . ." What had she been going to do? "These candles."

"Ellie said you've been out here in the dark for an hour."

"No, I haven't." Nora glanced at her watch. Almost ten. "Damn."

Mariana was wearing a ripped black leather jacket and a ragged blue scarf, the first one Nora had ever knitted. Her jeans were frayed at the knees. Her shoes were the exception to her outfit—they were purple leather boots that had probably cost more than all of Ellie's fall school clothes put together. How many times had Nora mentioned that her sister might do better saving money, rather than buying four-hundred-dollar shoes that couldn't be worn in the rain?

"You must be freezing," Mariana said. She took off the scarf and wrapped it around Nora's throat.

"You're not wearing your pajamas," said Nora. It had gotten cold, she suddenly realized. An ache had seeped into her lower legs, as if she'd been jogging too much lately, whereas the truth was she couldn't remember her last run. "I can't remember," she said.

"What?" Mariana's smile lit her whole face.

That face. Nora loved it—it was her own visage, reflected back at her but prettier. Everything a little better than her own. Mariana's eyes had more hints of cocoa and spice, whereas Nora's were plain crayon brown. Mariana's chin was defined and firm; Nora's was getting a little weak, she knew. Even though they were fraternal, they'd looked identical enough to trick people growing up. And now, it was just nice, seeing her own face look so pretty on someone else.

"What do you mean?" asked Mariana again. The wind lifted her long brown hair—smoother and shinier than Nora's—and she tugged it back.

"Nothing." Nora shook her head to clear it and then touched the scarf. It smelled of Mariana, of patchouli and gardenia, sweet and spicy at the same time. "I should make you a new scarf. This looks awful."

"Nah," her sister said. "I like this one. Let's go inside, huh?" Mariana linked her arm with Nora's and, as if it were her house and not Nora's, led her up the three steps and inside.

Chapter Four

Something was wrong with Nora.

When their eyes met on the back porch, Mariana could tell. Something was different—not missing, not even out of place. It was just off enough that Mariana couldn't quite touch it. It was just a feeling. Her friend Beth could read auras. "Hey, we should do lunch with Beth soon."

Nora didn't even look at her as she spilled the bag of lace on the kitchen counter. She poked through the pieces as if looking for something important.

Mariana lined up the candles and tugged at their wicks until they stood at attention. "Look. I'm turning them on. Get it?"

Nora rolled her eyes. *That* was more like her.

"Okay, tell me what you were going to do with these."

Nora's voice was defensive, as if they'd been arguing about it. "They're wishing candles. For wishes."

"Well, yeah. I would guess that's what wishing candles were

for. How do they work?" Mariana examined a bit of lace. She held it up to her eyes and peeked through the holes.

"You pick a word for the new year. Then you carve the word into the side of the candle, and when we burn them together, the words will come true the next year."

Such a Martha Stewart–Nora thing to do. "I like it," said Mariana, and it was true. "What's the glitter and the lace for?"

A short pause. "For whatever you like. Decoration."

"But if you cover the candles with lace, then where do we carve the—"

"Never mind." Nora swept everything back into the bag. "It doesn't matter. It's fine if it's not your thing."

"I didn't say—"

"Did you bring the screwdriver Luke was going to lend me?"

Mariana *knew* she'd forgotten something. As usual. "Crap, I'm sorry."

Nora folded the top of the bag tightly. "It's fine. I'll just buy one. Where's Ellie?"

"She said she was going up—"

"Ellie!" Nora bellowed up the staircase as if she'd lost her daughter on a crowded beach.

Something was definitely wrong with Mariana's sister. She didn't *look* different. It was like when a computer screen started that slight flickering. It was visible only when you looked sideways at it.

Mariana steered Nora by the shoulders to the refrigerator. "I'm *starving*." She wasn't, but her twin loved nothing more than someone asking for food. "I bet you have something amazing in there."

Nora blinked as if just noticing for the first time that Mariana had arrived. "I do. I totally do."

"Great. I'll eat just about anything at this point." Luke had brought home sushi, bags of it. He always bought twelve rolls, never believing her that they wouldn't eat more than three or four. Mariana couldn't imagine stuffing anything else in her mouth ever again. But she'd do it for Nora.

"I got figs and I made those bacon-cheese biscuits you like. Oh, and I have the best goat cheese. A local gal makes it."

This was better. "Yeah? Do you know how she processes it?" There was very little that Mariana could imagine caring less about than how a Marin local made cheese in her backyard dairy, but Nora's eyes lit up.

"She showed me everything, and I got to meet the goats when I went to pick up my second order."

"You're *kidding*. Get it?"

"They were darling." Nora took out a plate, prearranged of course, and knocked the door of the fridge closed with her hip. With her other hand, she slid two glasses off the wine rack, cleverly not breaking them the way Mariana would have had she tried that maneuver. "They jump, did you know that? Straight up into the air, like, well . . . like little goats, I guess. And their eyes looked like they were stuck on sideways."

Mariana looked at the plate with growing distrust. "Huh."

"The males and females are kept separate because they'll start to breed at six weeks old. Think about *that*. I met Wallace and Gromit in her yard, and then I met Cliff and Clair in the pen."

"As in Huxtable?"

"Oh!" Nora stopped pouring the white wine into Mariana's glass, the liquid splashing to the countertop. She laughed. "I didn't make that connection. One of the babies in the yard was Vanessa, I think. That's kind of great." She mopped up the spilled wine with a pristine white dish towel.

"So the woman who makes cheese is our age."

Nora tilted her head again, as if checking in with someone before answering.

Mariana felt a thump in the middle of her chest. "Nora?"

"Yeah. I guess you're right. I just assumed she was older than us."

"Why?" Mariana settled herself on a kitchen stool.

"Don't you do that nowadays?" Nora pushed the glass toward Mariana and filled her own. "Meet women you think are older, like middle-aged, and then you find out they're our age? And it's *us* who are middle-aged?"

Mariana nodded. "Oh, my god. Yes. And you're shocked, convinced you look better than them, but you can't be sure." It had happened just that afternoon at Luke's motorcycle shop. Mariana had caught herself noticing Eliza's roots, thin sparkles of silver showing at her part. Then she'd realized that if she let her own hair grow out more than four weeks, it would have exactly the same white shine. "I do it all the time. But you look great," said Mariana.

Nora glanced at her distractedly. "I don't."

"Really?" If Nora didn't think she looked good, it was a judgment on Mariana. Sure, they weren't identical, but they were close enough. "Did I tell you the other day at Whole Foods a woman accosted me and told me she loved my book?"

That got Nora's attention. "Really?"

"Yep."

"She recognized me?"

"Well, the point here is she recognized you by looking at *me*, but yeah."

"Oh." Nora twisted the stem of her glass. "That's so nice."

"I thought so."

"What did you say?"

"That I didn't know what she was talking about."

"You *didn't*."

Mariana longed to move to the couch, to sprawl. It had been a long day, and she was perched almost formally on the stool. "Of course not. I thanked her sweetly and told her she'd made my day."

"Thank you for that." Nora dampened a sponge and started scrubbing at an invisible mark on the countertop.

"Come on, you think I don't get PR?" Mariana had to be

perfect in the minds of her app subscribers. She'd known that when she'd started BreathingRoom, her meditation application, which was just starting to take off—she just hadn't known how hard it would be to continue pulling it off.

Nora didn't look up from the sponge. "Sorry. The app, I know. You get it."

"Hang on. If you scrub at that counter any more, you're going to reach the basement." Mariana slid off the stool and picked up both their glasses. "I've been sitting at my desk all day—" She saw her sister thin her lips. Naturally. Nora didn't believe it yet, but the app *would* be important. This time, this venture: Mariana could *feel* it. Everyone wanted to meditate, and no one knew how. Mariana might be a fuckup in a lot of ways, but she knew how to sit, how to be mindful, how to breathe. She knew how to say it, how to talk people through it. The app, with its instructional guided meditations, was going to be her ticket. BreathingRoom would take off. Any day now.

She chose the big red chair and a half Nora had bought on her advice years ago. "I still think this is the most comfortable thing in the house. Besides my bed. So tell me. What's wrong? I can tell something is."

"Speaking of your bed, are you staying over tonight?"

"I think so. I don't want to cross the bridge with the crazies after midnight."

Nora grinned at her. "Sleepover!"

It was silly. They were forty-four, and still the prospect of a sleepover with her sister and niece made Mariana giddily happy. Popcorn and silly movies and staying up too late (till midnight tonight, obviously, maybe later), followed by a lazy morning in Nora's perfect kitchen. Nora knew how much Mariana loved fresh orange juice and always had it made, squeezed by hand, by the time Mariana wandered downstairs. In return, Mariana—the pancake queen—would flip perfect chocolate chip pancakes, one after another, for Nora, who could pack away an astounding number of them. Once her sister had managed to eat seventeen while Mariana and Ellie roared with laughter. "I'll make pancakes for you."

"I hoped you would. But where's Luke?"

"Home," Mariana said shortly. He'd been going to come, but then they'd had that stupid fight. Again. She didn't want to talk about him, though. "Hey, you're avoiding my question. Are you okay? You're all distracted and weird."

"I'm fine."

"You're not." Nora had that face on, the one Mariana knew better than her own. The one that said she wasn't going to answer the question straightforwardly. But Nora was the other half of her coin. Mariana knew exactly how to flip her into the air. "Where's Harrison?"

Nora was ready for it. Smoothly, she said, "Next door, I'd assume."

"Has Ellie used her Christmas present from him yet?"

"Just once. Why he thought a sixteen-year-old would like a turquoise and yellow backpack, I'm not sure, but she filled it with her library books yesterday before she left and made sure she went to ask him a question first. Then she actually took it with her to the library, if you can believe it."

Mariana could. Ellie had always been good at taking care of other people's feelings. She looked over her shoulder at the front door. "So come on. Is he really not coming over?"

"He said he might but not to look for him. He might fall asleep early."

"When are you two going to fuck and get it over with?"

"Mariana!" One of Nora's legs shot out and kicked the coffee table.

With some difficulty, Mariana stopped herself from laughing. "You always say you don't think of him like that, but—"

"Stop."

It was the way Nora said it. Her voice was thready. Thin.

Usually Nora's next-door neighbor was a topic ripe for teasing. They laughed about him when he wasn't there, and Mariana was comfortable enough with him to tease him to his face. She liked the man, genuinely enjoyed his company, and she'd suspected for years that if Harrison weren't so into dating women with half his IQ, he and her sister would have had a fling a long time ago, getting it out of their systems.

The strange look that crossed her sister's face did more to unnerve Mariana than anything else had.

"Oh, my god. Nora. You slept with him."

"No," Nora started, but her word was cut off by something that sounded like a cough even though she maintained the same facial expression.

Mariana flipped her legs off the arm of the chair and slid into a seated position on the floor next to Nora's knees. "You did."

"I didn't *mean* to."

Mariana's spine loosened with relief. Just a man. Just a boy problem. Easiest thing in the world. Luke's hurt face flashed into her mind.

"Tell me everything." She rested her head against the couch's seat cushion. "If you leave one single word out, I will know, and I will bite you in the kneecap, I swear to god."

Chapter Five

*N*ora didn't know where to start. She couldn't believe she'd kept it a secret from Mariana for so many weeks.

In front of her, Mariana leaned forward and bared her teeth, aiming for her knee. "I'll do it," she growled. "I'll bite you so hard . . . *Tell* me."

"It was just once."

Mariana narrowed her eyes. "Are you lying to me?"

"No."

"Soooo hot," her sister drawled. "A one-night stand with your best friend."

"*You're* my best friend. Duh." Nora hated it when Mariana called Harrison that. It wasn't like you got a choice when you were a twin. Nora's best friend had been chosen in utero forty-four years prior. If Mariana had ended up being a psychopathic serial killer, it would have just meant that Nora's best friend was on death row.

She took a deep breath and placed a hand over her belly-button.

Mariana clapped twice. "Your best male friend. Whatever. Tell me."

"There's not much to tell."

"You're *killing* me. So. When?"

Nora felt her face color.

"Oh, Nora. How long ago? You didn't tell me?" Mariana's voice was hurt.

They talked to each other. Every day. They always had, about everything. And yet, even yet, sometimes nothing was said.

"Eight weeks. Maybe nine."

Mariana swallowed. Her neck was an inch longer than Nora's—they'd measured once, when Nora had realized she wasn't the same swan her sister was. "Wow."

"I'm so sorry—" Eight weeks was an eternity not to tell her sister something this big. She told Mariana when Whole Foods ran out of the local Zocalo dark roast she loved best. She told her about her bad dreams. But she hadn't told her about Harrison. Why?

Mariana waved her hand. "No, stop."

"But—"

"Really, you'll just end up making it worse."

The words made Nora want to take back the apology, as sincere as it had been. There was no *rule* she had to tell Mariana anything at all. She hadn't broken any laws. "It's really not a big deal, anyway."

Mariana's hand crept up to grip the edge of the couch cushion her head leaned against. "You didn't do anything wrong by not telling me. I'm sorry I reacted like that. Tell me everything."

Her smile was an antidote to everything that hurt inside Nora. "Okay."

"Most importantly, was it good?"

Nora folded her lips around her smile.

"Right *on*. More, please. Is he hung?"

Nora could only squeak. She held a finger to her lips and

looked over her shoulder toward the staircase. It had been years since Ellie had hidden there, listening, but it could still happen.

"The reason I ask," Mariana continued, "is because of his hands. They're small. But I think they're the deceptive kind of small, because his feet are frickin' enormous. Remember when we went to the lake a few years back with Ellie and him? I couldn't take my eyes off what was in his flip-flops."

"Seriously?"

"I mentioned it to you then."

"If you did, I blocked that out completely." Harrison had brought an intelligent-looking but not-quite-smart-enough law student who hadn't understood the importance of sunblock and had ended up with a blistered sunburn. Nora had shared her aloe vera gel.

Mariana shrugged, tucking her fist under her chin, catching it between her jaw and clavicle. "'Friends with benefits' isn't a phrase because it never happens. Happens all the time. Look at me and Luke."

"You met him in a bar and"—Nora broke off before almost whispering—"*slept* with him the night you met."

"Yeah, but then he became my friend. Okay, and then my boyfriend. But whatever."

Nora shook her head, but her heart felt light, like it was made of paper. She hadn't realized how much she'd hated keeping the secret from her sister.

"Anyway. This isn't about me. More." Mariana rocked forward and backward once, tapping Nora's knee with her forehead. "How did it start?"

"We had too much wine. Isn't that always how it happens?"

"Where was Ellie?"

"At Samantha's."

"Ah. So you had too much wine on purpose."

"No." But she had. *They* had. She knew that. It was nice to have something to blame it on. The next morning, Harrison had rolled over with such a *look*, and it had cut something inside her, sliced her heart in a way she knew she couldn't handle. He wanted more. She hadn't seen that coming. *Oh, man,* she'd said to him. *I drank so much last night. Can hardly remember a thing!* She'd seen him pull back, a hurt snail retreating into its beloved shell. *Yeah. Me, too.*

They hadn't talked about it. Not once in two months. He'd tried bringing it up one night, but she'd asked him not to. He'd complied.

"Whatever it was, I blew it."

"Oh, my god." Mariana sat up, wrapping her arms around her knees. "That means you're admitting there was something to blow."

"No, I didn't . . ."

Mariana scrambled to her feet. "I'm going over there and dragging his ass over here."

"No."

"What?" Her sister cocked a hip. "I thought he was your best friend. Your other one."

"Don't," said Nora, feeling as if they were in high school again and Mariana was teasing her, cajoling her to talk to boys when she could barely look at them. "Please don't." Tears thickened in her throat. Good grief, it wasn't that serious. Mariana was teasing. Nora sucked in a breath. She couldn't *cry* about it. God, don't let Mariana see . . .

But she had. "Oh, honey. No. I'm sorry. Please, don't . . ." Mariana sunk to the couch, pressing her knees against Nora's. "Please don't cry. You know how I get when you do."

It was true. Sometimes it seemed like nothing in the whole world could truly upset Mariana except for seeing Nora cry. When Paul left, Mariana would climb behind Nora in her bed, unable to look her in the face while she howled, wrapping her arms around her, able to console Nora only from the back, only from where she was safe from the tears. When hit face-to-face with them (in the kitchen, at the grocery store), her cheeks went pale, her skin tone almost sallow. Nora suspected Mariana felt physically ill when she cried, actually experiencing nausea. It must be nice to be so strong you felt queasy in the face of weakness.

"It's New Year's Eve," said Mariana desperately. "You can't cry. It's bad luck. Or something. Have some goat cheese. Think of the kids." A pause. "Get it?"

The damned crying—maybe it was a symptom of something. She *really* wanted to google it, but she was worried it would confirm a perimenopause diagnosis. Every day for at least the last five or six weeks, she'd either fought off tears or given in to them somewhere quietly, privately. Once Ellie had almost caught her, but she'd pleaded something was in her contact lenses, and Ellie, who didn't seem to be able to notice anyone but herself lately, had bought it.

Tears trickled down Nora's face. She wiped them away impatiently. "I'm not crying."

"You are. God, Jesus, you are. *Stop* it. Please?" Mariana's hands were fists in front of her belly.

"Are we going to box?"

"Will it stop you from crying?"

"I swear to everything holy, I'm not crying. This stupid water keeps coming out of my eyes. I think it's allergies."

From the direction of the kitchen came Ellie's voice. She'd sneaked down the stairs—when? How much had she heard? "Mom?"

She sounded young. Small. "We're in here. Just talking," called Nora, scrubbing at her cheeks with the backs of her hands.

"No, here. Don't." Mariana used a napkin, one of the cheerful poinsettia ones Nora had sewed herself, using discounted post-Christmas fabric she'd found one year. They had prompted an essay, actually, about finding joy in craft store sale bins.

Mariana blotted carefully. "There. Blink. Good."

"Where's that cheese?" Ellie poked her head into the room.

"In here, chipmunk. Come give me a hug," said Mariana.

Nora watched the two of them embrace. Her sister and her daughter. If Mariana couldn't handle tears, at least she handled happiness well. She was used to it, after all. Inside, Nora felt a tiny bloom of fear, a terrified algae spreading through her blood. She reached into her jeans pocket to touch the piece of beach glass she kept there. Smooth and warm, as usual.

Then she stood with them. "I want more wine. Ellie? Sparkling apple cider? It's your favorite." She ignored the eye roll that went along with her daughter's assent.

They'd celebrate the New Year, by god, even if she had to drag them both along behind her.

Chapter Six

"Ten, nine, eight . . ."

Maybe Ellie could tell Aunt Mariana about what had happened. Later. When the house was dark and her aunt was in the guest bed. Maybe she could sneak in and tell her.

"Seven . . ."

No. There wasn't anything to tell.

Three pairs of eyes were trained on Ellie's phone, which she'd propped up against one of those candles Mom had said she wanted to carve but then hadn't done anything with except light. She should have cleaned her screen. The black background of the clock was showing all the smudges, especially at the bottom where the keyboard normally was.

"Six . . ."

What would happen in the next year? A year and a half of high school felt like forever, but then she'd be somewhere else. Smith, if she was lucky, far away. Smith was her first choice, the college she'd spent the most time imagining herself at. It was the largest of the Seven Sisters colleges. Any school that had turned out both Julia Child and Madeleine L'Engle was a good place to be, Ellie figured. UCLA was on the short list, too, and she was considering Portland, even though she had no clue what she wanted to do. To be. It was only the rest of her *life* at stake.

"We know you'll pick the school that's best for you," her mother would say. "We stayed close to home, and we both regret it sometimes. You'll make the right decision."

No pressure, though.

It usually didn't bother Ellie to hear her mother or her aunt talk about herself in the plural form—both of them did it, practically unconsciously. Every once in a while, though, it made Ellie feel lonely. Like she was the only one who didn't get someone. She'd never have a person, not like they did. Mom and Mariana had been born together—Ellie couldn't compete with that. Her half sister, TeeTee, was eleven and a total brat. She competed in beauty pageants, for god's sake. Her stepmom totally did the whole makeup and puffy hair *Toddlers and Tiaras* thing. It was creepy.

Sometimes Ellie thought she could almost remember when her dad was actively still being her dad instead of just some guy who sent money to her mom and called her once a month to apologize—again—about how busy his life was and how he couldn't come pick her up to have lunch even though he lived only an hour away. Other days she wondered if she was just making up the memories, crafting them from photographs, stitching them together with wishes like her mom stuck rickrack to kitschy potholders.

Sometimes she just wanted to be the most important person to someone. That was all. If she'd said it out loud, Mom would have denied it—would have said that she loved Ellie best of all. But she knew the truth. She was okay with it, mostly.

Now that Mom and Harrison had done the deed, they'd probably shack up, too. They were probably already talking about her going away to college so they could have sex in every room. Loud, middle-aged, horrifying sex. You would think once anyone hit *forty*, they would give up on the idea. What was the point? Also, *gross*. Ellie had suspected it, sure, from the way her mom suddenly stopped going to Harrison's house for her glass of wine at night. Yeah, Ellie was out of the house one night and suddenly they couldn't look at each other? It had been pretty clear.

Ellie would have preferred it, though, if it had just remained a suspicion. Hearing it confirmed while she was coming down the stairs—that was just disgusting. It changed immediately from kind of amusing to just plain awful.

No whoring around. That's what she and Samantha said laughingly to Vani at school, who basically slept with anything that moved, up to and including the janitor, Simmons. The *janitor*. But that was hilarious. That was just Vani. She'd always been advanced, and she didn't mind that Samantha and Ellie weren't ready yet.

Ellie stared at the numbers on her phone, which were changing so slowly she could almost hear the electrons inside gathering, rallying to change shape and charge. She knew she'd never say the words to her mother in jest. *No whoring around, Mom*. Even thinking the words made her kind of want to cry.

What if they wanted to get married or something? What would happen to the house? What if Mom sold it when she went to college? College students went home for the holidays, and if there was no home to go to, didn't that just mean there was no point to having holidays? She'd be the one student eating in the freezing cafeteria, the women dishing out plates of turkey and mashed potatoes with a side of pity. One of the cafeteria workers would probably take her home with her that night, saying that any girl needed to be in a warm family home on Christmas Eve. For some reason, Ellie pictured this happening in New York City, even though she wasn't planning to apply to any school there. But the cafeteria worker who ushered her into an old station wagon driven by her red-cheeked husband lived just a bit upstate, and in her imagination, they sped through New York, the husband surprisingly good at jostling for road space among the bossy taxicabs.

He drove hard and fast until they reached a country road lined by trees covered with snow, and then, inside the cozy suburban home, they sat Ellie next to their four children and fed her Jell-O and slices of salami the dad had cured in the workshop out back. It was practically a story. Ellie imagined herself writing it out. Maybe she would try later. She kept trying to finish short stories, but the most she ever got was a few pages in before they seemed as lame and stupid as the pink baby-duck pajamas her mom had bought her. It was weird how good a writer she always thought she was until she actually tried to write anything.

"Five . . ."

Not knowing about Mom and Harrison hurt her feelings, that was all. She'd even asked her mom if anything had happened with him. Okay, Ellie hadn't been that blunt—she didn't say, "Did you fuck the neighbor?" which was what Vani probably would have said even to her own mother—but she'd very clearly said, "I don't understand why you're not going to hang out over there. Like you always do. Did something happen between you two?" The most important thing was to get her mom to start going over there again—as his friend—because sometimes Ellie felt like that hour or so her mother was out of the house was the only time she had to herself, ever. Every other minute of the day was consumed: by water polo practice in the morning, by the following seven periods of classes, then by homework at the study center her mom insisted was to help her learn study skills but Ellie knew was actually an expensive form of babysitting. Then her mother picked her up and took her home, where she had eyes in the back of her head. If Ellie was just lying on her back on the bed, her head hanging off, dangling toward the ground, Mom knew she wasn't doing anything productive and would be standing in the doorway before she knew it, suggesting she clean her room or do more homework. When Mom was at Harrison's, though, Ellie could sit and space out. Watch TV. Lie in the bathtub and consider the shape of her big toes—something was wrong with them, but she hadn't been able to figure out what it was. It wasn't for lack of trying. Were they just a bit too long, or fat in the base, or . . .

Her mother nudged her shoulder. "Four . . ."

It was something to think about. She didn't want her mom selling the house, no. But there might be pluses to this, if it happened. If Mom and Harrison lived together, they'd be too busy cooing at each other to notice what she did, right? And he had that whole third floor that he kept saying he was going to make into a separate apartment—maybe he would do that for her. That would be something. Sam and Vani would like that. She'd be the cool one, for once. They'd come spend the night, and she would lift a bottle of wine from Harrison's stash, and they'd watch the R-rated movies Vani's parents didn't let her watch and text the boys that Vani had slept with, teasing them with boob Snapchats or worse.

"Three . . ."

Ellie had done that only once, and honestly, it had felt less weird pushing the send button than it had lifting her bra so Samantha could snap the picture of her breasts. Not like Eric or Jake would even know which girl was which (except for Vani— her bra size went along with her experience), but it was still weird. Sure, the photo was supposed to last only ten seconds before self-destructing, but what if it didn't? What if Eric, who had built a working Tesla coil in his garage, had figured out how to get around the thing that disallowed screenshots, and a picture of her naked chest was out there? What if it *was* recognizable? What if it got into his parents' hands and was then eventually identified and sent back to her mother with a note, "Please teach Ellie to keep her shirt on at all times."

She would just have to kill herself.

"Two!"

On one side, her mother clutched her hand. It kind of hurt. On her left, Aunt Mariana took her other hand, her skin cool and soft, reassuring as always. Together, they said, "One!"

"Happy New Year!"

There was a flurry of hugs, and then her mother said, "Go on, Ellie."

It was her job to open the door and let in the New Year.

"Nah."

Her mother looked instantly hurt, as if Ellie was doing it specifically to pain her.

"Why not?"

Ellie shrugged. "I don't want to."

"But . . ."

"If it's that big a deal to you, why don't you just do it?" Ellie didn't mean to sound like a kid in the playground—*No, you play with Joel*—but it was too late to take it back. "I mean, I always do it. Time for someone else to have a turn."

"But . . ." Her mother just kept sitting there, looking like she was going to cry or something.

"I can do it—," started Mariana.

"Fine." Ellie stood and then stomped to the door. She flung it open. "There. Are you happy?" She looked at her mother, who looked horrified.

Ellie's cheeks were on fire and she knew she shouldn't say another word, but she couldn't stop herself. "Come on in, New Year!" she yelled into the darkened street. She heard fireworks and the faint pops of gunfire. "Do your worst!"

Then Ellie flounced—she could feel herself doing it even though she hated herself for it—upstairs, tossing over her shoulder, "I'm tired. You two just keep drinking. You can have my lemon and honey. Happy fucking New Year."

Two gasps. She got *two* gasps out of it. This year was going to suck, and she would never figure out where she was supposed to apply to college and for what, and it would be her fault for not opening the goddamned door when her mother told her to. But she'd gotten a rise out of them both. She mentally patted herself on the back so hard that if she'd done it for real, she would have knocked herself all the way to the ground. It almost made up for feeling so terrible.

Chapter Seven

EXCERPT,
**WHEN ELLIE WAS LITTLE:
OUR LIFE IN HOLIDAYS,**
PUBLISHED 2011 BY NORA GLASS

Valentine's Day

When she entered kindergarten, Ellie got her first taste of the way popularity works, thanks to Valentine's Day.

Ellie was well liked by the children in her class. Her teacher said she was a pleasure to teach. She got along well with most. I predicted no trouble for her.

But do mothers ever get that right?

That first year, one girl named Sissy got all the good cards. There were rules, of course, that every child had to give one card to every other child. (I wondered about the single mothers of five, the women who could barely get protein on the table at night, let alone afford two boxes of Valentine's Day cards for each kid.)

There were no rules, however, about what kind of card had to be given.

Sissy got five cards with chocolate attached. She got three oversized foil cards and two filled with glitter. One of her cards sang. Sissy was a pretty child, with long blond perfect hair. She wore black shoes that shone every day, never scuffed. She had a light singsong lisp and a way of dispensing random hugs that made even the playground moms smile at her harder, hoping to be graced with one. Everyone wanted to be her best friend, including Ellie.

Ellie asked if she could make Sissy a card, instead of giving her one of the *Peanuts* cards we'd bought. I didn't understand playground politics yet. I thought it would be sweet. I even thought perhaps Sissy would choose my daughter to be her best friend. I wanted that. I pictured kindergarten to be something like my yoga group. After you went a few times, you were accepted, greeted happily, and embraced upon leaving. In my mind, Sissy was the equivalent of my friend Lily, a woman who looked *right* into your eyes when she asked how you were, a woman I'd been so pleased to have been chosen as a friend by. So I understood.

I helped Ellie glue the handmade hearts onto the construction paper card. Ellie knew her letters by then and composed the words she often put in cards she made for me, "I love you." She added, "Your friend, Ellie."

Ellie told me later that when Sissy had opened the card from Yolanda that sang Christina Aguilera's "Beautiful," the construction card Ellie had made had slipped off Sissy's desk to the floor, where Rodney Byron had stepped on it, mashing it into three mangled pieces before he moved away.

Sissy never noticed.

What Ellie didn't know then—what *I* didn't know—was that she'd be hurt like this a hundred times before it would hurt less. She's only eleven as I write this essay, she'll be fourteen when this book falls into your hands, and her true romantic heartbreaks are still to come, all lined up in her future. How I wish I could see into each one of them. How I wish I could meet each man (or woman—I don't care one way or the other) she'll love, how I wish I could prep him—*this is the woman you treat well. I don't care about any of the others you've loved. This is the one who matters. Don't make this girl of mine ache for even the smallest fraction of a moment or I will tear your head off your body like a paper doll and then light it on fire.*

Sissy was just a girlfriend crush, but I wanted to step on that little girl's fingers. (Don't look at me like that. You've felt that way, too.) By the next day, Ellie had shrugged it off and sworn undying love to Yolanda of the singing card. I still steamed, staring holes in the back of Sissy's blond head as she swung delicately upside down from the monkey bars.

How do parents balance this love? On one side, it's crushing, completely and totally. The power of your love could flatten a star, could create a black hole—the vast, dense weight of your love sucking everything inward, even the radiance of light itself. On the other side, it's weightless. A breath against your cheek, a moment in time that slips through your fingers, as ephemeral as the quiet bubbles she blew as a baby.

That crushing, lightweight love fills and empties you within the space of a single blink.

Wish your babies Happy Valentine's Day. Look forward to watching them fall in love over and over again. And relax, resting in the sunlight, consoled by the knowledge you will never again love as desperately as you do now.

Chapter Eight

The funny thing was that Nora wasn't nervous when she went in to meet with Dr. Niles. She could admit she might have been a little obsessed with WebMD when it first hit the Internet, but she liked to think she channeled her hypochondria for good now. Using a combination of the Mayo Clinic Symptom Checker, the NIH, and the CDC, she'd successfully diagnosed her friend Lily's onset of Bell's palsy and Ellie's whooping cough. She was good at diagnosing the difference between a cold and the flu (it was usually a cold). She had all the markers of perimenopause: breast tenderness, urinary urgency, fatigue. Her period had been five days late last month, and the PMS had been horrible. Always driven to clean while premenstrual, Nora had taken down the ceiling fans—actually uninstalling each one—to swab each blade with her homemade vinegar–tea tree oil cleaner. (Her column "Does Green Really Clean?" had gone viral the year before, getting more than four million reads and pushing *When Ellie Was Little* back onto the bestseller list, and now, even if she'd wanted the industrial strength of 409, she wouldn't have been able to justify buying a bottle of it.) She predicted the doctor would tell her to start thinking about HRT (she wasn't interested), and then she'd get back to work on the column that was giving her fits, the one on how working from home could be just as productive as working from an office. In annoying irony, she kept wandering away from the computer, forgetting to finish it.

Dr. Niles's office could have doubled as a hotel lobby, full of healthy potted plants and watercolor paintings of boats and bays. When Nora was done filling out paperwork, the tan receptionist handed her a box of Valentine hearts with a conspiratorial smile. The pink *Be Mine* tasted like a preschool chalkboard might, granular and sweet. While she chewed her way through the small box, she played with the piece of beach glass she'd chosen that morning—pure, clear blue, and perfectly round. It was a good worry stone, made for a doctor's office. She put it back in her pocket when she started to put it in her mouth, almost confusing it with the candy heart in her left hand.

The doctor herself was as pretty as the office, with a blond bob and a manner so warm Nora thought she might have missed her calling as a preschool teacher. She could picture Dr. Niles bending down to stick a SpongeBob Band-Aid on a six-year-old, receiving kisses that smelled of peanut butter. She would be careful with germs and keep one of those tiny plastic bottles of Purell in the front pocket of her adorable smock, which she'd wear un-ironically. Ellie's preschool teacher, when Nora thought about it, had been someone who should have been a doctor. Mrs. Finchly's posture had been so rigid Nora had sometimes wondered if she wore a brace under her plain dresses. She'd smiled at the kids, but Nora had never seen her squat on the playground, arms wide open, like all the mother-helpers did. Mrs. Finchly took her job seriously. Much more seriously than the teacher in the other preschool class did, the one who was always wandering around with Play-Doh on her dress and her arms filled with finger-painted maracas and flutes made of bamboo. Yes, Mrs. Finchly would have inspired more trust as a doctor than as a teacher.

In Dr. Niles's office, Nora asked her, "Did you ever teach?"

The doctor shuffled a paper, pushing it underneath a brown manila folder. Was that where the answers were? The nerves Nora hadn't been feeling rushed in to fill their familiar place. She wanted to reach forward, grab the folder, and run. In her car, she would read the words that would tell her why they'd taken so much blood, why the phlebotomist with two-almost-three children looked at her so strangely the last time she'd sat in his ergonomically correct chair with the armrests made for tired elbows. If she didn't understand the words, she'd google them on her phone. She was a trained reporter, after all. She knew how to do research.

"Not really. When I was premed, I was a TA for a couple of classes. Once I had to teach a semester of childhood development but I wasn't that good at it." She smiled. A dimple darted into her cheek and then ducked away. "Why?"

"Do you have kids?"

Gamely, she said, "Not yet."

"But you will."

"I'd like to." Dr. Niles held out her left hand and looked at it as if the small, sparkly diamond still surprised her. "I haven't been married that long, actually. We do want kids. Someday."

"The sooner the better."

The doctor looked at Nora again with that sweet gaze. "You were young when you had your daughter?"

"Not too young. I was twenty-eight." Could this woman be any more than twenty-five? She was a doctor—was it even possible she could be that young?

Dr. Niles pulled out another sheet of paper. "You just have the one child, is that right?"

"Yes." Nora's blood chilled, as if she'd plunged her wrists into ice water. "Why?"

"And you're not married?"

"Divorced."

"Are your parents still alive?"

"We never really knew our father. Our mother died in a car crash when she was forty-four." Her age. God. She hadn't thought of that till right now.

"She never had these kinds of episodes that you've been dealing with? Memory loss or confusion. Any kind of mood swings?"

Nora frowned. "Mom was a little volatile, I remember, just before the crash, but she was still working two jobs and her boyfriend had also just moved out. She was tired. It just happened." What was the doctor implying? That if her mother hadn't died young, she would have had something? Had what?

"What about your sister? You're a twin, right? Identical?"

"Fraternal." Nora was confused. "Are you asking if she's married?"

"Does she have children?"

There was so much more under her voice, things that Nora didn't understand. Fear tugged at the base of her neck.

"No. Just my Ellie."

Dr. Niles nodded and leaned back in her chair. She steepled her fingers. In an older doctor, it would have come across as pensive. Knowledgeable. Instead, she looked like a child playing in a leather chair too big for her small body.

"You came by yourself today?"

"You're scaring me," Nora said with a smile. Maybe this would make the young doctor laugh and realize she was being too serious. *Oh, sorry! I didn't mean to frighten you. It's really no big deal at all, nothing to worry about.*

"We've found something." The words were blurted out rapidly, as if the doctor didn't know what else to do with them. "You have early-onset Alzheimer's disease."

Nora laughed at the words, relief soaking her like warm water. It was just a mistake, then. "I'm forty-four. Not old."

Dr. Niles's voice was tight as she said, "Early-onset is a different beast, I'm afraid."

"I don't understand. I don't have Alzheimer's. I'm *forty-four.*
You can't get it that early." She would tell the doctor her job.
That was always a good idea.

Dr. Niles reached forward, touching her papers again. Nora's papers. Her tongue darted out and wet her lips, and Nora
realized the doctor was nervous. Maybe even more so than
Nora was.

"In some unfortunate cases, it can start as early as midthir-
ties. I hate telling you this. I've actually never run across it in my
practice, and I've been up the last two nights at home, researching it."

Nora pictured her, propped up in bed with her laptop. She
would wear a peach negligee, something sheer enough to please her
new husband but decent enough to wear to the kitchen to make
coffee. Nora used to have one like it, in cream. Dr. Niles would sit
in bed, distracted by the sound her husband made gargling mouth-
wash. She would read about Nora, about what was apparently in her
blood, her body. She would read about how to get it out.

"What's your first name?" Nora asked her. It was suddenly
incredibly important that she know what her husband called her in
the middle of the night when he rolled over and found her ear next
to his lips. Nora must have known it, must have heard it when she
first introduced herself, but it had dropped out of her mind.

It had dropped all the way out.

"Susan," the doctor said. Her eyebrows came together and
her mouth wobbled for a split second.

Her husband called her Susie. Nora knew he did.

Nora picked up her purse, which she'd left thoughtlessly at
her feet. As if she wouldn't need it. She took out her Moleskine
and her favorite pen, the burgundy Montblanc fountain pen she'd

bought herself the first time her book hit the *New York Times* list. She would make particular, careful notes, and then this young doctor would fix it. Not a problem. "What does this diagnosis mean for me, Susan?"

To Nora's horror, Susie's mouth wobbled harder. She pressed two fingers against her lips. "Oh, god. I'm so sorry. This has never happened to me before." She spun in her huge leather chair so she was completely hidden. A child playing hide-and-seek, only Nora, the seeker, was more goddamned terrified than she'd ever been in her life.

Ten seconds later, when the doctor spun back around, she was normal again, the only telltale sign of any emotion a slight glassy sheen in her cornflower eyes. Her lips were steady. She placed both hands flat on the top of the papers on her desk. She looked directly at Nora, sizing her up. Nora made a reckless, unnecessary line on the blank page as if she had something to note.

"It means you have an incredibly rare, familial, incurable, fatal disease that we hate to diagnose in anyone."

Nora wrote the unacceptable words slowly. One by one.

Rare.

Familial.

Incurable.

Fatal.

"I'm so sorry," pretty Susie said.

Chapter Nine

On Valentine's Day, Luke took Mariana to the House of Prime Rib. They sat in a cracked leather booth and they both ordered a martini: top-shelf gin, very dry. The banquet room seemed to demand this. Mariana didn't usually eat meat, but she missed it. Sometimes she figured she could atone for slipping up in other ways. It was worth the hit on her karma. Probably.

With excitement in his voice, Luke pointed out the huge metal contraption that housed the eponymous meat. "Look at that right there. Prettier than a 2002 Harley V-Rod. And look at you. Even *more* gorgeous."

That might be a first, being compared to a metallic zeppelin full of meat. Not that she was complaining. There were worse things to be compared to.

Luke thickly buttered and chewed his bread thoughtfully, his eyes closing in pleasure. Mariana had always liked watching him chew—it was part of how he lived in his body, with conscious awareness. His lower jaw moved with a similar deliberate slowness. He made love to her the same way, with careful attention and long, measured movements.

Her sweet, rich, generous, motorcycle-riding gearhead.

Mariana had met him two years before in a bar south of Market—all dim sconces and velvet wallpaper, perfect places for making out with your new favorite person, places to slide business cards across dark maple bars and order drinks with never fewer than six impossible-to-find ingredients. She'd been there with Molly, another yoga teacher at the studio where she'd been working. That night at the bar, she and Molly had been playing their usual game of dividing the men in the room into categories of men they'd sleep with and men they wouldn't. As usual, Mariana felt a twang of conscience. "Isn't this exactly what we don't want them to do to us? Fuckable and unfuckable?"

"Come on, this was probably the first game in the world, and it'll probably be the last," Molly said. "We're going strictly on looks, and we're evolved enough to know that looks mean nothing and the ones we like the best are probably asshats. Doesn't make it not fun. Besides, I don't have the cash for another drink here if I don't flirt my way into the next one. And you need to get your mind off tomorrow."

Mariana felt sick again. The next morning, she was going to pitch her idea for BreathingRoom to two venture capitalists who looked, in their online profiles, like they weren't more than eighteen. Who was she kidding? *She* wanted to build an app? Her laptop was six years old and had been used when she got it, and her cell phone still flipped open. Not only that, but everyone who heard the phrase "meditation app" had laughed at her—everyone but the two young guys she'd met at a different, equally trendy SoMa bar two weeks before. They were the kind of guys who knew people who built ideas into apps and apps into money. Mariana had the idea. That, a rent-controlled apartment in the Mission, and a startlingly impressive collection of way-too-expensive shoes were really all she had.

Molly nudged her. "That guy, go."

The man at whom Molly pointed hadn't fit in with the place at all. Six foot four, thick necked, a leather jacket ripped at the elbows hanging from his enormous shoulders, he'd looked shell-shocked. He'd caught Mariana's eye once and smiled, a real smile. Not a SoMa one. There was no "what do you do?" about his gaze, just an interested "who are you?" vibe. She'd smiled faintly back, automatically nervous of a man who looked like he might club his women over the head before dragging them to his lair.

"No way," said Mariana. "Never."

"I dunno," said Molly, leaning on her fist. "He probably can't afford to buy any more drinks here than we can, but his eyes are kind of dreamy, and everyone likes a guy with a rap sheet, right?"

Later, in the hallway of the bar, as she was coming back from the bathroom, the heel of Mariana's Fluevog Mini Zaza had caught on a taped-down wire that crossed the carpet, and she'd tripped. He'd been there, a few feet away.

She'd been prepared to shoo away his offer of help. To get up on her own, thank him, and get back to her friends.

But instead of pulling her up, he dropped to his knees and then shifted to a cross-legged seat. Her impulse to leap to standing faded. She hadn't had that much to drink, just a whiskey and water, but in front of him, she suddenly felt unstable. He reached into the pocket of his leather jacket and pulled out a plastic package. Weed? Something harder? Was he a dealer or something?

"Gummy bear? To soothe the nerves."

"Oh?" Mariana found herself reaching for a green one. "What makes you think I need my nerves soothed?" She did.

The man with the silver eyes smiled. "Don't you?"

Surprised at his perceptiveness, she said, "I guess I do." Then she admitted, "I'm going after something big tomorrow. Really big."

"Like, a dream big?"

"Totally my dream big. I'm worried I won't pull it off," she confessed. "I have to make a really good impression."

"You kidding me? You'll knock 'em dead. I know it."

He'd given her a red gummy bear, the best one, he said, and they'd sat, comfortably chatting with each other about favorite mechanisms of sugar transport. Tootsie Rolls were high on both their lists. He liked a Snickers bar way more than she did. She liked the way his jacket creaked when he moved his arms, and the way his hands looked battered.

He stood eventually, taking her hand and holding it with his huge one for a second too long, a second that started heat to her core. Back in the bar, Molly shot her a thumbs-up but didn't break away from the small dark-haired man who seemed to be holding her interest. Gummy Bear Guy started to introduce Mariana to his friends and then they both laughed, realizing they'd never told each other their names.

"Mariana Glass," she said to his friend. She immediately forgot his name, but then she turned back to Silver Eyes. "And you are?" she said.

"Luke Clement," he said. Then he threaded her fingers with his and, without excusing them, pulled her behind him into an unused room full of broken chairs and one listing desk. He kissed her, a kiss so hot it seared her body with its strike of lightning. She felt heat on the soles of her feet. "H-holy *shit*," she stuttered in the dark room. "Come home with me."

His huge fingers cupped the back of her head. "Don't you have an early meeting?"

She did. The most important meeting of her life. She should have had an early night. Meditate. Prepare. "I've never needed that much sleep. Come home with me," she said again.

"Okay," he'd said, running his tongue to the soft spot under her chin. "You ever ridden on the back of a Harley?"

In bed that night, both of them still covered in a thin layer of sweat and utter satisfaction at getting something so right on the first try, Mariana had said, "What's your deal?"

Luke said, "Huh?"

She rolled so that she was naked on her belly and grabbed his hand. "You have a line of grease under your nails."

"I told you. Motorcycles. That's my job."

Mariana narrowed her eyes. "But your nails themselves are manicured. Over the dirt."

If a mountain of a man could blush, Luke managed to do so. "I guess I forgot to mention I might . . . own the motorcycles."

"How many of them?"

He shrugged. "All of them? I inherited a Harley dealership."

"Oh, shit!" She blinked.

"Just a thing," he said. He'd slid off the edge of the bed, his cock, even though now soft, still startlingly large. He stood in front of her, seemingly totally unself-conscious. "Want some water?"

She nodded. His revelation stirred something in her, something she wasn't proud of, but something she acknowledged. "If you put ice in it, I'll let you stay all night."

He smiled, as if unsurprised. "What if I wanted to stay longer than that?"

"You'll have to bring me ice cream."

He brought her a choice of the two she had in the freezer: chocolate chip cookie dough and caramel fudge. "Skip your meeting with the money dudes in the morning."

She laughed. "I can't. I'm telling you, this is the first idea I've had that's good. I have to hire someone to build this app."

"I'm just saying you might be able to find funding closer to home."

Mariana ditched her apartment, rent control and all, and moved into his Potrero Hill loft two weeks later. It wasn't just about BreathingRoom and the fact that he hired the developers for her. It was about him, about Luke. Mariana had fallen in love. The fact that he was wealthy was just . . . handy.

Now, in the House of Prime Rib, Luke was acting funny.

Suspiciously. His gaze darted around the room, as if looking for someone.

"Are we waiting for somebody?"

Luke rubbed the back of his neck. "No. Why?"

Mariana laughed. "I was kidding. What's going on?"

He shook his head. "Nothing. You want dessert?"

She thought about it. "Nah. Not really. That was amazing, but I'm full."

He frowned. "But you always want dessert."

"Usually. But not tonight. You go ahead and get something, though."

Luke ordered the chocolate torte. He fiddled with his watch. "How's the app?"

It had turned into shorthand for BreathingRoom. *The app, the app, the app.* "Fine," she said. She'd been trying so hard not to bring it up over dinner. Luke didn't care enough about technology to keep up with the details of her struggling business. She knew he didn't want to know how difficult it was to optimize an entire site so it was easy navigate on both iPhones and Androids. (Nora, who'd written a piece on the most reasonable phones and their various platforms, did—she was the one who'd told Mariana she needed a responsive site. Mariana hadn't even known what the term meant.) The third-party marketer Mariana had chosen for the pay-per-install had reneged on their quoted price, and she couldn't afford them anymore. And she was *not* going to ask Luke for any more money. Not this month, anyway. She'd just asked him for money to hire an in-house developer so the bugs could be more quickly fixed and . . . she wasn't going to ask for more. That was all there was to it. If she fucked it all up, well, it wouldn't be the first time she'd fucked something up so big she had to run in the other direction to avoid the avalanche's crash. She'd call her sister tomorrow. Nora was the best sounding board, anyway. She always knew what to do.

"I love you," Luke said, still tugging at his watch, pulling at the strap.

Mariana smiled. "I love you, too."

The waiter appeared, hovering tactfully. "Your dessert."

The bowl appeared to be holding multicolored beads, or maybe jelly candy. "I think he ordered the torte—," she started.

"No, this was what I wanted. Thank you, sir."

With a nod and—*was that a wink?*—the waiter retreated.

Mariana gaped. "What . . ."

"Gummy bears. I thought I'd offer you all the flavors. You can have anything you want in this bowl. Anything. There's strawberry and grape and blue, whatever that is, and if you don't like any of those, then I was hoping you'd consider accepting this." Luke reached forward, placing a diamond ring on top of the pile of bears.

"Oh, Luke." A gust of fear blew through her.

To Mariana's horror, Luke stood and went down on one knee.

Not here. Not in front of God and everyone. Not where she couldn't . . .

"Mariana Glass, I love you. Will you marry me?" His voice was choked, thickened. The diners around them, as if alerted by some subsonic engagement bell, dropped their voices to silence. Even the noise of the attached bar quieted.

Mariana's fingers clenched around her napkin. She heard a woman sigh. Then another. But she couldn't fix her face, couldn't get the right words lined up, couldn't, couldn't . . . She was going to, she would fuck it up, there was no way she could explain, she didn't even know—

"Mariana?" He was white around the eyes. "Don't leave me hangin' here, babe."

She felt the word "yes" in her mouth, tasted it. Then Mariana said, *"No."*

The worst part was her volume. As if an almost-silent whisper of the same word wouldn't have had the same devastating effect on him. But she practically yelled it, the terrible word hanging above them. Luke pulled his head back as if she'd hit him with pepper spray. He retreated a million miles just by blinking.

Confident, strong Luke. Never, in the two years she'd known him, had she seen him in retreat. Not once. He'd been so sure she'd say yes.

She'd thought she would, too. Up until thirty seconds ago.

Then she was on the floor with him, and her arms were around his neck. Her lips against his cheek, she murmured, "I'm so sorry. So sorry."

Luke stayed completely still, as if the "no" had turned him to stone.

The few gasps she'd heard when she'd answered changed into a swell of approval. She could almost hear them changing their minds. Perhaps they'd misconstrued her answer. "Yes," that must be what she'd said. Perhaps her "no" actually meant "yes," maybe that's the way they worked as a couple.

"So sweet," she heard a woman say.

A man offered a hearty "Congratulations!"

Mariana kept her face against Luke's neck. How could she stand up? How were they possibly going to be able to walk out of the restaurant and back to the car where they'd left it on Polk Street? When they got home, how would she brush her teeth next to him before getting into bed with him? Her fingers were pressed so tightly against his shoulders that she knew she would leave ten tiny bruises there against his skin, markers of the time he got it so wrong, so very wrong.

Luke didn't speak.

He still hadn't moved, still stuck in a kneel that now looked more like a crouch. No tears. Too hurt for tears.

"I'm so sorry. I can't. No, Luke."

Finally, he spoke. "I heard you the first time."

Slowly, so slowly, Luke stood, extending to his full enormous height. He carefully placed his credit card on the table, along with the car keys. The jacket he'd hung on the hook at the end of their booth creaked over his shoulders. "I need to walk."

"Wait . . ."

He left.

When Mariana presented the flustered waitress with her card—not his—the woman looked as if *she* were about to cry. Mariana didn't answer when the hostess automatically asked if everything was okay with the meal as she pushed her way out the heavy old door.

Fucked it up. She'd fucked it up. Again. She fucked everything up.

It wasn't until she got home—dark, no lights, he wasn't there—that she remembered the ring that they'd both left sitting in the candy bowl. He'd told her about it once, late at night, right at the beginning of their relationship. *I have my grandmother's ring. I'll only give it to the right woman, and I'll only give it away once.*

She'd dreamed of the moment Luke would ask her to marry him. Stashed somewhere in the house she had an earmarked *Brides* magazine, the product of an afternoon spent in Barnes and Noble waiting for a phone call that never came from a blogger with connections to the *Shambhala Sun*.

But she couldn't.

She wasn't . . .

God, the whole point was that Mariana wasn't enough for *herself* yet. How could she be enough for anyone else? She broke things. She was a fuckup, practically a professional one. It was a miracle the app was still running, that it hadn't put viruses on the phones of everyone who'd downloaded it. A marriage should be . . . something strong. If Nora hadn't been able to keep hers together—well, Mariana would probably blow up a marriage before the end of the honeymoon.

And she knew it was true: Luke loved her. She loved him back.

It wasn't enough, though.

If she could reach her purse to get her phone, she could call Nora, but her purse was in the kitchen, and she was stuck on the edge of the bed, frozen in fear she didn't recognize. Nora would know what to do—she'd know why Mariana had said what she'd said, and she'd know how to fix it, how to change it, how to turn back time so she could answer differently—but, god, Mariana wouldn't answer differently. That was the point.

Or if Mariana could reach her phone, she could open the app and hear her own voice telling her how to find calm, her sense of space. It was strange, yes, but she'd listened and relistened to the MP3s so many times in production that now the voice coming out of her phone actually sounded more like Nora's to her, and Mariana could just absorb the words. *Find the motion of your breath, and rest in that place.*

Mariana gripped the bedpost so tightly she could feel her fingernails denting the wood. Her eyes rested on the word tattooed on her inner forearm: *Now.* Normally a comfort, a reminder that the only moment to be sure of was this one. She took a deep breath, smelling the comforts of home, leftover coffee scent and the dryer sheets that Luke liked. Luke . . .

Now. Now was all she had.

Mariana held on tighter. Hopeful, despite herself.

Chapter Ten

$\mathcal{N}$ ora touched the Valentine's Day card she'd bought for Harrison. Three months since they slept together.

Three months since they were close, in any way at all.

The card was blue, anomalous for the holiday, with an ice floe on the front. Inside it read, *You melt me*. She wouldn't give it to him, even though he always gave her a card. He might not this year, as awkward as it had been between them.

Twelve weeks ago. Before she was diagnosed, before the earth had rotated on more than just its axis. Midfall. The leaves on the sycamore in front of her house had just begun releasing their tight grip on the branches, fluttering down in twos and threes. She and Harrison had been drinking wine, like they'd done approximately a hundred billion times before. They never drank too much, just a glass or two at the end of an evening. Friendly. She and Ellie used to both walk next door when the sun started dropping. Harrison always had Ellie's favorite brand of potato chips, Kettle Salsa. Ellie would take her book and her bowl of chips and read on the porch hammock while Nora and Harrison drank their glasses of wine, and then Nora and Ellie would walk across Harrison's lawn, jump over the low line of dahlias back into their own yard in the dark.

For the last year, though, Nora had gone alone more often than not. Ellie cited homework, but walking back home across the conjoined lawns, looking up at her daughter's window, Nora could make out the wide-screen on her desk. She could tell by the colors displayed that she was usually playing a video game. Fine. She figured it was better than a lot of other things her daughter could have been getting into.

That night, last fall, Ellie had been out of the house staying the night at Samantha's house. Nora had waved at Harrison over their parked cars and raised her voice to be heard over the kids riding their whining motorized scooters that zipped up and down the street. "Come to my house tonight, okay?"

She'd wanted to show him an article she'd written before she turned it in. It felt more like her earlier work, honest and raw. It had felt good to write, and she hadn't felt that in a while. She hadn't doubted her motivation in asking him over. Sleeping with him, she would have sworn, hadn't even crossed her mind. Harrison was just *Harrison*, well-worn and frayed like the right cuff of the brown sweater he wore from October to March every year. Harrison, for all his admirable qualities (which were many), tended to go for women who were quantifiably less intelligent than he was. They never stuck, and after the first three or four, Nora had given up on trying to be friends with the women who shot daggerlike looks at her when she let herself into Harrison's kitchen to drop off his favorite oatmeal–peanut butter cookies.

That night, his third glass of wine in his hand, Harrison had looked up from her pages, his dark eyes taking a moment to refocus on her. "Do you really feel like this?"

Nora had laughed lightly. "Sometimes. Do you think it's too much?"

"No."

"Do you think my readers will hate me? They think of me as light and funny. I talk about bathroom tiles and the way light falls on candles from the dollar store. I don't talk about . . ." *Sex. Longing.*

Harrison twisted sideways on the iron porch chair so he could drop the pages onto the small table that sat between them. Then he faced his own house, his dark hair longer over his ears than he usually kept it. Silver showed at his temples, and Nora was startled by how much she wanted to touch it. The planes of his head and jaw were dear and familiar—she'd known him how many years now? They'd moved into the house when Ellie was one. Fifteen years now.

"It's a good piece," he said. "I can't *believe* you thought about a Craigslist hookup, though."

It felt as if he'd knocked the wind out of her. "And that's what everyone's going to say. Damn it. I knew I couldn't send it in."

"No one else will say it," he said in a low voice.

"I can write something else, quickly. I can send it in the morning. Benjamin won't care if it's a few hours late . . ." She shuffled the pages, squaring the edges.

Harrison turned suddenly. His fingers laced around her wrist, and instead of light friendliness, the kind that was always between them when they were together, she felt an electric tension. "You placed a casual encounters *ad*."

"Well, it's not like it was a newspaper . . ." Nora wanted to pull her arm back and she wanted him to touch her wrist just like that, forever. She wanted to shut her eyes, but she couldn't look away from his.

"When . . ." He trailed off, a muscle jumping in his jaw in what looked like frustration.

"When what?"

He jerked his chin at his house. "When I was right *there*."

There was a thick silence, one Nora knew she couldn't fill with a laugh or a joke. She could only stare at him. "You don't . . ."

Harrison said, "I do."

"You don't like smart women."

He shook his head. "Not true. Sherry was a paleontologist."

"That's right." She'd forgotten about Sherry with the voice that sounded like a hive of bees, a glum buzz, Sherry who'd understood evolution and dinosaurs but who'd entrusted her every decision to the stars. "She was an astrologist, too, right? Why did you like her?"

"I liked her—" Harrison's voice was abrupt and low. "I liked them because you always said you were too busy."

For what? For him? She *had* been too busy to date, mostly. Besides, she'd always had Harrison, a glass of wine, and that incredible, wide grin waiting for her at the end of most of her days. Nora felt heat at the base of her spine. She spoke her next words slowly. "Would it be just this once?"

He didn't answer her. "Is that what you want?"

She didn't know. Maybe. No. "Yes."

"Then, yeah."

They were upstairs in her bedroom before she could even take another full breath. Then she was naked and so was he, and he was perfect, in every way, and then he was inside her, and the best part was that he'd stayed the night. No, the worst part was that he'd stayed the night. That he'd slept next to her, his head on the pillow next to the bowl of beach glass she kept on her nightstand, glass she and Ellie had picked up over the years. There was nothing finer than beach glass—function gone, only form left—everything worn away except opaque, occluded beauty. Nora's favorite place was Glass Beach, up the coast a couple of hours, a shore littered with sanded, colored glass. She usually tried to carry a piece of it in her pocket—to rub, to remember how strong glass was, how strong Glass was. Plastic bags biodegraded in twenty years, plastic bottles in 450. But glass took a million years to bio-degrade, to return to sand. The shards of beach glass she collected had almost nothing left of their former selves but had so much beauty and comfort left to give. And strength.

Harrison had run his fingers through the glass in the bowl just the way Nora did before she went to sleep, each cool stone clicking against the others satisfyingly. Of course he got it. Nora had wanted to take the glass away from him as much as she'd wanted to give him every piece.

She should never, ever have let him stay, even though the coast had been clear with Ellie out of the house for a night. How did you go from sleeping alone for thirteen years to warmth, twined arms and legs, to commingled morning breath? In the years since Paul left, she'd slept with exactly three men, and only a few careful times each. (The *planning* that went into sex as a single mother. It was an article she knew she should write some-day. *Forget hotels with their suspect comforters. Minivans are your friend. Tinted glass helps. If you park at the mall, choose a parking spot as far as you can get from the elevators to minimize foot traffic near where your groove-on is being got.*)

Harrison knew exactly how many men she'd slept with since the divorce. Two of them he'd met and approved of. That's what *friends* did. Friends didn't stay the night, naked, with each other. They didn't cuddle. God, how Nora had missed that part—the skin against skin, the simple equation of body heat plus covers equaling a sweaty animallike warmth that was both erotic and slightly embarrassing in the morning.

Now, three months and a whole new (non–sexually trans-mittable) disease later, she propped the Valentine's Day card for Harrison on the windowsill in front of the kitchen sink. She had to decide what to do with it before Ellie got home, that was all she knew. It would be fine to tear it up and put it in the recy-cling. She should do that.

But she didn't.

Nora scrubbed the sink drains with a paste of baking soda, water, and Dr. Bronner's mint soap. Nothing got the steel brighter, and very little usually filled her with more satisfaction. But something didn't feel right. She'd forgotten something.

How many damn times in her life had she made this scrubbing paste? A thousand? More? There was an ingredient, a small one. A few drops of . . . The frustration bit at her, nipping at the back of her brain. Something small . . .

The knock on the back kitchen door made her jump though it shouldn't have. She'd been expecting it, but her stomach still clenched.

"It's open," she called. Of course it was. She moved the stack of campus catalogs over so Harrison could take his normal seat at the kitchen island.

"Happy Valentine's Day," he said.

"You, too," she said, too flustered to look in his eyes. Her fingertips were smooth and slick from the baking soda.

"I moved your trash cans in."

He always did. "Thank you."

"I got you a card." He held out a dark red envelope. "I just wanted to drop it off and then I'll go."

A funny friend card, that's what he always got her. Something that said that year's equivalent of *As long as we're both single, let's eat lots of chocolate in honor of those too busy having sex.*

"Don't be silly—stay. Wine?" She put the envelope facedown on the counter.

Harrison swung the barstool so that he straddled it backward. "Sure."

Nora felt goose bumps rise on her arms, as if it had just gotten colder. As if he'd touched her.

"Where's Ellie?"

"Volleyball." Suzanne Carpenter had volunteered to drive the girls. Harrison knew as well as Nora did that Ellie wouldn't be home for another two hours.

But he just sat on the barstool, watching her with those dark eyes of his, taking the glass of wine from her as if they'd never been naked together, as if they'd never tasted the inside of each other's mouths.

"Whatcha doing?" he asked, pointing. "I mean, besides cleaning."

"Oh." Nora sat next to him and restacked the brochures, closing her notebook on what she'd been jotting down for Ellie. "Colleges. I ordered a bunch of their catalogs."

He pulled the stack toward him. "Berkeley."

Paul's alma mater. "Yep."

"Has he called her recently?"

It was kind of Harrison to ask, but of course Paul hadn't. "No."

Another catalog. "U of Mississippi?"

"Random. She heard something about it. I can't remember what."

"Huh," said Harrison. "UCLA. Portland. Dallas?"

"Another random one. Smith College is still her first choice. I don't know what she's thinking with the others."

"You always know what she's thinking."

If Harrison were Ellie's father, he would have a say in the college decision. He'd have an opinion and a right to share it. Nora knew he had an opinion, and like always, he'd keep it to himself until he was asked. "I don't," she said. "Not anymore. Not for a while now."

"Why are you doing this for her? She can't order these for herself?"

"She's overwhelmed, I can tell." Nora took the Cal booklet out of his hands. "I *want* to do this. I'm helping."

Harrison nodded.

"I am," she said again.

In a normal voice, as if he were answering a question she'd asked, Harrison said, "I can't stop thinking about kissing you."

The muscles in her thighs, the ones that would have to hold her if she stood now, warmed and weakened. "Tea tree oil," she said.

Harrison nodded. "Whatever you say. Open your card."

"That's what I forgot. In the cleaning paste." Her voice shook. As well as having to tell Mariana and Ellie, she would have to tell him. If the second opinion came in with the same diagnosis—the wrong one—she'd have to tell him. She could imagine his face when she did. That was the problem.

"As much as I adore you, I sure as hell don't care what you forgot in the cleaning paste. Open the card, would you?"

She carefully slit the envelope with the paper scissors as he sighed in impatience. The outside of the card was a large, red-foiled broken heart, jagged and torn. Inside, the heart was in one piece, sewn together with actual red thread. *You mend me.* So close, almost word for word, to the card she got him.

Harrison had seen it, of course, and he stood, reaching behind her to take it off the windowsill. He was so close to her she could feel his shirt brush her upper arm. One rip and the envelope was open. *You melt me.*

He didn't move his feet, just ducked his head so that he could kiss her, hard. He tasted like popcorn and cinnamon. Stubble scraped Nora's chin, and she wanted him to kiss her harder.

But she pulled her head back. She didn't remember reaching forward, but her fingers were clutching the front of his shirt. "I . . . What about Penny?" Harrison's latest was an ex–Hare Krishna who drove a red convertible Mustang.

"Over."

"Oh." He hadn't told her that.

"What's wrong?" he asked.

She didn't let go of his shirt. "This—we don't do this." When he'd asked her in the past why she didn't date more, she'd told him she was too busy, her life too full to give her heart to anyone but her daughter. She'd thought it was the truth, but now . . .

faced with the fear that ripped through her at the feel of his shirt. Maybe she'd just been a coward. Harrison would nod and say that's why it was easy to date women who didn't know Antarctica was a continent—he never had to get his heart involved at all. She'd thought he'd meant it. She'd thought he was just careless and sweet and really liked being the smart one in his relationships. This whole time . . . had he been . . . ? God, what else had she missed along the way?

Harrison said, "I mean, what's wrong with *you*?"

Nora's heart juddered. "Nothing."

"Something is. You've been acting strange for a week."

A week? She'd been acting funny for three months, since their night together—she knew that. "What do you mean?"

"It's like . . ." He tilted his head. He *looked*. Nora realized suddenly she wasn't wearing a bra. She wasn't even wearing ChapStick. She felt naked.

He went on. "You're quiet. You stopped chattering to me. You've always chattered."

Nora couldn't tell him first. She had to tell her daughter, her sister, she had to explain what she had, what she was carrying, but she had no idea how. She *couldn't* tell him, so she'd stopped her mouth in case she slipped. She hadn't thought he would notice.

"I think something's wrong and you don't want to tell me," said Harrison. He placed his thumb against the corner of her mouth. "I can tell by the way you're in some other place even when you're five inches away from me. I don't know if it's menopause or cancer or something else."

Something else. She couldn't make herself form the words.

"But I'm not going anywhere. Well, yeah, I'll go back to my house, but not until I kiss you a while longer."

"Oh."

"That okay with you?"

"Yeah," she said. "Yeah."

Chapter Eleven

*T*he music swelled through her headphones, and as Ellie raced her Healer back to the hut, she suddenly felt like crying with happiness. They were winning. The sick, dying Dragon Queen Ulra would be saved—healed—thanks to her and Dyl if they could just get this part right.

Everything should have a sound track. It would be amazing to take a test at school with violins and cellos upping the danger level. Or doing water polo practice with drums and cymbals encouraging speed. The best thing about learning how to drive was that you got to *pick* a sound track. Or, at least, she would when her mother finally let her drive with music. Right now she was still insisting—wrongly—that it would distract her. Her mother didn't seem to understand that it would actually make things easier. If she had a symphony, complete with organ and choral voices like in *Queendom*, Ellie knew driving would go smoother. The quietness punctuated only by the graunching of gears and her mother's audible terrified gasps made Ellie forget to check both her inside and outside mirrors. The last time they'd gone out to practice, it had been at night—like, pitch dark—and her mother had made her practice three-point turns using the white lines in the mostly empty Whole Foods parking lot. Two of the streetlights in the lot had been burned out and her mother somehow thought she should be able to use her headlights to figure out how to stay in the lines. Right. *That* hadn't gone well. Both of them had cried, although only Ellie'd had a reason to. She'd been *frustrated.* Her mother had just been a passenger. And why Ellie had to learn on Harrison's old Jeep was beyond her. She should have been able to at least learn on her mother's automatic Prius. Something about *if you can drive this, you can drive anything,* but since she didn't plan on driving a stick shift ever, it didn't make sense. What was the point?

Ellie directed her Healer up the grassy knoll and then over the covered fire pit. She entered the code to open her hut's door.

Inside was Dyl the Incurser.

Holy crap.

Hey, she typed inanely. She'd given him the code, like, five days ago, and he'd never stopped by, not while her Healer was there, and it had kind of hurt—hella other guys were trying to get in her hut, claiming all sorts of wounds and life-drains, but not Dyl. On the battlefield, Dyl was professional. Above the fray.

She'd looked him up in real life, of course. It wasn't like *Queendom* was Ellie's first MMORPG—she'd played a little *World of Warcraft* and had been into the new *Star Wars* game the year before. But *Queendom* was the first one she really loved at first roll, and Dyl was her favorite player. His real name was Dylan Hacker, which was possibly the best last name of all time. She'd found an article on his dad's flower business, so she knew he hadn't made it up.

And he was local.

Dylan Hacker lived in Oakland. He was nineteen, older than any other player she'd ever had a crush on except ChrisNINja, who'd said he was seventeen and in San Francisco but when she'd traced his IP, she'd found a married thirty-five-year-old man who actually lived in Mississippi. That had freaked her shit out.

Dylan, though. He was as hot IRL as he was online in his Incurser's body. He had light brown hair, high cheekbones, and sexy brown eyes with blue-gray smudges underneath them, as if he stayed up too late, or maybe as if he had allergies, though that was kind of less hot. He looked the tiniest bit like Ryan Gosling. Samantha didn't think so. His Facebook pictures were clean enough to show a mother, lots of shots of him standing in front of school-looking buildings with other guys. There was one where he had his arms slung around two girls, both of them pretty and happy looking, neither of them pressed very close against him. His Instagram pics were more relaxed—there were shots of him holding a red plastic cup, obviously drunk. He was even cute like that, rumpled and sleepy looking. Looking at what must be his tiny bedroom in the shared house, she wanted to *be* there. She wanted to be the one he was looking at.

Hey, he typed back.

You're in my hut, Ellie managed to respond. *I'm kind of surprised.* Ellie realized that Dyl was in Addi's hut on Valentine's Day evening. He wasn't out with a girl. He was, kinda, out with *her.*

        Why? You invited me. I'm sorry I
        didn't come earlier.

Ellie felt something sharp and delicious shoot down her fingertips, dancing over every keystroke. *You are?*

        You did well on the battlefield,
        Addi.

It was a ridiculous thing to say to someone, archaic and old-fashioned. It made him sound like a knight. And it made her feel like a warrior. Ellie loved it. *Thank you.*

```
         Really. How long have you been
         playing again?
```

Ellie moved her Healer to the rocking chair near the fire. Dyl's Incurser stayed in place, near the bed. *My mom gave it to me for Christmas.* She felt immediately juvenile and wished she hadn't said it. *So maybe three weeks. I've only done, like, five Sorties.*

```
         And you have all that Growing
         already? And the StarFlight?
```

I guess. Yeah. I like that part of it, finding the stuff.

```
         When you got in and healed that kid
         who had lost his mom? While the
         battle went on all around you? I
         thought the Dragon Queen was going
         to kill you for sure, but she just
         ignored you.
```

When we heal them, they protect us. That was the story Ellie had made up in her last Rendering—the part of the game players themselves got to write—and it was good. She knew it. Other players were telling her story now—she'd seen it in the forums. For the first time she kind of got what her mom did, maybe. It was intoxicating, the knowledge that you wrote something that made people want to act, to do. Because of your words that before you wrote them didn't exist. *The Queen is sick anyway. She's just trying to hide her eggs.*

```
I've heard that. So it's true.
```

Yep. It was her story. Her rules. Making up the game as she went was the biggest reason Ellie loved *Queendom*.

```
You'd make a hell of an Incurser.
```

Her back against the headboard, she felt as pleased as if he'd said she was hot. *Thanks.*

```
You live in Marin, right?
```

Had she mentioned that? Ellie didn't type for a moment.

```
You said in the game that glass was
your secret weapon. I could see
your real login name was Ellie, not
Addi . . . I guessed Ellie Glass,
and your mom came up.
```

Ellie pushed the laptop to the bedspread and took a moment to writhe silently, flailing with her hands and legs. *When Ellie Was Little.* Shit. Sure, she'd looked him up online and had scanned his photos, trying to read the titles on the bookshelf behind him, taking long moments to figure out if she thought the skateboard propped against the desk was his or a roommate's, but if he went back into her mother's archives—or, god forbid, bought the *book*—he would know that when she was little, she refused to poop anywhere but at home, scared of what could be lurking in a stranger's toilet bowl. Poop stories! There were stories about her *taking a shit* on the Internet. Every year or two, one of Ellie's friends would trot out an oldie but goodie (the plastic-wrapped tampon as fishing lure, the time she thought their bunny rabbit was possessed by Satan), reading the chapter in question aloud at a sleepover. Ellie learned early on that the more she asked them to stop, the more interesting her mother's stories about her became, so she'd gotten good at laughing along with them until they lost interest.

But this was a boy.

A man, actually. Not some kid in high school who relied on his parents for movie money. At least, she hoped he didn't.

Yeah. I live in Marin. Tiburon.

Cool. Are you near the water?

Pride she knew was misplaced but enjoyed anyway filled her. *I can see it from our back door.*

That's amazing. I might want to be a sailor someday.

Why aren't you one now? You're in Oakland, right?

Lol. You looked me up, too.

You used your last name, which I didn't believe at first, by the way, in the Guarding forum.

Smart girl.

Ellie grinned and pulled the laptop closer to her, shimmying it across her knees. Samantha was always telling her that no one asked Ellie out because she didn't know how to flirt. In real life, she knew it was true. As soon as a boy talked to Ellie, her tongue went gummy and her brain went to mush. She hated it.

But she was good at gaming. *I totally stalked you.*

        I'm glad. The stalking—the friendly
        kind, of course—is mutual.

Ellie took a deep breath. *Okay, I'm trying so hard not to overre-
act to that but can you not read my mom's book, please?*

        Okay.

        Okay?

        I only read half an essay before I
        felt weird about it.

        Weird how?

        Like I was reading your diary, only
        it was stranger because it wasn't
        even yours. It was just about you.
        I felt like a creepster.

        Thanks. For that.

        No problem. Are you as pretty as
        you are on Instagram?

She hadn't friended him because she hadn't wanted him to
know she had searched him out. *No. That's just some girl I hired to
play me online.*

        Wouldn't that be weird, if we did
        that? If we were our real selves in
        the game but fake everywhere else?

She responded, *Isn't that what we do?*

```
Yeah. I'm more me here than any-
where else.
```

Me, too.

Ellie's fingers went motionless on the keyboard. Did he hear the music at the same time she did? That soft, trilling flute part of the score, was that playing for him, too?

The music is pretty in here, he typed.

**Is it different from other Healer
huts?**

```
I don't know. I've never been in
any hut but mine.
```

The admission made Ellie grin. *What does it sound like in yours?*

```
Like guy music.
```

What's that mean?

```
You know in science fiction movies,
when the world is about to blow up
and the people on the spaceship
have to fix everything in the next
seventy seconds?
```

Yeah.

```
It sounds like that.
```

```
Doesn't sound very restful for your
Incurser.

Dyl's got to sleep there, not me.
```

Ellie didn't admit that since she'd started playing the game, she'd been falling asleep with her laptop open on the desk next to her, the music playing softly over her bed. She'd disabled the screensaver, knowing it would burn in the screen but not caring that much. The hut was just so beautiful, with its bottles of herbs and tinctures lined up on the wooden shelves and the crystal sun catcher in the window. At night, the Fernal moons rose and set on the other side of the glass, sending rainbow colors skittering around the room. Sometimes when she rolled over in the night, she'd catch the glow of the small green lamp next to Addi the Healer's bed, and she'd stare at it, wishing *she* were really the lump under the red velvety-looking bedspread, instead of just her, just Ellie in the bed her mother had bought her at the Sealy store on a rainy Sunday when she was ten.

Anyway, Dylan typed.

Anyway, she agreed.

Her mother knocked softly and pushed open her door. "Can I come in?"

Ellie made sure her laptop was facing her stomach completely. Not that she was doing anything wrong.

Her mother guessed, though. "Are you playing that *Queendom* game again?"

She made it sound like checkers or something. "Yeah. I guess."

"You like it." Her mother was so pleased with herself for buying it. It was beyond annoying.

"It's all right."

"So you don't like it?"

"Does this have a point?" She typed, *Stand by. Intruder.*

The response came instantly: *Let me know if you need the assistance of my knife.*

"I just wanted to say good night."

Ellie frowned. Usually her mother just stuck her head in and blew a kiss. Nora wasn't big on chatting at night, preferring usually to work on whatever she was writing until one or two in the morning. They were both night owls, and when she was younger, Ellie would lie on the little sofa in her mother's office reading until they both grew tired. Ellie would wake up being carried into her room. She used to love the feeling of her mom's hands tucking the cool sheets around her, and on the best nights, she'd grip Nora's hand until she gave in, crawling in next to her. Ellie had never been big on sneaking into her mother's bed, but she'd loved it when Nora had slept in hers. She used to like pulling her knees against her chest and pressing her shins into her mother's back.

Her mom hadn't slept in her bed with her for years, though.

"You're going to bed this early?" Ellie asked.

"I'm tired." She took one step into the room, tentatively. "How are you?"

Ellie frowned. "What's up?"

"Why does something have to be up?"

"You're acting funny."

"Can I see what you're doing online?"

No. She could not. But if Ellie said that, then for sure she'd look. "Yeah. But are you sure there's nothing wrong with you? Are you feeling sick? Getting a migraine?"

Her mother's fingers fluttered up to the small silver hoops in her ears and then back down again. "No. Of course not. I'm fine." She smiled. "Absolutely nothing wrong with me except that I haven't spent enough time with you lately. You don't need to show me your computer. I trust you." She narrowed her eyes, and for just a second, Ellie could see why people said Aunt Mariana and her mother looked like identical twins, not fraternal. "Unless you're hiding something."

"Mom." Ellie made herself laugh. "I'm not. I'm just talking to Samantha."

"About boys?"

Ellie nodded. "Of course. How we're planning to seduce them all and get pregnant just for fun. We get bonus points for STDs."

Her mother smiled. "Awesome. Best of luck in that." A pause, and the joke got serious, as it *always* did with her mother. "You'll ask me for condoms if you need them?"

Ellie groaned. "Do you really need to say that?"

"I just enjoy talking about condoms with my sixteen-year-old. What mom doesn't?"

"God."

"Happy Valentine's Day. I love you."

It was like her mother always wanted to *make* her say it back. "You, too."

The door shut silently, surprising Ellie. Her mother normally left her door open, and it was always on Ellie to get up and close it again.

Are you still there? Ellie felt as if she should apologize for her mother even though Dylan couldn't see her.

Is the Intruder dispatched?

She's gone. She just wanted to offer me condoms. There. If that wasn't hard-core flirting, she didn't know what was. He was gorgeous. He was a gamer. He lived across the bay. And he liked her.

Or at least he liked Addi the Healer, and that was a pretty good start.

Chapter Twelve

EXCERPT,
**WHEN ELLIE WAS LITTLE:
OUR LIFE IN HOLIDAYS,**
PUBLISHED 2011 BY NORA GLASS

Easter

When Ellie was little, we hit a turkey with the car on Easter.

The phrase is funny, isn't it? We hit a *turkey*. Who the hell hits a turkey in the Bay Area?

We did. We were on our way up the coast, headed to Glass Beach. It was just the two of us—my sister was out of town. Ellie was eight that year, and I thought we'd do something different for the holiday. We'd eat at a fancy restaurant in Mendocino. And Glass Beach, well, that was something special we'd done for years. It was, obviously, our beach. How tickled Ellie had been when she realized she and the tiny spit of sand shared a name. (How glad I was that I'd kept my last name when I married Paul, that I'd insisted that Ellie take mine when he left. Glass was bright and clear and so strong that not even the ocean could remove its brilliance.)

Located below what used to be an old glass-bottling factory, the sand at Glass Beach was literally made of beach glass, all the sharp edges smoothed away. From a distance, it looked disappointing. Just another gray shore. But if you lay on your stomach on the cold stones just as the sun dipped into the water, if you carved out a place for your chin in the glass sand, you could watch the sunset through pieces of cloudy, jeweled color, splinters of light, a homemade kaleidoscope made of glass and water.

In Petaluma, not even halfway to Glass Beach, we ran into trouble in the shape of Benjamin Franklin's favorite bird.

I was still driving my beat-up old Civic I've mentioned so many times in my columns (the floorboard fire! the brake failure! the radiator explosion!), and by then it didn't like going up hills much. I gave it as much gas as I could, so busy pouring my own futile mental energy into the old engine that when the flapping thing dove toward my grill in the heavy traffic, I didn't have time to swerve, not without endangering Ellie. With a thump as loud as a clap of thunder, the windshield was covered in blood and feathers and gelatinous goo.

Ellie screamed. I'm sure I did, too. I pulled over as quickly as I safely could. I told her to stay in the car, but she didn't. "What *is* that, Mama?" She pressed her head against my side and then peeked again. The traffic was a blur next to us. No one stopped, or even slowed.

"I think it was a turkey."

"You killed it."

"I did."

"On *Easter*."

"At least it wasn't a pig."

"What?"

"Ham? Oh, never mind..." I wished for my sister desperately. Mariana would have been hopeless with the cleanup, but she would have made me laugh. She always made us laugh. "Bad joke. Sorry, honey."

"What do we do now?" Ellie's voice was a wail.

I knew what I wanted to do: I wanted to walk forward on the highway, one arm around my daughter, the other arm thumbing a ride. I wanted to wail, too. I wanted to leave the car behind us, leave the carnage and blood, and go on with our lives as if it had never happened. I wanted a kind older man to pull up in his farm truck and offer us a lift to town, where he'd give us the old car he'd fixed up for his daughter before she married a car dealer. "Don't worry about the pink slip," the tenderhearted old farmer would say. "I have a friend at the DMV—she'll take care of everything."

What really happened was something I know you mothers will recognize: I rolled up my sleeves, literally. I got out the paper towels I kept in the trunk. While Ellie insisted on watching (and crying), I mopped dead turkey guts off my windshield, blood off the grill, and something even worse off the hood.

"I don't get it, Mama. Those look like eggshells."

They were. I'd just been hoping she wouldn't notice.

But of course she did. "They *are*. They're *eggshells*. The turkey was *pregnant*, Mama? You killed a pregnant turkey on Easter?"

I wanted to yell at her. I wanted her to understand I hadn't aimed for the bird, that it wasn't my fault, that I hadn't planned on getting turkey gore on my jeans that day. I certainly hadn't aimed for a turkey matriarch. I would have swerved around it if I could have kept her safe.

Instead, I had to hold my tongue. I had to clean up the mess.

That is, on many days, the only thing a mother can do.

Then, in what felt like a small miracle, the car started even though the engine had a new, worrying rattle. We made it to the coast. We blew off our Easter dinner reservations and ate McDonald's cheeseburgers on Glass Beach.

At the very last minute, right before the sun slipped into the water, Ellie and I threw our bodies onto the sand and dug holes for our chins. We scooped the bigger pieces of glass up into small piles so that we watched the sunset from behind a barricade of refracted color. The sand underneath pulled the warmth from our bodies, and when we sat up—the sun gone— we were both happily shivering.

In a motion that felt very much like grace, Ellie threw herself in my lap even though she was eight and perhaps almost too old to do so anymore. She hugged my neck. I thought she would say something smart, something that made me reflect on life, as she so often did. Something about the strength of the broken, worn-down glass, the way our last name was just as strong, just as hearty and beautiful.

Instead she said, "You stink like rotten baby turkey eggs."

I hugged her back. "I'm sure I do."

Chapter Thirteen

When Nora planned the Easter Alcatraz jaunt, she hadn't planned on the rain. Riding the ferry to the defunct jail was usually a pleasant crossing of famous waters. When they'd gone in the past, they'd always remained on the top deck of the ferry, no matter how strong the wind or thick the fog. But with the miserable damp that ranged from drizzle to downpour, they had to stay in the main cabin, packed inside, competing for room with tourists who jousted with elbows like padded swords as they attempted to get lousy photos of the city through breath-misted glass. The smell of sodden wool and wet dog wrestled with a cloud of cologne and fading excitement. "I thought no one would be here," Nora said in astonishment as they'd looked at the line of people trying to buy coffee at the inside counter. "It's a holiday. No one's supposed to be here."

At least Nora, Mariana, and Ellie had managed to score three seats together. All Nora had seen when they'd boarded was a mass of people circling like chum. Her boarding stub pressed against her palm like a tiny knife. Mariana said, "We'll never get to sit together."

"Yes, we will." Nora wasn't at all sure of this.

"Whatever." Mariana had that giving-up sound in her voice, the tone Nora hated the most. Ellie was the sixteen-year-old, not Mariana.

So Nora, who'd always been the one good at scoping out the overview of a situation and summing up what needed to be done, led them confidently to a section where two seats were available. A small child played on the edge of the third, hopping between it and his mother's lap. As gracefully as she could, Nora slid her purse onto the seat of the chair while the child scrabbled on his mother's shoulders between leaps. "You don't mind, do you? This is my sister and my daughter. Oh, isn't your son a *cutie*? You see, Mariana?" she said triumphantly. "Plenty of room."

"Sit by me, sit by me," said Ellie to Mariana, the same way she had as a child. Ellie had always loved her aunt, from the very first moment.

Well, not the *first* moment.

Mariana hadn't been there for that. She'd been in India for the second time (this time she'd communicated by e-mail at least), studying yoga and her third eye. She hadn't made the flight back home, the one Nora had booked and paid for, the one that would bring her twin back to her for the most important moment of her life, the moment Ellie entered the world.

A taxi problem, Mariana had said later. "Lost one tire, then another. I rode to town on the back of a motorcycle to grab another cab, but it was a tiny town, and the other cabdriver had died the week before. We had to wait for the guy's uncle to come back. It was kind of a big deal."

Nora had been in the middle of a much bigger deal, she'd been pretty damn sure. Ellie had gotten stuck and she'd almost needed a cesarean. She could hear her sister's voice when Paul held the phone up, but Mariana wasn't *there*. It didn't count. When

Ellie was finally bundled and passed into her arms, it had hurt to hold the baby without being able to show her to her sister. Ellie looked exactly like they had as a child: bright slapped red with a shock of black silky hair that stuck straight up. Sending the first video via e-mail to her sister wasn't the same. Nora found she couldn't even push the send button. She made Paul do it.

When Mariana had finally come to meet her niece, a whole three days late, Ellie's birth-pale eyes had already darkened. Angrily, Nora hadn't wanted to hand her sister the baby, who'd been crying most of the day. Most of her *life*, it seemed. Mariana didn't deserve to hold this bundle, this part of herself.

Finally, Mariana snapped, "I'm sorry I missed her birth. All right? I'll keep saying it if it makes you happy. Is that what you want? You know I would have done anything I could to be with you, and I couldn't and it wasn't my *fault*."

"You're just . . ." It was never Mariana's fault. Nora looked at Ellie's face, covered in angry tiny bumps. Her mouth was wide, busy with furious hiccups. Her hands were clenched in fists. "Sometimes . . . you're careless."

"Careless?"

"Not sometimes. You're always careless."

"You're worried I'll break your baby?"

Mariana broke lots of things. It was something to worry about.

But finally Nora said, "Here." She thrust Ellie at her twin. "Knock yourself out." Ellie would scream—she always did when taken from her mother's arms, not that she didn't do it in *her* arms, too.

Mariana's face had shifted, softening. Ellie immediately quieted and stared upward, as if trying to figure out the differences between this new woman and the woman who normally held her. "Oh," said Mariana. "Hello, my wee chipmunk."

Mariana's whole body held Ellie, not just her arms. A sudden earthquake could have tossed them all to the ground, and Mariana would have held up an unscathed Ellie seconds later,

Nora knew, taking the entire hit herself. Ellie was as safe in Mariana's arms as she was in Nora's. Safer, perhaps, without the mother's baggage, which came complete with a roll-aboard of concern and a carry-on of guilt.

Ellie calmed.

Cooed.

Her face smoothed, the red turned to pink, and her little fists relaxed into starfishes.

It would have been unbearable if it hadn't been Mariana.

Instead, it was gorgeous.

It was still like that, even now, on the ferry. Ellie leaned comfortably against Mariana's arm as they both looked down at something on Ellie's cell phone. Her daughter never did that casual lean anymore with Nora. They used to cuddle on the couch at night with their feet tucked under each other's. Now any physical contact was rare. Ellie ducked Nora's hands, which moved to smooth her hair, scooting out of hugs too quickly. Nora wanted to clutch but knew she couldn't; it would only make it worse. She remembered the feeling of ducking their own mother, of desperately wanting the hug offered and at the same time feeling like she might stop breathing if she had to take it.

Knitting might help. She took out the green sock she'd been working on for months. What she lacked in skill, she made up for in enthusiasm. Or at least she hoped her enjoyment of knitting would help hide the two holes she'd already left behind, one in the toe, the other at the heel. She was knitting them toe up and would stop eventually, when they were long enough. Her friend Lily had said they were ugly. "Puke green, that's what that is. That yarn should be illegal."

Lily. She'd almost told her. Almost spilled the diagnosis a few weeks before when they'd met at a coffee shop to knit together. "I know you're hiding something," Lily had said. Her nimble fingers made the lacework she was doing look easy.

Nora had held her sock in progress crumpled in her fist. She'd gotten as far as, "I . . . ," before her voice stopped as if she'd swallowed a cork.

She and Lily had met two years before, when Nora had shown up at a stitch-n-bitch. Nora herself knitted a little bit, just like she quilted and crocheted and scrapbooked. She knew how. These women were different—knitting was their language, how they moved through the world. They recorded what they believed by the yarn they held. Nora's recorder on the couch next to her, her notebook on her lap, she'd attempted to divine from the knitters what it meant to them—this yarn-as-life movement. *Is it a reclamation of the domesticity of the hearth?* she'd asked. *Does it bring you back to your roots? Were your grandmothers shepherdesses? Do you feel wisdom in the fiber?* Lily had pushed down her oversized black glasses and said, "Cut the shit. We just like to drink wine together. This is more fun than a damn book club. Put your recorder away, huh? Just knit with us." They'd been close friends since that moment.

But that morning, a few weeks ago, Nora hadn't been able to tell her. Lily had known something was wrong, but she'd just waved her ice blue yarn in her direction. "Just knit, darlin'. Tell me if you want to. I'm here. Till then I'm going to tell you how I found not one, not two, but *three* vaporizers in my son's room. I would think if you had one, you wouldn't need another one, right? How much weed can one eighteen-year-old smoke? Or vape, or whatever it is they're doing these days." She threw her yarn over the needle with a sigh. "Be glad you have a girl. Boys are the *worst*."

Nora had gone home, the destructive secret still caught inside her. She couldn't believe she'd even considered telling Lily before Mariana. Before Ellie. If she said it out loud, it might make it true, it might make her believe it, and while she was *almost* there, it still wasn't real. Not quite yet. When she told Mariana, it would be true. When she told Ellie, she might stop breathing forever.

The Alcatraz boat rolled with a wake and Nora felt her stomach answer. Ellie giggled and pointed happily to something on her screen. Mariana nodded and said something Nora couldn't catch.

Suddenly Nora couldn't remember the last time she and Ellie had slept in the same bed. Ellie always used to want her to climb in bed with her. God, could it have been two years? Was she fourteen the last time they fell asleep listening to each other's breathing? Or thirteen? Was this the disease? Or just a misplaced memory that anyone could have lost?

Nora missed Ellie desperately, and she was only a chair away on the other side of her twin. How much worse would it get? The balls of Nora's feet ached with longing. If only she could just reach around Mariana and wrap a tendril of Ellie's hair around her finger. For that matter, she wanted to grab the edge of Mariana's wool coat and dig her fingers in and hold on, long after the ferry docked and the tourists departed. They'd be the last three on the boat. Nora would be wrapped in and around Mariana and Ellie, her feet hooked around their ankles, her hands clutching whatever part of their clothing she could grab. The people who worked on the boat would come to move them along, kick them out to join the tour, and Nora would put her head back and scream and not let them rip her from the two people she needed most.

Mariana noticed, of course. "Is something wrong?"

"Nah," said Nora. She flapped the end of the sock.

"You're never going to finish knitting that thing." Mariana drew back as a child raced past. "And I don't believe you."

Nora smiled at her sister. "It's nothing. Nothing much. Tell you later."

Chapter Fourteen

"*En arrivant à Alcatraz, on donnait chaque prisonnier une carte de bibliothèque et une liste de livres disponibles.*"

The library was Nora's favorite part of the Alcatraz tour—it always had been. She loved standing there, listening to the narrator talk about the prisoners who had read behind the most infamous bars in the nation. The high ceiling above her, the narrow shelves, the complete lack of seating sans one hard wooden bench—all of it made it real. For the men in Alcatraz, if they'd read in the library, there would have been no lounging on a couch, feet up on extra cushions, a glass of hot tea at hand. Nora thought longingly of her own living room.

Nora wandered with the group, looking up to where the grenade blast was still visible in the ceiling from when the jail was taken over by six prisoners. She'd heard the audio narration so many times that last time she'd gotten the Spanish version. This time, French. "*Les prisonniers pouvaient emprunter des magazines aussi, cependant on déchirait les pages avec les nouvelles de crime,*" *et les journaux étaient interdits.*" She wasn't very good at either language, but she caught a lot of it. Mariana, still fluent from the two years she'd lived there, had chosen German. Only Ellie had gone with the tried-and-true English version.

This was Ellie's trip, really. It had been her turn to choose what they did for Easter, and she'd always been fascinated by Alcatraz. "I like thinking about them," Ellie would say, "because most people don't think about them anymore. I can't get them out of my mind, those men sitting in solitary confinement in D Block, watching the lights of the city."

They were criminals, Nora would point out gently. They'd done things to deserve to be there.

"But some of them were innocent."

Nora couldn't deny that. Some of them probably had been.

Ellie's eyes would fill up with tears. "Imagine them, away from their families, so close they could hear the music from dances on the Embarcadero. I read that some nights they could smell women's perfume if the wind was right. And they were here, alone." Nora and Mariana would gently tease her, but they loved this about her—her tenderness. Her empathy.

Now Ellie had that moony look again at the end of the tour, the same one she always got. "Can we stay?"

Mariana said, "Or we could go back and get clam chowder in a bread bowl."

Nora's stomach rumbled.

"Please? The next ferry leaves in an hour, and we could wander around outside."

"It's pretty dreary out there," Nora pointed out.

"But it stopped raining, and that's why we're wearing coats," said Ellie. "Please?"

Mariana said, "I don't mind if you don't, Nora. We can take our coffee out and talk." *You can tell me why you're being weird.* She didn't have to say it for Nora to hear it.

Nora couldn't tell them. Not here. What had she been thinking?

That she would introduce them to a brand-new personal grief in the place where so much sadness had lived for so long? "Okay," she managed.

At the door that led outside, a woman with a purple stripe in her black hair touched Nora's elbow. "Excuse me. I'm sorry, but aren't you Nora Glass?"

Nora swallowed. "Yes." She was. Wasn't she?

The woman broke into a delighted laugh. "Oh, I just *love* you. Johnny—that's my boyfriend right there—hey, Johnny, I *told* you it was her! I *told* him it was you. We're from Spokane, and I read your column every week. You look so much *younger* than your picture in the paper looks. Oh, my *god*. Is that Ellie? Johnny, that's Ellie! From the book! Hi, Ellie!"

With a cheery and very fake smile, Ellie waved on her way outside.

"You're just so *funny*. You know? Like that story about the stray chicken who got into your house. Remember that? Can you say something funny? Johnny, she's going to say something funny. Watch. She's hilarious."

Nora felt herself blush. "Oh . . ."

Mariana stepped forward. "I'm the sister. Yep. The twin." She shook hands with the woman and her boyfriend. "I know she'd love to spend more time getting acquainted but Nora here has the whooping cough."

Nora tried to make a coughing sound but it came out more like a manic yawn.

"Highly contagious."

The woman covered her mouth with her hand.

"So we'll just head outside where she can breathe a little better, and hey, Happy Easter to you!"

"Whooping cough?" asked Nora as they headed outside.

Mariana shrugged. "I heard about it on NPR. Making a comeback."

Under the cold, gray sky, Nora and Mariana watched Ellie

scramble on the rocks. She couldn't go out far—people weren't allowed out of the safely prescribed area—but she went as far as she could, and then, of course, a few feet farther.

"She's so tall," said Mariana, her hands wrapped around her paper coffee cup. "Almost as tall as us now."

Nora didn't answer. There was something stuck in her windpipe, something that had swept in off the bay and was choking her.

Mariana sidled closer on the bench. Their thighs and shoulders touched. "Tell me."

"I can't." The words were a whisper.

"I know it's not nothing. Your eyes have that look they had . . . when Mom died. And as far as I know, no one's died. And you're not looking at me."

"I am, too." But Nora knew Mariana was right. Since they'd met Mariana at the dock, Nora hadn't really met her sister's eyes. She couldn't.

"It can't be that bad."

"It is."

"Oh, no." Mariana turned and faced her. "Just tell me."

Nora stared.

"Cancer," Mariana said. "Is that it? We can't have it. We're too young."

The *we* was what made Nora stand up. They weren't together in this. They *couldn't* be. That was the whole point. Statistics bashed around inside Nora's head like heavy moths trying to get out. Nora knew so much now, terms she hadn't ever seen before: autosomal dominant, penetrance, presenilin-1, receptor binding, secretases.

It all added up to one thing: Mariana had to get tested, as quickly as possible. With the PS1 mutation, Mariana had a fifty-fifty chance of having EOAD.

So did Ellie.

It was too much.

Nora put one hand at her waist and the other over her stomach. "Alzheimer's," she gasped.

Looking confused, Mariana said, "Who?"

At the fence line, Ellie hopped from one broken chunk of concrete to another one. She crouched as if looking for tide pools, even though there couldn't be any, not up so high.

"Me."

Mariana gave a surprised yip that turned into a laugh. "Oh, my god, you just scared me so much."

Nora stared at her. She should have written this out. She should have had notes that she could refer to, so she could keep going. "No . . ."

"You're terrible." Mariana grinned wider. "I really thought you were sick."

"Early-onset."

Mariana barely looked at her, her eyes on Ellie. "What?"

"It starts early."

"Honey! I'm supposed to be the one who exaggerates problems! We're forty-four. We forget things now. It's normal. It happens to everyone. Deep breath."

"No."

"You worry too much." Mariana brushed away a strand of hair from Nora's face. "Ow." She laughed. "That's my own hair."

Anger burned in Nora's chest. Irrational, unwelcome heat. "I've been diagnosed."

"Is this like the Epstein-Barr?"

Nora gritted her teeth. She'd self-diagnosed with that, years ago. Her first WebMD accident. She'd been wrong, and she'd admitted that over and over again, usually as Harrison and Mariana laughed at her. "No."

"You're serious."

"Yes."

Mariana's face changed, straightened. "I'm sorry."

"It's okay." Nora twisted the silver ring Mariana had brought her years before from a trip to Mazatlán. Mariana had learned to surf there, she remembered.

"Tell me. Is this a big deal or a little one?"

"Not that big a deal," Nora said. "I'll just forget everything, including how to walk, eat, talk, and swallow. Then I'll die."

Her sister stood. Without saying a word, she turned her back and headed toward the concrete steps that led to the wide doors of the entrance. She walked with purpose, the same way Ellie did.

Ellie.

She was still by the rocks, pulling on a piece of ice plant. Out of earshot. She looked like a child playing with rocks one moment, and the next, she looked like a teenager again, checking her cell phone. On the other side of Ellie the bay was choppy and dark gray. The city was almost obscured by the fog, the skyline murky, Coit Tower only a suggestion.

Nora sat alone on the bench. The cold had seeped through her jeans and her bones ached with something more than the chill.

Her sister stopped moving, twenty yards away. A guide dressed like a prison guard stationed on the top step watched them both.

Mariana turned. She marched back. Nora stayed still.

Then she grabbed Nora in a hug so hard that it healed her very bones, the same ones that had been aching.

She said only one word, the word Nora needed her to say.

"No."

It was a relief, such a clear and light relief, to hear verbalized the only word that had made any sense to Nora for weeks. *No, no, NO.* She said it back. "No."

"Good. Agreed."

Nora looked down and then licked her thumb. She rubbed at a dark spot on her coat that might have been coffee. "Where were you going?"

"Dunno," said Mariana. "I just had to get out, and then I realized there was nowhere to go."

I know.

They sat in silence for a moment, watching Ellie tap something into her phone.

"Who's she texting?" asked Mariana, as if it were just another overcast day.

"No idea."

"Think of all the trouble we'd have gotten into if we'd had cell phones. Can you imagine?"

"How do I tell her?" *How do I break her?* How would Nora tell her anything, come to that? She watched her daughter's blond hair—too long, with the layers grown out—swing as she ducked her head to look under a heavy-looking piece of broken metal. Nora imagined for a moment what she would write later. In her Moleskine, with her favorite Paper Mate SharpWriter pencil, in very dark letters: *What I Haven't Taught Ellie.*

How to . . .

How to live . . .

Holy crap, she had no idea. She had essays, so many of them, telling people how to do things. She'd researched and then told her readers how to make a perfect crust, how to decorate cupcakes, and how to bake no-knead bread. She'd made budgeting seem easy, something her readers could accomplish. She'd given so many time-saving tips she thought she should at some point get at least one twenty-five-hour-day as repayment.

But what did *Ellie* need to know? Nora wrote for women, for working mothers, for adults. She didn't write about how to become a woman. That was something she'd been teaching her daughter as they went. What were the things she might forget to tell her?

HOW TO PUT ON LIPSTICK

Swipe your top lip first, following the curve on each side. Don't be afraid to coat thickly. Now mash your lips together three times, using the color on the top lip to fill in the bottom lip. If you need more color, add sparingly to the bottom. Use the tip of your first finger to clean the lines, to make sure that dip in your top lip (so deliciously perfect, thought Nora, remembering her daughter's rosebud-sweet mouth; strangers used to comment on it when she was little—a Gerber smile) *is clear of color. Now smile at yourself. Then check your teeth. If you're applying for a job, check twice. If it's a really important date, check three times.*

Such a small, tiny thing, but it matters.

She rewrote the last line in her head again. *Small things are what make a life big.*

Self-pity raked its talons across Nora's chest, tearing open her heart, leaving it beating, but just barely. She grabbed a breath of wet salt air that scraped her lungs. A *job*. Ellie would have a job that Nora would never know anything about. A writer? Ellie saw the world in stories, creating them where there were none. She always had. A journalist, maybe? God, Nora hoped not. It was a difficult, poorly compensated life, although now, with the Internet, some things were a little easier. . . . At least Nora had gotten syndicated just in time, right when Paul's alimony was going to end, right when she'd been worrying about how she'd keep the house, losing sleep thinking about what kind of second job she could possibly find.

"How long does—?" Mariana's voice cracked.

Nora jerked herself back to the present. The concrete bench where they sat seemed to be getting colder under her, not warmer. She shrugged. "No one seems to know. Maybe a year. Maybe three. One guy lived eleven years after his diagnosis, but he got it at thirty-four, so . . ."

Mariana bent at the waist as if the breath had been knocked out of her.

"I'm sorry," said Nora.

"They're wrong. Aren't they?"

"Maybe," she said lightly. She could give her sister this.

"You need a second opinion. That's what people do."

This is the second opinion talking.

"We'll fix it," Mariana continued. "We'll get you fixed."

She grabbed her wallet out of her purse, as if to pay for the remedy. She peered inside. "I have . . . I don't have much, but you can have it. All of it. But Luke has money, and . . ."

"We don't need his money."

"This can't *happen*."

Nora felt Mariana's fury prickle along her skin. Or maybe it was her own anger. She couldn't tell, sometimes, where she left off and Mariana began. It felt good—something she hadn't let herself feel yet. Rage.

"I'm staying with you tonight."

Startled, Nora said, "At my house?"

"What the hell else would I mean?"

"What about Luke?"

"We're barely talking now. Not since Valentine's Day and the ring. He's shut me out."

"Oh, Mariana."

"Screw him."

"Really?"

"No," said Mariana. "I love him. But he doesn't matter. *You* matter."

A thicker relief trickled down the back of Nora's throat. "Sleepover?"

Mariana took her hand and gripped it so hard it hurt. "Will you make me orange juice?"

"I'll squeeze a thousand oranges. Just for you." She could almost taste Mariana's thick pancakes, still liquid in the middle. Perfect.

Ellie waved from the top of a broken piece of concrete and then jumped down lightly, as if she were folded paper. Nora's origami girl. She shouldn't be out in the rain.

"We'll tell her tonight," said Mariana.

Nora nodded. "Maybe."

Mariana squeezed her hand harder. "Together."

Chapter Fifteen

We're not telling her today. We can't. It's not time. Not today. Soon. When we know more. Not today. Please. Not now.

Mariana would do anything for her sister when Nora's eyes looked like that.

God, please don't let her cry again.

She punched a pillow and turned it over. She lifted her hair so the coolness of the pillow soothed her neck, which felt rigid with knots.

Sick.

Sick.

Sick.

It was the only word Mariana would let rattle around in her brain. The other words—words that were too big, too hard—she let go of with tight breaths, breaths that should move more easily, if she could figure out how to breathe ever again.

Open hands cling to nothing.

They were words she'd said on the meditation podcasts how

many times? Hundreds, at least. It was BreathingRoom's catch-phrase. Two weeks ago, a blogger had quoted her on HuffPo, and their Web site hits had tripled. *Open hands cling to nothing.*

She couldn't help it. She was clinging.

She slid farther under the bedding. One breath in, one breath out, dropping the words *death, alone, gone, memory, light, Nora.*

Nora.

Another breath. Luke, if he were here, would lie in front of her. He would scoop both sides of her face in his big hands and put his mouth next to her ear. *Breathe, love.* She would take his breath, eating it right in front of him, accepting what he offered. She was supposed to be the Zen one, but he was the one who calmed her.

He wasn't here, though. He would have been, had she asked him. But they were on such uneasy footing since she'd said no to his proposal. He said he was okay whenever she asked him, but he barely met her eyes when he smiled. She worried she was losing him.

Or she *had* worried about that until she suddenly had to worry about losing the most important one of all.

Mariana put her nose under the top sheet and breathed.

Usually these sheets against her skin—the smell of them—filled her with a contentment she didn't find anywhere but retreat centers. Yoga was the closest she came to it in everyday life—the tired, heavy warmth of her limbs as she got into the car Luke had bought her for her birthday and used the seat warmer on the way home. Or postorgasm, when there was nothing to do but breathe and feel Luke's chest behind her, rising and falling. That's how good the smell of Nora's sheets was. Once, years before, Mariana had tried talking Nora into doing her laundry for her. She'd actually thought for a moment that Nora would do it. Of course, Mariana might have had a bit too much to drink, which had been the reason she'd stayed over that night. She was embarrassed now to think of it, the recollection a sharp poke in her mind. This was before BreathingRoom, before Mariana had to be better. "Please?" she'd said to Nora. "I need this. To *smell* this every night. Oh, the *heaven* of it. Please?"

Sitting on the edge of the bed, Nora had looked at her with wide eyes. "Are you asking me to be your *maid*?"

"No!" She didn't have the money, anyway. "It's just . . ." Mariana had clutched the sheets with both hands, pulling them to her nose again. "Maybe I am. I just want your sheets. Come on."

Nora's gaze had been amused. "I can't believe you're asking me to change your bed linens."

She called them linens! No one was as Martha Stewart as her sister, not even goddamn Martha herself. "Please? It won't take you more than an hour to get over the Golden Gate if you come mid-day. You come into the city once a week to go to the office anyway, right?"

Nora's chin moved from amused to cold. "Won't you be back here soon enough, anyway?" Ice rattled her syllables, the sign to back off.

It had rankled, that assumption her sister held that Mariana would fuck up again and have to move back in. Although, with the sun-scented sheets . . .

"I *have* a life," Nora continued, the implication that Mariana didn't have one. "A job. Your sheets can smell exactly the same as mine. Just get a clothesline. Amazon. Twenty bucks."

They wouldn't smell the same, though. Sheets line dried in San Francisco would smell of burritos and diesel, not ocean and blue skies. Nora's sheets smelled of Tiburon and morning hikes and afternoon picnics on sunshiny Mount Tam.

Now, her phone in her hand, the sheets over her nose, Mariana brought up a search window before she caught herself.

No.

She would *not* google early-onset Alzheimer's. She would *not*. Her fingers felt an ache at the tips, adrenaline surging in painful spikes. Before she could punch the letters into the search box, she threw the phone away from her so that it landed on top of the blanket at her feet.

Mariana pulled the sheets up higher, now to just below her eyes. One breath in, one breath out. She taught users of the BreathingRoom app to imagine their breath as the ocean, their thoughts as the waves. You didn't need to follow waves to shore to make sure of the sea. The water was always there, no matter what.

What if, one day, the ocean were drained bone-dry?

There was a knock at the door, and then Ellie stuck her golden head around. "Can I come in?"

Mariana threw off the covers and opened her arms. "Get in with me, you gorgeous chipmunk of an Ellie-bean."

Chapter Sixteen

*H*er niece ran at the bed like she had when she was a little girl, getting to sleep with her aunt on very special occasions. She leaped and slid in. Mariana noticed for perhaps the first time how long her niece's legs had gotten. "How tall are you now?"

"Five-five," said Ellie. "I feel like I'm going to get a little taller but maybe not by more than an inch or so." She put a pillow against the headboard and shimmied backward, comfortable in her skin. Mariana wondered if at that age, that terrible age of sixteen, she would have been able to leap into an adult's bed and cuddle up close. Then, the only person she had cuddled with was Nora. They'd always had their own beds, but every night Mariana had crept out of her own and into Nora's, folding her body to fit her sister's, falling into the thick, hard sleep that made her blood feel like maple syrup. The worst way Nora could punish her during a fight was to tell her she couldn't sleep with her. Mariana had a clear memory of standing next to Nora's bed one night when they couldn't have been more than eight or nine—Nora wouldn't let her in the bed, even though during the day Mariana had been the offended party, upset that Nora had let next-door neighbor Sven cut the hair of her garage-sale-but-precious-nonetheless Barbie. Mariana had been exhausted and too stubborn to patch up the fight. Nora refused to pull back the covers. Mariana's legs shook, trembling, as she stood next to Nora's bed for an hour—maybe more—until Nora's rigid posture wilted and Mariana knew she could creep beneath the blankets. She could trick Nora into cuddling her until the morning, when the fight would likely begin again with just as much spirit.

Now Ellie was the one she cuddled as often as she could. "Five foot five? How would you know you're close to done growing? You could go to six-two."

"I just know," said Ellie. "I can tell my body doesn't want to get much taller." She lifted the sheet and peeked underneath. "I think my boobs are going to get bigger, though."

"If you're anything like us, they will." It was a lament. Neither she nor Nora loved their abundant bra size. It was easier to go fast when you had less weighing you down.

"That'll be okay. I'll need a new bra."

Mariana sighed and wriggled her feet closer to her niece's. "I would never have been able to ask for that when I was your age."

"A bra? Why not?"

Why not? Because their mother hadn't liked to admit that her daughters' bodies were changing, and when she'd been forced to face it—the first bra, the first box of maxi pads—she'd made them feel like they'd done something wrong. It wasn't as if their mother had acted mad at them—she was usually too tired to be very angry about anything. Ruthie Glass had worked two waitressing jobs to pay for their small apartment, and when she was at home, she was usually sleeping as hard and fast as she could. Pads and bras were expensive, money that wasn't in the budget and—when the twins were twelve—suddenly had to be.

"Your grandma didn't like to talk about stuff like that."

"How did you learn, then?"

Mariana pushed a second pillow under her head. "We figured it out. Together, me and your mom."

"How? There weren't computers then, right?"

Mariana laughed. "You make us sound ancient." But Ellie was right—how *had* they learned about what was going on inside their bodies? The Internet hadn't existed in the mideighties. They'd learned from osmosis. They'd read Judy Blume books to learn about bras. Nora, a better, faster reader than Mariana ever was, whispered the words to Mariana at the kitchen table while their mother snored on the couch. At the library, they'd pored over the Whole Earth Catalog, staring at the products that might or might not have been vibrators. In seventh grade, Becca Tripton had told them she'd had sex with a ninth grader, but she'd been their only firsthand authority, and Becca had also thought you could get pregnant from a toilet seat, something Mariana and Nora had a hard time believing. "We read as much as we could. And we guessed."

"How did you guess about something like your period? She must have told you something."

"She gave us a brown paper bag."

Ellie made a sound like someone was tickling her. "What was in it? Oh! Did it have one of those sanitary napkins with the straps and the belt?"

"Are you kidding me? Do you think I'm eighty years old?" At Ellie's age, forty-four and eighty were practically the same thing. "I never wore a *belt*." Thank god. Mariana had always had a hard time with period management—she still did. Nora had always been good at it—she'd always known when she was going to start and always had in her purse exactly what she would need. She'd always had what Mariana would need, too, pressing a tampon into her hand in the hallway at school, not needing to ask why Mariana looked so panicked. Even now, Mariana could be at work and feel total surprise when she got a cramp. But why . . . ? It had to have been . . . oh, four weeks since the last one. Of course. Always a total fucking surprise. "No, in the bag was a box of tampons and a box of mini pads and a cartoon leaflet titled something like *Your Body and You.*"

"How old were you?"

"When we got our periods? Twelve."

Ellie nodded knowledgeably. "That's the median age."

"Really? It used to be thirteen, I thought." Poor girls. Everything was so hard at that age, and to have to balance sudden, new blood at an even younger age was just rude.

"Hormones," said Ellie. "In our tap water."

"What?"

"I wrote a paper about it. Female growth hormones are everywhere now, in our water and in the plastic things we buy and the animals we eat. It's why girls get breasts earlier nowadays. Some boys even get boobs. And it's why our periods start sooner."

Mariana glanced down at her own chest. "Unfair."

Ellie shrugged. "It is what it is. Did Mom ever tell you about when she taught me how to put in a tampon?"

Mariana barked a laugh. "No."

"Yeah. She was so uncomfortable about the whole thing."

"I *bet* she was." Nora might have always known when her period was coming, but she sure hadn't liked to talk about it. She liked to manage it. To handle it.

"I needed her to! I wasn't going to just put something up there without help."

Mariana couldn't contain her hilarity. "You're killing me. Did you make her put it *in*?"

Ellie laughed, too, her girlish giggle shifting to something more grown-up right in the middle. Mariana realized she was laughing like she did with a friend. "Oh, my god, Ellie, I'm dying."

"Of course I made her. And it hurt, so I made her take it out and put it back in. It took, like, an hour. It was awful."

"Oh, my god, if I didn't know you like I do, I would swear you were making that up."

Ellie looked surprised. "What's wrong with that? Who else is supposed to show me if not Mom?"

"You're right, chipmunk. I love that you don't give a shit." It came out of her mouth wrong. It wasn't exactly what she meant to say, but it was true: Ellie *didn't* give a shit about some things. She didn't seem to care about the way she looked, for example. She wore sloppy clothes that she liked, T-shirts with holes at the stomach that had dinosaurs roaring at robots on them. Her favorite pair of jeans looked like mom jeans, big in the butt, a little too long at the bottom, but with pockets that Ellie loved to fill with things she found when she was outside. Even when she was little, when Mariana "borrowed" her to stay overnight in her small, old apartment in San Francisco, Ellie managed to fill her pockets with rocks and sticks and leaves of plants that smelled good. Trees were set in sidewalks and gardens were more expensive to maintain than cars, but Ellie brought the natural world inside with her without really trying. She still did that. Tonight, she'd gone out on the porch after dinner to talk to someone on the phone and had come in with cobwebs in her hair, as if she'd been wriggling under the porch.

But Ellie didn't seem to mind what Mariana had said. She twisted a bit farther down the bed and turned on her side so she could face her aunt. She breathed softly, and Mariana wanted to wrap her up and hold her tight, but she didn't want to startle her. This was nice enough. This, in her sister's miraculous sheets.

Her sister . . .

Nora had said she needed to wait. That she wasn't ready to tell Ellie. She'd said she needed the exact words. *Maybe a counselor. I'm thinking of hiring someone to help me figure out exactly what to say.* That, as much as anything, had turned Mariana's bones to ice. If *Nora* needed help finding the right words, then the rest of them should probably give up on language entirely.

Breathe. Now. This moment was all she had, this moment with the sixteen-year-old she loved the very, very most. "Who were you talking to earlier?"

Ellie's expression was sleepy already, her cheeks soft, her lashes low. "Mmmm?"

"When you went out on the porch when we got home."

A different smile creased her niece's face. "Yeah."

"Oh, really? I know the sound of that 'yeah.' Who is he?"

She smiled more deeply. "No one."

"Hmmm. I know that guy, and he's usually pretty hot."

One shoulder lifted and dropped. Ellie kept her eyes closed, but her expression was complicated. Satisfied and worried, all at once.

"Okay, you want me to guess."

Ellie nodded once.

"He's a pirate."

Ellie's eyelids flew open, her face amused. "Kind of. But only in the computer way."

"Isn't that almost as dangerous as the high seas nowadays?"

"Nah. And if I tell you anything, you have to not judge him. Or tell Mom."

Fair enough, if she could wrangle info out of her. "So an online pirate."

"He torrented the game we play." Then Ellie covered her mouth with her hand.

"A gamer. I should have known. Is this *Mynga 7*?"

"No." Scornful. "I haven't played that in, like, months."

"That Queen-whatsit?"

"*Queendom.* It's awesome. The topography is sick and it's *totally* interactive. You get to make up your stories as you go. Like, I'm writing story lines, and other players are picking them and playing them." Pride lit Ellie's eyes. "I'm . . . He likes the stories, too."

"Okay. So this guy is a player. He . . . Let me guess. He rides a winged something."

"Close."

"He's a shape-shifter."

Ellie shook her head. "No."

"A dragon."

"I *wish* he was."

"He kills them."

Ellie looked admiringly at Mariana. "I wish Mom ever noticed what was going in my games."

"She does," said Mariana, knowing Nora didn't.

"It's okay. I'm used to it."

Mariana snuggled farther down, bringing the pillow with her. Ellie smelled adolescently like bubble bath and, faintly, like sweat. "So he kills dragons. And you protect them, right?"

"Yeah. I'm a Healer."

"So you protect and heal dragons and he kills them. I'm getting it. Star-crossed lovers, am I right?"

Ellie shifted, as if suddenly uncomfortable. She rolled onto her back and stared at the ceiling.

Mariana felt the pang of worry again. She could almost hear it, one note being struck deep inside her. Ellie was too young to actually think she was in love or star-crossed. "This is a crush, right?"

"Sure."

"You're saying it's more?" Mariana pushed up on her elbow.

"Nah," said Ellie, but she closed her eyes.

Mariana poked her in the shoulder. "Don't play a player. I'm not your mother."

"Is there . . . I'm not sure, but is there something wrong with her?"

"Are you trying to change the subject on me? Tell me about the boy."

"No, really. I think there's something wrong with her." Ellie rolled back onto her side and grasped the edge of Mariana's pillow lightly. "I do. She hasn't been acting right."

"What do you mean?" Mariana's fingers went cold.

"Distant."

"Like . . ."

Ellie released a deep breath. "Like she's having a hard time remembering who she is. I came home the other day and she was watching TV."

"Oh, my god. You're *kidding* me." Mariana tried to inject lightness into her voice.

"Don't laugh. It was weird. She never *wastes time*." Ellie put the last few words in air quotes. "But the TV was on an infomercial. About hair something. Like maybe to take hair off. Or get more hair. I'm not actually sure what it was. It was just making noise, and she was staring at it like it meant something. Like it was her computer."

Mariana couldn't do this. She wasn't prepared. *Dissemble, cover. Hide.* "Was she working on her next piece, maybe? Did you ask her? Maybe she's finally writing about the hold the tube has over normal mortals like us?"

"I thought maybe that's what it was, but I said hi, and she just looked at me weird." Ellie stuck the corner of her thumbnail into her mouth. Out of habit, Mariana gently pushed her thumb away.

"Don't bite your nails."

"I'm not. And then later, when I came down for dinner, I asked her about it. She said she hadn't watched any TV at all. She pretended like she didn't know what I was talking about."

"Oooh. I know. She's going hairy in places she can't mention, and she was trying to hide it from you." Mariana gave a laugh that felt as forced as it was. "Depilation happens, you know, even in the best of families."

"Fine. Whatever. That's probably it."

They were humoring each other.

"I'll find out," said Mariana.

"You will?" The hope in Ellie's voice melted Mariana inside. The sweetest thing, the most honest, true, and brave thing about the relationship between Nora and Ellie was how much the mother and daughter cared about each other. Mariana had always stood outside it, watching. Admiring. *Wanting.* Nora would kill for Ellie, that was obvious and natural. That's what mothers did. And Mariana knew she would lay down her own life for Ellie, too. In a fucking heartbeat.

But Ellie would die for Nora, too. A child didn't normally feel like that, did they? They hadn't felt that way about their mother, Ruthie, although both of them had tried their best. Ruthie'd always been too distant, too busy, trying to scrape nickels and quarters together out of thin air and thinner tips. Then Ruthie had died so young, when they were only twenty, falling asleep at the wheel of her car on the way home from Pedro's Cantina. They'd never known their mother as adults.

Jesus. Mariana lost her breath. Ellie wouldn't—might not—know Nora as an adult, either.

Jesus *fuck.* Without Nora to take care of Ellie . . . Without Nora to take care of *her* . . . Mariana's brain stalled, then spiraled in a downward dive.

Ellie said, "I think the migraines might be back. Or something. I think she's in pain and she doesn't want to worry me, but I'm sixteen, for Pete's sake. I can handle it. Doesn't she know that?"

Mariana stared at her niece. It was gorgeous to witness, all that love swimming in Ellie's eyes; it was like seeing sunshine break into diamonds, like watching emeralds run out of your kitchen faucet.

"I'll find out, chipmunk."

"When you do, tell me."

"Okay. I will."

"Promise?"

Was it a lie if you loved this hard? This brightly? "I promise."

Chapter Seventeen

Have you figured it out yet?

The pop-up box made a soft ping that felt like a shiver.

Ellie hadn't even seen Dyl's Incurser approach her
hut's window. Now she could see him, outside and swaying with
that rocking motion all the human avatars used. Cmd-shift-O
opened the door, and Dyl's character strode inside, his sword swinging wide. In the game he was taller than Addi the Healer. Ellie
wondered if that would be true in real life, if she'd be able to stand
under his arm. She bit the inside flap of her cheek. *Have I figured out
what?* Awesome. Was Dylan going to start being like everyone else
now? Would he ask her constantly (like her school counselor did)
what she wanted to "do with her life"? Would he try to guess (like
her mother did) what careers might suit her brain/hands/eyes/tem-
perament? Ellie couldn't figure out whether she preferred spearmint
or wintergreen toothpaste. How was she supposed to figure out
what kind of cubicle she wanted to fill in, like, five years?

```
Have you found out what's wrong
with your mom?
```

Oh.

Of course that's what he would ask. Dylan was, like, the nicest guy she'd ever met in her whole life.

Not yet, she typed.

```
How are you doing? Are you still
worried about her?
```

Seriously, what other guy would ask that? Guys didn't pay attention to parents, even their own. Ellie would bet that not one of her guy friends knew her mother's name, even though she'd picked them up from water polo about a hundred times, even though she'd bought them all pizza so often she knew their favorite kinds.

Dyl was an Incurser. And therefore he shouldn't be trusted.

But there *were* a few good ones out there. She'd read about them on the *Queendom* FanForums, stories of Incursers who'd inexplicably come to the unexpected rescue of fair maiden or dire dragon. At the last moment, when they should have been stabbing a beast to its gory death, they reversed and healed it, running away before their compatriots could turn their swords on the traitor.

Ellie was sworn to protect Ulra, the dying Dragon Queen, while Dyl was pledged to eradicate the entire species. Yet here he was, in her hut, asking about her real-life mother.

Ellie took a deep breath before placing her fingers back on the keyboard to answer. She'd had crushes before but they'd never felt so upsetting inside, as if her stomach and heart were in a slap flight. *She's just being so weird. And I saw her talking to my aunt today, and they were both super-upset. I'm totally not imagining it.* A part of her worried again about the way her mom and aunt had held hands—like one of them was trying to pull the other out of deep water—but another part of her was annoyed. She was still the kid. She hadn't called out, "Mom! Watch!" while she'd been on the rocks, but she'd assumed that's what they'd been doing. That was, like, their job.

What do you think it is? Dyl's head bobbed in that "I'm paying attention" way the avatars did. Ellie wondered what position Dylan was actually in. Lying down? Sitting at a table?

Dunno, typed Ellie. *I have no idea.* Her Healer sat on the bench under the crystalline window and then stood up again. The music was sad, a thin violin paired with something deeper, maybe a single cello.

Maybe she's pregnant.

HA! Stop it. She couldn't be. You're hilarious. But her throat tightened like someone was twisting it closed. Harrison.

How old is she?

Forty-three. Forty-four? Old. Too old.

You sure about that? My step-aunt had twins at forty-six. It wasn't pretty.

The slap fight in her stomach turned into a boxing match. *She did sleep with someone. Oh, my god.*

When?

New Year's Eve. That was when she'd heard her mother and aunt talking about it. *Like, three months ago.* When did someone

find out they were knocked up? No, no, no. Wasn't she in menopause or something?

> ```
> You're going to have a little
> brother! Or a sister!
> ```

> **NO.**

Just kidding. It's probably not that. Dyl shuffled, raising his
sword as if he were going to slice the long wooden table in half
and then lowering it again. *It's probably just money troubles or something. Parents get all weird about that.*

They'd been okay with money, though. That's what her
mother had been saying. They couldn't afford a new car right off
the lot or anything—even though Ellie wanted one of those new
electric Smart cars *so* bad, mostly because it was so cute she
wanted to put it in her jacket pocket and keep it there—but Ellie
could tell money wasn't as hard as it used to be before Mom got
syndicated, and it had gotten even easier since she got the book
deal. Ellie remembered when she'd had to bring home her ziplock bags for her mother to wash and reuse. Something rumpled
had smoothed behind her mother's eyes the day she told Ellie she
could throw them out at school, and she stopped being furious if
Dad's child support payments were late.

What if it *was* a baby? God, then her mother would never
pay attention to her again. Ellie sniffed and slid farther under her
sheets.

> ```
> What are you doing on Saturday?
> ```

Ellie's Healer jumped up from sitting, though Ellie didn't
have a plan for what she would do next. She made her juggle the
rainbow crystals she'd bought from a Ginkgo trader last week.

Nothing. Why? Her Healer dropped a red crystal and it melted through the hut's floor with an acidic whoosh.

```
I'm in a band. Wanna come hear us?
```

Ellie couldn't help the sigh that escaped her. Of course Dylan was in a band. *What do you play?* Oh, dumb! That was so dumb! But what else were you supposed to say to someone in a band?

```
Guitar.
```

She gulped. Desperately, Ellie wondered what Aunt Mariana would do if some cool guy asked her to come see him in a band. Breezy. She'd be breezy and casual and not let him think she was that into it. Or was that what she *wasn't* supposed to do? Ellie couldn't remember. She wiggled her fingers in the air in front of her face, using the same motion that her Healer did when fixing wounds.

Then she typed, *Sure. Sounds fun.*

Cool. The response was instant and gratifying. *It's at a cop bar in Oakland.*

```
What's a cop bar?
```

Dyl tossed his sword between his hands. *It's a bar. Where cops hang out.*

She typed slowly, hating the letters as they formed in the small purple box. *I'm underage.* He knew that.

Me, too. Believe me, no one there will care. I'm going to have to protect you from the old letches. Dyl dropped the sword to the floor of the hut with a clatter. *Whoops.*

Ellie wriggled her legs and pulled on both lobes of her ears with delight. Addi the Healer swayed serenely in place on the dirt floor of the hut.

Chapter Eighteen

EXCERPT,
**WHEN ELLIE WAS LITTLE:
OUR LIFE IN HOLIDAYS,**
PUBLISHED 2011 BY NORA GLASS

Mother's Day

When Ellie was little, I was one of those annoying people who assumed I would be a great mother. I knew what I would avoid and what I would do differently. I'd avoid drugs, for example. That was a pretty easy choice. Our mom didn't do the hard stuff, but she was never shy about taking a hit of her boyfriend's joint in front of us. My sister and I knew the best time to ask for movie money was when the adults' eyes were bloodshot and their reactions as slow as cold honey.

I would be more attentive than my mother had been. I would know my daughter's favorite color and what kind of shoes she loved best. I would never accidentally leave her behind at a Pak'n Save, getting all the way back to the apartment before realizing there was only one daughter in the back of her craptastic VW bug. (Mariana had kept her mouth shut because she thought it was hilarious and wanted to see how long Mom would continue to not notice she was missing a daughter.)

I would spend more time with my child than our mother had spent with us. I would *know* my child.

I would mother differently.

I would mother *well*.

When Ellie was eight months old, I got bronchitis. It was something I'd always been prone to—at least once every couple of years, I'd get a bout that would linger for months. It had always been a nuisance, but while nursing, it felt a million times worse. I was more exhausted than ever. I'd nurse, sipping water, praying not to get a coughing spasm, and when one would come, I'd unlatch Ellie's mouth and set her on the bed. She'd wail, and I'd hack for the next five minutes, and then we'd start all over again.

Worried, Paul insisted I see the doctor again. He thought I needed better, stronger medicine. I knew, though, it would go away eventually. It was normal for me. He put his foot down, though, saying that I *had* to go.

Oh, I fumed while I packed the car. It wasn't like *he* had to do anything to go to the doctor. If he wanted to ask a medical professional about a cold, he would just *go*. He didn't have a baby latched to him every second of the day. I could have, of course, insisted he stay home to watch Ellie while I went, but I'll admit that sometimes I enjoyed playing the martyr. "Fine," I muttered, loading Ellie's diaper bag into the car. "I can just do it all." Then I had a coughing attack while standing next to the open car door that lasted so long it actually scared me.

As I drove to the doctor's office, I talked to Ellie in the backseat. "He might be right, Ellie-belly. But let's not tell him. Do we have a deal?" I took her silence to mean we were in cahoots. I liked that about my daughter. She had my back, even at eight months.

In the parking lot at the doctor's office, I saw Paul's red truck. He got out as soon as he saw me, his eyes that sea green shade they took on when he was worried, as if the storm inside him were churning up emotions like a squall stirred the ocean's floor. "I felt terrible that I haven't been helping more with Ellie while you're sick. I canceled the meeting. Here I am." He touched my cheek and looked right into my eyes the way he hadn't in a long time. I remember how good that felt—to be seen by him as a person and not just as the mother of his child.

He continued. "I'll watch her while you go in. Or I'll take her home and watch her there. Whatever you want."

It was cold for May, and I'd worried about her being outside anyway, dressing her as warmly as I could before we left the house. "It would be great if you took her home." I opened the car door and reached inside to unlatch Ellie's seat.

It wasn't there.

Nor was my baby.

The backseat was empty of everything but my purse and the diaper bag.

I said an unprintable word. Paul repeated it.

"Where is she?"

It was clear, instantly, where Ellie was. "I put her in the car seat and set her on the porch steps while I loaded the other stuff."

I dove for the driver's seat of my car. Paul slammed himself in next to me. I wouldn't have blamed him for berating me the whole way home, but he didn't say a word. Not one. That was worse, I think.

Ellie was there when I skidded to a halt in front of the house. She'd fallen asleep, bundled to the ears in wool (a hand-knit sweater my friend Janine had made her, the purple blanket I'd crocheted while I was pregnant with her). The sun had broken through the clouds, and it was actually a lovely, warm place to nap.

But I'd left my baby outside, in the cold, all *alone*, in a place where anyone could have taken her. And worst of all—they would have been *right* to take her. If I'd seen a baby abandoned on a porch, I would have rung the doorbell, waited two minutes, and then taken that child straight to the police department, where I would have demanded justice for such egregious child endangerment.

"They should put me in jail," I said to Paul, sitting heavily on the step next to her. "I should go turn myself in." I was a wonderful housekeeper. If I had hired myself to clean our house, to make the rooms smell sweet, to coordinate dust ruffles to valances, I would have given myself a raise I was so good at it. I was made to hold an iron, to sew a curtain, to bake the perfect brownie. But I was a terrible mother. I didn't even want to touch Ellie. I didn't deserve to. I watched her breathing as if it might stop any minute, and if it had, I would have given her my breath, all of it, forever.

Paul, in a moment of kindness I don't think I've ever recovered totally from, didn't say anything. Not one word. He just kissed my head, picked up Ellie, car seat and all, and took her inside. He closed the door behind him.

I cried and coughed all the way to the doctor's office. I got a new prescription, which I filled while sobbing so hard I got lightheaded. I made it home and cried my way up the stairs.

The only thing that stopped my tears was the sight of them, both of them, asleep in our bed. Ellie's eyes were tightly crinkled shut like Paul's were—I'd never seen the similarity in the way they slept till that moment. They slept hard, as if it were their assignment and they wanted to do it right. I didn't want to wake them up. They were perfect.

No thanks to me, they were safe.

I prayed I wouldn't cough, and I didn't. I slid under the blanket and without opening his eyes, Paul made room for me next to him. He hadn't met Bettina yet. That wouldn't happen for another year.

Right before my eyes drifted shut, I thought of my mother. She hadn't ever cared about Mother's Day. She'd always laughed at the arts-and-crafts construction-paper creations my sister, Mariana, and I brought home from school. It was never an unkind laugh—she would just hold out the *Mom = Love* card festooned with glitter and say, *Mom equals laundry, that's what you should have put on this.*

I'd had no idea what it meant to be a mom. None at all. Since I'd lost mine when I was so young, I only knew it was hard—maybe impossible—and I also knew that this would be only the first of many unforgivable mistakes I'd make with Ellie.

Grace. That's all it was. That was the only reason my baby girl was all right. Grace was the only thing, perhaps, that allowed any mother in the world to make it past lunchtime. That same grace was the only thing that allowed me to sleep that afternoon, with my husband and daughter next to me, all of us in one piece—a family—for a little while longer.

Chapter Nineteen

*I*n her column a few years before, Nora had described what *didn't* go in her ideal picnic basket. Tiny cream cheese and cucumber sandwiches of the type made for high tea, wrapped in wax paper, none of that. A flask of strong, hot coffee and real porcelain mugs—why bother? Petit fours with fondant butterflies, bought fresh from the closest local bakery—cute, but too fussy. Seasonal fruit from the farmer's market—too much work to clean and cut; save that for home. *The point of a picnic isn't to spend hours preparing for a moment that will pass too quickly. Save that time for getting to your ideal location. Laugh in the sunshine with your family and friends.*

No, the ideal picnic basket was fast. *No lavish action here, please. If you have fancy embroidered napkins, this isn't the time to fold them carefully so that they nestle beneath your picnic silver. Paper works just fine. Peanut butter and jelly sandwiches smooshed into a ziplock will do. No fancy desserts—Hostess cupcakes will be appreciated by everyone. You don't even need a fancy picnic basket or wine bottle backpack, though those are fun, of course. A Trader Joe's paper bag will do. Don't worry about a pretty tablecloth to lay on the grass. An oversized beach towel that you grab from the laundry room on your way out will be perfect, and less stress to clean when it gets stained by new grass and grape jelly. The point is that you're together. Eating outside increases food enjoyment exponentially. It's practically scientific and has probably been studied by people in labs, but I'm telling you this: you should study it with your favorite people, and if you bring a Quiddler deck and play while boats chug past on your favorite body of water, it'll probably be the best picnic that ever happened in the history of the world.*

Big words. They were harder to live up to. In the car, on the way to Shoreline Park, Nora racked her brain. She'd forgotten something, she knew she had. She just didn't know what it was, and the feeling, instead of being irritating, was electrically terrifying.

"You should let me drive," said Ellie. "It's Mother's Day."

"That's *why* I'm driving," said Nora. "Because I get to do whatever I want today."

Ellie scooted sideways in her seat and put on a beatific smile. She folded her hands beneath her chin. "Mom. Dearest, beautiful Mom of mine. Don't you know I just want to chauffeur you around? You work so hard. Let me take care of you."

Nora lost her breath in a surprised laugh. "You *really* want to drive."

The act fell away as Ellie thumped back. "Come *on*. I'm good. Mrs. Lytton let me drive her minivan and she said I was a natural."

Nora made a mental note to discuss with Cindy Lytton what was and wasn't appropriate when she was on pickup duty. "I'm fine. It's my picnic, anyway. Oh, *crap*."

Ellie said long-sufferingly, "What?"

"I forgot to tell Mariana to bring plates and cups and cutlery. That was going to be her job."

Ellie didn't drop her feet off the dashboard even though

Nora had already told her to. "We can eat with our fingers. We'll drink out of the Martinelli's bottle! Like wine!"

But Mariana never brought anything—she never remembered to do so when asked and never thought to do so when she wasn't. How could Nora even begin to consider . . . Her stomach dipped as if they'd hit a pothole, but the road was smooth.

"It's just sandwiches, anyway."

"It's the point. I forgot to ask, and she won't bring them."

Ellie stared at her phone. "I don't get what the big deal is."

The big deal? Nora had forgotten to ask. She'd forgotten *another* thing. Another important thing. Another pinprick in the balloon that was supposed to be keeping her in the air.

The third and fourth opinions, the ones Nora had paid for out of pocket, had come back with the same result. Mariana was still unwilling to talk about anything except a cure, and Nora would lay money her sister hadn't yet accepted that all cases of EOAD—*all* of them—ended in death.

Well, hell. Life ended in death, didn't it? Nora was no different. She wasn't special. Spine stiffened with the spray starch she loved so much, Nora could do this. She would do this. She would tell Ellie the truth. The diagnosis. She'd finally tell her today, with Mariana at her side. *Mother's Day*. What a horrible day to do it, but she'd been waiting, hoping for a way out.

It turned out there was no good day to destroy your child's life.

If indeed that's what she did. Lately it seemed that Ellie only tolerated her at best. Like now. If it wasn't Mother's Day, Ellie would have rolled her eyes twenty times already. As it was, Nora could tell her daughter was working incredibly hard to stay polite.

It used to be easy to be together. It used to be joyful.

Mariana had to get tested, too.

Ellie . . .

God, please, not Ellie. No test for Ellie. Nora wouldn't—couldn't—chance her receiving a death sentence. It was bad enough for Nora as it was, at forty-four. To hear your fate at sixteen? Never.

Nora maneuvered around an old green Mercedes that had broken down in the right lane. Then she slammed on the brakes as a light turned red—had it even gone yellow first? *"Dang* it." Her throat felt tight; her eyes were hot like she had a fever. Her hands felt as if they were shaking as hard as her heart was hammering, but when she looked at them on the wheel, she could barely see the tremor. Thank god Harrison insisted on inspecting her car every month or two—her brakes were good, her tire pressure full. Her short stopping distance made up for the fact that she'd almost just run the light.

"Mom, what's going on?"

"Nothing," said Nora.

Ellie kept her face forward, her feet stubbornly on the dashboard. "Then why are we just sitting here?"

"What?"

"The light," Ellie said as behind them cars honked. "It's green."

"It just turned."

"It's been green for a while."

Time. How many seconds had she lost? "No, it hasn't." Was it possible her daughter was just messing with her?

Her eyes felt too dry. Symptoms of early-onset Alzheimer's disease include paranoia and suspicion.

No, Ellie didn't even know yet. And besides, she wouldn't do that.

To their right was an antique store that sold old marina collectibles, and across the street was a chocolate shop that specialized in fair-trade cocoa. Nora could almost taste her favorite treat there—they called it maple bourbon but she could never taste the alcohol. It was just rich and sweet. Jenny, the dark-haired woman who owned the shop, rode a purple penny-farthing that she locked to a chalkboard *Open* sign during store hours. It always looked as if she was on the verge of falling off while she rode it, but somehow the crazy bicycle, with its one huge (penny) wheel and its tiny trailing (farthing) one, stayed up. Maybe it was how Jenny moved her body, balancing . . .

A horn blared. Nora drove past the chocolate shop, then let an older woman with a walker cross in front of her, waving cheerily back at her.

She carefully braked for the next stop sign.

Her hands on the wheel went cold and slick with perspiration.

She had no idea where she was.

The SUV behind her blared, an impatient foghorn.

The terror was visceral, an animal in her chest, its talons hooked in the lining of her lungs as they wheezed. A headache blazed suddenly, insistent and sharp behind her eyes.

"Mom?"

Where was the ocean? Where were the hills? The damn buildings, as short and twee as they were in the little tourist town, were still too tall for her to see over them. If she could just see the foothills of Mount Tamalpais, she'd know which direction home was, but Jesus, where were they headed? Was it the grocery store? Which store? Had they already been? She glanced behind her but the unlabeled brown grocery bag told her nothing. She clutched the steering wheel tighter, unable in her panic to remember anything about the morning that had passed. She couldn't even remember waking up—she was able to recall only the middle of the night, when she'd woken from a dream about Harrison . . . or was that a memory of him? He'd been so tall in it, taller than she remembered him being . . .

"Mom!" Ellie's voice was sharp with fear. "What's going on?" Her feet thumped off the dashboard and down into the footwell.

"Nothing!" said Nora brightly. "I was just making a decision."

"Mom—"

"Just a second." Nora pulled to the side of the road and parked next to a fire hydrant.

"I don't think you're supposed to—"

"You're *right*. You should never, ever park in front of a fire hydrant. Consider that your first lesson today." She unbuckled her seat belt and opened her car door.

"Mom!"

Nora walked around and opened her daughter's door. "Yep."

Ellie's eyes lost their terrified look. "You're going to let me . . . but you've never let me drive on a real road before."

"You have to practice sometime, right? In a place that isn't a big, empty parking lot."

Ellie didn't even get out of the car; she just scrambled over the hand brake into the driver's seat.

Nora carefully breathed around the blade of dual-edged terror in her chest. "Now. Tell me what things you'll do before you merge into traffic."

Ellie's grin was even wider than her left turn onto Tiburon Boulevard.

Chapter Twenty

"*I* would have picked up the utensils and shit if you'd texted me." Mariana shoved her cell back in her pocket, ignoring the text from Luke. It wasn't right that Nora never let her bring anything. "I would have liked to feel useful."

Nora said lightly, "It was my fault for forgetting. I swear, I'm turning into you!"

Forgetting. Nora was going to tease Mariana about *that*? Mariana felt small and mean for even having the thought and said, "I know. But I do try, believe it or not. I even have a lot of stuff left over from the BreathingRoom party I could have brought. We broke ten thousand subscribers. Did I tell you that?"

This appeared to jolt Nora. "You're kidding."

Mariana grinned and bounced on her toes. "Nope. Isn't that *wild*? We're just about to hit the break-even point. Maybe it'll actually *work*." If they did that, if she could actually pay Luke back and stand on her own two feet—well, it would be a long cry from bouncing so many checks she went into collection from the bank fees alone.

Either that or it would fail. Well, she was used to *that*, right? Lightly, Nora said, "Good."

Mariana felt a jab of disappointment. Ten thousand subscribers were probably nothing to Nora, who must have, like, ten *million* readers. She watched as her sister pulled out a tall stack of sandwiches, carefully wrapped in wax paper. Was Nora planning on feeding the family twenty feet away on the grass as well as Tiburon's two homeless guys, who panhandled every day in front of the café? Was she going to hand a sandwich to every one of the joggers who bolted past as if being chased by zombies?

Then came the industrial-sized container of wet wipes. Nora handed her five, as if she thought Mariana had been picking up dog poop barehanded. "Am I supposed to take a bath with these?"

Gratifyingly, Ellie snorted.

"Germs are good for you, you know," added Mariana, but scrubbed her hands anyway. She and Nora would never see eye to eye on it. Cleaning, for Nora, was like some kind of religion, bringing her absolution nothing else could. Nora believed that cleanliness was right. Cluttered was wrong. Elbow grease expunged everything. It was as easy as that. It had been annoying when they lived with their mother, but when they'd roomed together in college, that conflict had often been the catalyst for nuclear explosions of anger on both their parts. Mariana's papers and books and half-empty coffee mugs filled with creamy curdled dregs would drift into Nora's neat half of the apartment, and Nora, instead of just pushing them back toward her, would "tidy" whatever it was. Half the time Mariana hadn't been able to find essentials: her calendar, her wallet, any bra at all. While Mariana ran around the apartment frantically, ripping into drawers and diving under furniture, Nora would say absentmindedly, "Oh, I put your debit card into the junk drawer."

"Why?"

"It was in the kitchen next to the cutting board. It didn't belong there."

"So it belonged in the junk drawer?" What made sense to Nora didn't make sense to Mariana. Her face would go purple with the effort not to yell, but Nora wouldn't even lift her eyes from whatever she was writing at the time, saying, "Just pick up after yourself. If you do it, then I don't have to."

"That's just it. You *don't* have to," Mariana would fume in the front hallway of that tiny apartment, the one that no matter what they'd done to try to mask the scent—candles, flowers, incense—had always smelled faintly of mold. Mariana had loved that place. She'd loved her mess, her sloppily made bed with its covers just right for smooshing all around her sleepy body, the tiny desk she'd picked up on the street on Big Trash Day. (The pulls were missing, that was all. She'd meant to buy or make new ones but never got around to it before selling it for ten dollars, years later at a garage sale, still pull-less.) Her mess held the contents of her mind; it was the real-life display of her thoughts, desires, and actions.

It was still that way. Mariana's home office was a small room in the attic of Luke's house with a slanted ceiling and one small triangular window that would be impossible to replace with thicker glass. It was hot in summer and cold in winter, but she loved it. She'd been going into the brand-new BreathingRoom office most days (it had its own office now! three employees and a water cooler and everything!), but every once in a while, Mariana worked from the attic, falling onto the small green couch under the window for a nap, knocking last week's paperwork to the floor. When the room held seven or eight water glasses, she'd take them down the stairs in a wicker basket her sister had given her. "I use my basket to tidy," Nora had said. "I just walk around the house and pick up what needs to go in another room and walk around till everything's redistributed back to its proper place."

Mariana had said, "I can't believe you're still trying to tell me how to clean," but surprisingly, she'd left the basket at the foot of the attic steps. It did come in handy, going up and down, carrying the piles she'd made.

Now Nora just shook her head in the sunlight and passed a plastic container of green olives to Ellie. "Germs are the work of the devil. Someday," she said, "I'll have a housekeeper."

"And you'll ride her ass into the ground," said Mariana cheerfully, not letting herself think that maybe Nora would need a housekeeper, and more. A tender. A minder. Someone to wash her, to dress her . . .

Ellie took the olives with one hand, dropping the container to the grass, never glancing up from her phone.

Will you be there? When I tell her? Nora had looked so panicked when she'd asked.

Of course. Of course.

Do I really have to tell her?

Yes. It had been the only thing Mariana knew for sure.

You have to get tested, then.

I will. What about Ellie?

Never Ellie.

Mariana tried to catch Nora's eye, but unpacking the food was taking all her sister's concentration.

Ellie's phone tapping slowed, and she looked up blankly, as if trying to remember where she was. "I have to . . ." She looked toward the public restroom. "I'll be right back."

"Really?" Nora asked. "You hate using that bathroom."

A flasher had exposed himself to them there, years before. He'd startled Mariana so badly she'd screamed, and he'd yelled back at them before cramming his dick back in his pants and hurtling out past them. Nora had predictably handled it well—she'd gotten his license plate number and had the man cited for indecent exposure.

"God, Mom. I'm fine."

"Let me go with you," said Mariana. "In case . . ." How did Nora manage it? The whole motherhood thing? How did you continue to breathe when the person you loved the most could be in imminent danger at any moment? She wanted to drape bubble wrap around Ellie's shoulders, a ridiculous plastic shawl.

Ellie rolled her eyes and clomped off in her Dr. Martens without even bothering to answer.

"Are those your old Docs?"

Nora looked rueful. "She took them off my feet. Literally. I was going to wear them to the office, and she asked me for them."

"And you can't say no to her."

"Please. I say no to her all the time. It's all I do."

Mariana moved closer to her sister on the picnic blanket as Ellie stomped farther away. "She's prickly today."

Nora said, "Like a porcupine. Every day."

Mariana fingered the woolen fringe of the picnic blanket. "You talk a big game, Glass, like you're the anti-Martha, but where did you get this blanket? This is no cheap beach towel."

"Oh, you know." A smile tugged the corner of Nora's mouth.

"I do know. I bet you got it from the back of your Prius from a matching plaid box where it lives when you're not sitting on it in bliss."

Laughing, Nora said, "Everyone has a car blanket. My friend Lily has a blue one."

It felt so good to see her sister smile. Mariana touched the fiber more carefully and kept teasing her. "Not everyone has a pure Scottish merino wool blanket in the car, one without a stain on it. You get it dry-cleaned between picnics, right? No stickle-burrs on this guy."

Nora fell backward onto the blanket in question. "I know. I can't help it. It just happens."

"What's to be sorry for? I love merino. I only know that's

what it is because Luke is crazy about these plaid ones. He has
five of them in a cedar chest in the hallway. We never get them
out. I asked him recently what he was saving them for, and he
said he didn't know. He just likes the idea of having wool blankets in case we're stuck in a blizzard. You know, one of those
good old San Francisco snowstorms."

"How is Luke?" Nora took out her knitting, the perennial
sock in progress.

Mariana twisted a piece of blanket fringe between her fingers. "Fine. Business is good. Everyone wants a Harley right
now, and he got some great Yelp reviews, so his phone is ringing
off the hook. I think he's going to have to hire another guy."
They joked, at home, about the day when she had more employees than he did. In the middle of the night, Mariana sometimes
couldn't believe where she was. She still didn't feel like a
grown-up, but she had a payroll clerk at BreathingRoom. She
had a publicist.

Her sister's smile was gone, and in its place was Nora's listening face. Earnest. Interested. "And how are you two?"

Mariana sighed. "Fine. The marriage thing is off the table. I
think."

"If he'd asked you in private, you would have reacted more
positively?"

Mariana stayed quiet.

Nora tucked a long piece of hair behind her ear and then
reached forward, doing the same to a strand of Mariana's.
"Why not?"

I can't fail at something I don't do. She shouldn't have to verbal-
ize this to her sister. Nora should just understand. Even if Mariana herself didn't, quite. She tried to change the subject. "What's
up with Harrison?"

Nora's eyes widened. Mariana wondered if her own face, so
like Nora's, was as transparent as her sister's. Somehow, Mariana
doubted it. She'd always been a better dissembler. "What?" she

said. "Did you sleep with him again? There's something you're not telling me."

"No."

Her sister was lying. But that was okay. Mariana didn't want to talk about her boyfriend, either. They were *supposed* to be telling Ellie her mother might be sick. Might be, because no doctor was infallible. Sure, four had independently corroborated the diagnosis, but all it took was one creative, open-minded doctor to turn it all around. Mariana would be sure to emphasize that for Ellie since Nora sure as hell wouldn't. The resigned, pulled look around Nora's eyes did nothing but tick Mariana off. Resignation was the same as acceptance. And while Mariana's app was based on helping people understand what to let go of (everything), she didn't want Nora to let go of a single thing. Not a memory, not a skill, nothing. She would collect them for her, if she had to, holding them in her cupped fingers until everything fell away but the two of them and her full and steady hands.

"Mom?" Ellie had come up behind them. "Aunt Mariana?"

She was holding hands with a boy.

Chapter Twenty-one

"This is Dylan," said Ellie. She was way more nervous than she'd thought she'd be. She'd imagined it a thousand times. *Mom, Aunt Mariana, this is my boyfriend.* It would come out as an inarguable fact.

Instead, she amended her first statement with "He's my friend."

She sounded like she was four, introducing her first playground pal. In a moment, she would arm-wrestle him and then they'd race for the sandbox where they'd avoid the cat poop and throw plastic shovels at each other.

"Who?" Her mother looked even blanker than she had been lately.

"Dylan," Ellie repeated, as if that would clarify it. They didn't know she'd stayed up late with him almost every night for the last month, talking in Addi's hut about everything and nothing at all. They didn't know she'd gone to meet him in Oakland when she'd said she was at Samantha's, and they *really* didn't know her first kiss from him had been in the back of a dimly lit bar located on a street her mother would have grounded her for being on at any time of day, let alone midnight. They didn't know that she was in love (probably) for the very first time and that he—with his skinny face and wide eyebrows and long fingers—made her feel special and pretty and completely—utterly—unique.

"Hi," said Mariana, leaping to standing from the blanket. "I'm Ellie's aunt. Nice to meet you."

"Oh," said Dylan. "You two really *do* look like each other. Wow."

Ellie's mother, still seated on the picnic blanket, said, "We're twins." Her voice was as flat as her expression.

"Yeah. Ellie said fraternal but . . ."

"Mom." Ellie didn't know what to say next. She'd assumed her mother would take over with her normal welcoming and polite questions. *Where are you from? Do I know your parents, maybe? What do they do? You look hungry, here.* She'd press a sandwich into his hand, and Dylan would be charmed by her. Everyone always was, even Ellie's friends.

"But *who* are you?" Nora's lips smiled, but warmth didn't reach her eyes.

"Mom!"

"Sorry, honey. But I don't understand. We had something to tell . . . I don't get it. Why is he here?"

Anger clawed at Ellie's throat and she made a strangled noise.

Her aunt stepped forward and motioned them to sit on her side of the blanket. "Make yourself comfortable. Would you like some Limonata? Or a Coke?"

Dylan said, "I'm fine, thanks. I just ate."

"With your family?" said Ellie's mother.

"Nah. With some friends."

"But it's Mother's Day."

Dylan shrugged and stuck a leg out onto the grass. He actually moved like Dyl did in the game, with a loose swaying of limbs as if he were a marionette, his arms and legs tethered to strings. "Yeah. I called her."

"You called her."

"And sent her flowers."

"A big bouquet?"

Dylan dipped his head. "The biggest I could get for what I had in my bank account."

Ellie saw her aunt smile.

"It was Addi's idea—I mean, Ellie's idea. The flowers."

"Addi?"

Dylan grinned. "I met her as Addi first, and it keeps coming out when I talk."

"So you talk about her a lot?"

Ellie was going to die. Right here, she was going to have a heart attack and stop breathing. If she didn't die on her own, she'd kill herself, hang herself with the playground swing's chain.

But Dylan didn't seem to mind. Did *anything* fluster him? Is that what his extra three years got him?

"I do. I like her."

Ellie's mother blinked. "So do I, as a matter of fact."

"So we have that in common."

"Eat." Her mother thrust the container of chocolate cookies at him.

Mariana grabbed the plastic tub and set it on the blanket. "Sorry. You don't have to eat. Nora's congenitally programmed to offer food. I think what my sister is trying to ask is how did you two meet? Online, is that right? That's why you call her Addi?"

"Addi Turbo," said Ellie's mother in a quiet voice.

"That's it!" Dylan shot an invisible gun at her with a *chhk* noise. "Addi Turbo. Such a great name."

"It's a knitting needle."

"Nora?" Aunt Mariana looked confused.

"She's right," Ellie hurried to say. "It's a brand she uses. Even when I was kid, I thought it was a cool name. Like a superhero or something. It's what I call my Healer."

"You're a kid now. Still."

No, she wasn't. Not anymore. "I'm sixteen. Almost seventeen."

"You're not seventeen for five more months."

"*Stop it.*" They were the only words Ellie could grab out of her whirling brain.

Her mother turned to face Dylan, her eyes still as fiery as Queen Ulra's. In a moment she'd spit flame and toast Dylan like a marshmallow, and none of Ellie's powers would be able to stop her. "How old are you?"

Dylan, for the first time, paused. "I'm . . ."

"You're over eighteen, right?"

They'd agreed what Ellie would say. It was important to her. Dylan had said he wasn't a good liar and wouldn't be able to back her up, but Ellie had said she'd handle it. She said, "He's almost eighteen."

Her mother didn't even look at her. "Care to tell me that yourself?"

Dylan stuck his finger in a hole at the edge of his jacket. "I'm nineteen," he muttered.

"Fantastic. Are you two having sex? Because that's *illegal*. I assume that's why you were going to lie about it? To avoid potential jail time?"

Ellie jumped to her feet. "We're out of here."

Dylan stood more slowly.

Then her mother stood. To anyone watching, they must look like they were playing a jumping-up game. "Why did you ask him here? Today?"

The question caught Ellie flat-footed. "Why not?"

"Because it's our day. We do this together."

"We can't change anything? In the future, it all has to stay the same?"

The vein that jumped in her mother's temple stood dark against her pale skin. "Yes."

"Why? When are you going to realize we have to move forward? Out of the past? You treat me like a kid because you're scared of the future." It was the first time she'd thought of it, but Ellie knew it was true the moment the words left her mouth.

"I treat you like a kid because that's what you are."

"Come on, Dylan."

"Where do you think you're going?"

Ellie slung her backpack over one shoulder. "He'll drive me home later."

"You do *not* have permission to leave."

"Then stop me." Ellie felt something catch at the back of her throat. Her breath, perhaps, or something even more important. She'd had plenty of fights with her mom. Tons. Weekly. Sometimes daily. But she'd never taken off like this, never openly defied her. It felt like the ground was about to open up, revealing a sinkhole that would dump her onto a winding pregreased slide directly to hell.

Instead, though, her mother didn't try to stop her.

She did the opposite.

Her mother turned and walked away. *She* left.

"Mom?" No answer. "Are you *kidding* me?" Childishly, Ellie wanted to chase her mother down, pulling at her hand until she took it. Instead, though, she hurled the words, "Well, you sure showed me!"

Her mother heard it—her back stiffened, and it looked as if she almost stumbled on the bouncy fake asphalt of the playground.

Aunt Mariana just stood there, her mouth open.

"It's okay. You can go. Choose her. She always chooses you, right?" Ellie's voice was so acidic her throat ached. She hiked her backpack higher on her shoulder till her neck hurt. Dylan didn't say anything. He just stayed next to her, his eyes surprised, his hands hanging open and loose.

"Ellie. That's not true."

How could her aunt say that with a straight face? Her whole life, when Ellie had heard those riddles—who would you save in a sinking boat if you could only save one: the old man with the wisdom of age or the child with the promise of youth—she'd thought of her mother and her aunt. "If the three of us were in a boat, you'd save each other."

Mariana looked mystified. "What are you *talking* about?"

Her mother had Mariana. Her father had Bettina. Even her half sister, TeeTee, had her terrible cousin Roxy, the awful one with teeth as bad as her attitude. Ellie, though, she'd always been alone. One summer, she'd played so many games of solitaire her mother had bought her a book of a hundred and fifty of them. And she'd played them *all*. Ellie thudded her toe against a clod of grass. With enough kicking, she'd be able to dig it up with just her shoe, no shovel required.

"She's . . . got something she needs to tell you," said Mariana.

Ellie froze, her foot still lifted. "What?"

Mariana closed her eyes the way Ellie's mother did when she was about to lose it. "I—can't. No. Not without her."

Ellie lunged forward and gripped Mariana's wrist. "What is it? Is she sick? Was I right?"

"You . . ." Mariana looked desperately over her shoulder. Ellie's mother was almost to the car in the parking lot now. "You have to talk to her."

"No." Icy terror flapped its way across Ellie's shoulder blades. "You told me you'd tell me. You *promised*."

Mariana looked at Dylan. "Maybe you should take her home after all. It'll give me a chance to calm her mom down."

"But I didn't *do* anything," said Ellie. Her mother was going to punish her for nothing by keeping the truth from her? How was that an acceptable thing for a mother to do?

Lifting one eyebrow, Mariana said. "He's nineteen? You didn't think she would flip out?"

"You're not flipping out."

"Oh, chipmunk. You have no idea."

The space between Ellie's shoulders and neck ached. Just a few minutes ago, when she'd walked over here with Dylan, his hand in hers, Ellie had felt light and open with happiness. She had imagined introducing him and then taking him over to the slide, where she'd make out with him at the top, not caring if anyone—even her mother!—could see. Dylan was a good kisser, an *excellent* one, no limp-noodle tongue, no sloppy dog licks. She'd kissed only two boys before, and both of them had been her age. Dylan was different. He was a man, and he made Ellie *feel* something different. When he'd kissed her inside the bar, he'd had . . . expectations. Not that he'd asked her to meet them. Dylan wouldn't ask that. Not yet. But that expectation had lit something inside her, something that felt liquid and quaked nervously in a place she could identify only late at night, when she thought about doing more with him. If she kept dating him, she'd sleep with him. She would. She wasn't even sure she was ready to, but what did that matter? Ellie did lots of things she wasn't ready to do. She hadn't been ready for calculus but she had the second-best grade in class. She hadn't been ready in swim class to go off the diving board, but when she had—free-falling through thin air—she'd felt a freedom she'd never felt before. She'd joined the dive team the next day, the water polo team the next week. Sex would probably be just like that.

Hopefully.

Dylan leaned sideways so that his upper arm brushed her shoulder. She felt braver then, under Mariana's gaze. "I'll be home by eleven." Her curfew was ten, and she knew Mariana knew it.

Her aunt's mouth opened once and then closed. She gave a nod and then made that angry face that meant she was sad.

That face scared Ellie more than anything else had so far. She held her breath for a second too long and then felt light-headed. "Please," she said. "Go get Mom. I'll be fine."

Mariana scanned her face, then turned and ran after Nora.

Ellie took Dylan's hand. Overhead, dark clouds gathered, rolling over Mount Tam like she'd summoned them with her will.

She stayed in place, watching Mariana catch Mom by the shoulders. Their hands flew, four arms rapidly arguing about something—about *her*. Or about something worse?

Dylan said, "Come on. Let's go fight evil."

Ellie tightened her grip on his fingers and took a deep breath of the wet air. "Well. When you put it that way . . ."

Chapter Twenty-two

*N*ora waited on the couch. She'd thought about calling her friend Lily to see if she was free, if she'd come over and knit with her. But she wouldn't be able to explain why she was like this, why she was so desperately jangled, why she must seem like she was seconds from flying apart.

She'd given up pretending to read an hour ago. She'd picked up her notebook and pencil and had doodled under her list of things to do tomorrow (check drain, buy shampoo, recover completely). She found the doodle becoming words: sex, love, flirt, man, boy.

HOW TO FLIRT

People will tell you it's about how you touch your lower lip, how you pull your hair forward or push it over your shoulder. Some say flirting is how you touch his arm, how you laugh at what he says, how you're just a little standoffish until the

*moment you're not. But flirting has very little to do with the
body. It's about your hearing, and your sight. It's about watching
his face as he talks, thinking about what he says, and asking
him the one question he wanted someone—anyone—to ask.
It's not hard. It should never be difficult. If it is, you're trying
it with the wrong person. Find someone prettier, or uglier, or
more interesting, or less so. Throw your best joke at them and
see if they laugh. Picture them crying with laughter and then
make it your goal to see it happen. Flirting is simple: it's
connecting with one other person directly, deliberately, as the
rest of the world spins on, unnoticed.*

She should have known about Dylan. Before. Nora stared
into the fireplace. She didn't know how long she'd been sitting
there, and after a while, she didn't care. Hours after the rains had
begun in earnest, the storm blowing up the way she wanted it to,
Nora finally heard Ellie's key in the iron security door.

"It's past midnight," said Nora, proud of how even her voice
remained. "It's pouring out there." When Mariana had confessed
to telling Ellie the fact that something was wrong with Nora
(and nothing else, she swore, nothing else), Nora had insisted
Mariana leave, cross the bridge and go home. "I was wrong. This
is something I have to do by myself."

"But we were going to tell her together." Mariana had
looked desperately hurt. "You shouldn't have to—not without me—"

Nora had been furious with her sister but had no solid
ground on which to stand. That made it so much worse. She
should have told Ellie a month ago. Two months ago. The minute
the first diagnosis came in from Dr. Pretty Susie.

Now, looking at her daughter's perfectly still face, the face
she knew better than her own, better even than Mariana's, Nora
said, "Come sit with me?"

"Mmm."

Was this what the rest of her daughter's teen years would be like? Tissue paper–thin veiled hostility masked by icy politeness? A hotel concierge who hates you but has to wish you good evening in order to get a tip?

"Come here." Nora pulled her feet up onto the couch. In the old days, Ellie would have laughed and hurled herself at the middle cushion.

"Tired." Ellie put her hand on the banister.

"You've never broken curfew before."

"Well." Ellie kept her eyes straight ahead, focused on the stairs in front of her. "Not that you knew of, anyway."

"Excuse me?"

"You heard me."

"You've been sneaking out?" The idea of it ached—another nail in the signboard that advertised her subpar mothering ability.

"When I feel like it."

She didn't believe it. "Ellie, come on." It wasn't fair, this part. Nora should be telling her truthfully what the future would hold. Nora should be comforting her daughter. No one knew how to dry Ellie's tears better. No one knew how to pet her until she fell into sleep, rubbing her shoulders in small round circles. It had worked from the first moment she'd laid baby Ellie in the hospital bed next to her, and it worked now. Even on really rough days—the ones when Nora couldn't say one damn word right to Ellie, the days of slammed doors and exasperated eye rolls and sighs so heavy they required handcarts to remove—if she went into Ellie's room after her light was out and rubbed her daughter's shoulders in those small circles, she would hear Ellie slip into heavier breathing, unable to hold any grudge all night.

It was the best sound in the whole world.

Right now, though, Ellie felt so far away. Miles, not just fifteen paces. She was three steps up the staircase. Ten to go. Ellie stared straight ahead, her face paper blank. "Anything else?"

It was childish, and god knew Nora should be trying her

hardest to be the parent here. But she couldn't help asking, "You don't want to know?"

Eyes still resolutely forward. "Know what?"

"Mariana told me she started—"

"No. I don't want to know. Keep your private life private."

And stay out of mine. Even unspoken, the words were loud and clear. "Honey, this can't be private."

"Just don't have *twins*—can I at least ask you that much?"

Nora spluttered, "What?"

"I know you're pregnant. Harrison's baby. Or babies. Whatever."

"Ellie!"

Her daughter still stared straight ahead. Nora could only see the side of her jaw.

"Harrison's a good guy. If you want to get married, that's fine by me. Don't make me be a flower girl or anything, but . . ."

Nora could hear in her daughter's tone, in the rigid set of her corded neck, that nothing was fine, nothing at all. But the truth was so much worse.

"I'm not pregnant. I'm sorry you thought I was. The truth is—"

"No!"

"We have to talk."

"Whatever it is"—Ellie put one foot on the step ahead and dragged herself up, as if she'd gained a hundred pounds in the previous thirty seconds—"I don't want to hear it. I don't care."

The blow was effective, cruel in its sharpness and thrust. *"Stop."* It was her mom voice, the one she'd never had to use that often with Ellie. It was the "wait for the light, don't run at the pool, watch out for that car" voice. Maybe in the future they were going to be that mother-daughter duo who couldn't stand each other, the kind she and Ellie had always laughed about in Target, the ones who bickered viciously over what kind of dorm-room throw pillow to buy, as if tassels or cords made any kind of real difference at college.

Then the tips of Nora's fingers ached as the realization surged through her blood again.

They weren't going to be that duo.

They had, what, two or three more years of this teenage discomfort? She wouldn't be around long enough to see it out, to see her daughter magically like her again, the way her friends told her she would, the friends who'd been through this teen-girl hell. Nora would be lucky if Ellie deigned to wheel her outdoors on a Sunday afternoon at whatever care home she landed in.

Anger ran her over then, like she'd once done to a possum on Highway 120. A solid *thunk* and the car rattled as if it would come apart. The thud was anger not just at the disease, not just at the fact that she had no idea what was going to happen to her, mentally or physically, but at the child in front of her who didn't seem to give a crap about *anything*.

"I'm dying," Nora said.

Ellie didn't even blink. "I don't want to talk about it."

It was the last thing Nora had expected. A scream, a wail, maybe sobs—those she would have been able to handle. Collapsing to the staircase, falling down it, she could have understood that. "Well. We have to."

Ellie shook her head. "I'm just super-tired."

"Are you kidding me? I tell you I'm dying, and you need your beauty sleep?" The word "dying," the one she thought would stop her heart the very second she said it out loud to her daughter, came easily. Gleefully. "Dying," she said again.

"We can talk tomorrow."

"You have school tomorrow."

"That reminds me, I have a test in physics." Ellie's nose went higher, something she always did when she refused to listen.

Nora wanted to threaten her with something, anything. *Turn out your light. It's after midnight. No studying. You blew it, going out with that boy instead of coming home. You should have been home talking to me. You're grounded for the rest of your life. No, for the rest of my life.*

But there was nothing she could say. It was selfish, and truly, if she could have spared her daughter ever knowing, she would have. She'd fantasized about suicide, leaving Ellie behind without a conversation, a note on the counter the only clue. *I love you. I'm sorry.* Then she would die (pills? gun? where? how? what was the kindest, easiest method?) without ever having to talk to her daughter about it.

Nothing was right, nothing at all. The anger left her in a rush, leaving a burned-out husk seated on the couch she'd picked out by herself after Paul left. "Okay, sugar. Good night."

Okay, sugar. Good night. How many nights had she said that? She could get out a calendar and add up the numbers, get an approximation of the total amount. What Nora couldn't do was estimate the number of times she had left to say it to her daughter. After she was gone, who would wish her girl sweet dreams? Because Paul—it could never be Paul. Even if Paul wanted to take care of his daughter, he'd fail. The one summer Ellie had gone to stay with them—*once*—Ellie had been back inside a week. Paul had left her at home, twice, while the rest of the family went to dinner and a movie. He'd blamed his wife, that she felt threatened by Ellie. But Nora knew—and Paul knew—it was him. He'd never asked his daughter back, just saw her when he came through town on business, never more than an hour at a time. When he'd left his first family, he'd left them for good. Paul couldn't have Ellie. He wouldn't want her, and that was utterly heartbreaking in and of itself. It would have to be Mariana. Nora's brain stalled, caught in the pain, still watching her daughter standing—seemingly stuck—halfway up, halfway down the stairs.

Wouldn't it have to be Mariana?

Ellie didn't look at Nora. Her chin just went higher in the air. "What is it, the thing you have?"

If Nora told her, Ellie would google it in her room. She would learn that EOAD ended badly. Worse than that, she'd learn that she herself had a fifty percent chance of having it. Nora couldn't say the words, not with her daughter halfway up the steps.

But she couldn't *not* answer. That would be the cruelest thing of all.

So she said it. "It's called early-onset Alzheimer's."

Ellie gave a terse nod and then continued up the stairs, her spine ramrod straight.

Her strength was what terrified Nora the most.

She drank the glass of wine she hadn't let herself have while she'd been waiting for Ellie to get home from god knew where. She sipped it slowly, the unshed tears a solid mass of pain behind her eyes.

A careful, deliberate fifteen minutes later, she went upstairs. She knocked on Ellie's door once, gently, before opening it.

The light was off in her daughter's room, a faint white glow coming from where the covers were bunched around Ellie's face.

Ellie dropped the phone, and then Nora could see nothing but her daughter's huge green eyes, as gorgeous as they'd been the day they'd handed her baby to her in the hospital.

"Mama," she whispered.

Nora pulled back the covers and slid in. Then she held her baby as the storm passed overhead.

Chapter Twenty-three

EXCERPT,
**WHEN ELLIE WAS LITTLE:
OUR LIFE IN HOLIDAYS,**
PUBLISHED 2011 BY NORA GLASS

Father's Day

When Ellie was little, Paul bought her a chemistry set. I thought she was too young. She was only nine, after all, and some of the chemicals were labeled corrosive or acidic. One was even toxic. I pictured her adult hands pocked with scars from a childhood chemistry accident. But Paul had a chemistry set when he was young, and he had clear memories of the way cells had looked under the glass. He'd loved the power of it—suddenly, he said, you were God, and everything on the slide was a world you'd invented and you controlled.

Of course, I told him he was wrong. If I knew one thing, I knew I controlled almost nothing. That was the year of things that crapped out—my old Civic blew its head gasket on the way home from Costco, the washer threw a hissy fit and flooded the kitchen, the refrigerator started smoking like a Vegas stripper, and the furnace wouldn't heat the house above subglacial temperatures. Paul, in the meantime, had a newish wife, a tract house with the tags still attached, and a cell phone that magically never rang when I called. (*Sorry, must have been out of range again.*)

For Father's Day, Paul sent Ellie the chemistry set.

She'd opened the package and then stared at it. I thought maybe she was scared of it, as I was. But it was my job to ignore that, to push the fear into the pocket I'd made in the lining of my soul, right between my ribs and lungs. "Oh, isn't that fun," I said, but I knew I had to do better than that. "Your dad loved his old set. He blew things up with it." He hadn't needed a chemistry set to blow apart our family.

Ellie had looked confused. "But I thought I was supposed to get Daddy something for Father's Day. Not the other way around."

We'd been planning on making the drive out to Modesto to see him that Sunday. That was my gift to him, as the father of my child: to deliver to him the daughter he couldn't *quite* find the time to see on a monthly basis. But then he'd sent the gift (Friday overnighted, express Saturday delivery) with a note that said, "To My Best Ellie, Happy Father's Day from Your Pop." I got a text that said, *Sorry, Bettina made plans with her folks, kiss Ellie for me.*

"This is *cool*," said my daughter. She took the box to the shed, a small room attached to the garage that smelled perpetually of putty. It had been Paul's workshop, where he kept his wood tools and saws and routers. I didn't go there often. But Ellie loved that little space. "Don't come in, Mama. No, come in an hour. I'm going to experiment until then."

Sixty minutes later, I found Ellie sitting on the little blue chair in front of the microscope, a bloody tissue pressed against her finger. Her smile was radiant. "Mama!" she said. "Give me some of your blood. I'm going to see if we're related."

I didn't ask a single question. I just used the same safety pin she must have stolen from my sewing box to stab myself. She pressed my thumb to the glass slide. We spent the next hour watching our blood cells squirm and wriggle, comparing the shapes we found to the other slide.

Eventually the cells slowed. "They're dying," Ellie confided.

I shrugged. "It happens."

Ellie nodded gravely. "I wish I had some of Dad's blood." She looked at me hopefully. "Do you have some?"

"Not on me, no." I was only a little disappointed.

"Oh." She looked devastated. "Then I could have seen that we're related."

"Trust me, kiddo. You are. Besides, how can you tell, just from looking at the way our cells move?"

She pointed at the eyepiece. "I can see parts of the blood that dance the same, but that's normal. You're my *mom*. With a dad I bet it's different. I just wish I could test it, that's all."

I was both tickled and dismayed. I was Mom. I was unnoticeable, an extension of her body, a part of her brain. I was normal. I was just me. Paul was practically a mythical creature, someone who blew through Tiburon on his way to occasional meetings in the city, dropping off gift certificates and promises that almost—but never quite—got fulfilled. But Paul's was the blood she wanted to watch more than plain old mine.

She wore out that chemistry set. I had to buy refills of litmus papers, glass slides, and filter funnels. She stopped using it only after a seven-year-old neighbor boy broke in while we were at the grocery store and dumped all the chemicals into one aluminum bowl to see what would happen. Nothing did, really, and the only damage was to the concrete floor (a permanent blue stain) and to Ellie: the magic of the set from her father was gone. She didn't play with it again.

Once, though, before that happened, when she was in fifth grade, I couldn't find her for bed. I thought the shed would be too cold for her to be in that night, but there she was, head down on the chemistry table. She'd been reading *Little Women* (her first time) and she'd fallen asleep, the book splayed open next to her. Quietly, I craned my neck to see what page she was on. Mr. March had just come home from the war, surprising everyone. Amy had cried all over his shoes, Beth had walked, and Mr. Brooks had accidentally kissed Meg. It was the perfect place, the happiest part of the book. I wanted to take it from her, so she wouldn't keep reading. So that would never change.

I was still so *angry*. I didn't want Paul—he'd broken my heart when he left, and I'd spent all the time I wanted to spend crying over him. But Ellie was stuck with him, and because of her, I was stuck with him, too. For the rest of my life, I'd have to include him in graduation photos, and his name would be on her wedding announcement, and I'd always have to remember the day he told me he'd met someone else.

I didn't want her to be reading *Little Women*, pining over Mr. March.

I didn't want her playing with the chemistry set, longing to test Paul's blood.

But the next time he showed up to take her to ice cream (an hour—an *hour* with his daughter!), I made him smear some blood on a slide for her and I didn't offer to open his vein for him.

And when she finished *Little Women*, she—like I had— reopened it and started it all over again. "Won't you be sad about Beth a second time, chipmunk?" I asked.

She flipped another page, barely looking up at me. "It's worth it."

Pain was worth it. My heart hurt as I looked at her—her ears shaped like his, her mouth a copy of mine—a perfect mix of her father and myself.

Ellie was right. As usual. It was, and is, completely worth it.

Chapter Twenty-four

*N*ora forgot the word "red."

She was in the food market, the expensive one on the corner, the one they never went to unless they wanted just one item: when they needed an egg for pancakes or one box of birthday candles. She was alone when she forgot the word, when she realized she didn't have it ready.

Nora had known she would drop words—they'd said she would. She'd lost only a couple so far, though, and they'd come back quickly: "cellophane," "winterized." Words that didn't matter much, words anyone could have lost. She was expecting to lose more of them, but she hadn't known she'd be able to feel the hole they left when they went.

"I need a . . . pepper," she said again to the young stock clerk who asked her what she was looking for.

He looked confused. She was standing in front of the peppers. Thoughtfully, he pointed them out, as if she had just overlooked them.

But Nora was missing nothing but the word for the color she wanted.

She remembered all the other colors. She knew she didn't want a yellow pepper: they were too sweet. She didn't want a green one: too bland.

She wanted to touch the pepper in front of her, the one that was the color she was missing. She could taste the color, slightly bitter and a bit tangy. A short word. Or maybe a long one?

She knew the other words—the words that lived around it. "Vermillion," "cerise," "scarlet," "ruby," "cardinal," "carmine," "maroon." Beach glass didn't often come in that particular color. The piece she had in her pocket today was pale gold when she held it up to the light. Pretty, but the wrong word. She could feel her brain tugging, shaking itself out upside down, like a purse that held the very last dime. Her brain knew the word was there, but how did you find the missing word when you didn't even know what it started with?

Nora moved her tongue in her mouth. She couldn't even remember what the word felt like.

She became more frantic, her pulse pounding in her finger-tips, but she didn't want to worry the nice stock boy, who was watching her carefully, as if he thought she was perhaps crazy enough to steal the vegetable she couldn't describe. Behind him was a bin full of apples the exact color she'd misplaced. A woman reached forward to take one, her fingernails the color of the lost word.

Nora picked up a pepper and bagged it. She tried sneaking up on the color, putting it in a sentence. *This pepper is . . .* Nothing. She tried again. *I like apples that are . . .*

When the checker rang up her purchase, she watched the electronic scanner to see if somehow, by magic, the color would show on the display, but all it said was GROC.VEG.MISC.

In her car (which was blue, very blue, such a *blue* kind of car, no help at all), Nora held the pepper in her hands. She ran through the letters, testing all twenty-six of them, but the word wouldn't come. She wanted to cry and felt tears of anger start. She held her breath for a moment until she pressed the tears back into her chest, and then she took a bite of the pepper, right out of the side, hoping the taste would fill in the terrifying blank.

But nothing came except the vague unease that she wouldn't have enough pepper for the chicken curry she'd planned and that she hadn't washed it before biting into it.

Home. She needed to be home. The word would be there for her. Surely it would.

"Early-onset," Nora whispered, her fingers playing with the end of her key ring, the rabbit's foot Ellie had given her years before cold and smooth under her fingertips. Most of its fur had rubbed off a long time ago. Nora hated to admit it, but she liked the lucky charm more this way. When she rubbed it, she felt the leather of the dead bunny's foot. It was strong, a surprisingly tough hide. Something strong that belied the softness of its fur. The rabbit, underneath that pretty pelt, was strong.

Nora, underneath her anger, was strong, too.

She was. She had to be. Fury, rage, hatred—that temperature of emotion had never been anything that had gotten her very far in the past, but now she needed the heat. She had to fight with everything that was in her. She wished for an agonizing moment (that she would never admit to *anyone*) that she had cancer. Cancer was fightable. Valiant. She could kick cancer's *ass,* and afterward, she'd be labeled a hero.

If she did have this thing—this hell of a disease—she'd end up a wandering idiot. Someone to be pitied. Hidden.

The Internet—the hateful, terrible, awful Internet—had told her that there wasn't much she could do. Drugs, maybe. A combination of Aricept and Namenda, the same drugs that Dr. Niles had put her on immediately. Then there were experimental trials, lots of them, but she'd have to be willing to accept a possible placebo, and that didn't sound like a great idea. Anyway,

why should she be in a hurry to take medications that just prolonged . . . what exactly? The agony? The desperation? At what
point would she be stripped of nothing but a desperate wish for
death? When would she start spending her days wishing for them
to end?

Questions, so many questions. What if you wanted to kill
yourself and you couldn't? What if you missed your window of
ability? What if you planned to take yourself out with pills or a
noose, and on the day you planned it, you forgot to take the steps?

Who would help?

There was only one person who could.

Nora was so upset she almost ran the stoplight at Tiburon
and Lyford. She slammed on the brakes. Her purse and the pepper flew off the seat into the footwell.

Then she laughed with sudden unexpected delight.

Red. The light was *red*. It was the happiest word, right up there
next to "Ellie" and "sister" and "Tiburon" and "pencil" and "sky."

Red, red, *red*.

Things could change. They could change quickly. As fast as
the storm came, the sun came even more rapidly. You never
knew—that's what she always told her readers in her column.
You just never *knew*. Red, red, red-red-red. Her heart sang the
word all the way home and her chicken curry came out so well
Ellie asked for thirds.

Chapter Twenty-five

"How long has it been?" It was taking too long. Mariana had made a mistake. She wanted to take it back. She didn't want to know anymore. Her jaw ached from clenching it for the last . . . "How long?" she asked again.

Nora looked at her phone. "Five minutes."

Screw facts. "No way. It's been, like, half an hour."

"He said he'd be right back. It'll be okay." Nora's voice was calm, soothing.

Mariana twisted her fingers in her lap. There should be *rules* for genetic counselors. They shouldn't leave patients in their offices alone. Too much time and the brain went crazy. *What if I have it?*

At BreathingRoom, her developer, Grant, had thought she shouldn't find out. He said knowing she might get sick would do nothing but scare her and take her out of the current moment. Grant was good at his job—not only was he in charge of making sure the app was up and running, but he believed in it. He meditated with purpose and ease, and while no one got meditation "right" (it wasn't a quiz, Mariana said over and over again), if anyone did, it would be Grant. He was openhanded and clear hearted naturally. Mariana sometimes wanted to put him in charge, make *him* be on the recordings, on the podcasts. She took his opinion seriously, and she agreed that knowing her genetic fate didn't secure any real fate at all.

She knew what Luke would have said if she'd asked him about it. *The more you know, the better.* He was working his way—alphabetically—through a list of the classics he'd never read. She pointed out that she'd never read *Moby Dick*, either, and she was doing just fine. "But what if it held something important, something you missed? Wouldn't you want to know that? Wouldn't you want to add that to what you have inside you? The more you know, the better." He would carefully insert his bookmark—a blow-in subscription card to *Rider Magazine*—and shut the book. He always closed whatever he was reading when he talked to her in order to make her feel important. When she'd told him about Nora's diagnosis, he'd listened so hard she thought he might be able to read her thoughts. For the first time since the proposal disaster, they'd made love under the skylight. With an almost-full moon overhead, Mariana had cried when she came. Luke had known it wasn't from the orgasm, and he'd cried, too.

But she hadn't asked him for his opinion.

The very fact that she hadn't talked with him about her choice to get tested felt like a betrayal. She loved him—nothing about that had changed. He *should* have been a part of her decision. But when they talked now, there was a space between their words, a space that both of them tried to fill with smiles and touches and small, daily jokes, a space that never quite got closed. Small talk was words thrown into the chasm between them—maybe someday they'd fill it up and be able to walk toward each other again.

The more you know, the better. That's what he *would* have said if he were there in the waiting room with her and Nora, so she said it to herself. *The more you know, the better.*

Most important, her sister, Nora, needed to know if Mariana had the PS1 mutation.

Mariana's stomach knotted, her guts tangled. This was why she didn't go to doctors. This. A person could find out terrible things from someone who'd paid a lot to get a bunch of letters after his name. That wasn't the real reason, she knew. She just hated facing the reality of doctors. They told you to eat right, to look to the future, to watch your cholesterol. Before Luke, she'd barely managed to remember to pay her electricity bill. She'd never had time to be too thoughtful about her triglycerides. Shit. Even if she *did* have EOAD, if she stepped in front of a Muni bus by accident, *that's* how she would die, not from the complications of Alzheimer's.

From the comfortable seat next to her (perhaps the designers had confused comfort with comforting), Nora said in that same soothing voice, "You don't have it. You can't have it. Besides, *if* you had it, you'd be showing signs. You're not showing signs." It had been Nora's catchphrase for weeks. *You'd be showing signs.*

How did she *know* Mariana would be showing anything at all, though? They were different in so many ways. They were fraternal, not identical. Mariana had freckles on her forearms, while Nora didn't have a single one. Mariana was half an inch taller. They hadn't walked at the same time—their mother had told them Nora had lagged by two months, something Nora had always seemed a little ashamed of. They'd gotten their periods three months apart, with Nora in the lead that time. Sure, they'd been knitted together in the same womb at the same time. That just made them very close next-door neighbors. That was all.

Now, though, Mariana noticed their legs were jiggling in exactly the same way—silently jouncing up and down as if they were both trying to entertain invisible fractious babies.

"We're just getting the facts, that's all," said Nora. If she'd had a baby on her knee, it would have flipped into the air with the bounce she gave the last word. "It'll be negative. You don't have it."

"For fuck's sake," Mariana said. Then she caught herself. This was such a bad idea. Mariana had been so firmly against doing this that she hadn't thought about what might happen next—what if she had the gene mutation? How was she supposed to react to the news? Would she scream? It didn't seem appropriate, given that Nora was already dealing with it. And what if she didn't have it? Should she celebrate? Again, that seemed wrong under the circumstances.

Mariana's teeth ground together, and her left foot began to jiggle harder. Under the smooth orange carpet, she could feel a floorboard thump in answer. It was reassuring, feeling the bones of the old building. "You know," she said, "they shouldn't have fake plants."

"What?"

She pointed at the fern behind the doctor's desk. "Plastic. I don't think it's a good idea."

Nora's eyebrows flew so high they almost ducked under her hairline, and Mariana knew she'd succeeded. For half a second, she'd distracted her sister.

"You're absolutely right."

Mariana nodded. "I knew you'd think so."

"This is a *doctor's* office."

"I know."

"They take care of their patients, and part of that care is making us feel as if they'll do a good job of it. What does it *mean* that they can't trust themselves to have real plants?" Nora stood, shrugging her bag onto her shoulder. "Let's go."

"What?" It was supposed to be a distraction, not an out, though she wouldn't look a gift horse in its genetic markers.

"Let's *go*. We'll find another doctor."

"Are you sure? With all the tests they've run already?"

A sheen of tears brightened Nora's eyes, and Mariana's heart thumped in her chest. Instead of distracting her, she'd upset her. This was so much worse. She was an idiot. She *knew* better. No crying. If her sister cried, it would end her.

"You know what? I think I'm wrong. About the plant."

Nora's eyes were still frighteningly glassy. "Don't patronize me."

Mariana stood and moved behind the doctor's desk. "Look. It's real."

"It isn't. I can tell from here. Probably from Target."

"It's totally real. It's in real dirt."

"What else would they put fake plants in, Cheerios? It's silk."

Mariana ripped off a frond, and it came off the base stalk with a viscously wet crack. She held it up triumphantly. "It's *totally* real."

The doctor entered, a large white envelope in his hand.

"Oh, shit." Mariana dropped the leaf. "Sorry."

Nora started laughing.

Dr. Ghanjit frowned but didn't say anything as Mariana scurried around the desk and back to her chair. She rubbed her hands discreetly on the sides of her pants, dusting off the dirt. Nora made a noise that was a choked giggle.

"Sorry," Mariana said again.

The doctor, a man in his midsixties with bright hazel eyes, shrugged. "It happens. We replace that thing every year or two."

Nora squeaked again and Mariana ignored her as hard as she could. She wouldn't look at her. If they went into a giggle fit now—no, it would be terrible. No matter what he said, it wouldn't be the kind of thing they should laugh at.

"Okay, you ready?" he asked, sliding the papers out of the envelope and onto his desk.

Mariana glanced at Nora, but her sister wouldn't meet her gaze. She'd banished the giggle squeak and her face was straight now, her expression stern. "Yes," said Nora. "We are."

"Wait a minute," said Mariana. She didn't have the diagnosis yet, didn't know what he'd say, but she felt all the air leave her lungs, as if she'd fallen from a great height onto her back. She leaned forward and tried to find where she stored that breath—*breathe into your belly*—but she couldn't find it. Sucking a small sip of air, she said, "Just one second. I'm sorry." Dizzy. She was dizzy. Fucking hell, was that a symptom?

Nora scooted her chair to the right and hooked a foot around hers. Her right leg tangled with Mariana's left one. They used to sit like this in school when they could get away with it, stronger against the class that way, winners in their solo three-legged race.

"Look at me," Nora said.

Her eyes were soft. Had Nora been this terrified when she'd learned her fate? Probably not. She hadn't known at that point how devastating the diagnosis would be. She'd been alone when she'd heard, and Mariana *hated* that fact. She should have been there.

Nora smiled and jiggled her leg just the tiniest bit.

Mariana smiled back and then turned to face the doctor. "We're ready."

"Okay." He looked down at the paperwork as if he were seeing it for the first time, which Mariana hoped to god he wasn't. "You're negative for the PS1 mutation."

Chapter Twenty-six

"I am," said Mariana flatly. She was supposed to feel something here, wasn't she? She felt a numb, lightweight thud, as if someone had thrown a beach ball at her head. That was all. "I am?"

"She doesn't have it." Joy lit Nora's voice.

That was it. Mariana was supposed to be happy. Overjoyed.

"Are you sure?" Mariana asked, unhooking her leg from Nora's and leaning forward.

"Yes. Completely. You will not develop EOAD. You can, of course, be at risk for regular Alzheimer's, just like anyone else, but that's an epigenetic question, and we can talk about that if you like. It's not at play in this, though."

"Holy shit," said Mariana. Disappointment, crisp and utterly shocking, filled her blood.

"Oh, my god." Nora covered her mouth. "Mariana. Thank you. Thank god you're okay. Thank you, Doctor."

It wasn't fair.

It wasn't fucking fair.

Mariana stuck her index finger into her mouth and peeled off a strip of skin that tasted of dirt from the fern frond. Bright blood bloomed, a single red star of it next to her nail bed. How dare she feel *disappointed*? How dare she feel what was flooding her, the emotion that was so much worse than disappointment.

"Mariana?" Nora touched her arm.

Mariana was *jealous*. It was so far beyond unacceptable she couldn't even be in the same room, contaminating her sister with it. She stood, saying, "I'll just—" Then she sat again.

"Honey, this is good." Nora was stroking her arm, gentling her.

Of anyone in the world, Nora would be able to see into her heart, to see the black jealousy that lay curled there, wanting to unfurl into diseased smoke. A jealousy flare—that's what she was about to shoot into the sky. To have the disease with her sister, to be together as they began to fade, to live together all the way to the shortened, devastated, smashed end—they would have gone out tougher, faster, better. The way they'd always said they would. "This is good," Mariana repeated, her tongue thick.

The doctor leaned back, appearing content to wait for them to process the information. How many lives did he change or destroy while sitting in that chair? Why did he get that power? Why couldn't *she* have some of it? Mariana would change this, reorder the deck, stack the dice . . .

Nausea churned her stomach, turning it over. Sweat broke at her hairline. The shame of it, of her terrible reaction, burned her throat like battery acid. What should have happened—her heart filling with joy that she wasn't sick—hadn't. She couldn't look at Nora. Nora would know. Maybe she already did.

She took a risk and glanced sideways. "Nora," she started.

Her sister's eyes were swimming, not overfilling with tears but simply leaking, like water dripping down a porcelain fountain. "I'm so happy," Nora whispered, but there it was—there, at the corner of her mouth, was the truth. No one in the whole world would have been able to see it, no one but Mariana.

Mariana saw it. Nora was jealous the same way Mariana was. Nora wanted to be well, like Mariana. And Mariana wanted to be sick.

"So happy," Nora said again before standing. "This is—I'm so sorry. I think I need a minute." She threw a wide, desperate smile at Mariana like a heavy blanket. Then she fled out into the quiet waiting room. Mariana heard a thud and knew Nora had crashed down the stairs and out the heavy door.

Nora wanted to be well. Mariana turned in her chair. "I've never lived farther than twelve miles away from her." When she'd been in the country, that was . . . She wasn't counting either India trip or the time Stephen had taken her to New Zealand for four months. . . . She shouldn't have gone then. She should have stayed close.

Mariana stood.

"Wait," said the doctor. "Before you go, hear me out. In every case of this type of familial processing, this is normal . . ."

This was a *type*?

"She just needs a moment to deal with this information. Alone."

Mariana nodded and wished that she had thought to bring the fern frond with her to the chair. She'd have been able to strip it with her strong, healthy fingers. Instead, she pulled at the skin of her second finger. A small stripe of flesh followed by exactly what she wanted—a bright second of searing pain, a tiny stab. She put her finger in her mouth. Blood. It all came down to this, didn't it?

"This is normal?" The word had almost ceased to have meaning to her.

Dr. Ghanjit, his face softening, his eyes sympathetic, said, "Yes. I counseled her to bring a third person. It can make this time a little easier. But she said she wouldn't bring her daughter.

Is she getting tested, do you know?" He looked down at the file. "Ellie?"

"No." Mariana remembered how clear Nora had been about it. "No, she won't be tested."

"That's fine, of course, if that's what they both want. I've known teenagers who want to know and others who didn't."

"Who makes the call?"

"The guardian parent. Most of the time. It can get sticky."

"So if Ellie wanted to know but Nora didn't want her to, she wouldn't be able to be tested."

The doctor shook his head. "She wouldn't, not until she was eighteen. Things can get . . . complicated, though. When guardianship changes." He shuffled papers on the desk. "Her father—he isn't in the picture?"

"Shit." Father's Day was coming up, wasn't it? "He's second string. No, he's last string. I don't know sports. Is that a thing?"

"Will that change, do you think?"

"I'm not the one to ask." Paul would never change. Nora might hope and Ellie would believe and Paul would let them down, and then Mariana would have to—finally—kill him with whatever came to hand, even if it was a rubber duck. She could do it.

"I often find the closest family member"—he looked over his glasses at her—"to know more than the patient does about family ties."

"Yeah, well, her dad's a dickbag."

Dr. Ghanjit nodded. "Then you are the most important one."

What did that mean? Did he mean . . . *custody*? Impossible—Mariana couldn't keep Luke's houseplants alive. She'd killed five African violets so far.

She couldn't think about it. They'd figure something out. Nora wasn't going anywhere without her. Swallowing down the burn in her throat, she said, "I have to go find my sister."

The doctor closed his eyes and rubbed the bridge of his nose as if it hurt. "She's probably in the garden in the back. There's a big swing. That's where most people go." Then he said, "You will be good at this."

Startled, Mariana said, "Pardon?" This man didn't know her. She wasn't good at anything except being the fuckup sister. Granted, she was pretty excellent at that.

"I can tell."

"How?" she challenged.

"It's your turn, I think." He smiled, and his eyes were so warm that Mariana felt strength start, deep inside her. Such a small tendril, barely alive. But it was there. As Mariana walked out of the office and down the hushed hall, she wished for it to root, like a blackberry, for it to grow tangled and fearsome without her trying. For it to be so big, someday, that no one could tear it out.

For now, she'd just be grateful it was green, and that she hadn't moronically ripped it from its stalk just to prove a point.

Chapter Twenty-seven

*N*ora wasn't sure if it was the swing or Mariana's diagnosis (the *non*-diagnosis) that was making her feel so queasy, but pushing with her legs was at least giving her something to do while she tried to get her thoughts to smooth. If she could iron them, put them on the board and hit them with the starch she loved so much, she could get them under control. It pleased her, thinking about getting the creases out of her thoughts, storing them in the linen cupboard next to the red (red!) Christmas table-cloth and the good hand towels she got out only for company. She wouldn't need to put water in the iron—she could just cry over the top opening, filling it with tears. Her fingers twitched in her lap. She wanted to write that down before she forgot it, taking a sick pleasure in how pathetic it was. She could make fun of herself later for having the thought, if she wrote it just right for a col-umn. But she'd forgotten her purse upstairs when she ran, and she'd probably forget the thought itself before writing it down.

She should get used to it.

Her sister pushed her way through the glass door and into the garden. Her step was uncertain, as if she thought Nora might be mad at her.

Mad at *her*.

"I'm sorry," said Nora. One hot tear dripped to her chin, and she swiped at it, as if it were a bug suddenly crawling on her skin. It was the most messed-up reaction ever. "I'm so sorry. It's like I can't control it, and I keep thinking, is this the way it starts? Is this when you watch me start to lose it? I can't stop *crying*." Fury lit her chest on fire—it felt like bronchitis made of anger.

"Oh, my love." Mariana sat next to her on the swing, tangling her left leg with Nora's right. Now they had only two feet touching the ground, one Nora's, one Mariana's. With those two feet, they began to push themselves back and forth, so slowly.

"How long do I keep trying to pretend I'm still normal? Because I don't *feel* normal. I feel like I'm fighting my brain every second of the way, and the worst part is that I feel like it's winning. That I'm losing myself, and with you"—Nora barked a thin laugh—"with you healthy, I'm losing you, too. I won't be able to find you." She took a long breath. They became still, so still, just their legs entwined, the swing barely moving.

Then she went on. "I have to be able to find you. But now . . . god, Mariana, I'm so happy that you'll be okay. There's *nothing* in me that isn't happy about that."

Mariana looked straight ahead and moved the swing with her free foot, a gentle nudge.

"But you're going to leave me," said Nora. The real tears started in earnest then, even though she knew they might break Mariana. "I'm leaving you, but I won't understand that. So it will be like you're leaving me." She couldn't stop the heaving in her chest— there was a train barreling toward her, and she'd never get the straps undone in time. It was the kind of crying that took over a body, and every part of Nora was weeping, her shoulders, her belly, her knees. Next to her, Mariana gasped and folded at the waist.

Then Mariana stood and straddled the swing so that she could wrap both her arms around Nora. Her face was dry and hot against Nora's cheek, and even though Nora kept crying, Mariana didn't let go. Her knee dug into Nora's thigh, poking her sharply, but it felt good. Something else to feel, something besides despair.

"I keep thinking about what I could use . . . how I would do it. But I'm too scared. And I can't leave Ellie . . ."

"Stop it."

"How does a person make that decision? To go?"

Mariana gripped her tighter. "You're not going anywhere. You're not making that decision. Fuck you if you think you are." Her voice shook, and Nora felt such tenderness toward her. Mariana wasn't good at this. This comforting, this holding—this was as difficult for her as a marathon, as scary to her as a skydive. No, her sister would have preferred either of those to these tears.

"But . . ."

"There. There," said Mariana, her voice still pale compared to its usual bright bluster. "I'm here. I'm right here."

She would continue to be there. That was the bitch of it.

They couldn't—wouldn't—do this together. Nora was on a one-way trip out of town, and even if Mariana had wanted to come, she couldn't get a ticket.

Mariana wouldn't be able to follow.

Nora wouldn't be able to take care of her anymore.

As if she could hear Nora's thoughts, Mariana said, "I'm not strong enough for this."

Nora started, and laughed around a sob. *"Crap."*

"You can swear, you know. If you want to. You're allowed to." Mariana used the back of her fingers to wipe off Nora's wet cheeks. It was the first time her sister had ever touched one of her tears. Nora wondered if it would be the last.

Then Mariana paled, the color leaving her lips. "Oh, god. Sorry." She held up her hand, showing where the tears had mixed with blood. "I bit my finger, and now . . ."

Nora grabbed Mariana's hands and inspected them. "I thought you'd stopped doing that."

"I did."

"When did you start it back up?"

Mariana jerked a thumb over her shoulder. "You know. In there."

Nora straightened. "I'm going to make you take up knitting. That's what I'm going to do. You can't say no to me. I'm dying."

Mariana's mouth stretched in a grimace that was almost a laugh, and Nora knew her face looked the same.

She went on. "At least you get something out of it, instead of ragged, bloody cuticles. Oh!" Relief swelled like music inside her.

"What? You thought of something?"

"No." Nora laughed. She couldn't fix this with Aleene's glue or with the right words. "I think I'm just fucked." The word felt pleasingly shocking in her mouth.

Mariana blinked. "Why that look, then?"

Nora felt her smile get wider. "I'm gonna start smoking again."

"Oh, *hell* no."

"Yes, I am." Nora stood and scrubbed her cheeks with the backs of her hands, but she could feel some of the dust from the rope transfer to her skin. "Let's get out of here. I have a 7-Eleven to hit." She thought of what she'd write in her journal to Ellie: *Don't smoke. It shortens your life, it makes you smell like a hobo, and it gives you wrinkles. If you must smoke, do the e-cigarette thing and quit before your thirtieth birthday. Then take up knitting—knit at the bars, knit when your friends look cool with their glowing blue tips, and then give them the hand-knitted socks when you finish them. If your aunt tells you I ever smoked, tell her she's full of crap even though she's not—it's what she gets for telling on me.*

Would she see Ellie at twenty? Given the medical regimen, given that her daughter was almost seventeen, it was possible. Only just, but still possible. She'd never see her at thirty. They still weren't talking about it, not directly, though Nora knew they'd have to start, and soon. "You still have to go to Smith,"

Nora had said the week before when Ellie had been deciding which schools to send her SAT scores to. They were phenomenal scores: *2210*. It was all Nora could do not to put a bumper sticker with the number on her car. She'd tried not to push Ellie to one school or another, but Smith, with its tradition of educating strong women, would be perfect for her. She knew it.

"Oh, god," Ellie had said, her pencil stilling in midair. "Should I not go there?" It was obviously the first time she'd thought about it. Nora should never have even brought it up. "I shouldn't go. I'm so stupid."

"No," Nora had said. "You *have* to go." Then she'd rushed into the backyard, where she'd stood in the cool air with her hands pressed to her cheeks for a long, long time.

Now, in the garden of the doctor's office, Mariana said, "Your face is covered in blood and dirt."

"Figures," said Nora.

"You're seriously going to buy cigarettes."

"You coming?"

"You're going to let me smoke? Shit yes, I'm coming."

"Oh, no," said Nora over her shoulder, already halfway up the walkway back to the reception door. "You don't get one. You're not dying. You have to stay healthy. It's me who gets to drive this car right off the edge of the cliff." Her grin as she pulled open the door was electric. "What do you think heroin is like? Maybe I'll try a little of everything. I think I'll try a little smack. I have no idea what it is, really, but I'll give it a shot."

Mariana stopped walking and put her hands on her hips. "Over my dead and totally disapproving body."

"Okay. Just cigarettes."

"Just one, and then you throw the pack away."

"Oh, my cancerous silver lining." The rapture felt like forgiveness. "I'm getting *menthol*."

Chapter Twenty-eight

Addi was getting closer to finding the Dragon Queen's clutch of eggs. She and Dyl, unknown to his group of Incursers or her group of Healers, had been leaving the game play every night to explore the outer edges of the *Queendom* Hinters.

It was her idea—Dyl hadn't believed her. *If we walk that way, won't the game just push us back into play?*

The only correct answer to that was, *Can't hurt to try. We write the stories here*—and by that she meant *she* wrote the stories—*why can't we tell it that way? Out there?* The Hinters wouldn't be mysterious if they knew the terrain. And if they were assigned there later in the game, then they'd be experts already.

When she was with Dyl, Addi was fearless. She leaped, swung, tore, raced, climbed, and jumped. She sailed carelessly off cliffs, landing in low waters with a laugh. She cursed, liking the way the game took her swear words and made them automatically into asterisks and exclamation marks. She even killed sometimes (but only when totally necessary).

When she was with Dylan the boy—no, the man—Ellie was three parts wreck, one much smaller part confidence. When he kissed her, his mouth strong and hot, she kissed him back with abandon, forgetting the brick wall they were leaning against, or if they were in his car, not feeling the emergency brake in the middle of her back. But as soon as his hands moved south, she tensed—every inch his fingers crept under her shirt or into the waistband of her jeans felt like another year of worldliness traversed backward. The first time he'd put his hand inside her underwear, she'd giggled like a freaking baby.

She was almost seventeen.

Mentally, she was good with it. Ready for sex, and specifically, for sex with him: Dylan. The flatness of his wide hands excited her, and she wanted to push his face down her body until she felt something . . . new.

Why, then, did she close like a poppy at sunset when he tugged at various pieces of her clothing? She wanted him to, so it didn't make sense.

It wasn't a question she could ask Samantha. Sam was remaining "chaste" for her someday husband. (It didn't stop her from going down on Randall Watson behind the ceramics classroom, something she and Ellie had argued about. It counted as sex, Ellie said. Sam said no penetration equaled no sex, and they hadn't spoken for a week after the argument. When they made up, they called it their Clinton fight.) She could ask Vani, who had no problem talking about sex, but Ellie felt the same shuttering of self when she was around Vani, too. She turned young again. Soon she'd sit in the middle of the floor and bang on a xylophone like a two-year-old while the rest of them had amazing grown-up lives.

She wanted to ask her mother.

And she couldn't. Her mom was sick.

Ellie thought she was supposed to have had wrapped her head around it, but she hadn't. It didn't make sense.

Sick was sick. Other people were sick. Mrs. Hill, her fourth-grade teacher, had gotten thinner until she disappeared and died. The librarian with the angry eyes had ovarian cancer and a seriously bad attitude—she was so mean she'd never die. Her mom didn't have cancer. The Internet said early-onset Alzheimer's was bad. Ellie couldn't google it a second time. She hadn't told Sam or Vani. She'd tried to tell Dylan twice, but both times she'd tried to type out the words, she'd erased them at the last minute. She didn't know what to say, and besides, maybe the diagnosis was wrong. Mom had said she was going for more opinions and that she was going to try all the treatments available. She'd said that Ellie could ask her anything she wanted.

Ellie didn't want to ask her anything. Mom got that look— that awful one—and besides, Ellie was busy. She had finals, and Mr. Lippman was no fucking joke. If she didn't figure out *The Sound and the Fury* soon, she was doomed. Her SATs had been good, thank god, and she'd listed Smith College to send them to, but she didn't know if she was supposed to hear back from them or just wait until admissions opened in December. And then there was Dylan. . . .

For the last few weeks since the Mom Catastrophe at the park, Ellie had begged off seeing Dylan in person. Instead, they'd been creating a story in *Queendom*. Inventing it as they went along.

The Hinters were beyond amazing, as if that part of the world had been designed for them. Being with him in-game every night until three or four in the morning sometimes—her mother never checked after she said good night as long as Ellie left her door open—was almost as good as being with him in person. Maybe . . . maybe it was even better, since she didn't have to decide how far to go with him physically. Online, there were just the boundaries of her screen and their imaginations.

Okay, her imagination. Every night he typed, *Tell me a story.* Then she would write. She told the story as it came to her. Sometimes she held up her hands, staring at them, wondering where the words came from. When she wrote papers for school, each word weighed seven pounds. But when she was telling stories in-game, the words came easier than breathing. She ran through the game, inventing it, Dylan at her side.

Now Dyl jumped across a river full of thrashing eels and held out his hand to help Addi. His text scrolled across the screen. *I get that last bit, about protection, but she could protect them anywhere, right? Like, she's the most powerful. Why do you think her eggs are out here, anyway?*

Doesn't it make sense? she typed back. *She has to hide them somewhere, to escape extinction. She's dying, and this is her only hope. The last clutch was found by Incursers, and they not only broke each egg, but they roasted the tiny broodlings on spits in the Queen's Square.*

With his sword, Dyl lopped off a branch of a magical Islan tree. Addi picked it up, tucking it into the herb satchel at her waist. *Thanks.*

Dyl typed, *I remember that.*

Did you take part in it? She wanted to know if he'd been one of the celebrants that night.

        I was . . . otherwise occupied.

Out loud, Ellie said, "Oh, my god!" Her fingers paused before she typed the command to race to the next HectaRock. She got to the top, protecting it so he couldn't join her. *You had another Queendom girlfriend!*

        Just for a little while.

        Who?

        You don't know her. She doesn't
        play anymore.

        Why not?

```
Her husband found out about us.
```

Ellie's jaw felt stiff. *Wow.*

```
She was forty-two. With three kids.
```

Holy crap.

Dyl ran around the HectaRock twice, as if playing ring-around-the-rosy.

**You know, if you do that ten times
counterclockwise, you find an
Easter egg.**

```
Now you're shitting me.
```

**You'll never know till you try,
will you?**

Addi sat with crossed legs on top of the giant rock, watching with great satisfaction as Dyl ran ten times around it. His sword kept striking the back edge of it and falling to the ground with a metallic clatter. He didn't even have time to type about it—he just kept running.

After eleven circuits, Dyl stopped, taking up his normal avatar swaying motion. *You're so full of it.*

Ellie laughed so loud it echoed against the pale peach walls of her bedroom. *Gotcha.*

```
Oh, man, you're going to get it,
Ellie.
```

She wriggled farther into the pillows behind her. It was

dissonant and super-hot when he used her real name in the game. Anyone could wander into their field of vision at any point—it was dangerous, this flirting where any member of the Revolution could see them, read their words. Yet no one would. They were alone in their land, the one she wrote and made and owned. Addi jumped so far off the rock it looked like flying for a minute. *I intend to make sure I do,* she typed. Her keystrokes felt bold. *And I'm going to collect interest, too.*

Dyl strode to stand in front of Addi. If she pushed her avatar close to him, his body pixelated, fragmenting before it pieced itself back together behind her. She walked through him. Then he walked through her, trying the same thing.

You know what blue balls are?

Ellie laughed again. *They're bull crap. You're not going to die.*

Feels like I am.

I don't feel sorry for you.

You wound me, Addi Turbo.

She drew the short blade she carried and parried a thrust in his direction. *No. But I could. We haven't checked the northwest quadrant of that copse of trees yet. She could have hidden them there.*

What do we do if we find them,
anyway?

Ellie hadn't stopped to think that far ahead. But she knew, instantly. *We guard them. With our lives.* Dyl, an Incurser, had one job—to kill dragons and their broodlings. Queen Ulra was failing, and there was no guarantee that after this last clutch of eggs

there would be any more. The next queen might be in an egg,
right now.

His reply was instant. *I will guard them with you.*

It might cost your life.

```
Not too high a price, I think, to
bring you joy.
```

Goose bumps rose all over her body.

This really might be love.

Ellie's mother stuck her head in the door. "I'm going to bed.
Need anything?"

"Nope."

"Thanks for my gift certificate. I love it."

That morning, Ellie had sent her an Amazon gift certificate
for Father's Day, a riff on an old joke. Years before, when she was
eight or nine, Mom had taught her how to ride a bike. Dad had
been saying he'd teach her, but then he hadn't shown up four
times in a row. Her mother running behind her while yelling
directions hadn't gone well, and there had been a lot of tears and
more than a little road rash, but once Ellie had gotten the hang
of it, it had felt like she was soaring. "You're a better dad than
Dad," she said, and while her mother had looked a little horrified
when Ellie had said it, she'd also looked amused. That year, Ellie
had given her a Father's Day gift (gumballs in a glass jar, obviously meant to share), and she'd given her something every year
since. The gift card this year was easy—she'd cobbled it together
from the amount she'd had leftover from her Christmas gift
cards. A couple of clicks, the typed words, "To the best dad
ever," and hit send. She'd heard the ding from the kitchen as it
had landed in her mom's in-box, and she'd felt like an ungrateful
child suddenly, something she hadn't meant to be. She still meant
the sentiment. Sure, she'd call her dad later, but chances were he

wouldn't answer—he rarely did. But Mom was the one she should be talking to, hanging out with, instead of playing *Queendom*, and instead, Ellie had sent her a gift card with money her mom had given her in the first place.

But her mother was still smiling, still looking grateful.

"You're welcome."

Ellie should have at least made her a card or something, like the ones she'd loved when Ellie was a kid. It hadn't mattered if the lettering was crooked or the doilies were mashed; Mom had treated the cards as if they were made of solid gold, carrying them with her all day, admiring them loudly whenever Ellie looked her way.

A pause. Her mother said, "You okay in here?"

The music on the game turned slow and sad—violins again—Addi and Dyl walked across a dark blue desert under the two three-quarter moons. "Yeah, I like it. I get to . . . I get to tell stories."

Her mother looked interested. "They let you write? In the game itself?"

Ellie nodded and made Addi take a small jump for no reason.

"Does everyone write in it? I don't remember anyone saying that when I was researching it."

"Most people don't, actually." She gave a quick glance at her mother, who looked too pleased. Great, this was going to start her on a whole *You're such a good writer, you could write, like me . . .*

She didn't look at the keys but typed as quietly as she could. *My mother . . . I don't know what . . .*

The response was instant. *Isn't Father's Day your thing with her? Tell her you love her.*

It was a good idea and she was ashamed she hadn't said it yet. "Love you, Mom."

Mom swallowed and leaned her cheek against the doorjamb. She looked thinner at the waist—or did she look heavier around the jaw? Ellie felt like she'd never seen her mother before. She was a stranger, visually. Nora was pretty, Ellie realized with a jolt. Other people might think so, too. It was an odd thought to have.

But then her mother said, "You, too, chipmunk," and her mother was just her mom again. Normal hair, normal eyes, standing in the normal hallway like normal mothers did when busy helicoptering.

Ellie went back into the game. Dyl was ahead of Addi, swinging his secondary ax at the top of a flower that looked like a collection of fuzzy plates. She wanted to pick the flower, roll its leaves up tight, and put them in her pocket. *Thanks,* she said.

```
Moms. Everyone has one.
```

Not everyone. For one long second, Ellie tried to imagine a world without her mother in it.

But she couldn't. Her brain wouldn't do it. It was like walking to the edge of her own, real world. The ground shivered and pixelated, her own bed glitched, the pillows behind her juddering as they struggled to remain solid. Ellie knew, if she kept walking that way, that the walls would artifact so wildly she'd fall through them into nothing. It was so much safer to push ctrl-fn-F and make Addi run so fast she passed Dyl, so fast no Incurser could hope to keep up. Her leather boots creaked below her, and the violins sped up into a low bass thudding. Her heart finally eased.

Catch me if you can!

She hoped he could.

Chapter Twenty-nine

here were always tests. Always. Something more to come in for. There was always a doctor she hadn't met with yet, someone else with an amazingly clickable pen who wanted to weigh in on her diagnosis. Someone else with a great idea. And Nora bought it every time, bought into the hope they folded into their charts and tucked into their computers while they pecked at keyboards and stared at computer screens, looking for answers. Sometimes she wondered if they were just googling, doing the same thing she did late at night. She wondered if they were looking for the same thing.

Hope.

Stubbornly, like daffodils planted on freeway medians, hope was what kept springing up over and over again. Hope that they were wrong, hope that something had changed. Sometimes Nora woke with the startling belief that a cure had been found. Somewhere—maybe Sweden, wasn't that where they were always doing something amazing with medicine?—somewhere far away, overnight, a young medical professional had stumbled over it, the one thing that would selectively lower levels of amyloid-beta 42 and make all the difference. The one chemical with innumerable syllables that, mixed with the other seventy-two necessary substances, would fix Nora, would bring her back to where she was supposed to be.

Every day, as she jotted notes of things to remember, to do, to keep, one word kept coming up, doodled in the margins, drawn in bold at the bottoms of the pages of her journal: "Hope."

It was a song. Hope, hope, *hope*.

She had it. It seemed more important than anything else she wrote down, more important than other worthwhile words like "fortitude" and "courage." "Resilience" and "strength" were good, too, but none were as necessary as "hope." She looped the *H* and drew out the last breath of the *E*, over and over.

One late spring morning, while she sat in the backyard watching the hummingbirds swarm the honeysuckle, Nora remembered with sudden clarity her very first diary. It had been small and pink, with a white and yellow spray of jonquils on the front. Her mother had bought it for her ninth birthday. Nora had been thrilled with everything about the locking journal, especially with the tiny brass key that fit so satisfyingly in the book's strap, opening with an almost soundless click. She wanted to swallow the key to guarantee she wouldn't lose it. She pictured the key deep inside her belly, safely stored away, safe from Mariana's curious fingers and eyes.

Mariana, for that birthday, had gotten exactly what she'd asked for—a box of Fashion Plates with their gorgeous colored pencils and snapping plastic pieces that each depicted one-third of a perfect woman's body. Talons of jealousy pierced Nora's soul. No doubt Mariana would accidentally crumple the paper and carelessly break off the tips of the pencils. Their mother had warned Mariana when the paper had been stripped off the box, "Remember, if you break these, I can't afford to get you another set. This is it."

"I know," said Mariana, her voice filled with flop-over-and-die joy. She'd clutched the white cardboard box to her chest. "I know, Mama."

Nora felt the clawing pain of jealousy again. The only things she and Mariana were good at sharing were the bedcovers. At night after they crawled in together, Nora pulled the afghan close, and Mariana used her feet to wind the bottom sheet around them both. There was enough room for both of them. Their hair wound around each other's and their fingers entwined. Sometimes they thought they had the same dreams. They shared the space, the very air.

Most other things they fought over.

That birthday, Ruthie sat back, looking pleased with how the gifts had been received. "Honey, I'm sorry your diary's pink. I know you like green better. But you said you wanted it to lock and that's all they had—I'm still not sure the lock is a good idea."

"It's perfect, Mama," said Nora. "I love it."

Her mother's mouth twisted. "But . . . the lock, I'm just not sure . . ."

"You can use the key whenever you want to," said Nora. She'd never lied harder in her life. The key was *hers*, no one else's. She'd wear it on a piece of string around her neck until she *died*. She knew it was what her mother needed to hear, though. "You can even write in it, Mama." She *couldn't*; only Nora's newly learned cursive letters would fill the book: all her dreams, her fears. All her hope.

"Oh, sugar," said her mother happily. "I would never ask to do that, but it's sweet of you to say."

Mariana got the look she got when Nora got the bigger piece of cinnamon toast. "I can write in it, too, can't I?"

"I'm sure your sister won't mind," said their mother, already moving toward her bedroom to change for the second half of her split shift. "Share, both of you. Happy birthday, girls."

Nora slipped the diary under her shirt, the metal lock cold against her stomach.

"You have to share with me," said Mariana, her voice chilly. "Mama said."

"She did not."

"She did. I have to share my Fashion Plates with you, and I don't want to."

Nora sensed a power play in the air, a way she could turn this to her advantage. "I *really* want to draw some dresses." She did.

"I know you do," said Mariana in satisfaction. "I'll let you. If you do what I say."

"But if you promise not to write in my diary, I won't touch your Fashion Plates."

Mariana glared suspiciously. "But you want to color."

Nora made her eyes wide with need. "I *do*. But I won't, if you leave my journal alone."

"You'll never use them once? You won't sneak in and make a Fashion Plate while I'm in the bathroom or something?"

Nora gave up her thought of being sneaky and getting around the promise. There was nothing—usually—that she didn't have to share with Mariana. From jeans to hair bands to the rare chocolate bar, everything got used up between them both. Nora was so tired of sharing. The journal—it could be filled with secrets. Secrets that Mariana wouldn't even know, couldn't even dream of. Secrets that were hers, Nora's, alone.

"Deal," said Nora. "I promise I'll never use your Fashion Plates, ever."

Still looking distrustful, Mariana stuck out her hand. "Deal."

"And you won't ever look in my diary." She should stop talking. Nora knew she should. A better plan would have been to pretend she'd never use it, didn't care about it, but she hadn't thought of it in time.

"Okay."

They shook hands, and it felt official. A business deal between the sisters.

It hadn't worked, of course. Within a week, Ruthie had needed a piece of paper to make the weekly shopping list and had popped the lock in order to rip out a sheet. To Nora's broken-hearted wail, she'd assured her, "I used a bobby pin to open it. It'll still lock—don't worry."

The fact that the tiny cunning key still worked was beside the point. The safety was gone. Nora wrote in big block letters at the top of every page, STAY OUT, but then she found seven diary pages used for Fashion Plates stencils—women with blue eye shadow and incredibly short skirts—shoved under a couch cushion. In a fit of sheer rage, Nora found her mother's thick black marker, the one that gave off fumes she knew she wasn't supposed to breathe (thereby making inhalation terrifying and thrilling). She struck out every page in the journal.

If she couldn't find privacy there, in the locked book, then no one would.

She was hit by remorse the very second she ruined the last page. She should never have done it—she'd ruined everything.

Again.

Nora wiped tears off her cheeks and looked up to find herself in her office.

In her home. She was in her Herman Miller chair, the one that had taken years of paid writing to justify to herself. She looked out the round window in front of the desk, down to the top of Harrison's kitchen roof.

Hadn't she just been in the garden? Watching the brilliance of the tiny green hummingbirds as they zoomed blurrily past? She'd been lost in the birthday memory for how long? When had she walked upstairs? Her phone said four o'clock, but she couldn't remember what it had said the last time she looked.

Her own Moleskine journal was open on the desk in front of her. No lock. Nothing to keep anyone out.

Where am I?

The words were in her handwriting. She didn't remember writing them. The page wasn't dated. She'd left herself no clue.

In an online *New Yorker* article she'd found, Oliver Sacks had said, "Though one cannot have direct knowledge of one's own amnesia, there may be ways to infer it: from the expressions on people's faces when one has repeated something half a dozen times; when one looks down at one's coffee cup and finds that it is empty; when one looks at one's diary and sees entries in one's own handwriting."

Carefully, she wrote the date at the top of the next page. June 30. It felt good to write because it was true and verifiable by her online calendar and the fact that it matched the smudged date on her wrist, which rested above the word of the day, "obstreperous" (which had almost too many letters to fit on her skin—the smug *O* almost met the sinuous *S*). Every morning, first thing, she wrote the date along with the day of the week. Every day, she flipped open the pocket-sized *Merriam-Webster* she kept on her bedside table next to the bowl of beach glass and picked a word. She wrote it on her wrist under the date. She tried to pick a word she didn't usually use in conversation so she wouldn't accidentally run across it in daily use. She had to *try* to think of the day's word: "cellulose," "fulvous," "prototype."

Throughout the day, she said the word to herself. Today: *obstreperous, obstreperous.*

But Nora didn't know what to write next in her journal, and she *always* knew what to write next. She couldn't remember what she'd come up to her office to work on or if she'd even had a plan at all. She'd finished the column on the dementia village in San Luis Obispo. She'd turned it in to Benjamin. She knew that. But for the life of her, she couldn't remember her next column idea. She popped open the lid of her computer and searched her calendar for Benjamin's name.

Ah. The piece, due in a day and a half, on mothers who smoked through pregnancy.

That was all it took, really, Nora thought with satisfaction. A careful methodology. With the tools available nowadays, she could orchestrate a way to not forget things. An iPhone reminder app and her Google calendar plus lots of notifications—set minute by minute if that's what it took—and she wouldn't put anyone out. It would be fun, actually. It would be a really important game. And that, perhaps, was the best hiding place of all for hope. Hope lived tucked in the base of one question: If Nora played this vicious game against herself, even if she always lost, didn't it mean (since she was both the player and her own opponent) that she also always won?

Chapter Thirty

EXCERPT,
**WHEN ELLIE WAS LITTLE:
OUR LIFE IN HOLIDAYS,**
PUBLISHED 2011 BY NORA GLASS

Fourth of July

When Ellie was little, her favorite thing was fireworks.

It was to be expected, since Paul was the biggest fan of fireworks there ever was. He loved the noise, the light, the flash, the *grandeur* of the presentations. He was never good at shooting them off himself—he got nervous even lighting sparklers—and I think it was because they were so important to him. Besides, he always wanted to be in the middle of the action, to be directly underneath as they exploded overhead, not in charge of the not-very-important small arms that popped and sparked on surface streets.

The first big show we ever took Ellie to was in Sausalito, on the water. She wasn't even a year old yet, and I'd argued that it would frighten her. Most children were terrified of fireworks. I'd read this in a magazine. (Everything I read I spouted at Paul with the surety that motherhood gave me. All mothers are like this. Even if they act like they're not sure what they're doing—they are. They're one hundred percent sure they're right and that the other person is wrong. This would be good for new fathers to note.)

My husband ceded most decisions to me. I was the one who decided on cloth diapers even though we couldn't afford a service and I had to rinse them in the toilet, gagging every time. I decided how to swaddle her, and god help Paul when he didn't do it tight enough. I knew what every look on her face meant (even when I didn't), and confidently, I told him, "That's gas," or "She's hungry," or "She won't like fireworks."

But he insisted on this one. "We're doing this. We're going tonight. By we, I mean Ellie and me. You can come if you want to, but we're going." It was so unlike him to press his hand that way that I gave in. I can confess it now though I'm still ashamed of it—I wanted to be right. I wanted Ellie to scream. I wanted her face to go plum with howls of fear. I wanted to comfort her and I wanted Paul to be wrong and sorry about it. (Don't judge. I hadn't slept in eleven months.)

The crowd was terrible. We drove as far as we could get, but the traffic was terrible and we had to park a mile away from the shore. We followed the hordes of people on foot ahead of us in the dusk. I rehearsed how right I would be later and cheerfully carried the bag that held a bottle of wine and half a pizza.

Night fell. We sat on the salt-eroded grass at the water's edge and watched the bay expectantly. Far, far away, in San Francisco, the first show started. Muffled thumps traveled over the water. I watched Ellie expectantly. She sat up. In the baby backpack on Paul's back, her eyes focused on the blips of lighted color. She looked startled, just as I'd known she would.

Then overhead, our Marin show started. Rockets exploded. Gunfire thumped my chest and I worried that the percussion could damage Ellie's tiny internal organs. I was about to insist we leave—about to grab her out of the backpack and run, never admitting what I'd just realized for the first time, that I was the one terrified of fireworks—when Ellie burst out laughing.

She'd been a quiet baby up till then. Her chortles at home were low and satisfied but never loud.

This was different. She howled with laughter. Other families looked at us and laughed at her joy. Every time a mortar went off, shaking us with impact, she laughed from deep in her belly. She laughed so hard that the tears streaming from her eyes jiggled on the way down her fat face. At one point, she fell over sideways in the baby backpack. "Is she crying now?" he asked, suddenly worried he'd been wrong, that he'd scarred her for life.

I could have lied—her laughter almost sounded like crying then. But it wasn't. It wasn't hysterical or out of control. Ellie was simply laughing in joy, as hard as she could, hiccuping between giggles, and I had honestly never seen anything as beautiful or as funny in all my life.

"No. She's perfect."

Our tiny family turned our faces up to the explosions bursting in air. Ellie hiccuped and laughed, and we laughed with her. We watched, the three of us delirious, as happy as the men whose job it was to set the sparks to the fuses.

Chapter Thirty-one

"Okay." Dylan ducked his head and pushed back the heavy brown lock that always flopped over his right eye. "You said you wanted to see a dive. This place is a *fuckin'* dive."

Merchants Tavern, in downtown Oakland, was the type of place Ellie would never have set foot in six months ago. Even if she'd been with someone cool—like her aunt or something— even if she'd been dared to go inside to use the restroom, she would have declined, not caring if she looked chicken.

But things had changed (so much had changed, with Mom and school and college coming up), and Ellie was a lot older now. This gorgeous guy *liked* her. Not only was he her friend, but he thought she was hot. It made it way easier to go with him into the bar.

Inside, the space was long and narrow, dark and humid. Men with high round bellies pressed tight against the wood, not even looking up when the door slammed behind them. In their ball caps and dingy sweatshirts, they looked as if perhaps they'd grown there, tired fungi growing straight out of the barstools.

"Back here." Dylan took her hand and led her around three pinball machines, past the open door of the smallest, dirtiest bathroom she'd ever seen. It was so small the sink was stuck in the small hallway as an afterthought. She just wouldn't drink much. No matter how bad she had to pee, she wouldn't be using that. The whole bar smelled like piss, anyway—the bathroom was obviously just a suggestion.

To the right, the space opened up into a wider, taller room. The walls were covered in graffiti, from the floors to the beams along the ceiling. It smelled of cold dirt as well as urine. The air itself felt muddy and sticky. Without thinking, Ellie leaned against the wall while Dylan ordered them drinks. She had to peel the shoulder of her shirt away when they moved.

She coughed. Almost every person in the bar had a cigarette hanging from their lips, dangling from their fingertips, or resting in an ashtray on the bar. "I thought you couldn't smoke indoors in Oakland." *Or in all of California.*

Dylan pointed at the glass elephant next to the tip bell. "If you smoke, you chip in. That's how they pay off the fines."

Ellie frowned. "You'd think that with enough violations, they'd eventually shut the place down."

"Nah," Dylan said. He turned and handed her something that looked way more fancy than a simple beer. It was clear, and it was served in the kind of glass her mother served at her book club when it was at their house.

"What's this?"

"Martini."

She took a sip. It *burned*. The burn crawled up into her nose and singed the tip of it. She wanted to swear, or spit it out, or both. But she wasn't a baby, so she didn't. She steeled her face to remain as still as possible and tossed back another swallow. She blinked once, hard enough to clear her eyes of the tears that wanted to rise. "I like it." Her voice came out almost normal.

Dylan grinned and leaned his shoulder against hers briefly.

"Knew you would. Come back this way." He smelled good, like mint.

The big room held a shabby stage that looked as if it was held together with plywood and black duct tape. Two pool tables stood in puddles of dirty yellow light that dripped from ancient beer signs overhead. The guys playing seemed to be making the old tables work in their favor, taking their shots so the raised pieces of torn felt played into their bank shots.

"Maybe we'll play a game," said Dylan.

"Totally," said Ellie, lifting her chin. That was just about the last thing she wanted to do.

Dylan introduced her to a younger group at the second table. Ian, Holly, Vinyl, and Toast. The last two were his roommates, and she'd met them briefly at the cop-bar gig. She'd been sober that night, terrified of how she was going to get back to Tiburon—her mother had thought she was watching movies with Vani that night, but she'd still had to get home before curfew.

Tonight, though, she hadn't told her mother a damn thing before leaving. They'd had a fight, a huge one. That morning, her mother had given her money and asked her to pick up four chicken breasts on the way home from Vani's house later. She'd said she wanted to barbecue chicken and have Harrison over and watch the fireworks down in the marina from the backyard.

Chicken. Her mother had said chicken.

When Ellie'd brought the chicken into the kitchen, her mother had *lost* it. She'd wanted to know where the pork chops were. She'd been very clear, she articulated with her teeth visibly gritted, that she wanted pork. Pork chops with applesauce.

But her mother had asked for chicken. Ellie had even *clari-fied*—breast, not thigh—but apparently having pork chops was, like, the most important thing in the whole universe because Mom had slammed a bowl full of some kind of spice mixture into the sink. The bowl, a blue one with a yellow rim that Ellie knew her mother loved, had cracked when it hit the porcelain. A small dust devil of spice had risen into the air, and her mother had turned toward Ellie, a storm of rage clouding her expression, making her into someone else, someone with Mom's hair but not her face.

Ellie had stumbled backward, smacking her hip on a chair. "You said chicken," she'd insisted.

"Pork!"

"Remember?" Ellie started. "I think you forgot, that's all. I asked if you wanted thighs or—"

Her mother slapped her.

Right across the face.

The sound of it was as loud as the bowl had been when it hit the sink, but thinner. The crack hung in the air, and Ellie— before she could help herself—moved into her protective stance, the one she'd learned from the self-defense class her mother had made her take. She bent her knees slightly, and her hands went up, open, palm out.

The next thing she would do—the terrible thing she almost did—was a nose thrust with the heel of her palm. She was less than a second away from doing it without thinking. And if she had, she would have broken her mother's nose. If her mother had slapped her twice, she would have been startled into doing the heel-palm-thrust strike automatically—she could *feel* it.

Her mother cried out, but the noise wasn't a word—it sounded more like a strangled animal stuck in her vocal cords.

Ellie's breath was caught somewhere in the pit of her stomach and she couldn't get air. Mom looked at her hands—they'd taken the class together. She knew the strike as well as Ellie did. She knew what Ellie had almost done.

"Mom—"

Her mother turned. She ran from the room, right out the back door. Ellie stood in place, her hands still in front of her, breathing so fast the pepper in the airborne spice blend grabbed at her lungs, choking her.

She'd gone upstairs, back into the game. Breathing hard, she tried to ignore the pain in her cheek. She texted Dylan. He responded almost immediately. *Jack London fireworks? I know a guy with boats. I can come pick you up.*

Yes.

Then she'd waited until she heard her mother clattering in the kitchen, tossing the pottery chunks into the trash, running the garbage disposal. While the water ran and cupboard doors slammed, Ellie had simply walked out the front door. She'd stood by the mailbox until Dylan pulled up; then she'd gotten in Dylan's car. She'd silenced her phone when they hit the on-ramp to the bridge and then tucked it into her back pocket, resolving to not look at it again until she got home. Whenever that was.

Mom had *hit* her. She'd never hit Ellie before, not ever. Not even a swat on the butt, as far as she could remember.

Maybe she'd wanted to. Maybe in the past Ellie had been such a pain in the ass that her mother had wanted to but hadn't thought she'd get away with it. Maybe her mother was *using* her sickness as a way to get what she wanted. It was a terrible thought. Ellie hated that she'd had it. But once she'd had it, she couldn't *stop* thinking it. Not that Ellie wouldn't use the sick card if she had it in her pocket. Hell yes, she would. She'd drop out of high school and write an amazing novel about the pain of life and the glory of love or something. There had been a kid named Walter at her school who had died—actually *died*—of lung cancer, but before he kicked the bucket, he got everything he wanted, up to and including a Camaro. The kid could barely breathe or move, but his Camaro came fitted with a steering wheel with button controls. He got a ticket for going ninety-five on the freeway. He got his wish, and good for him.

At the bar, Dylan had driven onto the sidewalk and parked next to the wall.

"Is this legal?" As soon as the words came out of her mouth, Ellie regretted them. How juvenile could she possibly sound? It was a miracle she'd swallowed the words she'd almost said: *What about wheelchair access?*

Dylan grinned and said, "The bartender doesn't mind, and OPD's *way* too busy tonight to fuck with anything as stupid as parking."

"Right?" she'd said, nodding hard. "Totally."

And now she was drinking a martini in a bar.

She could tell Toast and Vinyl had obviously been drinking for a while. Both of them were sweating slightly even though the iron-barred windows were open to the wet night air. Holly and Ian were one of those annoying and probably new couples who couldn't do anything without sticking their tongues down each other's throats first. "Hi!" They dove into a slobbery kiss before she could respond. "So you live in Marin, huh?" Back into another kiss so wet Ellie wanted to put a bucket at their feet so their drool didn't rise over her ankle boots.

As a gust of smoke blew past Ellie's face, she caught her breath, choking on her own saliva. A man spit on the floor behind her. It was the mouth-drippiest place she'd ever been. She turned sideways and spoke quietly to Dylan. "Are you sure we're not going to get in trouble here?"

"Dude, we're all underage. Except Holly. She was, like, twenty-one last month. Nobody at this place cares, not if you've been here before or if you came in with friends." He waved at a man sitting on the stairs who was smoking a joint the width of a carrot.

"That old guy keeps staring at me."

Dylan looked over his shoulder.

"No! Don't look," she hissed.

"You mean Jasper? The bald one?"

"Yeah."

"He's cool. He's the one with the boats. Come on. I'll introduce you."

Jasper didn't seem cool—when she shook his hand, his skin

was clammy. But he smiled, and when Dylan asked if he had space on the boats, he said, "Hell yeah, there's room. Chug that."

"What?"

When he smiled, Ellie saw he was missing important molars. "Chug your drink so we can go."

Everyone was watching her by then, so she did. Her eyes teared again.

"Let's go."

Dylan bought two huge cups of beer from the bartender and then poured them into the empty Snapple bottles. "Smart, right?"

She didn't know if she'd call it smart. Smart was stealing the tapers of war, smart was breaking into the metalsmith's shop while he slept, smart was using her Maker tokens to create a steel box to hold the tapers so they didn't burn through Addi's bag when she ran. Smart was getting into your first-choice college and finding enough scholarships online to pay for it all. No, smart was as simple as knowing what your first-choice college *was.* Carrying beer in a Snapple bottle—that was only kind of high school–level smart. But when Dylan grinned and kissed her, his mouth sweet from the Life Savers he kept in his jacket pocket and bitter from the cigarette he held in his left hand, Ellie nodded. "Super-smart," she said.

As a group, they fought their way through the crowd to the marina, weaving their way through families carrying kids who were already tired of waiting for the night to start. One man had a child on his shoulders and was pushing two more in a baby carriage, and all three of the children were screaming. The man looked like he might join them.

"Wait till the bombs start going off overhead," said Dylan. "It'll get worse. Kids hate that shit. Fireworks terrified me when I was little."

"Not me," said Ellie. But no one seemed to hear her.

"This way," Jasper yelled over the mariachi band as he led them past two mediocre jugglers. "Past the boats."

She'd thought they were going *to* a boat of some sort, so Ellie was surprised when Dylan pointed out the kayaks. "Isn't this great? Jasper has, like, five of them."

"I don't know how to do that," she said. Her mother had tried to get her out on the water in a kayak, touting the wonders of a night ride through the estuary, but Ellie had always been a little too worried about what could be underneath them. It wasn't like whales came into the bay and knocked over kayaks, and as far as she knew, sharks weren't really known for attacking big pieces of plastic in the water, but what if she overturned and fell out? What then? Anything (a crocodile, an alligator, a homeless junkie) could grab her and take her down, especially at night.

"You'll be fine."

Ellie felt dizzy with fear. She dug her balled fists deeper into the pockets of her sweatshirt. She wanted to say it again, louder. *I don't know how to do this.* Just one more thing she didn't know how to do, how to navigate. But he was already walking down the ramp. So she followed.

Jasper seated her in her own pale blue kayak.

"I don't know how to do this," she gasped, but Jasper and the man next to him—a tall redheaded guy wearing a Grateful Dead T-shirt—lifted her boat with her inside it, sliding first the front, then the back end of the kayak off the wooden dock and into the water. The kayak splashed and bobbed and she screamed, a girly noise that she hated. Behind her, the men laughed.

Fuckers. Fuck them. She wanted to flip them off and paddle away, stealing the kayak, but she didn't know how to paddle and she'd never managed a good flip-off in her life. Sam and Vani always laughed at her when she accidently threw "I love you" or "Hang loose" instead of getting the bird right up there.

So Ellie just smiled as hard as she could until it felt almost real. Dylan was next to her in his own kayak. "Look. Ellie, check it out." His face was kind. "It's going to be okay. I'll be right next to you. I won't leave you."

"Promise me."

"I promise." He pressed a kiss to the tip of his index finger and then rocked sideways in his kayak, touching her bottom lip. It should have been a silly gesture, but Ellie was moved almost to tears.

"Okay, then," she said. "Show me."

"Hold your paddle like this. Now, watch, you do a figure eight to move forward. Easy does it. Not too hard on the right, that's your stronger side—no, not so hard, you'll knock yourself out of the kayak."

Ellie made a smaller motion, and sure enough, she felt more confident in the kayak. The less she moved, the more stable she felt.

"That's it," called Dylan, looking over his shoulder at her. "Now paddle a little faster, because the boat behind you wants to get around us."

Swallowing a scream, Ellie paddled harder to get out of the way of the white yacht with its chugging engine. "If I *do* fall out, what happens?"

"Nothing," said Dylan. "These are ocean kayaks; they float. It'll turn right side up, you'll climb back on board, and you'll be fine. Wet, but fine."

"Unless a shark gits ya," said Jasper in a loud voice on her left. He'd come up behind her soundlessly. "Been a long time since a shark took someone from the estuary, but you never know, do you?" He laughed louder so everyone could hear him and paddled past, leaving her behind. Two girls she hadn't been introduced to barely glanced at her as they worked to keep up with him.

Everything except for Dylan felt wrong. It was *wrong* out here. She should have said she didn't want to go, she should have just asked if they could stay at the bar . . . For a moment Ellie wished she were at home with her mother, and then she remembered. She touched her cheek. Still tender, like her skin was feverish. She wondered if her mother was looking at the bay from the backyard. If she was wondering where Ellie had gone.

Ellie couldn't even *see* the bay, just the estuary. She could see the lights of Oakland behind her and something that might be Alameda in front of her. No matter what that asshole Jasper said, she wasn't scared of sharks, but if she fell overboard, what would prevent a boat with a motor from running over her and cutting off her legs before she could get back into the kayak? Then she'd die in the water and her mother would have to bury her and the grief of it would probably kill her even faster than she was already dying . . .

But Ellie kept paddling. Dylan thought she was a warrior, a healer with fighting prowess. He'd told her so when Addi and Dyl sat in the hut together late at night. Maybe someday Ellie would ask if he'd ever tried to make his avatar come to her, to sit on the bed with her, if he'd ever attempted to make his avatar kiss her. *She'd* tried. She'd made Addi walk toward him a million times, but there was a space that had to be maintained between them, a space the game makers didn't allow them to breach. There was no way for Addi to touch Dyl in the game if she didn't wheel into a roundhouse kick or launch into a forward closed-fist punch.

In the middle of the estuary, Jasper and the red-haired man lit three lanterns and stuck them on the ends of fishing poles. Dylan waved her in closer and she managed to clumsily turn her boat so that she was on the end of the row of kayaks. A rope was passed around, and the group of seven made themselves into a flotilla of sorts. They weren't the only groups of kayaks doing it—two other similar groups, including one that had to be comprised of at least thirty kayaks, had made themselves into floating parties.

Ellie pulled up her knees and rested her paddle on her thighs. A flare went off overhead, shooting from so nearby that she jumped, almost unseating herself.

"It's starting!" said Dylan.

"Nah," drawled Jasper, holding something up in the dark. "That was my flare. Let's get this party started, right?" He took out a huge bottle of dark-colored liquor and passed it to the woman on his left. Then he lit a joint and passed it to his right. Dylan took a hit off it and passed it to Ellie.

Ellie held it, considering the weed. She'd never smoked it before, but given the way she already felt dizzy from the martini and the two sips of beer she'd had, she wasn't sure she was cut out to be the partying type.

"Hit it, little girl," said Jasper. "Hit it and then show us your tits."

Dylan said, "Shut the fuck up," but the other men laughed.

Ellie held up the joint, examining the glowing red end. If she held it close to her eyes, she could cover the whole Oakland skyline.

"Come on," Jasper said, sounding more exasperated. "If you're gonna be a fuckin' baby, pass it back. That's good shit."

She wasn't a baby.

Ellie didn't really know what she was, but she knew she wasn't a fucking baby.

She considered the lit tip for another few seconds. Then she carefully dropped the joint into the water. She waited until Jasper was done spluttering and hurling epithets at her, and then she said, "You don't fire flares into the night sky on the Fourth of July. You ruin the show that way, you fucking *idiot*." Directly over her head, the first sky flyer exploded and she turned her face up to the light.

Chapter Thirty-two

*H*arrison folded his hands behind his head and leaned back. "So let's walk through it again. Did you hear a car?"

"I heard a bunch of cars. I didn't think about it."

"And you've tried her cell."

"Five times. Fifteen texts."

"She'll be back."

Nora shook her head. "She'll never forgive me." She would never forgive herself.

"So, what, you just think she's going to go live on the streets? Because you gave her one slap?"

Nora sighed and pressed her fingers against her forehead. "I don't know. Maybe."

"You're overreacting. Where do you think she went?"

"Probably out with Dylan. He's in a band—did I tell you that?"

"Yes."

"Guitar. Of course it has to be the guitar player. If she's out at a club right now, underage, I'll . . ." But her voice trailed off. There was nothing she could do.

Harrison left his seat, going to stand behind her.

"Oh," Nora said. "God, will you . . . ?"

"Of course."

She leaned back against her chair and closed her eyes. Harrison's hands were in her hair, his thumbs and the pads of his strong fingers rubbing exactly where it felt the best. He'd taken a massage class years before. He'd gotten two different girlfriends out of it, too, if she remembered correctly.

His hands were perfect. Nora groaned and said, "If I were a millionaire, I'd hire you to do this all day long."

"This knot is the size of a coffee cup. What are you doing to yourself?"

She had to tell him. It would explain so much—how she hadn't been able to touch him, to let him touch her. How she'd been avoiding him, going in from the garden when she heard his car pull into the driveway next door. She hadn't been able to, though. Not until now, now that she'd fucked up so big with Ellie, now that she had her back to him and she couldn't see his face. "I'm sick."

His hands stopped moving.

God, it wasn't fair to him, not to face him with this. She spun in her chair. Harrison's hands hung helplessly in the air. "I've been trying to think of a way to tell you . . ."

"Okay." He sat heavily, placing his hands carefully on his lap. "What is it?"

"Early-onset Alzheimer's."

"*Fuck.*" His voice said he knew what she meant. She wouldn't have to explain it to him, thank god.

"How do you know it?"

"I knew a family with it."

"In your practice?" Harrison was a psychotherapist. A good one, she knew.

"Yeah."

"Ahhh." Nora thought about that for a second. "How many of them were affected?"

"Five of the six siblings."

"Oh."

Harrison nodded.

"How old were they when they came down with symptoms?" Why hadn't they ever talked about this? Why wasn't EOAD something people talked about at dinner parties? *Did you know there's a disease that takes your brain away from you in the middle of your prime? No! Tell me more!*

"Two were midforties, I think. One was over fifty. One was thirty-six. She was the one who was my patient."

"When was that?"

"A while. Maybe five years ago?"

"How many are left?"

Harrison's look was soft. "How many do you think?"

Nora threaded her fingers in her lap and wished for her knitting. It was in the living room, much too far away. "Just the one sibling who didn't have it."

"Yes." His voice was kind, too.

"I want to talk to her."

"Nora," Harrison started.

"Can you help get me in touch with her?"

"It's not a good idea. Besides, I wouldn't be able to find her now even if I wanted to."

"Why?" No, Harrison didn't get to say what a good idea was and what wasn't. That was up to her. Only her. "Are you her therapist now?"

"No, I only saw her sister."

"So put us in touch."

"No."

"Maybe she needs someone to talk to." God, no. It was a ridiculous idea. "I'm losing it. I bet she has someone to talk to. A shrink. A husband. Maybe I need to get some of those. I should go to one of those care homes and see what it's like. Talk to a patient. I'm a journalist, I know how to research things. No, I don't want to—I can't . . . I'm totally losing my mind." Nora paused. She'd hit her *daughter.*

Harrison said, "I'm a shrink. Just talk to me."

Nora tilted her head and looked at him. Harrison. Even now, with his lower lip stiff from emotion, he was calming to her. She loved the way his hair stuck straight up by the end of an evening, strangely confident curls breaking free of whatever hair product he used in the morning to keep them under control.

He lifted her hand and kissed the back of the knuckles. "Do I get to cry in front of you?" His voice was thick but didn't shake.

"Absolutely not. Thank you for asking."

"There are better drugs now, better than what was available even five years ago."

"I know. I'm on all of them. One makes me poop like crazy. One stops me up. The Namenda, get this, can make you feel confused. Ha! Isn't that funny?"

Harrison didn't look up. While keeping his gaze on her palm, he ran one finger from her wrist over her lifeline, all the way down her middle finger to its very tip. "How's Ellie doing with it?"

"Well, considering that she'd already hit the apex of her teenage career of hating me and I just made it a thousand times worse, I think she's . . . doing the best she can. I thought . . . No, it doesn't matter what I thought." Nora smiled but her mouth felt crooked. "She thought I was pregnant."

Harrison's whole body jerked. "What?"

"I'm *not.* Obviously."

"Right." He rubbed his face.

"But she thought I was. She told me not to have twins."

Harrison pointed at Nora and then back at himself. "So she knows . . ."

"Apparently."

"I thought we'd been so careful."

"She's smart."

"Scary fucking smart," agreed Harrison with a grin, and Nora felt a lump rise in her throat so sticky and sweet it felt like she was choking on syrup. She hadn't expressly chosen Harrison to be the man in Ellie's life, but for all intents and purposes, he'd been the one. He'd been the man snapping her picture at her grade school and then middle school graduations. He was the guy cheering at the top of his lungs at her water polo games. He was the one who picked Ellie up on the rare nights Nora got stuck at the paper at meetings. When Ellie had gotten her period, Nora had been at work, and she'd run to his house. And the thing that got Nora, the thing that made the lump even bigger and sweeter in her throat when she thought about that now, was that he'd had supplies in his house in the guest bathroom, along with a little instruction book for teens. *How did you know to do that?* Nora had asked him. He'd said, *I didn't think I'd need it, but what if I did? I've got lots of little plans you don't know about.*

"It doesn't matter that she knows," said Harrison. "She's old enough to understand that grown-ups make their own choices, and . . ."

"It matters," said Nora.

"Damn it. It does. I'm sorry."

"I'm not. It's just one more thing for her to process. That's the only part I don't like, but honestly, with the weight of my diagnosis, I don't think she's worried about my sex life right now."

"Is she going to get tested?"

"No." It was impossible. She'd never let Ellie be tested.

"What did she say to that?"

"We haven't talked about it."

Harrison groaned and stood, picking up the plates. As usual, since she cooked, he'd clean. It had always been so sweet, so familiar. Now that they'd slept together, it felt different somehow. She hadn't predicted that, and she didn't like it. An image of him, naked above her, holding himself up on his arms just before he entered her, his dark eyes so startlingly intense, flashed through her mind, and she felt the spot between her thighs dampen. It wasn't *fair* that while her body was betraying her in so many ways, it included this one—she'd like to be able to control her sexual urges in the same way she'd always controlled herself, carefully, with great thought.

She stood. "I'll do them."

"It's okay." He grabbed the water glasses. "I'll get them. The fireworks should be starting soon. You want more wine?"

"No. And I said I'll do the dishes." Her voice was too strong, too angry.

He placed the glasses carefully next to the sink and then turned slowly to face her. "I know you're upset, Nora. What happened tonight with Ellie—"

"You don't know anything," said Nora, wishing she could stop talking, but she couldn't, not just yet. "I'm so sorry, but you know crap, Harrison. You knew someone with this disease once, but beyond that, you know shit about what's going on inside me. No one knows. This is July. You know how long I've known? Since February."

Harrison opened his mouth as if to speak, but Nora held up her hand. "Don't," she said. "I didn't even tell Ellie and Mariana till six weeks ago. Don't feel bad or apologize or do any of the other things you might feel like doing right now. Whatever it is, I don't think I can take it."

"Easy, tiger. You're forgetting who I am."

She'd thought he was her closest non-blood-related friend. She hadn't *forgotten*. Not that, anyway.

"What symptoms are you presenting?"

"You even say the right medical words. *Presenting*."

"I'm a doctor. You should have come to me, Nora."

He was hurt that she hadn't. She could see that. She should have told him earlier. She shouldn't have held on to it for so long, keeping it away from him like she'd hid the bottle of Miracle-Gro she'd sprinkled on his roses when he wasn't looking (that said, they'd sprung back to life gorgeously). "Not many symptoms. I forget where I put things."

"I do that, too." He smiled lightly.

"Don't *do* that. Don't trivialize it. I forgot where I was when I was driving last month. I got completely lost in downtown Tiburon."

"What did you do?"

"I made Ellie drive. Called it a lesson."

"Smart. Quick thinking."

If it was designed to make her feel better, it was working. She scowled at him. "I'm having trouble sleeping. Insomnia. It could be a side effect of the Aricept, or . . . I've forgotten to pick up Ellie twice, and now she won't let me pick her up at all—she's arranging all her rides with friends until she gets her license."

Nora held up her wrist and showed him the smudged black ink. *Minstrel,* she said now in her mind while she held her wrist toward Harrison, grateful to have remembered the word again without looking. Eventually, the inside of her wrist had become blue-gray, the Sharpie ink never quite washing off at night. It was something she would have worried about in the past. All that ink, seeping into her blood. Strange chemicals with many letters. Now Nora thought the more letters in her blood, the better. Maybe she would hang on to them longer. She slept with *Q* clutched in her fist, wrapping the tendrils of *S* around fingers, memorizing the way *A* jutted up forcefully, the way *P* could be used as a hammer if necessary.

"I'm not me anymore. I don't feel like myself—I'm snapping when I never snap, and that's part of the disease, they say. Personality changes." He touched her wrist so lightly it felt like a breath. "I could blame hitting her on that, but I don't think that's fair. *I* did it. Not the disease. She knows that, too. You can't make this better, Harrison." That was Harrison's thing—she had to cut him off at the pass, before he made a run at fixing her. It was what he did, after all. He made things better. He helped people, whoever was in front of him. He helped his patients, staying late and wiping out bills that couldn't be paid. Nora had seen him carry groceries out of the store and pack them into the cars of the elderly and mothers who had more children than bags. He always, always had cash in his front pocket for panhandlers. He mowed Nora's lawn every week, even though she'd told him a million times she could do it herself. She couldn't remember the last time she'd put her own garbage can at the curb. As much as she teased him for dating women less intelligent than him, he was kind to them, too. He *liked* his girlfriends, even if they didn't stick around longer than a spin around the calendar. He'd given his old Ford to Sherry the astrologist, Nora remembered now. Sherry's car had broken down, and he hadn't even thought about it, just took out the pink slip and signed it over to her. They'd broken up a week later (Sherry had dumped him for not wanting to move in with her) and he hadn't even asked for the car back. How could you not love a guy like him?

And *that* was it. It was infuriating and terrifying to realize how much she loved him when she'd never agreed to do so. It was just one more thing that had happened while she hadn't been watching.

"Anything else, other symptoms?"

He should be snapping at her. She deserved it. She didn't deserve the look of patience he gave her. "Just the confusion, so far. I get it in the middle of the night, mostly." Horrible long minutes where she woke and couldn't remember where Paul was. Twice she'd thought she heard Ellie fussing in her crib. Once she'd thought she was in the room she'd shared with Mariana in high school. She'd been frozen, the scratchy nightdress bunched at her waist, fear inside her teeth and tongue. Her feet had searched the bed; then her arms had turned over her pillows, throwing them to the floor. Where was Mariana? Where was her sister?

Then she'd come back into place, standing next to her own bed in her own house, wearing her own normal soft cotton T-shirt and panties. Her heart had thumped in her ears so hard she thought it was the pipes in the wall banging.

She hadn't slept for the rest of the night.

"And anger. They said it was a thing. I have a way lower flash point."

"That goes with stress, too, so combined with the EOAD, that could be hard to deal with."

Of course he just *understood* it. "Do you have any idea how frustrating *you* are to deal with?"

"You know what?" His voice was tight, the words like chips of glass.

"What?" Nora stuck her chin out and scowled.

Instead of responding, Harrison took a deep breath.

Nora was furious, the inside of her brain a dark red. "What? Just say it already."

"What about Mariana?"

Angry tears sprang to her eyes. "She's fine. She doesn't have it. Of course."

"You're *mad* about that?"

"No!"

"Not what it sounds like to me."

She covered her face with her hands. It was dark and quiet for one long second. Then she looked at him. "I don't know what I am. I don't know how I am. I just want to get off the ride, and I'm terrified I can't make it stop. I'm on one of those spinning things, you know, in the playground—what are they called? *Damn* it."

"Carousel?"

"No, no." Was this another symptom? "The metal thing. You can fit, like, five kids on it, and then you push it . . ."

"Merry-go-round."

"That. I'm on a merry, go, round, and someone's pushing it and I can't jump off because I'll die if I do, but the problem is that it's speeding up, and in time it's going to throw me. I'm smart enough to know that, and not smart enough to figure out how to get off."

"Nora," Harrison reached for her, pain in his eyes.

"I'm fine," Nora said quickly.

"You're not. You can't be. *I'm* not."

"I'm just worried because Ellie isn't home. That's all. Thanks for hanging out with me, though. And thanks for eating the chicken. I needed your help with that—"

"God*damn*, you're an idiot."

"Hey!"

His stood, his forehead red. "This is what you do? You hit me with the fact that you're dying of an incurable disease and then get pissed off when I have a reaction to that fact? Fuck off, Nora." Harrison's voice shook. She'd never seen this particular expression on his face, savage in its unvarnished fury. "Fuck *all* the way off." He barreled out the kitchen door.

Nora didn't realize she was crying until she wondered what the snuffling noise was. For more than a few seconds she was tempted to stay there, in her chair, feeling sorry for herself, feeling angry at him. The two simplest, most boring feelings in the whole world.

Then she stood. She walked out her door, across their lawns, and into his kitchen. She was still crying, and so was he, standing next to the sink, the water running, his arms loose at his sides, tears streaming down his face.

Nora reached around him and turned off the water; then she kissed him.

Their tears tasted the same.

"Just for a little while," she whispered. "I'm not staying."

"None of us are," he said, which made her cry harder. Then he bit her lower lip until she gasped and pushed against him. He tried to carry her up his stairs, which made her laugh.

Then they stopped talking. They took up his enormous bed,

using all of it, every inch. For one moment, Nora considered the other women who had swum with him across the flatness of his sheets, the other women who had pressed their shaking palms against this exact mattress while his mouth moved against their clits. Expansively, she forgave them all, knowing she had his heart, that she'd had it as long as he'd held hers. When Nora came, explosions literally lit the sky outside. No wonder fireworks were shorthand for sex in movies. Every blast was a little death, every breath another reincarnation. Harrison and Nora laughed with stolen joy—a tenuous tremble of happiness, a kiss shared while balancing on a wobbling tightrope high above a waterfall that didn't suffer fools.

Chapter Thirty-three

"Hi," said Ellie.

"Holy crap," said Ellie's aunt. Her eyes raced up and down Ellie's body as if counting the number of extremities she still had. She opened the door wider. "Get *in* here. Your mom's about to call the cops, you know that? She already called CHP to ask about accidents."

Even at almost two in the morning, Ellie's aunt looked great. Her hair was long and loose, her skin dewy like she'd just moisturized it. She wore a soft gray shirt that swung out at her thighs and black yoga pants. Her toenails were deep plum. She looked like Ellie's mom, only newer and fresher.

"What would the cops do? Put out an APB for an AP student out late with her boyfriend on a holiday?" Ellie swept past her aunt as coolly as she could, but her neck and forehead ached with tension.

"Maybe. Yes. That's exactly what they'd do."

"I didn't break any laws." She went into the huge kitchen

without a plan. It was her favorite room in her aunt's house—Mariana and Luke loved cooking together, and it showed. It was always neater than any other place in the house, the dishes done and the pots hanging above the industrial stove, and it always smelled faintly of cumin and rosemary.

"Really?" Mariana followed close at her heels. "Because you stink like an ashtray."

"Is Luke asleep?"

"Of course he is. He's a reasonable person. All reasonable people are asleep." She didn't say why she was still awake.

"You love cigarettes."

Aunt Mariana sighed. "I should never have told you that. We loved—no, I loved them, past tense. I don't smoke them because they're bad for me, and I swear that's true. And marijuana will kill your brain cells, in case you were wondering."

Ellie crossed her arms over her chest. "I didn't smoke anything."

"Did you drink?"

Ellie raised her chin and fixed her eyes on the blinking red lights on the stove. "You should set that clock."

"I don't know how. I've tried, like, twenty times, but since the remodel I don't know how to do anything in here at all. I got the oven stuck on kosher and couldn't cook for two days. I keep meaning to ask Luke . . ."

Ellie punched buttons until the blinking stopped. She checked her phone for the time and then corrected it on the stove: *1:53*. The numbers were accusatory.

"Thanks. Now call your mother."

Ellie couldn't. She literally could *not* hear her mother's voice right now. "Can't you just text her for me?"

"Ellie . . . ," Mariana started, but she didn't finish the sentence. She picked up her phone from the counter and flicked it on. While Mariana sent the message, Ellie fake texted, just for something to do with her hands, her face. *SKJiiSK2*. Delete,

delete, delete. She made sure she kept her gaze on the phone's screen, serious. Intent.

An eternity later, Mariana said, "Fine. I texted her. I'll take you home in the morning."

"What did she say?"

"She hasn't answered. I bet she's asleep."

"Thanks a lot," Ellie said. She meant it and hated how it came out of her mouth, as fake as one of the blond surfer girls in her PE class. "Really, thank you."

In the guest room she'd slept in many times before, she stripped off her black V-neck T-shirt. Her bra even smelled like smoke. She stripped to her panties and pulled on a blue T-shirt she found in the closet. It fell to her thighs and had red advertising printing on the front, OIL DECK TO SHIP. Something from Luke's shop, male words that probably made sense when said with a wrench in hand.

Mariana came in, a glass of water in her hand. She put two pills on the bedside table. "Ibuprofen."

"I told you, I didn't do anything." The taste of vodka, or gin, or whatever that had been, still sat thickly on the back of her tongue.

"Just take them. They can't hurt, and you might thank me in the morning. Who drove you here? Dylan?"

"Yeah."

"Had he been drinking?"

Of course he had. That was the whole point of going out, wasn't it? He hadn't seemed drunk, though. Ellie would never have gotten into the car with a drunk driver. She wasn't stupid. "No."

Of course, her aunt wasn't stupid, either. "Oh, chipmunk." Her aunt brushed the hair off her forehead, the exact same way her mother always did. "What are we going to do with you?"

"Nothing." Tears rose to her eyes. "That's the point. Nothing. You don't have to do anything about me."

"Did something happen?"

Ellie shook her head.

Her aunt persisted. "You want to talk about it?"

The words surprised Ellie, coming in a torrent, cascading out of her. "What would you do if someone hit you?" She knew as soon as she said it that she'd said it wrong.

"I'll kill him." Mariana's voice was like a shard of broken glass, but her hand was soft on Ellie's sore cheek. "I'll fucking kill him."

Ellie raised her hands as if she could grab the words back. "No! Not Dylan."

"Who? Where were you tonight? Who hurt you?"

Ellie couldn't imagine even her mother being more upset than Mariana looked. A small part of her glowed—it was nice, to be loved like this. The rest of her just felt sick, wishing she'd never brought it up. "No, nothing like that. It was—" She couldn't say it. She couldn't tell her aunt why she didn't want to go home. It wasn't fair.

Her aunt tilted her head and looked at her. An expression of something Ellie had never seen flickered across her face, and then Mariana said, "Once someone tried to hurt me."

Ellie's breath caught in her chest. She gulped heat.

Mariana went on. "He didn't get what he wanted, though."

"Who?" This wasn't what she'd wanted . . . Her aunt still thought—

"Bill . . . God, I've forgotten his last name. I never thought I'd be able to do that." She rubbed the top of her nose. "We were on a date. He tried . . . more than he should have."

"What happened?"

Aunt Mariana made an unamused sound. "We were at a party at his friend's house. He got me behind a door that locked, and he . . . Well, let's just say that I broke his thumb."

Ellie's mouth fell open. "You *did*?"

"Yeah."

Even though fear prickled her scalp, Ellie had to know. "What did he try to do?"

"We don't need to—"

"Please." She didn't want to say *I'm old enough*, but she was.

Mariana shifted on the bed and looked at her as if she were weighing something. Then she said, "He told me he knew I wanted him. He said he didn't want to wait. I told him no, that he was wrong, but he pushed me down. I was . . . terrified. He was a big guy."

"What happened next?" The need to know was an itch under her skin.

"He held me down on my stomach. I waited until he lifted his weight . . . and then I fought as hard as I could. Like I said, I broke his thumb. I also bit the shit out of his upper arm."

"How did you know what to do? Did you have the class we had?"

Mariana shook her head. "I don't know how I knew. But I'm glad I did."

"What did Mom say?"

Another weird look crossed her aunt's face. "Nothing. I never told her." She paused. "She was at the party, but . . . Your mother always liked him. She always thought I should have kept going out with him. *What happened to Bill? You two would be good together. Why isn't he around anymore?* She must have asked me that ten times. More."

A quarry's worth of space opened below the words, and if Ellie yelled, she'd be able to hear an echo. *She* knew something her *mother* didn't? Why hadn't her aunt told her mom? Ellie thought they knew everything about each other. Then something else, something even bigger, occurred to her. "Is that why you won't marry Luke? Because you're . . . scared of men?" It sounded way more dumb out loud than it had in her head.

"Why I won't . . . No, of course not."

Confusion made the words jumble together in Ellie's mind.

She spoke without knowing what she would say, and then the words were out and she couldn't take them back. "Mom hit me."

Aunt Mariana's whole body jerked. "Are you serious?"

Tears filled Ellie's eyes again. She couldn't help it. It wasn't like her face even hurt anymore. "We have to get Mom well." The words rushed out of her, a knife-sharp release.

"Shit." If a voice could be pale, Aunt Mariana's was white. "I know."

"How?" Ellie knew she sounded babyish, her voice high and tight, but she couldn't help it. "There has to be something she's not doing right. We have to help her fix it. I know they say it's genetic and everything, but there has to be something she did that triggered it. Environmental something. I read about exposure to DDT. Maybe it was that. And if that's it, then maybe it's something surgery can take out. Or something." Tears came hot and fast now, and she struck her cheek with the back of her hand, harder than her mother had. She smacked the wetness away.

"Oh, love." Aunt Mariana lay down next to her on top of the covers and shut her eyes. She even smelled like Ellie's mother, as if they used the same shampoo or something. Ellie realized that if she was quizzed, she couldn't name the brand of lotion Mom used. It was in a yellow bottle—she knew that. But if Mom left and wasn't there to ask, if she wanted to go to the drugstore and buy the same lotion, she wouldn't be able to. The thought made her cry harder.

The difference between her mom and her aunt, though, was that Mariana just closed her eyes and let her cry. Her aunt had never been able to watch Ellie cry, not even when she'd had to take her to the emergency room for her broken ankle. She'd just shut her eyes as if she could pretend it wasn't happening.

She was doing the same thing now. If Ellie had been at home, Mom would have been holding her tight, rocking her, telling her everything was going to be okay. Ellie had always thought that was the way you helped someone.

But it was kind of okay, this way. Just crying, with Mariana next to her, her eyes closed, her face as sad as Ellie felt.

Finally, when the majority of the stupid tears had stopped, Ellie said, "What are we going to do?"

Mariana opened her eyes carefully. "I don't know."

"You're supposed to."

"I wish I did."

"Can't you just make something up?"

"Is that what you want? For me to lie to you?"

Ellie thought that would be just fine. *It's going to be okay. It's all going to work out. Don't you worry about a single little thing.*

"I can't, honey. I can't just tell you that."

"It's hereditary," said Ellie. "I bet you knew that."

Mariana nodded slowly. "I did."

"Do you have it?"

Mariana sucked in her lips for a second. "Did you talk to your mom about this?"

"She's barely looking at me. I don't think she trusts me to talk about anything. She tries to bring up being sick, but I . . . I kind of get nervous and—I just hate it when she brings it up. She gets those pink spots on her cheeks, you know, when she's trying to keep something bad from me. Anyway, she's already told me she's going to *die*; what could be worse than that?"

"Did she say that?" Aunt Mariana had the same bright patches on her face.

"No. I mean, yes. She didn't say no when I asked her." Ellie felt a heaving in her chest and worried she was going to lose it entirely. "What about *me*?"

"Honey, it's all about you. Everything she does is about you."

Ellie rolled onto her back and took a deep breath that tasted like salt. "Bullshit." But it felt good to hear. Especially if it wasn't her mother saying it. "You didn't answer me. Do you have it?"

"I'm going to open this window," said Mariana, hurrying to fumble at the latch underneath the slats of the blind. "Hot in here."

"Do you?"

The window slammed up so hard, Ellie was surprised it didn't shatter.

Mariana turned and wiped her hands on her leggings. "No. I don't."

Instead of being comforted, as she thought she'd be, Ellie had to fight back the urge to draw an invisible weapon. If she were in the game, Addi would be holding her bronze knife by now.

Ellie had considered it, the idea that her aunt didn't have it. She'd thought about it, too, living with her aunt, in this gigantic house on Potrero Hill. Luke had money, like, serious money, not just safe money like her mom. If Ellie lived with Mariana and Luke, she could probably get a car, a new one. But Ellie would have to change schools, and the idea of meeting new friends seemed exhausting. She'd just keep her old ones. And Dylan. No matter what, she wanted Dylan. And maybe Mariana wouldn't even stay with Luke, anyway. Maybe she and her aunt would both be fuckups together. Mariana's business would flop. Ellie would drop out of high school. They'd live on the street. Ellie would learn how to play guitar, and they'd busk in BART stations. Not Civic Center, where the junkies slept wrapped in newspaper like slabs of fish, but out in Walnut Creek or Pleasanton, out where poverty made commuters feel guilty.

Ellie suddenly wanted *Queendom*. Her fingers itched to play, to make up a story and have it come true. What she wouldn't do to slice the heads off a dozen Cyrnals or two, to watch their purple blood splashing to the ground, the oily blue smoke rising from the earth as the beasts turned into dead, headless husks.

Her aunt didn't have it.

"I want to get tested," she finally said.

Mariana didn't say anything, confirming what Ellie had suspected. "What? She won't *let* me? She can't just tell me I can't get tested. I mean, that's what she said when I asked, but, dude. I have the right to know."

"It's a mammoth thing to consider. It's so big I don't think your mom has even thought her way through it yet."

That figured. "I'm not considering it. I'm going to have it done." It would be negative. She could *feel* it. She was healthy.

"What are you going to do about Dylan?"

The subject change was abrupt and unwelcome. "What about him?"

"Are you going to sleep with him?"

Ellie's face burned. She *thought* she was going to. She wanted more of those feelings she got in her midsection when he kissed her, those wild flips that felt like tadpoles wriggling right under her ribs. And sex had always been something she'd planned on talking about with her aunt, never her mother, even before her mother got sick. But now that Mariana's eyes were on her, she felt angry. Tricked, somehow. "I don't want to talk about it with you."

"That's fine, little one."

Ellie tensed, her legs and arms stiffening. "I'm not *little*. I'm so fucking *sick* of you and Mom treating me that way. Can you just go away, please?"

"But . . ." Whenever Ellie had spent the night with Mariana in the past, Mariana always slept in the bed with her, not that she'd ever shown up this late before. It was part of the fun, part of the girls' weekend fun. Ellie had never asked to sleep alone there before. And if truth were told, Ellie didn't *really* want to sleep alone tonight in this big old house that didn't sound like hers. But she couldn't—wouldn't—ask her aunt to stay with her. Like a baby.

"Okay," Mariana finally said. "I'll drive you home first thing. And you better be wearing chain mail. Your mom is gonna be pissed like she hasn't been since I crashed that stupid car."

Even though the story of how Mariana had failed to set the parking brake on her mom's old beater Civic, allowing it to run away, unoccupied, down a hill, across a highway, and into a copse of trees where it smashed into tiny pieces, was one of her favorites, Ellie didn't smile. She closed her eyes and gave a fake yawn.

When she opened them again, her aunt wasn't in the open doorway anymore, and the only sound was the distant, mournful bleat of a foghorn through the open window. Ellie was alone. She pulled her feet up, tucking them against her butt.

She closed her eyes and prayed to have no dreams at all.

Chapter Thirty-four

After the fireworks stopped, Nora crawled out of Harrison's bed, her limbs heavy. "I have to go home. I have to wait for her." Harrison nodded and pressed her hand, barely waking.

At home, Nora didn't sleep. She sat on the sofa downstairs, the television on the Home Shopping Network, the volume off. When her eyes drifted closed, she propped them open using determination born of fear. Her leg muscles cramped with disuse. She straightened and shook them, then stuck her heels under the couch cushion Ellie liked to hold against her belly. From outside came random pops and squeals followed by the occasional M–80 blast that set off car alarms and made neighborhood dogs bark.

How could she possibly go to bed? Her daughter was gone, missing. It might be her fault. No, it *was* her fault. Ellie had probably been right—she'd probably asked for chicken. She shouldn't have argued with her daughter about it—oh, god, she remembered it all over again. Ellie hadn't left because of the chicken.

Ellie had left because Nora had hit her.

Confronted with the reality of her newly untrustworthy mind, she'd hit her own daughter across the face as hard as she could.

She didn't blame Ellie for not coming home.

The analog clock on the wall read a time, but it had been getting harder and harder to decipher it lately. Maybe she needed her contacts prescription checked. She knew what was important: it was predawn—the morning paper had just slapped against the front stoop, and cars were still using their headlights. And her daughter still wasn't home.

Nora placed her fingertips against the blank piece of paper in her journal. *Responsibility.* She could write that to her daughter. *Responsible women . . .*

Didn't hit their children in anger.

No, it was even worse than that. It hadn't been anger. Nora had hit Ellie in fear.

Fear was displacing the hope. Every day less of one, more of the other. Nora couldn't control it, she couldn't iron it out, she couldn't deep clean it, she couldn't paint over it, she couldn't make it pretty and tasteful. She couldn't write a funny column about it. She couldn't make it anything else but what it was, which was . . .

Even now, she was having a hard time staying on track with her thoughts. She kept thinking that she'd get up and do something *useful* while she was waiting, but then she needed to finish her tea, and then she got caught up in whatever the HSN girl was displaying. Even with the volume off, the whapper-icer-dicer looked interesting enough to warrant watching for a while.

Or hours. In the dark, with just the clock she couldn't read to tell her where she was in time, Nora didn't know how long she'd been sitting there. She was completely alone. Technically, she knew that on the other side of the globe, whole nations were awake and functioning—laughing, loving, dying—in daylight hours. But here, in her living room, it was possible it would never be light again. That's what she was scared of. Every night, and especially this night, the night she'd struck her daughter because she was scared that Ellie was right about everything, right that Nora had asked for chicken, right to be horrified at her mother's tantrum, right about all else that would ever happen, ever.

Ellie would be the right one from now on.

Nora's shoulders ached from the tension in her neck. She rolled her head and heard a satisfying pop. No, Ellie wasn't even responsible enough to check in to tell Nora where she was, which proved both her ignorance and her youth.

Then the seesaw tilted again, and Nora thumped down to the hard ground of truth. She had struck Ellie. It was her fault. Good for her daughter to take herself out of an unsafe situation. How many drills had they run on that over the years? *What do you do if your boyfriend hits you?*

Ellie would roll her eyes. *Leave.*

What if you're married to him?

Do you really think I'd marry an abuser, Mom? God.

What do you do?

Run. Leave. I know this.

What if he only hits you once and you know it was an accident and that he'd never do it again?

On a groan of exasperation, Ellie would give her the right answer. *Leave forever anyway. If he does it once, he'll do it again. Can we go back to the movie now? Please?*

Nora was the guy. Nora was the abusive boyfriend, the violent husband. And her daughter had done exactly the right thing. The pain of that realization lacerated her gut as if she'd swallowed a razor; the only thing that kept her alive was the stubborn, low-grade pride that knitted her partially back together, sloppily lacing up the wound that kept slipping open.

Ellie was a good girl. She'd be a good woman.

Nora picked up her pen, finally ready to commit the words to the page. She wished for humor, like she injected into her columns. But the pen wouldn't move on the page until she found the right words. They weren't the ones that would make her daughter laugh.

Responsibility is a thick woolen coat. We don't wear those here, so you probably don't know about the weight of a peacoat. They were popular when your aunt and I were growing up, and we sweated through way too many dates while wearing them. I gave mine to the Salvation Army as soon as I realized I couldn't afford to have it dry-cleaned and that the smell of sweat would never come out of its armpits. Too heavy, too warm, too much.

One day, though, it might get actually cold. Maybe it will snow. (Have you ever seen snow fall? I think you haven't. I've failed you in this, too.) When the blizzard hits, you realize it feels good to pull that thick coat on over your cotton sweatshirt. You won't believe me now, but responsibility is like that, too. You're scared of paying bills until you're grown-up, but the day that your checkbook balances and you're left with a dollar or two more than last time in savings, you realize you enjoy the heaviness on your shoulders. Calling the plumber gives you a sense of satisfaction, and if you manage to fix the leak yourself, without calling him? It's even better, the coat even warmer.

I don't think I'm leaving you my coat. It's already gone, or at least, it's going. You're going to have to find your own. I'd tell you what thrift store I donated mine to, but I can't remember anymore, and besides, your shoulders are wider than mine ever were. You were born stronger than me.

You can do everything.
And I'm so sorry you'll have to.
I'm so sorry.

Nora closed the book and wrapped her fingers tightly around it. She went to the front door and made sure it was unlocked, just in case Ellie had forgotten her key. Upstairs, she undressed slowly, deliberately. She put on her pajamas, the ones she'd worn on New Year's, and she got into bed.

If Ellie never came back, she would never get up again. That was the easiest answer. The only one, really.

Chapter Thirty-five

The morning drive over the Golden Gate Bridge was quiet. Mariana told Ellie she could choose what they listened to on the way. She prepared herself to listen to KMEL. That was fine. She was forty-four, not ninety-four. She actually liked Jason Derulo and Pitbull. She could even sing along with some of the lyrics. That came from hanging out with Luke in the shop, not because she was cool, but she wouldn't tell Ellie that.

Instead Ellie turned her head to gaze out at the water. "Okay." She dragged headphones out of her jacket pocket and stuck them into her phone.

"I meant you could choose something on the radio."

Ellie froze her with an iced glance. "I thought you said I could choose."

"Fine. Go ahead. *Fucker!*" A red convertible—probably a tourist in a rental—cut her off as they took the slight turn at the foot of the bridge. "Him, not you."

Ellie turned up her music so loud Mariana could almost

make out the words. She countered by turning NPR up so that Scott Simon's voice thumped the bass speaker at her left knee. He was reporting a news story on a plane that had crashed in a jungle somewhere. Or at least Mariana thought it was a plane. Maybe it was a boat. Or a bus. All she could hear was the tinny beat Ellie's earphones emitted. "God," said Ellie, at a volume that was almost—but not quite—inaudible over the radio, "NPR is so *stupid*."

How did mothers do it? How did they put up with solid years of disdain broken only by occasional glimmers of a better future? Ellie was a good one, as teens went. Nora had lucked out. But when Ellie pushed back, she was as talented as any other sixteen-year-old girl at making someone who loved her feel as low as slug bait.

At least new mothers with small babies got to get used to being the one in charge. The slights were small at first. They probably hurt less. The first "no." The first "I hate you." You started small and got bigger.

Mariana held the wheel tighter, wishing she could play the alphabet game with Ellie like they used to, grabbing an *A* from a license plate and a *B* from a passing billboard. But Ellie's eyes were closed, and she was busy moving her lips along with the song in her headphones.

How did anyone leap into motherhood feetfirst?

In Tiburon, Mariana took the winding road into town at a safe speed, even though she knew Ellie loved it when she drove just a little too fast. In front of the house, Ellie was out of the car before she'd shut off the ignition. She ran up the driveway, ignoring Harrison's wave next door. The front door opened and then slammed.

"She all right?" Harrison called, shutting off his hose.

"She's sixteen. Other than that, she's fine."

Harrison nodded. He hadn't shaved yet, and there were silver patches in his stubble. It suited him, Mariana thought. He'd always looked older, even when he was younger. He was just growing into himself.

"Nora's been a wreck."

"She knew Ellie was with me."

Harrison glanced at the door Ellie had just run through. "I don't think she did."

"I texted her."

Shrugging, Harrison said, "I don't think she got it. She woke me at seven a.m. She's not acting like she got it."

"You're shitting me." Mariana fumbled for her phone. Proof. She'd show him. "I texted her, look. Oh, god*damn*. Shit." A little red dot indicated the text hadn't gone through—it was something she'd been having trouble with lately, something she'd meant to figure out, but it had only been happening inter-mittently, and she hadn't remembered to check . . . "She's going to kill me."

Harrison grimaced. "I'm thinking your living trust should be in order before you go in."

"What should I do?"

She wanted him to say, *Apologize.* But she knew, like he did, that it wasn't going to be enough.

Nora's face, when she pushed open the door, was white. "You had her. And you didn't bring her home."

Mariana had never seen Nora so furious, ever. "I am *so* sorry, Nora. I texted you, but—"

Nora stood in the doorway, blocking it with her body. She shouldn't have been able to do it—the doorway was large and they had narrow shoulders. But the entire entrance was closed by the combination of Nora's body and her rage. Mariana wasn't coming in. "You should have put her in the car. You should have driven her to me. Last *night.*"

"She wanted to stay with me. She was upset. And I texted, but my phone—"

"She's a *child*," said Nora. "You bring children home. Do

you have any idea how worried I was? How terrified? It was the Fourth of July. You know how many drunks were out there? I thought she was dead."

"Ellie's okay," Mariana said. "She was with me."

"But where was she before she was with you? Do you have any idea how common meth is nowadays? It's more common than underage drinking—did you know that?"

Mariana shook her head. "First, I can't believe that's true." She wouldn't mention the smell of weed and cigarettes that had risen off Ellie's clothes. "And second, she's fine."

"This is why you can't be trusted with anything." Nora's voice was calmer, but the words were devastating. "You can't be trusted with *her*."

Mariana tried to inhale. She focused on her belly, on the motion it made as she attempted to find oxygen. Then she said, "That's not true." Was it? It might be—that was the worst part. No, she'd texted her sister (even though it hadn't worked) and she'd made sure Ellie was safe, in one piece. She'd hugged her. She'd put her into a warm bed. She'd talked to her.

That wasn't much. Jesus. She'd been the cool aunt, playacting at being in charge of Ellie a few evenings a year. It counted for exactly nothing in the end. BreathingRoom was the only thing that had ever flourished under Mariana's hands, and it was still just a fledgling, still just a wish. "That's not—"

"You don't know how to protect a child."

The bay wind was cold, straight off the water. Mariana managed, "She's almost seventeen."

Nora's voice was brittle. "So what? Do you remember what you were like at seventeen?"

Mariana's heart sunk. Nora at seventeen—as at all ages—had been just fine. But Mariana at seventeen had been reckless, never listening to Nora's cautions. At nineteen, Mariana had been the one tossed in jail for being so drunk she thought she'd try to climb the police officer like a palm tree. By twenty,

Mariana had been the one who'd racked up tens of thousands of dollars of credit card debt before claiming bankruptcy, the same year she was stupid enough to go into that room with Bill, the asshole who almost raped her. At twenty-one, she'd been the one who had dropped out of college in her very last semester, she'd been the one who'd run away to India with Raúl—even Mariana could see the daddy issues she'd wrapped around that man—leaving Nora with having to pay full rent on their apartment without warning or help. Mariana was the one who hadn't come back for three *years*, with only two postcards to prove to the person she loved the most that she'd still even been alive.

A whole life's history of Mariana's fuckups hung between them, unspoken.

Then Nora shut the door in her face. Mariana heard the deadbolt turn with two outraged clicks.

She bent forward at the waist and breathed in again. Then she shouted, "I texted you!" Then, childishly, she yelled as loudly as she could, *"I have a key, you know!"*

The door remained closed.

Chapter Thirty-six

"She'll never forgive me."

Luke grabbed Mariana's hand. "I know you feel that way."

He said it all the time. Mariana hated it. "You *don't* know."

"Look. You didn't do anything wrong."

"She didn't know where Ellie was." Mariana had ruined her chance. Her only chance.

Luke sighed. Again.

It had been sweet earlier, when Luke had asked that they stay at home instead of going out. They'd been planning on going to a picnic at their friend Savannah's condo in Oakland, but when they'd looked at traffic, it would have taken them an hour and a half to get there, and who knew how bad it would be on the way back? Luke had nuzzled Mariana's throat, his scruff making her shiver. "Let's stay home and make some belated fireworks of our own." Mariana had laughed in surprise and spun in his arms.

It had felt like Before. It used to be they'd spent full days in bed whenever they could steal the time. Since the proposal, though, they'd been so wretchedly polite. The few times they'd had sex had felt perfunctory, bodily needs met, that was all.

Today, though, was different. It had been old times. The windows shook with another reverberation outside. A full week after the Fourth of July, the Potrero neighborhood was still beating a staccato rhythm of airborne blasts punctuated by whistles. The bed swayed and thumped joyfully along with their movements. She kept her eyes open while she came, and he'd done the same. That had been the worst—and the best—part.

Lying on his back, Luke spoke toward the ceiling, "Honey—"

Mariana sighed. That simple noise was enough to take a bit of light from the room. Luke didn't finish his sentence. He got up. The water ran in the bathroom. She could see him in profile, leaning forward, his wrists on the sink, his head down. He stayed like that for a long, unbearable moment.

She was going to lose him if she kept this up. There was no relief in the thought.

He finally left the bathroom and sat next to her on the bed. "Mariana—"

"Why do you stay?"

"You still don't know?" His laugh said that things were the same, that he still loved her the same way.

She was—what were those rocks called? Where ships wrecked? She was those. "Your proposal . . . You shouldn't . . ." *You're wasting your time with me. Why bother? Why are you here with me now?*

"I love you, you idiot." He tugged on a lock of her hair. "I love the way you cuddle yourself into me until sweat runs off me in the middle of the night. I love the way you laugh at more than half of my jokes. I love the way you fit on the back of my Harley. I love the way when you're at the shop, you have your own work to do on the app and I don't have to worry about you. I love your sexy walk, and I like this slick spot right here." He slipped his hand to where he'd so recently been, and Mariana gasped. "I love that you like to cook but can still manage to burn rice."

"Hey!"

"And I love that I can see how much you love me by the way you buy the baking soda toothpaste instead of your damn Colgate."

"I hate that baking soda shit," she said mildly.

"But you buy it for me." Luke smiled.

"Let's have a baby instead," she said. It was a thought that had flickered through her mind two or three times a week for the last month or so. When Luke had been inside her earlier, she'd imagined it, a child made by them—a little extension. A piece of them, held to the side. Just in case. It was a stupid thought, one she couldn't stop having.

Luke scrambled, crablike, backward and up the bed so he was sitting against the headboard. "Are you fucking kidding me?"

She kept her voice light. "Why not?"

"Why *not*? You're forty-four. I'm forty-eight. You won't *marry* me. We've never even talked about babies. You bring it up *now*?"

"There are ways."

"You realize you're being insane. I know you're not serious." He wiped his forehead, swiping his hand down to his mouth.

She wasn't really serious, or at least she hadn't been, not up until about sixty seconds ago. She'd been pregnant once in her early twenties and she'd never regretted the abortion she'd had. She'd never thought about getting pregnant on purpose. Not till now. "We could do it. Think about what it would be like."

"God. *Everything* is about your sister."

Heat filled her mouth, burning her tongue. Mariana held up a hand. "Ex*cuse* me?"

"I know you love her more than anyone in the whole world, and I've always accepted that."

Anger flared low in her belly. She folded her arms. "You had no choice but to accept that." Of course she loved Nora more. Of *course* she did.

"That's what I'm saying. I've been mostly fine with that up until now. But, Jesus, Mariana." He wiped his lips. Normally he would reach out and touch her leg or she would twist and put her head in his lap. But neither of them moved. They were frozen. They didn't jump when a firework mortar blasted somewhere outside, rattling the glass again. "A child that you"—he waved his hands in the air—"give birth to or buy or adopt or whatever, that won't make Nora think you're good enough to take care of her daughter."

It hit her with the force of the sun. He was right. It was literally the only thing she hadn't tried in her constant quest for her sister's acceptance.

How naive of her. "Holy shit."

"Love—" He started to reach for her and then took his hand back, pulling the sheet over his lap. Luke was almost never conscious of his nakedness. Then he took a deep breath that Mariana could almost feel. "It'll be okay. Having Ellie here. It'll work great. We can move your office into the spare bedroom, and she can have the attic. She's always loved it up there—"

"No, no, no, no. *No.*" She wrapped her arms around her knees, realizing that she was freezing even though she was still sweating at the armpits. "It won't—she won't—we won't need to do that. It's not going to come to that. She'll be fine. I don't know how . . . But I'm not . . ."

Luke's answer was his silence.

Mariana went on. "She *will* be. We have no idea what kind of breakthrough drug is about to be released. They've been researching it, just throwing buckets of money at it." She'd read so much about it. Millions of dollars had to add up to a cure. Eventually. Soon. "And besides, she doesn't want me to have Ellie. I'm not good enough." Her voice trailed off. She wasn't.

"Well, she sure as hell won't want Paul to have her."

"I *hate* that you thought of this."

Luke shut his eyes.

She scooted forward then. She put her hands on his knee and shook it. "Nora's going to be fine." He smelled like them, like sex and sweat and faintly of the rosemary shampoo they both used. "She's going to be okay. Eventually."

When he opened his eyes, she saw the truth.

Fuck him, anyway. She scrambled off the edge of the bed and lunged for her robe.

"You're going to have a kid whether you like it or not," he said.

"Stop talking."

"Paul's never going to help. You all know that. You're going to have to take care of Ellie when your sister isn't here."

"Stop." They didn't yell at each other. Ever. She was a professional in the field of mind-body balance. And she didn't care that she was screaming. "You're so full of *shit*. You don't know *anything*." Her hands fumbled with the robe's tie—she couldn't make a bow. She'd forgotten how.

He stood and made the bow for her as she shook in front of him. Then he led her back to bed and pulled the blanket up over both of them. Mariana's teeth chattered so hard she bit her tongue and she tasted blood.

"I love you," she said against his neck.

"I know."

Another explosion roared outside. The smell of gunpowder drifted in through the open window. "No, I really love you." She wanted to tell him she loved him more than Nora. She wanted to say it so badly.

"I know." His hand was heavy on the back of her neck.

Open hands cling to nothing.

What a bullshit mantra. She wrapped her arms around him as tightly as she could.

Chapter Thirty-seven

EXCERPT,
**WHEN ELLIE WAS LITTLE:
OUR LIFE IN HOLIDAYS,**
PUBLISHED 2011 BY NORA GLASS

Labor Day

When Ellie was little, we went camping. The first time she slept in a tent was the first time Paul ever had, too. Such a city boy that he could sing along with car alarms, he was convinced right down to his toenails that we were doomed to die a terrible, outdoor death.

"How?" I said, pulling a citronella candle out of the pantry.

"Bees."

"Bees are a drag, but they won't kill you."

"What if a *swarm* of bees attacks us? What's your fancy-pants idea then?"

"Then we go into the tent and zip it closed," I said while I filled the food box: string cheese, Goldfish crackers, red apples, and perfect green grapes. We'd been playing this game for a while now, and I'd realized I didn't have to pay him my complete attention—I could pack for the camping trip while I listened to his galloping fears. We'd already checked bear-escaped felon–mountain lion off the list, and I figured it would take him a while to get to white lady–ghost-man with hook for hand.

"What if the bee swarm follows us into the tent?"

It was a ridiculous worry. They all were. That's what I wanted to tell him. But the camping trip was my idea, and thus, it was my responsibility to assuage him. I didn't have real worries yet. I had no idea I'd be for all intents and purposes a single mother in less than six months. I had no idea this man I loved so much would become a stranger not only to me but to the little girl he seemed to love so much. "Bees hate the sound of a zipper," I said. "They're more scared of being in a tent than you are."

Paul raised one thick eyebrow. "Now you're lying."

I had no firm science to back up my claim, but I believed it. Bees probably *did* hate the sound of zippers.

He scrolled down his mental list. "Okay. What if a spider crawls into Ellie's ear?"

I winced. "They don't do that."

He grabbed a chocolate bar out of my hands and unwrapped it. "Aha! Now I know you're lying. Remember the Schwartzes' kid? Didn't that happen to them when they went camping in Tahoe?"

"Those are for s'mores."

"You have, like, twenty of them. And tell me I'm wrong about the spider."

Jennifer Schwartz had been convinced a spider had wriggled its way into her ear while she slept, and no one had believed her until they'd gotten down off the mountain and she was *still* alleging she could hear it moving inside. Sure enough, at the hospital they'd flushed out a small, harmless, but probably very surprised arachnid. I still got chills thinking about it.

"No bug will climb into our daughter's ear."

"You don't know that for sure."

"You can have her wear earplugs if you're worried."

"Oh." Paul brightened and hopped up onto the counter next to the sink. He took a huge bite of the Hershey's. "Good point. I'll wear some, too."

"So really," I said, moving so that I stood between his knees, "you're concerned about getting something in *your* ear."

"No . . ."

"And being stung by a bee yourself."

He used those long, strong legs of his to pull me against him. "I could be allergic," he said.

"But you're probably not."

"Who knows? I've never been stung."

"Chances are good that you're not."

"But if I am, I could *die*." He made a tragic face, and I remember this: I laughed at him. Six months later, I would be wishing for his death. (Don't look at me like that, dear reader. If you'd seen the way he looked at me when he told me I couldn't be enough for him, that *we* couldn't be enough, you would have offered to dispose of the body.)

"We're camping in the *backyard*. We're two minutes from the closest fire station. I think you'll probably pull through."

"What if—"

"Shhhh." I kissed him. I remember so vividly the taste of that kiss: equal parts cheap chocolate and warmth, a mixture of exasperation and love. All of it tasted the same to me:

safety. I heard a shuffling behind me, and I knew almost-four-year-old Ellie would be standing there when I turned, one thumb in her mouth, trailing Paul's old Cal sweatshirt behind her, the sweatshirt she used as a binky. "There's nothing to worry about."

"Lions or tigers?" said Ellie's small voice. "Bears?"

I spun to face her, my happiness beating full, wide wing-spans in my chest. This was my family. My *family*. My own little world, and they came to *me* with their silly worries in the day, with their real fears at night. Me. *Mine*. "There are no creatures from *The Wizard of Oz* in our backyard. None. I promise you that."

"What about the downhill?"

Ellie had a nebulous fear about the slope below our house: that a bogeyman would walk up it and into her room, that ghosts roamed under the oak trees at night. "The only thing down there is deer. Maybe a raccoon or two."

"What about skunks? What if we get sprayed by one?"

Paul slid off the counter and tried—too late—to hide the chocolate wrapper. "Yeah, Mom. What about *skunks*? Huh?" He handed the last piece of candy to Ellie. Her face lit up, and she dropped her hold on the sweatshirt. I could try to grab it off the floor to wash it, but I suspected she needed it for getting ready to sleep outside.

"A skunk would not be ideal," I admitted.

Ellie's face was both horrified and thrilled. "What if it came in the tent and *sprayed* us?"

"Then we'd go in the house and wash off."

"It doesn't come off with soap," said Ellie. "Steffie's dog got sprayed and it had to stay outside forever and ever."

It had been more like a week, according to Stephanie's mom, Janice. "It comes off with tomato soup," I said, though I didn't know if that was exactly true.

Ellie screeched in joy. "A *bath*? In tomato *soup*?"

I nodded. "I'd make those crunchy bread crumbs you like. And I'd put them in the bath with you." I gathered my little girl into my arms, and I pressed my nose into the crook of her neck, right where she smelled like sunshine and No More Tears. I gave her neck a soft bite, loving the way she wriggled against me. "Then I would get a spoon and I would eat the soup!"

The hiccups she always got when she laughed too hard started, and I held her tighter. "What if—*hic*—you ate me, too—*hic*?"

"Then I would eat you up and you would be all gone!"

"All—*hic*—gone!"

Paul tickled her and I squeezed my little girl harder as she kicked and flapped and the three of us stood there in the afternoon sunlight that streamed through the west-facing windows, and none of us knew that it would be the last time we'd stand in that exact spot in the late summer sun, still a perfect, unbroken family.

That night, after roasting marshmallows over the portable hibachi Paul used at Niners' tailgate parties, we slept in our brand-new tent. The night was dry—we didn't attach the tent fly. Paul and Ellie stared up through the overhead mesh in wonder, watching the stars. I swear they were twinkling at us on purpose, as if they knew we were there watching, light-years and universes below.

"The stars see us," said Ellie, right before she fell asleep, still on her back between us.

Paul and I counted four satellites and three falling stars before I fell asleep. When I woke in the morning, he was still watching the sky, then streaked pale blue and pink with sunrise. It was perfectly silent. (Now I wonder if he was thinking about her, the woman he left us for. I hate wondering that.) Ellie had wiggled to our feet in the night, and I felt one small arm clamped around my ankle. Paul turned on his side to kiss me. He had morning breath. I remember I wrinkled my nose but kissed him anyway.

"Let's go camping again soon," I said. "Real camping."

"Bees," he said.

"I'll protect you," I said. That was my thing. That's what I knew how to do.

Until I didn't.

Chapter Thirty-eight

Nora stood in the evening sunlight, spraying down the house. It had been so hot, reaching the midnineties every day for a week, something it rarely did for more than a day or two in Marin. So hot, and so dry . . . Nora couldn't stop worrying that something would catch the house on fire. It was silly. Most of the year's fireworks had stopped as local kids' stashes dwindled. But some of her neighbors used those weed torches, and what if a piece of flaming Bermuda grass sailed up and over a fence, landing on her roof? What if someone tossed a cigarette out carelessly, and the wind blew it into her siding?

If there was the slightest possibility she could make her home safer, she would.

It was more than silly. It was ridiculous.

And it was normal, apparently. Just one more fantastic symptom of EOAD. "Hypervigilance can present in some cases, leading to excessive worry where little if any is warranted," said one Web site. One of the dozen new meds she was on could actually exacerbate anxiety. Of course. On a forum she'd reluctantly joined, she read that one man who lived alone had gotten so paranoid about break-ins that he'd booby-trapped every window with hair-triggered nail guns. He said that if he ever needed the fire department to come in and help him, he knew they'd get hurt on the way in, but he hadn't been able to quiet his mind enough to take down the traps.

Nora felt the same way about the hose. If she weren't out there when the thermometer rose above ninety-five, the house would burn down. It would spontaneously combust. If she wasn't paying attention to everything at all times, she'd lose everything. It was four weeks since she'd hit Ellie. She'd almost lost everything that day. Four weeks of not believing Ellie really forgave her the way she said she did. *Mom. Get over it already. Move on. I have. You're acting crazy. It's fine. I understand. Whatever.*

Nora sprayed the southern side of the house this time, what she could reach of it. There was a spot that she couldn't quite reach on the far side of the chimney. That part up there was as dry as old parchment, she knew it. At least she'd be able to spot smoke rising quickly. *Crazy.* She kept her head on a slow swivel—she checked the siding and then she scanned across the tree line below the house to see if any tendrils of smoke were curling upward. Then she checked her roof, especially around the chimney and the part she couldn't reach with the water, and then started the whole scan over again.

It felt crazy.

Crazy.

This was how insane people acted. This was how people with Alzheimer's—old people with the normal kind of Alzheimer's—acted on their good days. They worried about crazy things, things that didn't warrant such care or attention. In all her life, Nora had never had more than a passing worry about fire. For the last three days of elevated temperatures, it had been all she could think about.

She sprayed water in the air, enjoying the immediate shiver that ran through her body as the droplets smacked her skin on the way back down.

What if instead of drifting apart—like the fibers in unspun wool—her mind actually fractured? What if it splintered suddenly and violently? What if this—right now—was the beginning of the end?

What if this was her last summer?

Okay, with the drugs she was on, she might have longer. This might not be her *last* summer. There were people who had two good years. Three. There were a couple of men in Texas and one woman in Rhode Island who had been on the treatment for more than five years and still weren't all the way gone. The longest holdout, though, a woman who had said she'd been cured by a combination of the treatment and a holistic healer in Colombia, had died two months ago in a care home. No one in the online forums was talking about anything else. She'd been a poster child of health, the only real EOAD success story, and now she was dead at fifty-one, her fairy tale morphed into a nightmare.

Nora shot the hose at the wind chime Ellie had made when she was in summer camp. Built from driftwood and beach glass, it only clunked, but Nora had always thought it was the prettiest sound in the world. She sprayed it again, trying to memorize its particular wooden *bonk*.

She'd decided to visit an Alzheimer's care home. Googling "caring for an Alzheimer's patient" wasn't very goddamned helpful. It either brought up cheery-looking ads for dentures and care homes for the seventy-and-up crowds or it brought up terrifying stories of wandering elderly parents who were found dead of dehydration, days later, under freeway on-ramps.

Being the one who was cared for: nothing—*nothing*—made her feel worse to think about. The other day (what day? she couldn't remember . . .) she'd woken up on the couch, Ellie shaking her shoulder.

"What? What? I was just napping."

"Your eyes were open."

Nora had tried to laugh it off. "No, they weren't."

"You were stuck." That's what Ellie called it when Nora lost time.

That day, Nora had blasted into the kitchen and made a double batch of almond macaroons. No one who was losing it, no one who was "stuck," could possibly pull them off without ruining them, and it gave her pleasure to offer Ellie a plate of them, hot and rich and perfect.

Ellie hadn't even looked at her, just kept her eyes on her *Queendom* game, tilting her laptop slightly so Nora couldn't see the screen.

Nora was *Ellie's* caretaker. No one else was. And it did *not* go the other way around.

She chose a facility in San Ramon, an affluent community in the East Bay. She told the care home management it was research. "A piece I'm writing for my column in the *Sentinel*. I'd love to come by and ask a few questions. I write about domestic issues, and many of the women baby boomers I write for are starting to think about elder care . . ."

On her way, Nora had made a side trip to the fire station and spoke to the paramedic unit assigned to the area. Each firefighter said no way in hell would they let a loved one be taken care of at that place. Well, then, she asked, where? *At home,* they said adamantly. The only place to be was at home.

"What if they don't have that option?" Nora had asked. "What if they're too young to have children old enough to take care of them?"

Confused glances all around. "You mean, like their kids are too far away?"

"Sure. Whatever," she said.

The firefighter with the biggest mustache chuckled as if the idea was humorous to him. "I'd eat a bullet before I got shuffled in there. Oh. Don't quote me on that. Off the record, right?"

On one hand, the care facility was a "nice" place. You could tell upon entering, it was the kind of care that would cost a small fortune. Bright metal wind chimes tinkled cheerily on the front porch. Inside, it smelled good, like pinecones and vanilla. Nora wondered exactly how much they spent on air deodorizers every year. Was it a line-item expense? Did it fit under "Facility Maintenance"? Because someone was *on* that beautification shit. On it, literally. The norovirus had run through this place a few times already this year. No matter what, no matter how many masks you issued and how many gloves you made your staff wear, feces and vomit traveled faster than BART did under the bay.

Her mask carefully in place, Nora asked the head nurse about the patients. "What about the ones with Alzheimer's?"

"Which ones?" The nurse was Filipina and reminded Nora of a fire hydrant in her short squatness. Over her head hung red streamers. Faded Fourth of July banners decorated with gold foil clung to the white walls. They should have been removed weeks ago. One banner had lost its stick on one side and hung drunkenly toward the floor, a half-flapping, almost-dead symbol of freedom.

"The ones with Alzheimer's." Nora spoke more clearly.

"I heard you the first time, honey. I meant which one? All of them have dementia."

"Excuse me?"

"They all got it. All of 'em." She waved her hand to include the five or six elderly patients grouped around the nurses' station in their wheelchairs. If Nora didn't know better, she would have wondered if they were zombies. Their eyes were vacant, their mouths moving slowly as if trying to form words they'd once owned, once used with authority, confident their wishes would be carried out. Now they were lucky if they got themselves cleaned quickly after crapping themselves.

"How old are these people?"

The nurse didn't look up from the computer. She clicked boxes as quickly as Ellie texted. "Old, honey."

"No, I mean the range. What's your inpatient range, from youngest to oldest?"

The nurse's tired gaze finally met Nora's. "They all old, honey. All them."

Nora kept pushing. "Who's your youngest resident?"

"Simone."

"Can I meet her? For the article?"

The nurse's expression was tolerant. She'd seen reporters come and go. They all did the same kind of article, the shock-the-boomers piece, the article that was meant to get the reader to buy that much more life insurance. "Sure, honey. If you wanna."

Simone was asleep in her bed when the nurse led Nora into her room without knocking. "She our youngest."

Nora felt as if she wanted to sit on the floor, collapse to it, even though she'd promised herself she would touch no exposed surface in the residence care home. "God."

"She forty-five."

The woman could have passed for late fifties, easily. Her skin was good, yes, and her hands looked better than Nora's. But the muscles in her face had degraded to the point at which it seemed her cheekbones were trying to escape. Simone was sound asleep, her mouth hung open, and a raucous snore ripped from her, the sides of her nose flapping with the exertion of it. Something green clung to her cheek, something Nora tried very hard not to stare at.

"Simone!" The nurse didn't bother with niceties—she went in with a shout and didn't back down. *"Simone. Wake up, honey. You have a visitor."*

Simone's eyes opened slowly. *Blink.* One, two, three. Her mouth didn't close, and Nora could see that no silver gleamed as it had in the skeletal grins of the two elderly men who'd smiled at her in the hallway, her dental work new enough to include only porcelain fillings.

"What." Simone's word didn't sound like a question as much as an autonomic response.

"You have a visitor. She wants to say hello to you, honey." Now that Simone's eyes were open, the nurse's voice was kind, lower in volume.

"Hi, Simone," said Nora. She didn't hold her hand out to shake—it didn't look as if Simone could move. Instead, Nora thrust her hands into her pockets and gripped the piece of beach glass she'd chosen that morning. Green, she remembered. Foggily glazed, with a smoothed chip on one side. It had once wheeled and spiraled in the waves, too.

"What."

"I'm just here to check to see if you need anything." Nora hadn't planned to say that; if she had, she would have had questions prepared for this astonishingly young resident. *How did you get here? Who dropped you off? Do they still visit? Are you still in there, Simone? The one you were before?*

"What." Simone's voice was a croak, and the sound ripped into Nora's chest.

"Okay, then. I'm not going to bother you anymore."

"Did you know."

Nora ceased her backward crab step. "What, Simone?"

"Did you know."

"Did I know what?" What if this was the moment they made a connection? Simone needed someone to talk to, someone who would understand. Nora stepped forward and picked up Simone's cold, waxy hand.

"Phhffbt."

Spittle touched her forearm and Nora jerked back her hand. "Simone . . . ," she started, but she had no follow-up. She'd interviewed hundreds of people over the years, one of them a sitting president of a small island nation. Nora was known for bringing her warmth into her questioning, making even politicians feel relaxed enough to share their favorite pumpkin pie ingredient even while the red light glowed on her voice recorder.

But she had nothing to ask Simone.

Fear scrabbled at Nora's windpipe, choking her. The terror didn't so much run through her as it coagulated in her veins, slowing down all her bodily processes. She wanted to smile professionally at the very helpful nurse and then run down the hall, bashing through the heavy glass doors until she was out, out, out, back in her car, back in a world where the sick were taken care of, invisible. Forgotten.

"She just like this, honey. You know." The nurse grabbed a washcloth from the tiny, badly lit bathroom and rubbed briskly at Simone's cheek. "You got some peas here, honey."

In the parking lot, when Nora finally—politely, professionally—made it out, her hands shook too much to put the keys in the ignition. *She's just so young,* Nora had said to the nurse as they'd walked back toward the front door. *Nothing good about early-onset,* the nurse had said simply, as if Nora had been asking for reassurance that there was.

She probably had been.

"Mom?"

The hose jerked in Nora's hand. She'd forgotten where she was. She'd been right there for a moment, back in that care home. She could almost smell its acidly sweet tang. "I'm fine," she said to whatever Ellie was asking.

"Do you think you've watered the porch enough?" Ellie's voice was softer than her words. She was humoring her, something Ellie shouldn't ever have to do.

"I'm fine, honey." Nora smiled. "Really."

"Yeah?"

Her daughter was so beautiful. So *alive* and so gorgeous. She didn't even know it.

Ellie said, "You should call Aunt Mariana."

Nora knew she should. They hadn't spoken since that night, the night she'd hit Ellie, the night Mariana hadn't told her where she was, the night Mariana had failed to do what any reasonable adult would have. When she'd failed to bring her daughter home immediately. Whenever Nora thought about it, she felt heat bloom in the center of her chest. Mariana had said she hadn't known her text had failed, but Nora couldn't believe that. Mariana's whole life was her phone. She checked constantly to see how many were using the app. The first time BreathingRoom had a thousand people meditating at once, Mariana had bought the office pink champagne from Trader Joe's. Nora and Ellie had gone over to celebrate with them. It had been lovely to see her sister that happy. Nora had a picture on her desk that had been taken that night. They—all three of them—looked beautiful in it, even Nora. They'd been delirious in that moment, yelling *Breathe* instead of *Cheese*.

Mariana had texted her a million times since bringing Ellie home (all of *those* had come through). She'd called her every day. Every night, Nora erased the messages without listening to them.

She'd never gone a day without talking to Mariana, except for the times Mariana had been overseas.

"You should call her," Ellie said again. "Instead of . . . whatever you're doing out here."

"You know I love playing with the hose. And don't worry. Your aunt and I are fine." They weren't. But Ellie didn't need any additional worry. "Go in before I soak you." She moved the hose threateningly.

Ellie gave that soft laugh. "Okay. I give. I'm going inside."

Nora waited until the screen door slapped shut; then she turned and shot spray at the back fence. She wasn't worried about losing the fence to fire, but it felt good to watch the water darken the wood, to directly affect something. To make something change, even if it was only from dry to wet.

Chapter Thirty-nine

"Are you sure you want to do this?" asked Dylan. "You're ready?"

Ellie sat on Dylan's bed. Both his roommates were out with their girlfriends, and the apartment was theirs for at least another couple of hours. The timing was right.

"Yeah," she said. "I want to."

"I'm here," he said, and his eyes stayed on hers. Clear. Dylan was so *clear* in everything. Sometimes Ellie felt like everything her mother did or said had layers of meaning Ellie couldn't hope to identify, stratifications that were probably important but impossible to read. Dylan was sweet. Uncomplicated. He liked Ellie, his guitar, the city of Oakland, and his job at the pizza place three blocks away from the apartment. He didn't like reality TV, women who pretended to be stupid just to get attention, and tarantulas. It felt like a rest to be with him. A mini-vacation complicated only by sexual tension.

But now she had to call her dad. Dylan nodded reassuringly as she held her phone to her ear.

Ellie's dad answered on the first ring. Bad sign. He never answered her calls, always calling her back when he was in the car. He said it was so that he could fully concentrate on their conversation, but Ellie knew he did it because in the car he was away from Bettina and the kids, none of whom liked sharing their time with him.

"Kiddo! How's it going over there?"

His tone was way too cheerful. "So you know," she said.

"About what?"

He was *so* fake. Ellie looked at Dylan. He nodded. "About Mom."

"Oh, yeah! She called me."

Oh, yeah. That old thing. That old life-threatening nightmarishly horrible *thing.* "When?"

A pause. "Not that long ago."

"What does that mean?" Had he known for a day? A month? He should have *called* her; wasn't that what fathers were supposed to do? He should have driven to her side the moment he heard— he should have wrapped her up in his arms, lending her fatherly strength and wisdom and hope.

"I don't know. Not that long." His voice changed, like he was looking over his shoulder. Probably changing lanes. "How you doin' with it?"

"Me? Not good." Ellie spoke briskly. "Mom's losing her mind. She waters the house, but the houseplants inside are all dying. She's not driving much because she can't be sure she'll remember where to go. She writes the date on her wrist. She gets stuck in one place and doesn't move forever, not unless someone touches her or speaks to her. I do see her writing but—" Some of the rigidity left her voice. "I'm not sure . . ."

"Well, I know if anyone can handle a rough situation, it's you. You've always been a strong kid."

Rough situation. This was a catastrophe of nuclear holocaust proportions. Ellie's mother, whom she *loved*, was losing her fucking *mind*. All her brain cells just running out of her like radiator fluid had run from their old Civic. And her father thought it was rough?

Dylan put his hand on her knee and left it there. Ellie's whole body was frozen except for that one warm spot. She leaned into him, hoping to steal more of his body heat. "Shit, Dad. I don't know what I'm going to do." *When she's gone. No,* if, *if she's gone.*

"I know, Ellie-belly, I know. When your stepmom lost her mother last year, it wasn't easy for anyone. Look. I'm happy to help out."

A bright yellow hope rose in Ellie's chest and she tilted her head so she could flash a quick smile at Dylan. "Yeah?"

"Sure. You need some money?"

The hope popped with a soft hiss. "No."

"Does your mother need money?"

She had no idea. *"No."*

"I mean, she's got good insurance, right?"

Ellie hadn't even thought about the insurance. She added it to her list of things to worry about—how could she have gone five months without thinking of it? Would her mother have to stop working? As far as Ellie knew, her mother's columns were still being turned in on time, but how long could that last? What would happen if her mother lost her job? Was there something her father would have left her . . . ? No, they'd been divorced too long. Mom didn't even get alimony anymore, just the auto-deposit child support. Holy shit.

"I don't know anything about her insurance." And that wasn't why she'd called him. Jesus Christ.

"What else can I do to help? I'm going to be out that way in October."

It was late August. "You live ninety minutes away." The flatness in Ellie's voice matched the stark expanse of nothingness she saw in her mind—the drive to Modesto was unimpressive in every way unless you really had a thing for cows and dust. It wasn't a difficult trip, though. Her father drove a BMW. It would eat up the miles just fine. He could be with her before Dylan's roommates even came home.

"I know. I'm sorry it's so far, babe."

It wasn't far. It was hardly any distance at all. He could . . . He should say . . .

Then he said it. "You can stay with us—you know that, right?"

She didn't trust him this time. "Yeah?"

"I mean, I have to run it past Bettina, of course, but yeah, if that's what needs to happen, then that's what we'll do. I'll have her call you. Or e-mail you."

Ellie's father sold roofing. He didn't put it on the house or even handle the material himself. He bought and sold parts that turned into roofs, built by other men. She'd heard this tone of voice from him before, when she was his occasional passenger while they were on their way for a quick ice cream sundae. *Yeah, Jones has got it. I'll have him call you. Wait—e-mail's better for you, right? Great, we'll do that. Take care, buddy.* His car phone would beep off and he'd quarter turn toward her. "That guy thinks we're gonna go with him. I guess someone should have thought about that before he took the Hill subcontract, huh, Ellie-belly?"

Ellie had always thought it was funny, the way her dad said what people wanted to hear and then did his own thing. In a strange way, she almost admired him for it. He'd made a family, wasn't happy with it, so he'd made another one that he liked better. She'd always thought, though, that dads would come to the rescue.

She'd never needed rescuing before. *Mom hit me,* she could say. *Right across the face. I said I understood, but I don't. I don't.*

But her dad wasn't the rescuing type, apparently. "So anyway. Talk soon?"

"Yeah, I gotta go, too, Dad. Love you."

"Love you, babe—"

There could have been more words after those from her father, maybe better ones, but Ellie hung up before she could find out. Her fingers were so cold the phone slipped out of her hand, landing on the bed. She didn't want to hold it anymore anyway. She wanted to lose herself: in a kiss with Dylan that made her eyelashes melt, in writing a story line about Queen Ulra that would somehow save her, in getting drunk, in smoking weed, in doing anything that took her mind off the solid lump of fear in her heart that felt like physical pain. Was it possible for a sixteen-year-old to have a heart attack? Her breathing came faster and the pain in her chest heated. Her dad wasn't going to help. He couldn't help. She, Ellie, would have to save them all. She didn't even have her driver's license yet. She didn't know what she wanted to do with her *life*. But she would have to save them all.

Chapter Forty

Nora was going to meet Lily at the parking lot of the Golden Gate and they were going to go yarn shopping at Imagi-Knit after their walk. But after Nora had waited in her car for twenty minutes, she got a text. *Sorry, car won't start. Again. I have to go shoot my mechanic aka my husband. I might need bail money later.*

She decided to walk the span anyway. It had been too long since she'd walked the mile and a half across the water. The bridge was—always had been—one of her favorite things about the Bay Area. The way it was suspended between heaven and earth, the way it looked like it shouldn't work but it did. Like a bumblebee, it defied laws of gravity and floated. The new Bay Bridge to the east with its stark white sailboat girders and fancy new palm trees couldn't ever hope to compete with the sheer elegance and grace of the classically perfect Golden Gate.

Nora zipped her Windbreaker to her chin as she walked briskly through the heavy fog. Ellie called this "disappointed tourist weather." Visitors hoped for clear days to walk across the bridge, but Nora knew what they really wanted was the view from Hawk Hill in Marin or Fort Point, down below. They wanted the photo of the bridge itself, which they couldn't get from the span no matter how hard they tried. As Nora walked, she wove through dozens of couples taking photos of themselves standing in front of metal girders. She darted around school groups clumped like flocks of chickens in front of the rails. They'd get home, download their cameras, and flip disappointedly through the images on their computer screen. *You didn't get that shot of the bridge, Harold? I can't believe you didn't get that shot.* Maybe they wouldn't even be able to identify where they'd been when they took that picture—nothing visible behind them but the gray fog, as thick as upholstery fabric.

The fog comforted Nora. She liked the way it became sodden only after prolonged exposure. She didn't feel the dampness until she pressed her finger against the fabric of her running pants and felt the wet sponginess. Her hair got heavier with it and she could feel the moisture collect on her eyelashes.

She stopped midspan and looked up, but the tower tops were gone, lopped off by the lowering cloud. The ends of the bridge were missing, too. The only things that existed in the whole world were this section of the bridge, the cars that whooshed by in both directions, and the people who clicked and snapped their way past her. The water below was almost invisible, the same non-color as the fog.

Nora wrapped her hands around the wet red rail and held on until the metal slowly—so slowly—warmed under her hands. She liked the feeling of it, her hands growing colder as she put her own energy into it. Her hands lost, what, one degree? The iron absorbed it, impervious. The bridge sucked it out of her, but she didn't mind giving it away. Everyone else only leaned against the metal as they posed in front of the gray blanket of fog. They weren't giving it anything, like she was.

"Ma'am, can you tell me about how your day's going today?"

Nora jumped. "Excuse me? Fine."

To her left was a police officer. He was tall, with a wide mouth to match his wide chin. "Whatcha planning on doing tomorrow?"

What was this? "I'm . . . not sure."

"I sure would love it if you turned around so we could talk." His badge read Briggs, and his dark eyes were kind. "Nothing bad will happen if you let go of the rail, I promise. I'm here."

"Did I do something wrong?"

Another voice, female, came from her right. This police officer was short, wearing a pink lipstick that didn't suit her complexion. "We just want to talk. We're not going to hurt you."

She hadn't imagined they would. "What is this about?" Maybe she matched the description of someone wanted. Wouldn't that be something, if they'd confused her for a bank robber or a . . . Nora couldn't think of anyone else the police might be looking for. Was that a symptom of the disease, that she couldn't? Or did it just prove that she was basically—and boringly—law-abiding?

The male officer said, "What if we talk about what you're doing tomorrow. And hey, if you don't have plans, let's make some, huh? We can help. Hell, you can always come back another day, right?"

Nora released the rail, suddenly realizing that she was freezing. Shivers racked her and she rubbed her hands together. "Seriously." Her teeth clacked. "What is this about?"

There was a gentle touch at her elbow. The woman officer said, "Come with us for a second. We're just going to talk."

A cluster of people stared at the trio they made. Several phones were held in the air, as if something interesting was happening. "A jumper," someone hissed to someone else. Nora twisted her head to look around, to see if she could spot the person they were talking about, but Officer Briggs guided her forward, his hand in the middle of her back, as if he were guiding her firmly from a dance floor.

"Oh," she said, the realization dull and painful, like a hang-over. "You thought *I* was going to jump."

The female had a small computer tablet in her hand. "May I have your name, ma'am?"

"Nora Glass. I wasn't going to jump." She looked over her shoulder again. "I don't even think I could from here. Don't you have that safety barrier?" No, maybe they hadn't built that yet. She couldn't remember . . .

"Date of birth?" Officer Briggs smiled at her. "You don't have to give it to me—it's just something I gotta ask."

"You don't have to—I don't need—" Nora didn't know what she needed. Sunshine winked off his badge. When had the sun burned off the fog? She hadn't noticed it happening. "What time is it?"

"Four fifteen."

Nora had gotten to the bridge at twelve forty-five. She and Lily had planned to meet at one. It didn't take more than an hour to walk the whole bridge, round trip. "God. I got stuck again."

Chapter Forty-one

*N*ora found herself writing a list of all the ways Mariana had let people down over the years. It was a terrible list, one she'd never show to anyone, and it was one she couldn't keep herself from writing.

They still hadn't talked. Her cell phone had stopped ringing, and Mariana had switched to sending e-mails. She sent those dorky Hallmark e-cards, the ones that sang and bounced around the screen. She sent a picture of her and Luke, both of them making faces. She e-mailed a list of ways she sucked (*I'm too loud, too careless, too quick to throw out glass instead of putting it in the recycle bin. I got way drunk at that Christmas party you had five years ago. I forgot to pay the PG&E bill and we only found out when the lights went out*). Each e-mail Nora read melted her anger. Her rage was now just dirty slush, but it was still there. She loved her sister. She loved her daughter. How—and where—did those intersect?

Nora needed to make her own list. She'd always thought they were a perfect circle—all three of them living within the same diameter. Now she imagined they were a Venn diagram, with her own crooked, broken circle draining, becoming more and more empty as theirs filled with colors she couldn't compete against.

She took out a yellow sheet of legal paper and a red pen she'd dug out of the bottom drawer of her desk. Normally Nora didn't use red ink. She didn't like its accusatory nature. When she was catching her thoughts for her columns, she needed blue or black ink in her Moleskine journal, or even better, her soft, dark pencil.

But for Mariana's sins, she needed red pen.

Eddie. The goldfish they'd shared in high school. They'd argued so badly about whose turn it was to feed him that finally their mother—exasperated—had ordered them to divvy the chore. Nora got the even months, February and April. Mariana got the odd ones, January and May. When it was Nora's month, Eddie got his pinch of food every morning at seven a.m., even on the mornings they didn't have school. Nora would roll out of bed, feed the fish, and roll back into bed, pressing herself up against Mariana's warmth. But during odd months, Eddie sometimes got skinny and pale. One November morning, Eddie didn't move. Nora had thought fish went belly up when they were dead, but it wasn't the case with Eddie. He'd been in the same position for days—Nora had noticed but thought it was just chance that she'd managed to see him always sleeping in the same spot in the bowl. It wasn't until one of his fins had broken off and floated next to him in the water that they'd noticed he was all the way dead. Mariana hadn't fed him in two weeks.

Timothy. Against Nora's better judgment, they'd adopted Timothy when they moved into their first college apartment. He was black and small and very, very stupid. They called him Antonio Banderas, because even with all his faults, he was pretty. He stayed inside because if he'd been let out, he would have rolled in front of the first dog he saw, begging to play. One night while

Nora was at work at the college paper (putting out a piece on the Persian Gulf cease-fire), Mariana got wasted with two girl-friends. They drank cheap vodka and smoked a joint and left the window in the hallway open. Timothy, curious as always, jumped on the ledge, fell out the window, and died, proving once and for all that not all cats landed on their feet.

College. In their last year—only six months before graduation!—Mariana had disappeared with Raúl. She sent Nora post-cards from places like Thailand and Bangkok, finally ending up at the ashram in India. Nora didn't think she'd ever been more angry at her sister. Nora had hauled Mariana to class, sometimes almost physically when she didn't want to get out of bed, and she'd tutored her (even though Mariana usually did better on the tests than Nora did), and then Mariana had given it all up. For nothing. Raúl had jilted her, Mariana said when she walked back into the apartment without even a phone call of warning, her eyes bright with something that made Nora wonder if Mariana wasn't in recovery for more than just a broken heart. But she'd been so *furious* with her, for throwing *everything* away, that she hadn't talked to her, hadn't said a word when Mariana asked, "How's tricks?" Nora had left the room without a hug or a kiss of greeting. She'd slammed her bedroom door and locked it behind her.

The next day the doorbell rang. Nora stayed in bed, her door still locked. She didn't care who'd come by. Mariana could handle whatever it was. Nora was done handling things. A few moments later, Mariana knocked on her bedroom door. Then she banged. Then she started screaming something Nora couldn't understand, hurling her body against the wood. Nora was still too furious to open it, and it felt good to hear the franticness in Mariana's voice. How could she have *left* her?

Then the door crashed down. Not open, but *down.* Mariana had rammed her body against the door so hard that it came off its hinges and ripped off the latch, collapsing inward, the door and

Mariana thumping to the ground to the sound of both of their screams.

"She's dead," shouted Mariana to Nora. "That was a cop. At the door. He told me. She smashed her car. I yelled for you. I screamed for you! Why didn't you come *out*? Mom's dead."

Every muscle and every cell in Nora's body froze, turning into sudden ice. She was a floe, adrift. She pulled back the blanket and Mariana crawled in. They spent the next twenty-four hours doing nothing but eating frozen burritos and sleeping wrapped around each other like week-old spaghetti, impossible to pull apart without breaking. They'd left the door where it was on the ground, and when they stood the next day on shaky legs to plan their mother's funeral, they stepped on and over the door like it was nothing more than a rug.

Antonia. Mariana's friend Kim asked her to be her baby's godmother. What Kim was really looking for was a babysitter who couldn't say no, which she got, but when Mariana managed to lose Antonia at the zoo one rainy afternoon (the child was safely turned in to lost and found), her godmotherly rights (and the friendship) were revoked.

Every houseplant God ever made. When Mariana moved into her first San Francisco apartment (the first time they ever lived apart, both of them stubbornly taking leases on tiny spaces that could barely be called studios and were only two blocks apart), Nora bought her a pothos. It was black within a month, which was probably some kind of world record. Next, Nora got her a ficus. That one took six weeks to kill, its brown leaves spiny and brittle on the floor. When Mariana managed to kill six geraniums within three months, Nora gave up and just brought her orchids in bloom from the grocery store (a tip she'd recycled for a column about what to give people with black thumbs). When the blooms fell off and the stalks withered, Mariana quietly threw them out, the space remaining clear until Nora gave her another one.

Every feeling ever. This wasn't fair. Nora's fingers cramped. She scratched out the words three times and rewrote them again a fourth. When Nora had a strong emotion, Mariana evaporated like mist. Tears could chase Mariana out of a room faster than pepper spray. How she made a business of catering to thoughts, feelings, the inner workings of human beings all around the globe, Nora could barely fathom. It wasn't fair.

But none of this was fair. None of it. It wasn't fair that she was going to have to leave her daughter to the care of someone who couldn't take care of a geranium. (The fact that it wasn't fair that she'd have to leave her daughter—period, full stop—wasn't something Nora could face yet, and she still didn't know when she'd be able to. It wasn't something to write down. Ever.)

Nora folded the yellow sheet double, then triple, until it wouldn't bend any more. She stuck it into her pocket and then looked out the window. Harrison was reading under the willow in that old ripped hammock he liked so much. It was Thursday, his light day. The heat had broken, and it was seventy-five degrees out there. Perfect for a nap outside. On Thursdays she usually tried to finish her writing early, too, so both of them could work in their gardens, calling back and forth to each other before sharing their glass of wine.

She knew Harrison was upset with her, upset that they were still sneaking around, upset that she wasn't taking him seriously when he said he wanted to help. At some point, he'd want more. Or worse, he'd want to give her more while she could only give him less and less.

She'd never do that to him. Besides, she told herself, what guy didn't want a casual, easy hookup every once in a while? Nora would sneak over, they'd have amazing, mind-blowing sex, and then she'd sneak back before Ellie got home from wherever she was for the night. There was no harm in it.

Nora almost believed it herself.

He was coming on their camping trip, like he always did.

Nora realized she had no idea how to spend that time with him.
On previous trips, he'd always been cast in the role of friend. She
wasn't sure he'd allow himself to be placed there again.

Her hands were cold even though the sun shone through the
window. She held up the piece of paper that held her sister's faults
and tore it into tiny pieces. She couldn't think this way about
Mariana. Not anymore. Nora had to get over it, get over the fact
that Mariana had screwed up by not bringing Ellie home that
night. There would be a night when Ellie would have no home
to come to.

Ellie had to have someone to look after her. Paul, since that
terrible conversation she'd had with him, a phone call in which
he accused her of making up her illness just to get some time off
from being a mom, wasn't in the running. Even if she'd wanted
him to be (which she didn't), he wasn't. When he'd left them,
he'd left them so thoroughly there was no door leading back in,
no cracked window for him to squeeze through. The occasional
ice cream cone wasn't enough and Paul would never want to be
more than that to Ellie; he'd made that *perfectly* clear on the
phone. And even though he hadn't been a real father to Ellie since
she was three, Nora had wanted to kill him again, for the first
time in many, many years. It was one thing to leave your little girl
in the care of her mother. It was another entirely to essentially
orphan her when that mother was dying. Unforgivable.

Some high school senior girls were old enough to take care of
themselves. Nora saw them at Ellie's water polo matches. They
drove like adults; they reasoned as full-grown women. Some of
the girls in Ellie's class had been working since the age of fourteen.
Those girls' mothers were housecleaners who had started working
at the same age. They were in the same high school in Tiburon but
they were part of a different world. They didn't socialize with Ellie's group, the richer, whiter group. Nora was ashamed that Ellie's
core group of friends was made up of kids whose parents made
enough to lease a new car every year, but what could she do? *Go*

make friends with the poorer students. She couldn't say that. But if Ellie had counted among her confidantes girls who worked nights and weekends, girls who had to weigh paying for a movie with buying a meal that would otherwise be skipped, wouldn't that in turn make Ellie more grateful for what she had?

The yellow scraps of paper littered her desktop like judgmental confetti. She typed her sister's name into Google and scanned the first results. "Life changing. Powerful. Transformative. An up-and-comer to watch. You need this app. Redemptive."

Her sister was redemptive?

Of course she was.

How many times had she redeemed a day for Nora in their lives? How many times had the only good, only real thing been the moment Nora saw her sister? Until Ellie, Mariana was what Nora knew of love. Falling in love with Paul had been wonderful and good and it had brought her her daughter, and when he'd divorced her, he'd left a massive, moon-sized crater. She'd never seen the crash coming, and the dust of it had darkened the skies for a long time.

But dust settled. Craters got filled.

The only thing she wouldn't be able to recover from was losing Mariana, the only true love of her life. Or Ellie, who was her very soul.

She had to face this. Head on. With truth, or at least as much of it as she could manage.

Nora was going to die.

Worse than that (funny, that there was a worse), Nora couldn't protect Ellie from everything—or really, from anything. She couldn't protect her from Mariana's carelessness. She couldn't even protect her from herself, not anymore.

Nora picked up her cell phone. She hit speed dial number one.

Mariana answered, and her voice was so happy when she said, "Nora?" that it made her burst into tears. "I'm sorry," Nora said.

"You *should* be," said Mariana. "You know I hate it when you cry."

For the next hour, they said words that would have made sense to no one else, babbling at the same time, a twinspeak made of regular, common words tumbling over one another like rocks, like beach glass, like love. Each word meant the same thing: *I need you.* Each response meant the same thing: *I'm here.*

Chapter Forty-two

Packing for the Labor Day camping trip to Yosemite had been easier in years past. It had been simpler. Tent, sleeping bag, water bottles, some food in a brown paper bag, hibachi and long fork to hold first the hot dog, then the marshmallows. That was about it. Ellie always packed her own clothes and picked out the games. Mariana always brought nothing but a backpack for her clothes and usually a bottle of Scotch. Harrison had come on the trip for years, and he was good for bringing handy things Nora never thought of as essentials: Kosher salt and vermouth and toothpicks. This year, probably, Luke would come and with him bring his box of tools, which always came in handy. A heavy hammer could do a lot for a tent stake.

Nora used to enjoy packing for the trip. Now it felt epic, like her own personal video game. For every item she found and corralled into a box, she should get a *ding* or a *tweet* or a *bong* in reward. Remember the citronella candle? *Ding-ding-ding!* Pack the toasting fork, *zipzipzipBAM*. She had a camping packing list that was a full two pages, printed in ten-point type. There were categories and subcategories, moved and augmented as the years had passed and become more complicated. She had a kitchen box and a washing-up box. A bathroom box (tampons, wet wipes, toilet paper, shovel) and a sleeping box (eyeshades for the early sun, earplugs for the silly but now unshakable spider threat). Nora had a plastic storage bin full of quarter-sized spice jars. Every spice she had in her home kitchen was also available at her camp kitchen. Her propane stove had three—not two—burners. She could make the pancakes, heat the syrup, and boil the cowboy coffee at the same time.

Nora had not only a patch kit for the inflatable beds, but also an extra bed just in case one tore so badly a repair wouldn't work. As she shoved the air pump into the bin she kept the tent supplies in, Nora remembered that the first night in the backyard in Tiburon, they hadn't even put a tarp under the tent. They'd slept in their sleeping bags with only the thin ripstop fabric between them and the ground below.

Now they had beds in the wilderness, beds with their own fitted sheets. She had three down duvets—one for each of them, Mariana, Ellie, and her—that she used only for camping.

It was ridiculous, Nora knew. But she loved her list, as complex as it was ("double-check cumin level, don't forget six extra quart-sized ziplock bags, enough ChapStick?"). She drew comfort from printing it out every year before their Labor Day trip. Crossing each item off it made the muscles in her neck release.

This year . . . Well, the list felt even better in her hand this year.

Efficient. That's what she was. She had this down to a science.

Nora stared at the list, trying to figure out what she'd been planning on packing next.

"Mom?"

Nora whirled. She hadn't heard Ellie getting up from her nap . . . She hadn't even thought out her afternoon snack. Maybe peanut butter on an apple . . .

But Ellie was so tall, and she wasn't dragging the Cal sweat-shirt behind her—she was wearing it. No, no . . . Nora closed her eyes for a moment and thought. That wasn't the same binky . . . It couldn't be. No. This was the sweatshirt they'd bought together at the college bookstore last spring. They'd laughed about it being the same color as that long-ago disinte-grated sweatshirt Ellie had loved.

"Mom," Ellie said again, her voice quieter. "Are you okay?"

"Fine." Nora brushed at the air in front of her face. "Just packing."

"You've been staring at that piece of paper for, like, ten minutes."

"No, I haven't."

"I was in the living room. Watching you. You didn't move." Ellie's voice was tight.

"I was just thinking, honey."

"You got stuck. Again." Ellie's voice was a mixture of con-cern and faint but undeniable disappointment. It embarrassed Nora as much as if she'd caught a whiff of her own body odor.

"Maybe," said Nora. "Maybe I did just for a second." It was a game of freeze-tag, only Nora was the only one tagged. In this round, anyway. She tried to make her eyes bright, tried smiling with a twinkle. "What's up, chipmunk?" Ellie still wanted per-mission to get tested. They'd had the fight twice already. For their second round, Ellie hadn't talked to her for two days. That was fine. That was easy. Denying her that permission with every fiber of her body, with every neuron of her still-functional mind, was as simple as breathing. Until she checked out completely, Nora would keep refusing it. She steeled herself to hear the ques-tion again.

"I'm going to sleep with Dylan."

Nora felt her bare toes curl slightly into the cool tile and understood, for the first time, the phrase "caught flat-footed." "Oh," she managed. "When? On our camping trip?"

"Ew! Gross. No."

Relief swamped her. There was no way in hell Nora would have been able to take listening to her daughter make sex sounds two thin pieces of tent material away from her. "He's got his own tent."

"Yeah. I told you that."

"You'll sleep in my tent, though?" Nora couldn't help asking hopefully, even though Ellie'd had her own little two-man tent for years now.

"No."

"What are you saying, then?"

Ellie yanked open the junk drawer and rummaged through it. Then she slammed it closed. "I don't know."

Did she want approval? Nora could try to understand it, but she couldn't approbate. "What are you looking for from me?"

"Why? Would you even know where to find it?"

The stark, unclothed vitriol of Ellie's words turned the hope stubbornly lodged in Nora's heart into anger. Her blood felt heavy with it. She couldn't contain her words, and she didn't think she should. "Are you this mean to me because you're scared? Or is it that you just don't like me? Because what I'm getting from you is that you think I'm a fucking terrible person." She leaned back against the counter and crossed her arms. She rarely swore, and the word felt heavy and appropriate. She didn't want to take it back.

Ellie's eyes widened.

Nora went on. "And honestly? I'm sick and tired of it. I've given you a pretty generous pass because I'm sick and I know the world is a terrifying place to consider without your mother. I've been there, believe it or not. But I'm here now. Packing this god-damn box for this goddamn camping trip that you're not acting happy about going on at *all*, and I'd really like to get a signal from you as to how long I have to put up with your attitude."

Ellie looked as shocked as the moment Nora had hit her. Her mouth opened, but no sound came out. Ellie's face was exactly the same as it had been that moment—as pale as paper. Nora could almost see the pink stripes she'd left across her daughter's face, as if she'd hit her a second time. Had she truly apologized? Had she? "Ellie. I'm so sorry I hit you that day. God, I'm so sorry, baby."

"Mom." It came out as a gasp.

"I'm so sorry."

"You've said that."

Nora pressed her hands to her cheeks. She didn't remember. "I have?"

"When Aunt Mariana brought me home. And two weeks after that. Remember?" Ellie's eyes looked desperate.

Nora couldn't remember. It wasn't there. Was there something even worse about the disease, something that hadn't shown up in her research, something that said heightened emotion made you lose things faster? How could she have forgotten apologizing for physically attacking her daughter?

How could she trust herself?

And how the hell could she be trusted?

"Do you . . . ?" Ellie's voice was soft now, all traces of anger gone. "Anyway. We've done that. I said it was fine. I meant it. I know you didn't mean to. You told me. Let's just talk about the other thing, okay?"

Sex. Of course. "Okay," Nora said as lightly as she could. "So . . . sex. You're not looking for my blessing, I take it."

Ellie tucked in her lips and shook her head.

"No. You're seventeen in two weeks?" At least she wasn't lost on dates. Not yet. Today was Thursday. She glanced at the clock. In two hours they'd be on the road, and she still had so much to check off, to make sure got done. Then she looked at the list on the counter. Everything was checked off. Even the cumin.

She didn't remember checking the spices. God.

"In eleven days." Nora corrected herself quickly. "In eleven days, you'll be seventeen. You don't need my permission. Oh, I guess technically you do, don't you? After all, he's over eighteen and you're not. Obviously, that's statutory rape."

"Mom—"

"If I chose to pursue that. Which I never would."

Ellie's slim shoulders dropped a good two inches.

Nora went on. "But why are you telling me, then? Why not just do it and tell me later? Or do it and never tell me? Isn't that the way kids do it nowadays?" She was thinking out loud, something she caught herself doing more and more lately. "Sex is casual, no big deal."

Ellie ducked her chin. "It's a big deal to me, all right?"

"I'm sorry," said Nora. "Talk to me."

"No."

Well, then, why had Ellie brought it up? She just wanted to present it as a fait accompli?

"Okay. You're going to have sex with Dylan. Do you love him?" Lord Jesus, please, every deity that ever was, *please* don't let Ellie have already told her, don't let Nora have forgotten something that important—that would be unbearable, completely unthinkable.

But Ellie's face softened. No, they hadn't already had this talk, then. "Yeah."

"And he loves you."

Her daughter nodded.

"He told you?"

Ellie nodded again. "How old . . . ?"

Nora waited. She moved her toes again, touching the tile with first her big toe, then the little ones. She couldn't get stuck if she could feel herself moving, if she kept track of herself.

"How old were you?"

"The first time? Eighteen."

"Oh." Ellie's voice held disappointment. "How about Aunt Mariana?"

"She was earlier. Seventeen when she had her first real boyfriend." Mariana had beat her in the race to devirginization. But she'd told her everything, every single detail, sparing nothing, so that Nora could picture the boy's freckled thighs and the way his penis smelled of Drakkar Noir. They'd laughed for weeks over that, the way he'd put cologne on his balls.

"What was his name?"

Nora poked around in her mind, but it was gone. It was a fair thing to lose. He hadn't been her boyfriend. "I have no idea. Nice. Very blond. Skateboarder, I think?"

"No, *your* first."

"Oh. His name was Max. I actually considered marrying him."

Ellie gave her a flabbergasted look, her hands open at her sides. "Why didn't you ever tell me this? About him?"

"What, I should have told you I had a pregnancy scare right after graduating?"

"You did?"

"That's all it was. A scare. But I was a week late, and I was terrified." Funny, back then she'd thought nothing in life would ever be scarier than the thought of herself with a baby.

"I could have had an older brother or sister!"

"That's what you get from this story? Nothing about safe sex? Contraceptives?" Nora bit her bottom lip and took a breath. "Do you want to go see Dr. Rimes?" She was the pediatrician Ellie had always gone to, and at seventeen, Ellie was about to age out of her practice. Dr. Rimes, though, adored Ellie and had said she could come to her as long as the insurance company didn't throw a fit.

Ellie looked down at her fingers and picked green polish from a peeling nail. "I went to Planned Parenthood."

It hit Nora then. "You're on the Pill already."

Ellie nodded.

"How long?"

"Two months," muttered Ellie, scratching at her nail harder.

Nora covered her hand with her own. Ellie's skin was cool. So familiar. "Nail polish remover."

Her daughter jerked her hand back. "I like peeling it."

Funny, just last night before she went to sleep, Nora had written in her journal; she could barely see the paper in the dark, but she didn't need to see well. Her hand knew the letters, knew the space of the margins.

Sex is a big deal, it began. *You have to . . .*

No. The point in these notes to Ellie was to be honest. Totally. She scratched it out.

~~*Sex is a big deal. You have to . . .*~~ *Sex isn't as big a deal as everyone makes it out to be. That might surprise you coming from me. I've always been the heavy when we have those talks that make you roll your eyes and pretend to gag. "Just wait," I've said. "Save it for when you know it means something." And I meant that, but what I didn't say—what I didn't know how to say—was that it doesn't matter that much in the long run. The first guy you have sex with likely won't be the one you end up marrying.*

At eighteen, Nora had sex with Max, a nineteen-year-old classical pianist who had the most amazing hands. She'd chosen to lose her virginity to him because he was sweet and handsome, and she thought she would never see him again after that night. She'd failed, though, at being a one-night-stand kind of girl. She and Max had fallen in love and for a little while she'd thought they'd be together forever. It seemed silly now, but it had felt so real then.

Nora balanced the pen in her fingers in the dark. She'd forgotten to teach her own daughter the most important thing about sex—that it could be good. She'd kept their sex talk dry, sterile. *This is a tampon. This is a condom. This is how herpes is transmitted.* How the hell had that happened? Had she been PTA'd into it? Responsible, professional women didn't teach their daughters how to have sex for fun. Only irresponsible hippie mothers with too much sexual confidence did that.

God, she'd failed in so many ways, she couldn't count them anymore.

Ignore what I've told you in the past. Have fun. Be safe (I can't not say that—there's a strain of gonorrhea nowadays that can't be killed by antibiotics. I know you know that) and know that it's your choice. Whatever you decide to do is right. Enjoy yourself when you get to that point in your life.

Ellie was sixteen. She was going to be having sex with a boy. Naked. With a man. Nora's immediate reaction to the thought was to feel a protective rage, an anger that started under her fingernails and raced through her blood to her heart. Impossible. Not her daughter, not *her* Ellie. She was too young, so young.

Then Nora took a breath and thought about what she wanted her daughter to know most of all. If she could tell her only one thing.

Slowly, she wrote the words, *When you love, love. It's all that matters.*

Now, in the kitchen, Nora rummaged in the cabinet. Somewhere in here, next to the defunct phone book that she kept around just in case . . . "I have some nail polish remover right here. It's bad for your cuticles to do that."

"It's fine, Mom."

"Your nails will break."

"Not the end of the world."

They weren't talking about the nail polish remover.

"I'm sorry," said Nora. *For everything.*

Ellie said, "I know." She accepted the nail polish remover Nora thrust at her.

Then, awkwardly, Nora held out the beach glass she'd put in her pocket that morning. It had been a simple Coke bottle at one time, probably, but now it was warm amber, clear on one side, occluded on the other. Ellie didn't say anything, but she took it. Then, in a move that took Nora's breath away, Ellie leaned forward and kissed Nora's forehead.

It was just the way Nora had always kissed Ellie.

Just exactly the way.

Chapter Forty-three

*L*uke was made for camping. Mariana watched him drive another tent stake into the ground with his boot—one solid backward heel thrust. He looked like the kind of man who could build a cabin from trees he knocked down himself with his two bare hands.

He looked up and grinned at her. "This a good place for it, baby?"

"Great."

Meanwhile, Ellie and Dylan were arguing. It was kind of adorable, actually. Ellie didn't know how to argue with a boy—a man—she liked yet. She'd learn. For now she was still stuck in the passive-aggressive mode of sweetly suggesting ideas. "Is that maybe a little too close to their tent?" What she meant was, *If we go in your tent to fool around, I don't want them hearing us.*

"Nah, this is fine. It's super-flat here," Dylan said obliviously.

"Does the fly maybe go the other way? With the point to the back?"

Dylan kept doing it his way, ignoring Ellie.

Maybe he was good for her.

Mariana wondered if they'd already had sex. She would have asked Nora, but . . . And she would have asked Ellie, but every time she'd seen her in the last week or two, Dylan had been tagging along behind her like an eager groupie. Good. At least Ellie wasn't the one tagging along behind a guitar player, the way Mariana had done so many times. That never went well.

She helped Luke unfold the third camping table. Nora was busy unpacking the kitchen supplies, and Harrison had taken one of the cars to go buy the specially treated firewood the campground required them to use.

"We shouldn't have come."

"It'll be fine," said Luke, but he wasn't listening to her. She followed his gaze.

Nora stood still, looking down into the blue plastic bin that held the camp cutlery and plates, her body rigid, thrumming with contained energy, her face slack. Rigid tension and abject looseness held in one body, a space too small for both.

Mariana felt fear knife its way through her guts.

"Shit," Mariana said.

"How long does she do that for?" Luke's knuckle was bleeding from putting up the tent fly. He sucked it absentmindedly. Mariana knew if she asked him how he'd hurt himself, not only would he have no idea, but he'd be surprised to see the blood.

"Ellie said it's going for longer now."

"Like an hour?"

"No! No."

But truthfully, Mariana had no idea how long Nora would stay frozen in that glazed position.

Ellie rolled her eyes at something that Dylan had just said, something about how to properly light a fire. Mariana waited to hear Ellie's smart-assed answer. She'd been the master of lighting their fires for years now. She had the touch. She'd even taken a weekend class last year on survival living and could start a fire with nothing more than two dryish sticks and a determined glare.

But instead, disappointingly, Ellie got her eye roll under control and nodded along as Dylan showed her how to find kindling, as he explained the concept of tinder.

Oh, girls. Mariana called, "Hey, Dylan, did you know that Ellie can start a fire with two sticks? She doesn't even need a match."

Ellie's face fell. Mariana wanted to suck the words back in. Such a jerk move.

"Oh," said Dylan, dropping the stick he held onto the pile of kindling. "Oh, never mind, then."

"I was just—," started Ellie. She glared at Mariana. "Everyone does it differently. I liked hearing your way."

Dylan brightened with the soft eagerness of a nineteen-year-old boy. Mariana's heart ached, and she glanced at Luke, now stringing up the hammock Nora always insisted on bringing, the one they never put up because they didn't know the knots.

Luke knew the knots. All of them. She wondered, as she had many times before, what he had been like at eighteen. She could imagine him, just like this, but thinner, gawkier. Eager to please, and eager to laugh.

He was still like that.

Mariana went to him, threaded her arms as far as she could reach around his thick rib cage, and kissed him.

He pulled back and looked at her. "What was that for?" he asked. But then he kissed her again. "I'm not complaining, mind you."

Mariana pressed her forehead into his neck.

He held her tighter. "What?" he whispered. "You all right?"

She nodded. "I'm good," she said. "I'm just glad you're here."

Chapter Forty-four

It was a full-time job, having a boyfriend along for the camping trip. Ellie took a walk to the big bathroom near the lake just to get away from him for a minute. She only had to pee, but she made it last, sitting on the cold toilet seat until it warmed up. She dragged the toe of her sandal through the dirt on the concrete floor, making swirls and curlicues. She walked back through the campground the long way, waving at families who'd been camping here as long as they had. There were always strangers, of course, tourists who managed to grab a spot on Labor Day weekend, but most of the campers were familiar to her, as familiar as kids at school, the kids in other grades. She might not know their names, but she knew what they looked like as they laughed, how they fought with their brothers and sisters.

Each campsite had a theme, and she walked past Camp Pig Out, checking to see if they'd brought the full-screen TV back. They had—she could see it through their open RV door. *What's the point?* her mother always said. *Why bring the indoors with you? The point is to get away, not bring it with you.* The next camp was Camp Rainbow Song. The group was big and loud and cheerful, always in the middle of something that looked like a fun project. Today it was tie dyeing. Three kids were dunking pieces of fabric bound with rubber bands into buckets of gray-blue water. Two shirtless guys who had matching scraggly beards strummed guitars, and a woman wearing red cowboy boots played a ukulele.

Back at camp, Dylan had crashed out in his tent. She peered in the open door flap to see him openmouthed on his sleeping bag, softly snoring. She could smell weed and hoped to hell her mother couldn't smell it, too.

Boring. Sleeping was boring.

All of this was boring.

Her mother and aunt were sitting at the long picnic table, playing rummy, wineglasses at their elbows.

"Are you drinking?" Ellie hated the tone in her voice, but she'd just read that excessive drinking could accelerate the symptoms of Alzheimer's. Then again, another article had suggested the opposite, so what was anyone supposed to believe? Better safe than sorry, though, right?

"Honey," said her mother. "It's just a glass of wine."

"You shouldn't be drinking. I thought we talked about that."

Mariana laughed. Her mother's eyes flashed to her sister's, and then she looked back at Ellie.

Ellie felt herself flush. "What?"

"Oh, chipmunk, she's not laughing at you."

"Yes, I am!" Mariana said, still giggling. "You sound like you're twenty years older than we are."

Well, it wasn't like she *wanted* to be the mother. She hated it. She just wanted to be a kid again. Simple. Uncomplicated. Really, was that too much to ask? She was seventeen—almost—and she was having to live her life like she was thirty or something.

She was supposed to be figuring out how to take care of herself, wasn't she? Vani's mom was teaching her how to cook on nothing but a hot plate, so Vani would be able to feed herself healthy food while living in a dorm. Moms took care of their children until their children could take care of themselves. It wasn't supposed to be this way. "You have no idea what it's like. To have to watch her. All the time."

The card her mother was laying down snapped to the table and then skittered sideways and off the table into the dirt. "What?"

Mariana sat up as if tugged by a wire. "What are you talking about?"

"Nothing," said Ellie, fear moving through her like wind. "I didn't mean anything."

Her mother swung her legs sideways and stood. "Ellie."

"No," said Ellie, backing up, her hands palm out.

Her mother's voice was small. "Is it worse than getting stuck?"

Ellie maintained silence.

"Is it bad?"

Mariana said, *"Ellie."*

"No. Uh-uh." She wasn't going to tell anyone. It was going to stay locked inside her until she needed help, but she didn't need help. Not yet. "I just play my game. As long as I can play my game . . ."

Mariana cast a wild glance at Ellie's mother. "What is she talking about?"

Her mother stayed quiet now, fixing her with a look that made Ellie ache inside. "What is it, sugar? What's going on?"

You go away and no matter what I do I can't make you come back. I lose you. "I just meant I play my game around you now."

"I don't understand what you mean."

I have to be near you. "You know how I told you I like to use my laptop downstairs better than in my room?"

"You said it helped you think. To be out of your room with all its distractions."

Her mother had believed it, then. "Yeah . . ."

"What?"

Ellie couldn't say it. To say it out loud would be a betrayal. To her, to her mother, to her aunt . . .

But her mother got it. She wasn't *stupid*. "You have to watch me."

"That's not . . ." But she'd never been good at lying to her mother.

"You think you have to take care of me."

She didn't *think* so. She knew so.

"Oh, god."

"Mom—"

"Have I done something? Something that scared you?"

"Not . . . You're just different. You lose track of things now. And you never used to." Ellie was furious at the tears that threatened to rise in her eyes. "I just worry."

Her mother reached for her arm, to touch her, but Ellie's anger grew. "No! Don't! You don't get to soothe me now. You don't get to tell me it's going to be okay. It's not."

"Sweetie—"

Ellie had a visceral memory of what it felt like to lie on the ground and have a tantrum. The feel of the dirt on her arms, the way the ground thumped as she beat at it. She couldn't remember what her last tantrum had been about, of course, and she was sure it had been something stupid. Probably about the last bite of cotton candy or whether she could have pizza for breakfast, a five-year-old's problem, solved with empty calories or a hug.

She hadn't known then that there would be such huge things to rail against. It wasn't *fair*. To have a mom like this. To have this happen to her. To have this happen to *Ellie*. They were so sad, her mother and her aunt. They had given up, and that was fucking bullshit. As if they weren't going to fight. As if they weren't going to at least *try* to stop the disaster that was lurching toward them. She hated them for a dark moment, a feeling that was more familiar now. The sunlight draped through the pine canopy above them, dappling her mother's face, making her look so goddamned *normal*.

"I just want to play my game."

"Here?" Her mother looked confused again. Great. Just like always. "I think you could borrow electricity from the Pig Out camp, maybe. They have all the other electronic stuff going . . ."

"No. I just want that to be my biggest worry. Whether or not I'll save Queen Ulra. Why is that so hard for you to understand?"

"I'm so sorry—"

Her mother's hand went out again. Ellie dodged.

"Don't touch me. I shouldn't have come." She looked toward Dylan's tent. "We shouldn't have come. We should have stayed at the house and"—she wanted to say *fucked* but she couldn't get the word out—"had sex the whole time you were camping."

"Ellie!"

She threw herself at the opening of Dylan's tent. She scrabbled at the zipper until she remembered it wasn't closed. She fell forward and landed on top of Dylan, who awoke as cheerfully as he'd fallen asleep. He didn't ask questions. He just wrapped his arms around her and pulled the end of the sleeping bag around her lower legs. She could feel his erect penis against her stomach, and she pushed against him. A promise. *Soon.* Soon, when she needed to forget everything. Wasn't that the way sex worked? In the movies, in books, people had sex to escape.

She felt him take a breath to speak and dreaded the words that he'd say. *Are you okay? How's your mom? You want to talk about it?*

Instead, he said, "If the Queen leaves the castle, you know the Incursers will run her to ground. She's not strong. Do you think we could change that? She trusts you. You think you could write that for the game?" His voice was sleepy. This *was* all he had to worry about.

Ellie clutched the fabric of his T-shirt and felt a low-grade happiness flow over her like music. It wasn't trustworthy—when she woke up, it might not be there. But for now, it felt good to drift off, talking desultorily about the game while the top of the tent rocked slightly in the soft wind.

Chapter Forty-five

Ellie's face, when she'd been talking about taking care of her—her face had made Nora want to kill something. Maybe herself.

Taking *care* of her. Watching her as if she were a child. As if Nora weren't the parent.

How would she know when it was too bad to keep going?

Thank god Harrison was there. He made it all feel normal. Just a campout. He'd grilled the burgers and the hot dogs—so many more than they'd ever eat; there were only six of them, for Pete's sake. He'd actually gone through a whole package of dogs and had made at least ten burgers. "We can share them with the guys next door," he'd said when she protested. The site next to theirs was full of young guys who seemed to have brought only beer and tequila. So far it seemed to be doing them just fine.

At the picnic table, Mariana whispered to Luke. Was it about Nora? "What do you think they're saying?"

"Chill," said Harrison in her ear.

"I can't."

"You have to."

She looked at him, meeting his eyes for the first time all day. Heat lit the inside of her body, and she was half pleased, half upset. Harrison was still a secret, mostly. Mariana knew, of course. And because she did, Luke did. And Ellie might suspect something was still going on and so her boyfriend Dylan probably . . . Okay, everyone knew.

God. Shouldn't she be too upset to think about sex? She was practically past *thinking*, for god's sake. That was the damn point. But she thought about his mouth on hers, the way his fingers— so surprisingly long—pushed inside her, the way he knew how to bring her to orgasm within seconds, literally. He knew exactly what she liked, the exact pressure, tempo, rhythm. As if instead of books and friends and politics, they'd been talking about sex over those years of glasses of porch wine.

Maybe, in the pauses between their sentences, they had been.

"How?"

He pushed a plate full of meat at her. "You need to eat something. Then another glass of wine."

She took it, knowing she wouldn't consume more than a bite or two. "No wine. It freaked Ellie out."

"None of her business, is it?"

"You know that thing you told me I should think about doing?"

Harrison tilted his head, thinking. "I can think of ten things. Which one?"

"That *thing*."

"Oh! The pot card? You got it?"

"*Shhhh.*" Nora looked over her shoulder at Dylan's tent. Please, God, let them have all their clothes on in there. "I did." She still couldn't believe she'd been able to walk into the office, talk to a "doctor" on Skype for less than a minute, and get issued a medical marijuana card. It had been easier and faster than getting a library card.

Harrison gave her a silly double-fisted thumbs-up. "Let's fire it up!"

"I'm nervous." She hadn't yet dared try what she'd bought at the dispensary. All she could remember about the one time she'd smoked marijuana (at twenty, and at Mariana's insistence, of course) was that it had made her paranoid and dry mouthed. She'd gone to bed and pulled the covers over her head and prayed that the cops didn't come to raid their apartment. Nora didn't do *drugs*. She hated to take so much as an Advil. And even though she'd read the study Harrison had sent her—that cannabis combined with ibuprofen or another COX-2 inhibitor could actually delay the long-term memory effects of Alzheimer's, actually improving neuron capacity—it was too counterintuitive to make sense. Potheads didn't remember anything, right? Wasn't that her whole problem?

"Nothing to be scared of. I'm here."

He was. Thank god.

"What about . . . ?" She jerked her thumb toward Dylan's tent.

"Grab your stuff, and we'll take a hike."

Nora was going to get high in the woods. Who *was* she?

Besides nervous and worried, she wasn't sure anymore. Pot probably wouldn't hurt. Not once, anyway. She'd try it.

At the lake, as she showed Harrison what she'd bought, she had a sudden memory of being right there with Ellie at the edge of the water, years before. Ellie loved to look for frogs in the shallow, plant-filled murk. Every year, as they'd "hunted" frogs (which meant grabbing them, holding them for a second to marvel at their shiny sliminess, and then releasing them), she'd smelled the teenagers' weed drifting through the reeds. It was a good place to hide from the grown-ups.

And now she was here, about to toke up.

Harrison showed her how to put the concentrate on the vaporizer's element. "Just a little bit."

"I don't get it. What's the difference between this and one of those e-cigarettes?"

"No difference. Then you just push this button, here. When it's blue, you inhale."

"Hard?"

He laughed. "As hard as you want."

"How do you know how to do this?"

Harrison's left eyebrow rose. "I have a couple of secrets left."

What if Ellie saw her doing this? What if she acted baked for the rest of the evening? Nora rested her forehead on her knees. "No, I can't. I'm not going to get high in front of my kid."

"She's not here. And this is medicine."

"Yeah, right."

"Nora."

"Fine." She took the small metal tube, pushed the button, and inhaled.

Harrison did the same. Then he leaned back on his arms, watching the far dock, where at least twenty children jumped, splashing and screaming.

"How long does it take?"

"As long as it takes." He threaded his fingers with hers, and Nora felt her heart lazily thump in awareness.

"Oh, no!"

"What?" He didn't let go of her hand.

"I forgot to take the ibuprofen."

"That's fine. I thought about that."

"I'm supposed to take it together. At the same time. To prevent it from impairing my memory and so I don't feel stony. Oh, *no*." Was it too late? Could she run back to camp and grab some? Would she forget what she was doing on the way?

"Just feel it, Nora."

She could feel it then, a downiness in the front of her mind. A lightness, a lifting off of something she didn't know she'd been holding.

"Oh."

"Not bad, right?"

It wasn't bad. It was nothing like it had been twenty years before. Maybe now the formulation was more precise. God knew the dispensary where she'd bought it had seemed to know exactly what she needed. "Indica, not sativa. You don't want to get stoned," the young man had said. "You want to feel better and not stress as much."

She hadn't thought, then, that it would actually help.

But it did.

After a few long, stretched-out moments during which she felt her hands—always restless—lie still in her lap, Nora said, "I love you." She was surprised. She never said it first—he always did.

"I'm glad," he said simply.

"Why didn't we do this a long time ago?" she asked.

"Weed?"

"No." She moved her hands slowly between them. "This. Us."

"You said you wouldn't."

"I did?" she said in startled surprise. "When?"

"When you said you wouldn't date a man who had never been married. Or a man without kids. When you said you didn't like tall guys, and when you said you were never dating again because you didn't trust men anymore."

"You listened to me."

He inclined his head, a silent *yes*.

Nora felt her heart get wider, more broad. "I didn't mean any of it."

"How would I have known that?"

She leaned against him. It was easy. That's what it was. Nora's tongue didn't get tied. She didn't feel as if she were losing track of time. She reached in her pocket for her beach glass, the one she'd planned on keeping there all weekend. Instead, though, she skipped her green piece of glass across the still water. It had come from salt water, and she sent it whirling into fresh just because it felt right. When the sun was almost all the way set, she suggested going back to camp to see if everyone had eaten.

Walking back, it just didn't hurt as much. The knowledge of everything, the weight of it all, was easier to carry. Walking single file when the trail narrowed, she could hear Harrison behind her. Maybe he always had been.

Chapter Forty-six

Nora wondered if she should keep hold of Harrison's hand as they came into sight of the campsite, but he dropped her hand first, reaching to pick up a couple of good pieces of kindling.

"There you are," said Ellie. She and Dylan both held long metal forks over the fire, roasting marshmallows. "Want a s'more?"

Did she? "*Hell* yes." They laughed at her eagerness. It sounded like the best idea in the world. That part of smoking weed hadn't changed, apparently.

When Ellie handed her a roasting stick, Nora put her marshmallow as close as she could to the wood without putting it directly in the coals. When it caught on fire, she let it burn a second before blowing it out.

"Tiki torch!" cried Ellie. There was approval in her daughter's voice. Ellie had always preferred her marshmallows blackened before she pulled the hardened crust off with her fingers.

Then she'd complain mildly as the melted sugar burned her. Then she'd stick it back in the fire and do it all over again.

Luke, who'd been leaning back in his camp chair so the front legs were raised from the dirt, shoved his marshmallow farther into the flames. "That's the right way." His lit, too, and he held it up in the air, smiling at it.

He looked . . . Luke looked a little high, now that Nora noticed it. A little soft around the edges.

So did Dylan. He was reclined in another chair in much the same way, Ellie curled on his lap like a kitten.

Jesus, even Mariana had that soft, inward look.

Nora tried to work on her knitting, but even just the simple knit stitch seemed fuzzy in her brain. She held the sock loosely in her lap. "Is everyone here as stoned as I am?"

Ellie fell off Dylan's lap to the dirt with a thump. "Holy shit."

Luke started laughing.

Mariana goggled at her. "Nora?"

It was ridiculous, but her heart tickled, as if she wanted to laugh. So she did. She felt the ghost of shame—a recognition of something she *should* feel but didn't. "Sorry. I shouldn't have said that, maybe."

Ellie, her face still shocked, her eyes wide, said, "Mom?"

"Yes, chipmunk?" Even that was funny, and she giggled harder.

"Harrison!" Ellie leaped to standing. "You got her stoned?"

"No," said Harrison slowly, the grin on his face brighter than the fire that lit his face. "She got *me* stoned."

"Mother?"

Nora should feel terrible. She should be horrified that her daughter knew. Instead, all she felt was expansive. "Do you want some, honey?"

Ellie's mouth fell open and stayed that way.

"It's not normal pot. It's concentrate. Kush. For sick people."

Nora touched her own nose. "Like me. I'm sick, so they gave it to me. And you shouldn't do drugs. But if you wanted to try some, then at least you'd be with me when you tried it . . . And everyone else here is high . . . so we could . . ." Somehow, it seemed like a good idea, a sweet one, to share this feeling with Ellie.

"Nora!" said Mariana, her voice tight and thin. "We're not high."

Oh, no. If Mariana was shocked, then it was really shocking. Sudden despair twisted like a serpent in Nora's chest, roiling and thrashing in her blood.

"I'm just kidding," Nora hurried to say. "She's only sixteen. I'm not going to give *drugs* to my daughter. *God*." But for a second, she'd forgotten it was wrong. And that second was the worst second of all, and all the stoned expansiveness in the world couldn't change that. She'd gotten it so wrong. So wrong.

But then Ellie barked a laugh. "Is this seriously my life? This is fucking nuts."

Nora didn't know what to say. There wasn't an "I'm sorry" big enough to cover it, no groveling that would be low enough. To have offered weed to her daughter in front of everyone who was important, everyone who mattered . . .

Then her daughter passed another blackened marshmallow to her, and Ellie's eyes were soft. The marshmallow was sweetness, turned inside out, and it tasted like impossible forgiveness. It was as easy as that.

Luke leaned far back, way behind him, and pulled out a guitar, all without getting out of his camp chair. He started strumming softly, as if he could change the subject with the instrument. After a moment, it seemed that was exactly what he was doing.

Dylan was busy saying something in a low voice to Ellie, and Ellie was saying something back. Then she sat on his lap again, wrapping her arms around his neck.

Soon her daughter would have sex with that boy, if she hadn't already. Soon, even though Ellie wasn't high now, she'd try marijuana. She might try other things, too. Mushrooms, coke, ecstasy. Worse. Things like bath salts and whippers and things Nora hadn't even yet read about online.

And Nora wouldn't be there. "I wouldn't be able to help anyway," she said.

She caught the look that flew between Ellie and Mariana.

"What could I do? Encourage you? Discourage you? How is a mother supposed to know what to do?" She wasn't supposed to ask it out loud, she knew that, but the rules felt skewed. Inside was out. Black was red. Her daughter was her mother and her sister was her, had always been her . . .

"Mom, it's okay."

Nora nodded. She couldn't remember what she was agreeing to, but it felt right. She poked the fire with the metal stick, the marshmallow having already burned and dropped off in a plasticky black bump of molten sugar. Her knitting fell to the dirt, and she didn't care.

Mariana, who had been hovering next to Luke, watching his fingers on the fretboard, came to Nora. She sat down next to her on the ground.

"Our pants will be dirty," said Nora. It seemed important to say.

"It's okay," said Mariana. "We're camping. We're supposed to get a little dirty. That's what we do."

"Will you sleep in my tent?" asked Nora.

"But . . ." Mariana looked at Luke, who answered with a slow dip of a nod.

"Please? Ellie, you, too."

"Mom, I brought my own tent—"

"Please. What if this is . . ."

A pause. Nora didn't want to play the sick card. Even lightly stoned and not tracking well, she knew she didn't want to lay it on the table.

So she didn't. But they heard it. She knew they did.

"Okay, Mom."

"Okay," said Mariana, bumping a shoulder against hers.

In the tent that night, her high worn off to a paler shade of shame, Nora listened intently to the sounds of the forest around them. The night wind had picked up, soughing in the pines overhead. Teenagers cawed outside, running in groups, probably toward the lake. In years past, Ellie would have been with them, running from the younger kids, emulating the older ones.

But tonight, Ellie wasn't with them. Neither was she in her boyfriend's tent.

She was here, her body pressed firmly against Nora's back. She sighed in her sleep, sounding like a smaller, rounder version of the wind.

Mariana lay with her back against Nora's chest. They were a set of three spoons, with Nora in the middle. It was so warm they'd kicked off the top sleeping bag without discussing it.

Their breathing moved together, as if their lungs weren't only related by blood but by a set of bellows that inflated and deflated them mechanically. Three breaths in, three breaths out, a sighing in time.

Tomorrow, they would spend the day fishing in a rented boat on the lake. Nora would hopefully finish the sock that was almost done and immediately cast on for the next one. She'd brought a drop spindle and some fiber to play with, though she wasn't good at spinning yet. For the first time she wondered if she'd have enough time to learn to do it well.

Tomorrow night, they'd cook whatever they caught or they'd cook more burgers if they came up empty-handed. The next day, they'd repack all the supplies they'd carried up the mountain, dump their trash and recycling in the cans at the entrance of the campground, and drive home.

All this work. All this *effort* to pitch a tent and sleep with stuffy, recirculated air in a tent whose interior walls would be damp with breath by morning.

But all the work was worth it, for this moment of warmth, for this moment of being so close to her girls, both of them. Given a choice between this moment in a national forest and an all-expenses-paid trip to a tropical resort, she would choose this. She would choose the dirt tracked into the tent, the possibility of scorpions in their shoes in the morning (she would remember to tell them to shake their shoes). She would choose burned marshmallows over any chef's crème brûlée. Any day.

Three breaths in, three breaths out. In tandem. Together.

Then.

Someday . . .

Nora held her breath.

Two breaths in, two breaths out.

Just two.

In her sleep, Ellie kicked the back of Nora's leg and then tightened the arm that was draped around Nora's waist. At the same time, Mariana pushed harder backward and tangled her foot with Nora's. *Breathe,* they said in their sleep. *Breathe,* they encouraged her.

Nora breathed with the two she loved most of all.

Chapter Forty-seven

EXCERPT,
**WHEN ELLIE WAS LITTLE:
OUR LIFE IN HOLIDAYS,**
PUBLISHED 2011 BY NORA GLASS

Ellie's Birthday

When Ellie was little—no, when she was still in utero—I wanted her to have her own day. She was due to be born on my birthday, but since I'd had to share mine my whole life, I didn't want her to have to share it, too. She deserved her own.

I'd been in labor for two days by the time I was finally fully dilated. Two full days of exertion, two full days of off-again-on-again pain that made me feel like I was going to split into violent atoms, two full days of the strong conviction that I would have her before our birthday, September seventh.

Mariana, of course, didn't see it that way. From India, after her missed flight, she'd sent more and more frantic texts from a borrowed cell phone. *Wait. Hold on a little longer. If you just wait three more hours, we'll all have the same birthday forever.*

Like I could possibly slow down. I pushed harder, even though the doctor said I wasn't supposed to. It increased stress on the baby, she said. Birth, I figured, was a big enough stress, and my pushing couldn't possibly hurt that much. Besides, how were they going to stop me? By saying "No"? Good luck to them.

Paul said, "I'm here."

I looked deeply into his eyes and pretended I cared.

I'm here, texted Mariana, even though she wasn't.

The truth was, I didn't care. It was the first and only moment in my life I didn't need her. I didn't need my husband. I could only hear what was inside me, the roaring ocean kicked into tsunami mode by the tiny person earthquaking inside me.

She would have her own day, I swore.

Her *own* day.

At eight p.m., the midwife thought she was finally coming. I agreed—I knew she was. I was wheeled into the delivery room. At nine p.m., I pushed more. I gave every ounce my body had to give, and as a mother giving birth, that was a lot. Two hours later, the epidural had worn off, and they couldn't give me another one. They put a heating pad on my belly and I couldn't find the words to scream that it was hurting me until I had second-degree burns. That pain didn't matter, compared to what was happening inside me. At a quarter till midnight, the doctor talked in low tones to the nurse, and then the midwife told me that my baby was in distress.

The guilt that landed on top of me with that accusation was like nothing I'd ever felt before. My first failure as a mother, and my daughter wasn't even breathing air outside my body yet. I didn't want to fail her again, so quickly, by taking away the chance for her to have her very own birthday.

I grabbed the midwife's hand—it was hard and calloused, as if in her off time she gardened without gloves. "Do it now." I looked at the clock on the wall. Twelve more minutes. "Pull her out now. Use those forceps things."

"We tried that, Nora."

"If it's surgery, can it wait? Till the day after?"

She thought I was joking, so she laughed.

Thirteen minutes later, as they prepped me for a cesarean, Ellie speeded up her entrance. Given the very last-chance go-ahead from the midwife, I pushed with my brain and heart and liver. I pushed with the strength I wouldn't find for years, borrowing from it like it was a bank. There was nothing, no one in the whole world but me and my little girl. Mariana on my phone, Paul on my left—they both disappeared into a red twilight of background pain and noise, leaving me with no one but my Ellie, who was born one minute before midnight on September sixth, securing her very own day, all to herself.

As they caught her, suctioned her nose, made sure she had all her parts, I panted like a racehorse pushed past its limit. I wanted to say *Happy birthday* to my new little girl, but just like that, sixty seconds later, my daughter's birthday was over and it was ours, mine and Mariana's.

Paul couldn't say anything. Not one word. He just squeezed my hand and his tears rained onto my forearm. He went up on his toes, bobbing up and down, looking for a glimpse of our daughter, who was already unhappy about her ordeal, screaming like an injured kitten.

There would be time to examine her, to check every little part, to kiss every toe, to count every whisper of birth-black hair. I wasn't worried anymore.

"Ellie," I said. We hadn't decided on a name, hadn't been able to narrow our list down. We'd hoped that when we met her, we would know. I hadn't even properly held her yet, but I'd known her name while giving my final roar. *Ellie*. Strong, intelligent, willful. It hadn't even been on our short list. I don't think we'd ever spoken the name aloud before to each other.

"Ellie," said Mariana, her hiccups clear even from India. "It's perfect."

"Ellie," said Paul.

Then the nurse handed her to me and I was finally who I was supposed to be.

Chapter Forty-eight

For her birthday dinner, Ellie always got to choose where they ate. It was part of the fun of it. This year she'd chosen Forbes Island. She'd rattled off her reasons to Nora as if ticking off a list. "Some rich old geezer built it a long time ago and it floats, and it's an island with a lighthouse, and he lived on it in the San Francisco Bay for years and years, and he had huge parties on it, and now it's anchored and turned into a restaurant facing Alcatraz, and I *really* want to go."

Nora was surprised. She'd heard of it, of course—they'd seen it when they'd gone to see the sea lions at Pier 39. It looked like a standard tourist trap, like a five-and-dime version of Hearst Castle—glitz with all the glitter rubbed off. "Are you sure?"

"Yes. And I want Dylan to come."

"Anything you want. It's your party." Easy to say. Harder to believe. Nora still fluctuated between hating Dylan for what he represented—an attack on her child's very innocence—and what he was—a nice, sweet boy, a bit too old for Ellie but not by much, honestly. "Who else do you want?"

"It's your birthdays the next day, too. Invite whoever you want." Ellie had stuck her earbuds back in and gone on killing dragons or whatever she did in *Queendom*. Then she pulled one out. "Harrison. Is he coming?"

Nora's brain cycled slowly once. "Yes. Is that okay?"

Ellie rolled her eyes. "*God*. It's Harrison."

Nora said, "What does that mean?"

Her daughter only said, "Sheesh," and went to her room.

Nora had no idea how to interpret that word. Was it good, a "sheesh" of acceptance? Or was it a "sheesh" of irritation? Shouldn't she be able to tell the difference between the two? Harrison and Ellie had been fine on the camping trip, fishing and laughing together like the old days, but since school had started again (her senior year! how could that be possible?), Ellie had been spending all her time either studying with Vani and Samantha or playing her game with Dylan. She'd refused to continue with water polo (she'd made varsity the year before), but to pad her application she'd been volunteering with a food bank on the weekends. She hadn't allowed Nora to volunteer with her, pitching an honest-to-god fit when she'd suggested it. And whenever Nora and Harrison asked if she wanted to have dinner with them on Harrison's porch, she did that "sheesh" noise that was a cross between a word and a curse. Nora had been choosing to ignore it, but she needed to figure it out sooner rather than later, especially since the week before, Harrison had said, "I want to move in."

"Salt," she'd said. "I think that's what I forgot to put in." She'd poked at the lasagna she'd made and pretended he hadn't spoken.

"Here," he'd said. "I want to move into your house."

Nora had been noting the dates they had sex on her day planner. There were plenty of them, little blue *H*s, circled at the top of the square that held the day. She didn't want to forget a single time. But if she did, how would she know? It used to be that they'd drink a glass of wine and watch the lawn grow. Now they had sex and laughed and then gazed up at the long crack in his ceiling. Then they laughed more. Nakedness did that to old friends. Once Harrison had choked sobs into her hair, and once, after what had been possibly the biggest orgasm of her life, she had cried against his chest until the pillow had been as wet as the sheets below them. But mostly they laughed. That was the best part of it, even better than the actual sex. Naked, uproarious laughter.

"Did you hear me?" Harrison asked.

She shook her head. "No."

"I want to—"

"I *heard* you. I just don't want you to say that."

"Why not?"

"Because." There were so many reasons, the primary one being Ellie. Not that Ellie didn't love Harrison like a . . . She still hadn't admitted (out loud) to Ellie that she and Harrison were . . . were doing whatever it was they were doing. She was still hiding him in plain sight. "Just no. I'm fine."

"But you won't be."

There were grooves at the corners of his eyes, fine lines she'd never noticed before. "I know. *Then* you can help." Even that hurt to say. "Not before."

"Let me help now."

"When it's time," she said.

"How will we know when it is?"

She'd watched a video of a forty-eight-year-old man who'd been diagnosed four years prior to the filming. His voice shook when he spoke, and his words trailed off before the end of his sentences. "It's hell," the man had said, "knowing that I'm leaving them. Knowing I can't . . . What is it I'm saying?"

"Knowing he can't stay." His pretty wife, a grim look belying her bright smile, filled in the gaps.

In the kitchen, Nora had said to Harrison, "We'll know."

Now the bargelike party boat ferried them the short distance from Pier 39 to the fake island. Ellie sat with Dylan, snapping selfies with no flash. Harrison sat on his own bench and sneaked peeks into the storage area. "Empty wine-cooler bottles," he whispered at Nora. "People still drink those?" Luke stood next to Captain Mac, a hungover-looking young man who wore a captain's costume that looked two sizes too big for his narrow shoulders. Mariana sat next to Nora on the flat bench seat.

"This should be fun," said Mariana brightly. "How are you feeling?"

Nora took her knitting out of her purse. "If you're asking about the functionality of my brain, it's working. Firing on most of its cylinders."

"Most? How was yesterday? At the doctor's office?"

It was funny that she forgot random things—like the fact that she'd been making toast until she went to put the bread in the toaster and found cold, hard bread inside the slots—but she remembered every bit of that office visit. "Fine."

"Really?" Mariana looked so happy to hear it. "Really fine?"

Nora couldn't bring herself to tell her the truth: that she'd failed more tests than she'd passed. She'd screwed up the NYU story recall test and barely passed the Boston Naming Test. And that wasn't even the worst of it. "Yep," she said, patting her sister on the knee. She knitted another round.

"God, that's getting long. Is it a kneesock?"

Nora decided right then. "Yes, it is." It was easier to keep going than to decide to stop.

The island itself rocked more than Nora thought it would. Given that it was really just a huge floating pad, it made sense, but the roll and sway underneath her was unnerving. Nora liked to keep the ground steady underneath her. Lately it was her full-time job. This island seemed treacherous. Islands should be moored with long earthen limbs dug deep into dirt below—they shouldn't sway like a hula dancer.

Before they were seated inside, the six of them trooped up the stairs of the lighthouse. Up top, a small beacon rotated and four or five other tourists snapped pictures of Ghirardelli Square. "If this is a real lighthouse, no wonder people crashed on the rocks around here," said an old woman in a loud voice. "Imagine! I couldn't put on my makeup in this light."

Well, maybe that was the explanation for the wandering eyeliner and the lipstick on the tip of the woman's nose.

"Let me get a picture of the birthday girl and the almost-birthday-girls." Harrison, who always remembered to take photos of important moments, held up his iPhone.

With her back to the lights of San Francisco, Nora wrapped one arm around Mariana's waist, the other around Ellie's. They felt too thin to her. She, on the other hand, had been putting on weight—thanks to the meds—and felt like the solid one. She smiled at the camera and felt her roots grow down, down, down, through the lighthouse, through the wooden floor of the barge, through the water, past the plants in the murk, and into the mud far below. Somehow, she'd hold them all in place, safely through the storm.

Chapter Forty-nine

*M*ariana loved the dining room of Forbes Island. "We should have come here years ago," she whispered to Luke. It was straight-up kitsch, but the best part was that it was completely un-ironic. The lighting was dim; the tables stood askew. None of the plates or silverware matched except in era (late fifties?), and the chairs creaked as they moved in them. Small hurricane lanterns flickered below the portholes over their heads. The waiter pointed out that down here they were actually below the waterline. When Mariana had walked to the strange ladies' room earlier (located in a tiny room that used to be a berth, it still had a small bed, a fireplace, and an enormous stone bathtub), she could smell mildew. Imagine fighting wood rot on an island that was actually a boat. Mariana admired the chutzpah of the owner, who apparently still dropped by now and then, still treated like the captain he was.

Now she clapped her hands. "Presents!" She'd been looking forward to this for weeks. It was the best idea she'd ever had for a birthday present, and the fact that Ellie was in on it made it that much better.

She flagged down the waiter to clear their plates. The waiter clucked his disapproval at the basket of unfinished bread and clucked harder as he swept dropped salad off the tablecloth. "Thank you so much. It's a celebration, you know. It's all three of our birthdays! Well, it's hers"—she pointed at Ellie—"and it'll be ours in a few hours."

The waiter made a face that looked like he didn't believe a word of that kind of coincidence and took the plates away, still grumbling.

Nora, who'd been so quiet over the meal, so worryingly darkened like a shuttered room, brightened. "Presents! Oh, good!" She pulled out two envelopes and handed one to Mariana, one to Ellie.

Opera tickets. Season passes, two each.

Mariana looked at them blankly, turning them over and then staring at the front again. Ellie was doing the same thing with hers.

"The four of you can go," said Nora excitedly. "Together. Double dates."

"I don't get it," said Ellie.

"It's your new thing!"

"What?"

"You know how when someone gets really into something and has to drag everyone else along? I figure at least one of you will get really into opera because of this, and then you'll get to spend the time together. It was that or seasons passes to Six Flags in Vallejo . . ."

Ellie's face fell. "Oh."

Nora slipped two more envelopes out of her purse. "Yeah, I got you season tickets for that, too."

Laughing, Ellie waved them in the air. "I *love* Six Flags."

"I know."

Mariana felt a sideways lurch in her belly. Luke tried to take her hand, but she pulled away from him. "You got tickets for your-self, too, right?" she asked. "For you and Harrison?"

Ellie laughed. "Of course she did."

Nora's wriggled her nose and then rubbed it. "They're for *you*. And your dates."

Mariana watched Ellie realize what it meant. Her face fell below the waterline. "No way," said Ellie.

"What?" Nora looked honestly surprised.

"I'm not doing *shit* without you."

"Honey, I'm not saying—"

Ellie threw the envelope back onto the table so fast she knocked over her water glass. "I *know* what you're saying and I hate it."

"I'm sorry, but—"

None of them moved to right the glass, to stop the waterfall. The opera tickets were soaked.

"Seriously? You're playing the sick card again?"

"Again?" said Nora in an aghast voice.

Mariana wanted to put her hands over Nora's ears. "Ellie. Stop it."

"She does it all the time."

Nora's face was white except for two brilliant red spots shin-ing at the tops of her cheekbones. "I would never play that card."

Ellie shook out her hands in front of her as if she'd been typ-ing too long. "But you *do*. The other day you said, 'Clean your bathroom because . . .' and then you just walked away from me."

Mariana felt a wild rush of relief. "That's not the same thing at all!"

"Honey," said Nora, leaning forward, "I didn't mean . . . I don't even remember that. I think I must have just wandered away, maybe I just forgot what I was—"

"Whatever. You *forgot*. How much worse is this going to get? I know it's rough on you, I know, I know, but how much of *my* life is going to be affected by this?" Ellie glanced sideways at Dylan as if she was embarrassed.

Embarrassed? Maybe Ellie thought they should keep from being real in front of her boyfriend, but that was bullshit. Mariana would show her embarrassment. She stood, knocking over her chair, which crashed into a wicker loveseat behind them. "Your life?"

"Mariana," warned Nora.

"*Your* life, little girl? This disease is taking *everything* from her, and you *know* that. You think it's affecting *you*?"

Ellie's chin went up in exactly the same way it used to when she was learning how to be defiant, when she'd been learning exactly how far she could push either of them. "Yeah. I know it's the wrong thing to say. We're all supposed to be thinking about her. All Nora, all the time. And when they're not thinking of her, they're thinking of *you*. The twin. How can this affect one and not the other? Oh, how does the *twin* feel?" Huge tears welled in Ellie's eyes, and Mariana felt her heart break in two, split right down the middle. The fake island pitched under her feet, and she felt like she might throw up.

Ellie went on. "And I've been so quiet, trying to do everything right, trying to take care of everything. You know what? Every single night, I go through the house and shut things off."

"Oh." Nora put her hand over her mouth. Her voice was muffled as she said, "Oh, chipmunk. You said it was okay."

"She leaves lights on all over the house, even though she's always nagging me to turn them off. She never does. She opens the freezer door and walks away from it and when I get there, all the meat has defrosted. I check to make sure she leaves her keys on the hook when she gets home."

Mariana and Nora spoke at the same time:

"I always leave them on the hook."

"She always leaves them on the hook."

It was a thing her sister did, like Windexing when she was

stressed, like always having a craft of some sort in every room to work on when she had downtime. Nora never lost her keys, ever.

"She doesn't. Not anymore. I couldn't find her keys when I was going to bed, so I looked around the house, but they weren't there. I finally found them outside. In the car."

Mariana's body physically hurt, as if she'd suddenly contracted a high fever. Her eyes burned.

Nora, still with her hand over her mouth, said, "I left them in the car?"

"With the door open. It was running. In the driveway. Almost out of gas. You seriously don't remember me telling you that?"

Nora shook her head.

Ellie echoed the motion. "I can't believe you don't remember me telling you that."

"Don't get angry with her!" Mariana wanted to haul Ellie out by her ear, pull her up the steps past the stupid, foul-smelling waterfall, and leave her out in the cold to bark with the angry sea lions. "You don't get to get mad at her. It's a disease."

Ellie grimaced. "That's the worst part. I can't get mad. I'm not allowed to. I can't get mad at anyone but myself for being such a terrible person that I wish this had never happened because it's ruining my life." Oh, the *sound* of the disapproval that dripped from Ellie's voice. It was viscous, a toxic yellow tinge to the words.

"Don't you dare talk to her like that." Mariana, still standing, touched Luke's shoulder. He said nothing but raised his hand to touch her fingers. *Open hands cling to nothing.*

Nora kept her eyes on Ellie as if she'd never seen her before. Pain swam in her eyes, and Mariana felt like she could drown the child. Happily. If Nora cried, she *would* drown Ellie like a kitten in a sack.

Tell her, Nora. Tell your daughter she doesn't get to act like a child even though she is one, tell her she doesn't get the luxury of being an insolent teenager with an attitude, tell her that she lost that right with your diagnosis.

Tell her.

Mariana remembered suddenly the fort they'd built in second grade out of three pallets they'd found behind the diner their mother was working at. It had been so simple to lean the pallets together against the wooden fence near the Dumpster, and just like that, a tiny place with walls, just for the two of them. There had been nothing comfy about the space, the ground just dead grass, no roof over their heads, but that made it easy to watch the clouds sail overhead. They'd read books out loud to each other, taking turns one chapter at a time—*Freckle Juice* and *The Giving Tree*. It had felt like home, that tiny fort. Safe.

Mariana's heart ached.

Ellie scowled.

Then Nora said, "I'm sorry. I'm sorry you're scared. I'll buy a ticket for myself to the opera and to Six Flags."

"I'm not going without you," said Ellie with a catch in her voice. "You can't make me."

"I won't try."

"I'll probably hate the opera anyway. In case you're wondering, which apparently you're not."

Dylan, in his first non-mumbled sentence of the evening, said, "I love it. *Rigoletto* is great. And *The Barber of Seville* is hilarious."

They all stared at him. He raised and then dropped his shoulders. "My sister's a professional singer."

It was the first thing Mariana had heard about the kid's family, and she liked it. "Good. That's great."

"I want to get tested," said Ellie.

"No," said Nora. "I won't have you possibly ruin your whole life before it's even started. No way."

"For my birthday gift."

Mariana clapped her hands. "Jesus Christ, not *now*, Ellie." She tried a smile, and it didn't wobble overly much, so she continued. "Can we just try to have a nice time?"

She could almost see her niece contemplate the question.

She could almost see her need to say "no" wriggle under her skin. Then Ellie inhaled sharply and said, "Okay. Yes."

She didn't apologize, but Mariana didn't want to, either. So she said, "Now my present for Nora."

"*Our* present," corrected Ellie, and she was right. This present was from both of them. Ellie had done an amazing job, actually, collecting the names and e-mail addresses, sneaking into Nora's computer when she was in the bathroom or drinking tea in the garden, copying and pasting them into one long list. But it had been Mariana's idea. A good one, for once. Something she could give her sister that she needed, that wasn't wrong or inappropriate.

Luke righted Mariana's chair and held it for her as she sat. The waiter poured more water and offered desserts. "One of everything," said Mariana.

"Ma'am?"

Hearing it made her want to push nonexistent reading glasses down her nose to look at him. "We'll take one of every dessert you have. This is a celebration, and we're going to goddamn well celebrate. Put a candle in each one of those suckers, too. Do you sing here?"

"Sing?"

"The birthday song?"

The waiter just blinked.

"Never mind," said Mariana, sighing. "We'll do our own singing."

As the waiter trundled away, Ellie said, "Dang. That was fun to watch." There was a pause. "I'm sorry." It was a real apology. Mariana could hear it.

She felt her own anger deflate like a balloon. "I know. Me, too." She pulled the bag up from underneath the table. "You have your half?"

Ellie nodded.

Nora, who had just been watching them, leaned forward. "What's going on?"

"Remember when you said you didn't want to have a big party?"

"I didn't *want* a party." Nora spun, looking over her shoulder. She looked frightened—too much so—her eyes wide. "No party, please."

"No, no, I didn't mean to—no surprise party."

"We knew you would hate that," said Harrison.

"Something else. A silent party of people who love you." That sounded even weirder, so Mariana pulled out one bundle of vintage white envelopes with red and blue stripes at the edges. She thrust the stack across the table toward Nora. "Here."

Ellie gave over her bundle, almost as high.

"What are these?" Instead of picking up the envelopes, Nora held on to her napkin, folding and refolding it.

Ellie bounced in her seat. "What do they look like?"

"They look like letters."

"That's it!"

Mariana felt Luke grab her hand. "That's exactly it."

"I don't even *know* this many people."

Mariana wondered why Luke was trembling and then she realized her fingers were shaking, not his. "Yes, you do. And they love you."

Chapter Fifty

*I*t was awful.

Nora could understand why they'd done it. Hell, if Nora had known someone diagnosed with a bitch of a disease like EOAD—if it hadn't been *her*—she would have attempted the same kind of gift. But this, all the letters for her, addressed to her specifically, each one written in a different hand: it was too much.

She opened the first one. "I can't believe . . . these are from . . . *everyone*. How did you . . . ?"

Ellie bounced harder in her chair. On another day, Nora would have told her to sit still so that she didn't knock anything over. At this point, though, Nora realized she didn't mind if Ellie accidentally punched a hole in the wall. Since they were below water level, the frigid bay would stream in, rising first to their ankles, then to their waists, their necks . . . And they would all sit there, politely, watching Nora open sodden envelopes, one by one.

"What does it say?" Harrison's voice was low at her ear. She caught his eye, and she saw it then: such a look of love. It was so warm he glowed with it. "Go on," he encouraged her.

"Come on, Mom, read it out loud."

"Maybe just a few lines . . ."

You wrote in pen, never pencil, always sure your answers were right. (Mrs. Fisker, third grade, Oceania Elementary)

The way you so beautifully organized your home. Your pantry alone! The way you designed your spice rack made me so determined to make my house prettier that I went back to school and got that interior design degree. (Jan Heinhold, mother of Aubrey, Ellie's sixth-grade best friend)

My girl. When I told you off at that stitch-n-bitch, I had no idea how many times I'd have to rely on you to prop me up. The almost-divorce, the time Johnny rolled his car and we thought he wouldn't make it . . . I remember the day you picked me up when my car died in the Maze. Do you remember how fast the traffic whizzed past us? Do you remember how unafraid you were, while I shook like a dang leaf? If you forget, I'll keep telling you. That's what friends are for. Buck up. Fight. And try to remember the only thing that matters: We, your friends, so many of them, are here for you. (Lily, darling, treasured Lily)

Nora read a few snippets out loud. She was proud of how even she kept her tone. In pen, that was how she read it. No trepidation. She let no fear weasel into her voice, even when she read from Lily's note, which made her want to put her head under the table and howl. Mrs. Fisker's letter, though—it felt good, to be reminded that she'd been that headstrong girl, so sure of herself. So *cocky*. She'd take a little of that right now. That would be just fine. There was no way in *hell* she was going to read any of the other letters, though.

"How many of them are there?" She lifted one pile. There had to be fifty or sixty, just in that one stack.

"Over a hundred, and more are coming in every day," said Mariana proudly. "Written letters, for their favorite writer. I had them sent to my office so you wouldn't know."

Nora slid down in her chair. "I don't even know that many people. How did you possibly . . . ?"

Ellie, in her pleased voice, said, "Facebook. You don't want to know about everything else I found out about you while I was prying into your computer."

Nora felt ice slip down her back. "What did you find out?" She couldn't remember what was in her hard drive, what she'd left open. Which essay had she been most recently working on? What could Ellie have found?

"Mom. I'm kidding."

A light laugh. "I know." She hadn't known. She flipped through some more of the envelopes. More teachers. Friends she hadn't seen for years. More than one boss. Two of Paul's sisters. Many, many coworkers, all of whom, she knew, would have something good and embarrassing to say about her. There were probably some nice memories in the stack, too.

It really was a lovely thought. A gorgeous, generous gift.

And she hated it so much she wanted to claw her way out through one of the upper portholes. She'd pull herself through and land on the surface of the oil-skimmed water and splash as fast as she could to one of the small floating docks. She'd push away the sea lion in residence and she'd strip off her clothes. She'd bark like mad—she'd make all the same rude old-man throat-clearing noises that the sea lions did, and after a while, she'd get dark from thin sunshine radiating through fog, and then after long months, she'd become the tourist attraction, not them. Since the Bushman had died, no one had been jumping out from behind carefully arranged twigs at the passing Chinese tour groups. Where was the fun for the random San Francisco tourist? Really, she'd be doing the city a favor.

"Nora?"

"Mom?"

Harrison placed his warm hand on the back of her neck, something she normally loved the feel of. But she shrugged it off—too heavy, too confining. "You know what's funny?" she said.

"What?"

"I've always spaced out."

Mariana squinted at her as if trying to pull her into focus, but it had always been Nora with the weak eyes, not her sister. "Yeah . . ."

"I've always gone off in my own head, flights of imagination. I think it's part of why I'm a writer. I like to sit and think about things before I do them. Remember, Mariana, Mom always said I'd practice in my head what I was going to try until I was good at it, and then I'd do it. I whispered words to myself as I learned them until I pronounced them correctly."

Mariana nodded.

"But now, when I do it, when I rest and think, you all panic." Nora laughed. "You should see your faces right now. So concerned for me. God, take a breath, would you? I'm not dead."

Dylan, bless his heart, was the only one who followed her instructions and took a loud, deep breath.

She wasn't dead. Even if they'd just staged her own funeral.

Nora excused herself to go to the bathroom again, this time using the one downstairs that was attached to a small room that had a tiny bed, still made up with sheets. Someone, the chef, or the manager, or maybe Mr. Forbes himself, probably still slept in that bed sometimes, watching the lights of the harbor out the thickly paned window. Someone got laid in that bed. Or she sure hoped someone did.

In front of the mirror, she looked at herself. She'd forgotten to do that recently, content to wash her hair, drag a comb through it once, and slide on some lipstick every once in a while. She hadn't *really* looked at herself in a long time. Not in memory, actually.

Well. That was a laugh.

Nora had always compared herself to Mariana. She was used to looking at Mariana, so used to it that when she saw herself in the mirror, the differences were so plain as to be startling. Mariana was beautiful. She had great hair. Perfect skin. Lips that never chapped unless she had a cold, and then her nose got sweetly pink to match. Nora, on the other hand, turned beet red with every cold, sweating from every pore, her nose running like a hose.

She pulled her hair back, lifting it. She had crow's-feet at the corners of her eyes. Had she ever noticed that before? She'd seen them at the sides of Mariana's eyes, she knew that. She'd noticed them with some satisfaction, actually, meaning to check her own skin when she got home to the lighted mirror. She'd never remembered to look before now. Strangely, even in the watery green flicker of the fluorescent lightbulb, even looking like the older not-Mariana, she looked pretty. She could probably pass for forty, maybe younger.

Leaning forward with her palms on the cracked countertop, she looked in her mouth as if she were a horse. She still had a young person's teeth. Only one filling and one very expensive cap.

They'd thrown her a *funeral.*

She bet they didn't even know that's what they'd done. They thought the gift of handwritten memory was clever, and it was. They thought it was kind, and it was that, also.

But they were eulogies. She'd seen on the envelopes the names of moms she used to carpool with, and the name of the woman who used to live next door, the one who sold Avon products much too aggressively. *Oh, how tragic,* they must have all said when they got the request. They'd told other mothers, women who didn't know her, about how honored they were to comply with the family's request. *Well, at least this way she'll know how I feel before she passes.*

There was a peace to *not* knowing how someone remembered you. If the one single thing Mrs. Fisker really remembered about Nora was her propensity to do her math homework in pen, that was sweet, but limiting. Nora was someone who loved pencils, too, loved their soft scritch and how impermanent they were.

She loved how, if you were careful, when you erased no one knew anything was missing. And, conversely, if you pressed just hard enough, the indentation could never be ironed flat again.

Chapter Fifty-one

"So how much trouble will you be in if you don't go home tonight?"

Ellie tightened her grasp on Dylan's hand as they walked past the moored boats toward his car.

"It's my birthday. Or at least it is for another hour or two. Why, you wanna knock over a liquor store?" She felt a whisper of nerves in her larynx followed by a grip of lust felt lower.

He laughed.

Ellie tugged his hand. "Or we could steal a car. You know how to steal a car?"

Dylan shook his head. "Besides what I've seen in *The Fast and the Furious* movies, I'm not that sure about hot-wiring."

"Oh. Okay. What did you have in mind?" That same shiver moved from her throat to her spine. His roommate Ian was always home. Like, *always*. The guy didn't even work, except for the ads he made for porn sites, but Dylan said that mostly just kept him in free smut and didn't leave much over for partying. And no

matter how much Ellie liked Dylan—or loved or whatever anyone else in her position called this feeling that made her want to
crawl inside his coat and all the way under his skin whenever they
were in the same space—there was no way in heck she was losing
her virginity in a bed while a porn-obsessed mama's boy listened
from two feet away. Dylan had, of course, suggested his car. *Nothing on wheels, nothing without a ceiling, nothing without a locking door.*
He'd looked disappointed when she'd said it, but Ellie didn't care.

She wanted to have sex. In particular, she wanted to find out
what it was like to fuck someone. She didn't think she believed
in making love, which was where she departed from her friends
(everyone but Vani, of course). They all wanted their first times
to be perfect, this idealistic sweet and sexy night where they got
to wear Victoria's Secret lingerie. A night when everything felt
good, a night that ended in something magical, but what that
magic ending was, no one seemed to be able to say.

Ellie was more pragmatic. From what she read, the first time
never went smoothly. And it wasn't like she expected to have a
simultaneous orgasm or anything. But yeah, she wanted it to be
safe and as fun as possible. That desire, in itself, made her feel
hopelessly old-fashioned.

"So? Where are we going?"

He pointed. "Dude, you're gonna love it."

"Dude, don't call me dude." She was his girlfriend. Not just
a gamer pal.

He smiled. "Sorry, I forgot. There's this old-school twenty-
four-hour Internet café that just opened in the FiDi. They have
Queendom loaded, and I reserved two computers. We can play next
to each other all night. Have you written any more about that
burning punishment thing? BlueRazor and his gang hit me up
earlier about it—he can't wait to read what you've come up with."

"Um."

Under a streetlight wreathed in fog, Dylan turned to tug her
against him. "What? Doesn't it sound awesome?"

She could almost hear the *dude* he swallowed at the end of the sentence. She hid her disappointment, feeling awkward and too young as she rose on tiptoe to kiss him. She was a good writer. Was that all she was to him? A good player? Wasn't there supposed to be . . . ? Oh, well. "Sure," she said against his mouth. "I'll never turn down a chance to watch your friends get burned at the stake."

"But not me."

"Never you," she said, tugging on his belt loop. "I'll keep you off the pyre if I have to throw myself on it."

He pulled back, looking honestly touched. "Aw, man. Don't let Addi die like that. What a waste of a great Healer. I'd reroll my character before I let you do that."

A bubble of happiness rose in Ellie's chest. Him rerolling was the equivalent of him throwing himself in the way of a speeding bullet for her. "Oh," she said. She thought of the forms she had lying on her desk at home—she was vacillating between applying for early decision to Smith College and Mills College. Both were good for English and creative writing.

It was just that . . . she didn't *know* that she wanted to write. Like her mom did. Wasn't that too . . . obvious? A cheat?

How were you supposed to plan your whole life when it was falling apart?

The distance to Smith was twenty-five hundred miles. Hours of expensive plane travel. Mom would freak if she didn't apply (Ellie had been talking about it for years—Mom had even ordered a book for her about famous Smith alumnae), but Mills College was also a great school, and it was only a ferry and a BART ride away. She could be home in two hours if her mother needed her. Faster, if she got a car.

Early decision was a commitment—an actual contract—not like early acceptance. She could only put in her ED decision to one place, and if they accepted her, she had to go.

Mills was in Oakland. Like Dylan.

Dylan growled happily at her, kissing her once more, and then said, "Come on. It's only about six more blocks."

They passed Lombard and the Fog City diner. The only people left on Embarcadero were late-night joggers, a few wandering couples like themselves, and the hardiest of panhandlers. One said in a low voice as she passed, "So cold." She didn't even have a dollar in her pocket, though, only her mom's debit card.

"I'm sorry," she said. She tried to meet his eyes, to make sure he knew she meant it, but he turned his head and spat on the ground she'd just walked on.

"Almost there." Dylan turned right at Justin Herman Plaza.

"I know where we are! Have you ever been in the lobby of the Hyatt? It's gorgeous." Ellie walked faster. "My mom took me for lunch once after she had a meeting. She gave me a sip of her champagne. I think it was when she signed her book deal."

"Let's go in," Dylan said.

"Really?"

"Sure. We have all night, right?"

The door opened automatically, the doorman wishing them a pleasant evening. Ellie smiled at him and he grinned back.

"Mom said this is the world's largest lobby. Or atrium. Something like that. When we were here they made it look like it was snowing with twinkle lights." She gazed up as far as she could, and still the rooms rose higher. She felt tiny and fragile, surrounded by so much indoor air held up by concrete and well-made plans.

"We can try to get a drink at the bar," Dylan said.

Ellie laughed. "This isn't Merchants. We're the youngest people here. They'll card us for sure."

"Over here," said Dylan, and his voice sounded funny.

"What?"

He was walking straight toward the registration desk. Ellie looked over her shoulder. No one seemed to notice them. No one was watching. The people closest to them, a trio at a low couch, seemed miles away. "What are you doing?" she whispered.

He said good evening to the desk clerk. Like he did it all the time. "Reservation for Dylan Hacker."

Ellie sucked in her lips and bit down, keeping them gently locked between her teeth. She said nothing as he filled out a card and signed something else.

The desk clerk's eyes looked tired as she passed over the key cards. "Room 1215, sir. Do let me know if I can be of any other assistance." She didn't sound convincing.

Ellie waited until they were alone in the elevator to let out her squeal. "Holy shit! You had this planned all along!"

Dylan looked inordinately pleased with himself. He preened in the glass of the elevator, brushing off imaginary specks of dust from his shoulders. "Why, yes, perhaps I did. Perhaps I'm an evil *genius*. Happy birthday, Ellie."

Ellie launched herself at him, wrapping her arms around him as tightly as she could. "I thought we were going to play."

"We are. It's just a different game. Are you disappointed?"

"I'm *so* disappointed." And she kissed him as hard as she could to show him exactly how not disappointed she was.

Chapter Fifty-two

Ellie had said she'd be home late.

Nora lay in bed, staring up at the black outline of the fan she never used above the bed. When she'd asked Paul to put it in for her, she'd had the idea of menopause someday in mind. She'd lie next to him, bearing her hot flashes quietly, her naked, wet body stretched on the sheet below the turning blades. If Paul rolled over and noticed, maybe he'd bring her a glass of water. A clean, dry T-shirt, maybe.

She'd never turned the fan on. Not once.

Now she probably never would.

What had Ellie meant by *late*? Why hadn't Nora thought to clarify?

Nora checked her phone for a text. Maybe she'd spaced out—that's what she called it to herself now; she'd needed a better term for getting stuck—and hadn't heard the ding of a message received.

Nothing.

She checked Facebook. Seventeen friends had posted inspirational messages on their boards, but nothing for her, nothing from Ellie. Kids didn't use Facebook, anyway. She clicked onto her secret account on Instagram, the shameful one. Candi Wells. She'd opened the account with a fake Gmail address, using the name of a girl Ellie had gone to school with in first and second grade. Candi had moved to Texas, and as far as Nora could tell by a pretty in-depth Web search, didn't have an Instagram account or even a Facebook page. She'd heard a rumor through the mom mill that the Wells family had become ultrareligious and had seven more children and that Candi was either close to getting married or actually wedded with a kid of her own.

Ellie had accepted the friending on Instagram within minutes. She'd sent a sweet message about one of the houseboating pictures Nora had attached to the account, a picture full of generic-looking kids she'd pulled randomly off the Internet. The ruse allowed Nora to look at Ellie's pictures, which she did, more often than she liked to admit to herself.

As usual, Nora's throat got tight as she flipped through the photos. It felt as if she were about to cry, but it was from shame, not sadness. Ellie was a good kid. No, she was a *great* kid. The kind of kid who said no when Nora had asked if they could be Instagram friends, but the kind of kid who wouldn't have put up a fight if Nora had insisted on access to her pictures. She would have just shrugged and allowed it. Ellie wasn't the type to open a secret account to hide it from her mother. Nora had Ellie's computer password written down in her desk, just in case she ever needed it. Ellie hadn't seemed to mind overmuch giving it to her. She wasn't devious.

No, that kind of sneakiness belonged to her mother.

Her throat so tight it felt hard to breathe, Nora checked the most recent photos, posted tonight.

A sob snuck up on her, painful, like a hiccup gone wrong. There was a gorgeous shot—beautiful, really—of the three Glass women outside the restaurant. Harrison had taken it with Ellie's phone while Nora, Ellie, and Mariana had grouped themselves around the life-sized pirate wench holding the ashtray. Ellie was pretending to stub out an imaginary cigarette, Nora was standing at attention, smiling in a way that she'd hoped didn't make her look as tired as she felt, and Mariana—she saw now—was tweaking the pirate's nipple with a leer. A light from a tiki torch illuminated their hair so they all looked somehow radiant.

Blessed.

Well, goddamn it, she hadn't meant to cry tonight. That hadn't been on the agenda.

She slid the photo off the screen, and the next one populated. Again Ellie was lit from above, her hair shining golden brown, as she kissed Dylan. Obviously a selfie, the shot was a little crooked, and both of them were smiling. It was the kind of kiss you gave someone you really liked. Loved. The kind of kiss where your teeth clacked against each other's and you just laughed. The photo was two hours old, taken at eleven p.m.

Candi Wells "liked" the photo.

Nora was about to turn off her phone and stare back up at the motionless fan when a text message bounced onto the screen.

I'm going to stay out tonight.

Nora coughed. She would have typed back but she was too angry to move her thumbs. She needed to breathe, to recover. *Stay out.* She was seventeen and about a minute, not an adult. Yeah, it was a Friday night, but that didn't mean anything. Staying out? All night? In *Oakland*?

If that's okay, came the next text. *I'm still in the city. With Dylan.*

Nora knew she was with him. Of course she knew that.

We're at a hotel.

This, at least, she knew how to answer as a mother. *Which hotel? Address.*

Hyatt. Embarcadero.

Jesus. It felt as if Nora had taken off her helmet in space, all the air vacuumed out of her lungs.

We did it.

And at those words, with that admission from her baby girl, Nora could breathe again. This wasn't boasting, though Ellie probably thought it was. This was her girl reaching out to say, *Is this okay? Am I doing this right?*

Is he asleep?

Yeah.

She could let her daughter think that. *Are you okay, chipmunk?*
No response.
Maybe she wasn't a chipmunk when she was naked in a man's bed. Fair enough. *Ellie? It doesn't have to be good. Remember we talked about that? Most first times don't go that smoothly.*

It was kind of . . . okay.

Good. Was that good?

You're not mad at me?

Nora wasn't. Not at all. She was glad to her very bones that they had this moment, this exact one. There was no one there but the two of them. *It's always me and you, chipmunk.* She didn't text it. Instead, she thumb-typed, *Of course not. I'm glad you texted.*

You're not mad I'm not coming home tonight?

Oh, that. The sex thing had thrown her off the not-coming-home thing. *Yeah, you're in trouble for that.* Trouble. What did that even mean anymore?

The response was immediate. *Love you, Mama.*

As Nora fell asleep, she kept her phone in her hand, a new kind of rock to hold. If she needed it, she could swipe the screen to unlock it and stare at that last text from the girl she loved.

That word, "Mama."

That word was blood, was power, was strength. That word was memory. It was life.

Chapter Fifty-three

The next day, Nora had a normal Saturday, as normal as she could, anyway, while she lost more of her mind and Ellie—home at ten a.m. and sleepy eyed—pretended she wasn't watching her like a hawk. As usual, Nora felt nauseous for an hour after she took her Aricept, and she curled into the big chair in the living room with a book she felt too queasy to look at. Ellie played her game from the couch. The mantel clock (always a bit fast) chimed, and Nora was surprised to hear the three o'clock bongs. Where had one and two gone? Had they been in the living room the whole time? Was that why her back hurt? She smelled banana and peanut butter. On the coffee table was a peel, a peanut-buttery knife resting on it. Nora didn't remember which one of them had eaten it. She checked her mouth for the taste and caught Ellie watching her. She pretended she was yawning.

That night, she and Ellie would probably argue about doing the dishes after dinner, and maybe Mariana would come by and watch a movie. Nora would send Harrison overly flirtatious texts and maybe go sit on his porch for a while and ache with the need to feel his arms around her. She'd leave before he tried and then after she was sure Ellie was sound asleep, she'd cross the lawn silently and they'd fuck standing up in his laundry room—it was still easier to pretend to everyone including herself that he was still a secret even though he was so much more.

But it was still Saturday afternoon, and she was with her daughter.

Her daughter, who wasn't a baby anymore. Not after last night.

Maybe right now—this moment—would be the closest she'd ever be to Ellie again. Maybe they'd drift further and further apart as Nora's brain cells ran into one another, leaving pile-ups and traffic jams and twisted pieces of metal wreckage behind.

Then maybe Nora wouldn't care, and that was the worst, hardest, darkest part of all.

But right now, she cared with all her heart and soul and mind. Nora burned this memory—*this* one—deep into herself, as if she were branding her flesh with it. She'd write it down, before she forgot. She'd put it into her journal in her own handwriting that she'd recognize later (wouldn't she?) so that she could read it again and again. *Ellie's big eyes as she stares, the way she tucks her fist under her chin when she's worried.*

"What's wrong, chipmunk?"

"Did your mom have it?"

Nora didn't expect the question, but it was easier to face than she thought it would have been. "We don't know. The car crash was when she was my age."

"Could your dad have had it instead?"

It had to have come from somewhere. They'd probably never know, though. "Maybe."

Ellie closed her computer and tapped the top of it. "I want to get tested."

Nope. Still no. Nora couldn't—wouldn't—allow her daughter

to ruin her life that way. To find out how she would die . . . Impossible. Unless—maybe she could steal a sample of Ellie's blood (the old chemistry set came back to her, the slides, the finger pricks that hurt so sweetly) and get it tested, and then, if it was negative, only then would she tell Ellie she was safe, she would live, she would *live*.

Nora steepled her fingers, as if considering it. Then, "No."

"I'm not giving up on this."

"Fine."

Then Ellie made a face at her, crossing her eyes and opening her mouth in a silent scream, and Nora laughed, unexpectedly. Ellie laughed, too, and then pulled another, even better face, sticking out her tongue, bulging her eyes.

Moments like this. Moments of grace, that's all they were. Nora didn't deserve them, but she got them anyway. She had to thank someone, if she could just figure out who that was. It certainly wasn't any god she'd ever read about. Maybe she could make up her own now—wasn't that a sick-person prerogative?

"Don't leave."

Nora's knees jerked. "What, baby?"

Ellie closed her eyes and kept her fingers on the top of the computer resting in her lap. "Don't just go. Don't chicken out and run somewhere. Or . . ." Her eyes stayed closed. "Or do anything else. Anything worse."

Everything was implied in those words. Nora's chest ached. "Oh, honey. Sometimes I wish . . . Wouldn't it make it a little easier for you? If you didn't have to . . ."

Ellie's eyes flew open and took on that enraged look—the one she'd gotten when she'd read the end of *The Diary of Anne Frank*, when she'd learned what the Ku Klux Klan was. "It would make my life hard *forever*. That's what you would be doing."

"I'm not going anywhere, Ellie-belly."

The corners of Ellie's mouth twitched. The old nickname fit perfectly in Nora's mouth, like a sweet marble.

She thought about telling Ellie about Clive Wearing, the British man with one of the worst cases of amnesia ever observed. He could only remember new information for thirty seconds or less. Everything behind was a black void, everything in front of him was darkness. He knew what someone was saying and could understand the words—he could even respond—but during the time he uttered his answer, he'd forgotten the question. He had semantic memory—he could walk and talk, though he couldn't have told anyone how he knew these things. To him, it felt as if he'd just woken up from blackness. Every thirty seconds, he experienced it again—once more waking up from nothingness.

But he remembered two things. He'd been a musician and could still play the organ, sing, and conduct.

The second thing he remembered was his love for his wife.

Every time saw her, he was delirious with happiness. He'd been in the darkest void, for years, and here she was, the love of his life, the literal light in his darkness. "Oh, look who's come, oh, darling! Oh, wonderful! Can we dance?" Every time, one hand went to his wife's cheek, the other behind her head as he drew her in for a long, overjoyed kiss, from which he would draw back each time with a laugh full of relieved delight. "Oh, look who's come!"

And if his wife walked into the next room, his face would go slack, and they could play the game all over again.

In the videos Nora had found, no one had asked his wife, Deborah, *How badly does it hurt? To be forgotten over and over again? Did being the only person the patient loved make up for that? Would that make it better or worse?*

Ellie was still staring at her.

Nora repeated herself. "I'm not going anywhere." What a happy, perfect lie. It felt soft and comfortable, and Nora wanted her daughter to have as much comfort as possible. In every way.

"Fine," Ellie said, finally. "You better not."

Nora wouldn't be like Clive Wearing, forgetting everyone but his wife. Nora wouldn't forget Ellie or Mariana. It was absolutely impossible. She would know Ellie anywhere, at any age. It had to be true. And Mariana. Mariana *was* her. She didn't have to worry about forgetting her. She couldn't.

"It's just like death," Clive Wearing said in the video, over and over again. "No thoughts of any kind, no dreams, no difference between night and day, no sight, no sound, no taste, no touch, no smell, exactly like death." He babbled, perhaps because it grounded him, perhaps because it was something he could participate in. He repeated himself, like a record. They were, of course, new thoughts to him every time. "It's been like death. I've never seen a human being before, never had a dream or a thought."

Ellie was saying something now about a school Samantha was thinking about applying to, but Nora couldn't focus. She tried. She really tried. She nodded along with Ellie's words, and said things like, "Really?" and "Why's that?"

She reached into her pocket and tumbled the three pieces of beach glass she'd taken from the bowl that morning. Two more than usual. They were warm from her body heat. They clicked against one another, tumbling just right. A family of glass, broken and perfect.

What if their roles were reversed? What if Mariana was sick and Nora wasn't? If a day came when her sister didn't recognize her, when their eyes met with no history . . . it would be the same as death.

Nora would, she knew, want to die.

There was only one solution (Nora had the solution, she'd always had the solution, it was what she *did*, what she was known for—she couldn't lose that now), and the solution was so simple she didn't know why she hadn't gripped it before now: *I will not forget these two.* She would hold tightly every memory of them. She would do it with gritted teeth and brute force and ignore the niggling voice that said maybe the choice wouldn't be hers at all.

Nora *couldn't* be wrong.

"Are you listening to me?" *Mama, watch. Watch me!*

"Yes," said Nora, bringing her gaze back to her daughter's bright eyes. "Sam losing her UCLA app. Hey, Ellie. I love you."

Ellie focused. She looked right at her, into Nora's eyes. Suddenly Nora could smell the Bath and Body Works peach soap Ellie used. "I know."

Nora said, "I will always love you."

"I know."

"Don't forget, chipmunk." This, then, would be the journal entry she wrote for Ellie tonight. No how-tos, no you-shoulds. She would tear out the whole journal, all the Ellie entries. They were all wrong. Ellie would find her own way. There was just one thing to write to her daughter. Just *I love you I love you I loved you then and I love you now and I will love you always with everything I ever was. I will love you for so much longer than forever, I will love you so long forever will be done before I stop.*

Ellie took a sharp breath and said, "*You* don't forget."

"Okay, then."

"*Okay,* then." What Ellie meant was *I love you.* Nora could see it on her face, hear it in her voice.

"Okay." What Nora meant was *I promise you this: I love you I love you I love you I will love you so long forever will be done before I stop.*

Chapter Fifty-four

EXCERPT,
WHEN ELLIE WAS LITTLE:
OUR LIFE IN HOLIDAYS,
PUBLISHED 2011 BY NORA GLASS

Halloween

When Ellie was little, she hated the dark. This was after Paul left. A night-light wasn't good enough. She needed the overhead light left on. After Paul left, she was scared of the night sky in the backyard and of the night wind when I drove with my window down. She wanted the night turned off and the day turned brighter.

So the idea of Halloween was completely out, I thought. Trick-or-treating, sure. We could go while it was still light, before sunset, when the other gangs of sweet princesses and scallywag pirates were out marauding. But the haunted houses? They were a no-go, obviously. They were too scary for a little girl who saw bogeymen in the back of the closet at four in the afternoon.

The problem was that the biggest haunted house in Tiburon was right up the hill from us. It was so close we could hear the terrified screams from inside my kitchen. At five years old, Ellie was *finally* starting to get over her fear of the dark. Listening to the sound that made her cringe like a startled kitten, I wanted to march up the hill and murder all the screamers myself.

Ellie whispered, "Screaming is *awful*."

"I know, Ellie-belly." I fixed her tiara. "We'll go down the hill. We won't go there."

"I want to go to the haunted house," said my sister, Mariana.

I straightened. Stared. "You what?"

"I want to go. I love haunted houses. They're hilarious."

I felt like covering Ellie's ears with my hands, as if Mariana were swearing. "No, thank you. I don't want to terrify my poor *daughter*."

Mariana shrugged dismissively. "Nah, I can go by myself. I'll catch up with you on Robbins Street, how's that?"

"I wanna go with Auntie."

"Come on, Ellie, Auntie's being ridiculous."

Ellie dug the backs of her tiny wedge heels into the grass of our front lawn. "No. Haunted house. With Auntie."

"No," I said.

"She can come with me if she wants to, Nora." Mariana's voice held an edge, and I wanted her to stop talking. Mariana wasn't a mother. She didn't *know*. Not the way I did.

"No." It was the only word I felt sure of, anyway.

"So maybe what's going on here is you're the one who's scared?"

"No!"

But it was true. My daughter got her fear of the dark from me. Her fear of monsters under the bed was mine. Back then I still checked behind the shower curtain when I got home (what I would do if a serial killer jumped out at me, I had no idea—I just hoped one wouldn't). I was frightened of the inky blue shadows in the laundry room after dusk. I didn't even like going to the movies because when they dropped the lights, anything could happen.

"Mama, I want to go house haunting."

Mariana lifted Ellie, her light blue dress sparkling in the falling twilight. She put her on her shoulders, and we all looked down the hill toward the edge of the sunset. Red swaths of low cloud dressed the marina. I thought it looked ominous. Mariana said, "Man, that's beautiful."

I sighed.

"Okay," my sister said. "We'll go do this and come straight back."

"Stay here," shouted Ellie. "Stay here. I'll take care of you when I come back."

I sat on the front porch and smiled at mini Yodas and crooked-hatted witches. I gave each trick-or-treater three mini–candy bars, listening to them exclaim in joy as the weight hit their plastic buckets or pillowcases. Tortured screams filtered down the hill from the haunted house. Did Mariana really not care that she was scarring her niece for life? It really didn't matter to her at all?

Of course, I was wrong. When it comes to how I think about my daughter, I so often am. I'm at the age now when I can look back and see that just as a child doesn't know where the divide from their parent is until they hit the developmental separation phase, I didn't really know until that moment that Ellie wasn't actually an extension of myself.

When she came tearing up the lawn, she slipped. She almost went down in her ridiculous kiddie heels, but she righted herself at the last second, and she launched herself at my knees and held on tightly. I bent at the waist to comfort her. I went to dry her tears, and it wasn't until then that I realized she wasn't crying. She was laughing and hiccuping so hard it took a full five minutes before she calmed down enough to tell me that she loved it.

"There was a guy all wrapped in bandages, and—*hic*—he came out and ran at me—"

Mariana grinned back at me, unrepentant.

"An' I was supposed to scream, because that's what all the other little kids were doing, and some of the grown-ups, too, but I—*hic*—just laughed because it was actually the guy from the bank, Mama, and he had black and red stuff on his face under the bandage, and he was so *silly*."

I hugged her hard. "You liked it, chipmunk?"

She wriggled out of my arms and fell backward on the lawn. She made grass angels with her arms and legs, and I knew I'd never get the green out of the blue sateen, but I didn't care.

"No, I *loved* it."

"Huh," I said, handing the bowl of candy to Mariana so she could fend off the next herd of wee Harry Potters. "I think I would have been really scared." I threw myself on the lawn next to her and looked up at the stars. "You weren't frightened?"

"No," she said and kicked harder, poofs of her dress floating up into the air. I wished for my own fairy dress.

"Why not?"

"Because Auntie was there. *Hic*."

That night when she went to bed, screams still trickling down the hill like the cries of uncanny birds, Ellie said, "Turn it out."

"Your light?"

"Yeah."

"You're going to sleep all right without it?" I asked. (This is the worst part of all: When Paul left and Ellie slept with the light on again, a small, secret part of me was glad. I was glad that I wasn't the only one afraid to be alone. We both slept with the full wattages burning above us, burying our faces in our pillows only as the night went on and darkness became a greater need than courage.)

"Yeah," she said, turning on her side and tucking her hands under her banana-covered pillowcase. I wanted to know *how* she was ready. (*How did you do that, Ellie? How did you reach that point? How did you know you were there?*)

"You just want the light off tonight? On Halloween?" I couldn't help pushing.

"It's time."

That was all she had to say.

Ellie always gets where she's going at the exact right time. Me, I'm always a little bit behind the curve.

When I went to bed that night, I snapped off my own light. All I could hear was my own terrified heartbeat. Alone. So alone in the dark.

Then I slept harder and sweeter than I had in years.

Chapter Fifty-five

"I don't understand," said Nora.

Behind Benjamin Matthews was a view of the Yerba Buena Gardens. The construction going on in the street served only to make the fountains look more idyllic. As the fog melted in the October sun, light winked cheerfully off the glass walls surrounding the carousel. A small part of Nora had dreamed once, long ago, that she'd rise through the ranks at the paper and someday sit right there. That was before she started writing her own column, of course, which was where she belonged. She knew that, but it didn't get rid of the slight longing she felt when she saw the desk's mahogany smoothness, when she heard the grandfather clock ticking from where it had stood in the corner since the newspaper started, seventy-six years before.

Benjamin leaned forward and put his head in his hands. "God, Nora. Don't make this hard on me. It's hard on me, too."

"Excuse me? I think—although I'm not totally sure—that you're firing me. You're asking me to make it easy?"

"I'm not firing you. That's what I'm saying."

"You just told me—"

"I encouraged you—"

"To take a sabbatical to get better."

"Yes."

"I'm not going to get better." For the first time, Nora said it clearly. Her voice didn't break. She didn't tear up. It just was.

"I know."

"Then what—"

"Look. I can't fire you, because . . ."

"Because I could sue your ass off. ADA. Discrimination." The idea was novel. She hated it.

Benjamin jammed his hand through his hair, always too long. It was his one vanity, besides the paper itself, and journos laughed about his coif behind his back. Around town, though, he was known for being kind and smart. He was probably being both right now.

"Don't fire me, Ben."

"Nora—"

"I need the job. What do you need? A note? I've brought those in. I'll bring more." It wasn't exactly true that she *needed* the job—she and Paul had bought long-term disability insurance long ago when they were young enough for it to be inexpensive, and thanks to his life insurance, her job, and careful investments, she'd have enough to leave some over for Ellie. She'd run the numbers ten times. Maybe more.

The skin around Benjamin's mouth was white. "Nora, I just—"

"Did I screw something up?"

"No—"

"Bullshit," said Nora.

Benjamin jerked backward. His gaze flicked over her shoulder. Good. He *should* be worried.

She paused. "Just tell me. What did I do wrong?"

Benjamin closed his eyes and kept them that way, as if he were frightened she'd be able to change his mind if he looked at her.

"Tell me." Anger dissipated like the fog outside the window, and the rigid fear, so normal now, slid under her skin in its place.

"You keep turning in the same piece."

"What?' Nora laughed. That didn't even make sense. "I have no idea what you're talking about."

"The piece on the old-age home in Los Angeles."

"Dementia village," she corrected. They were huge in more civilized countries like the Netherlands, countries actually committed to caring for their elderly. And they were amazing, true villages in which the store clerks were actually nurses, and the "house cleaners" were caretakers. Fully fenced and safely inescapable; buses arrived and picked up the people waiting at the bus stop, drove them around the village, and then dropped them back off at the same stop where they'd been waiting. It worked for some, and they trundled back to their cozy apartments. Others stayed sitting on the bench, happy to grab the next bus to nowhere. "It's fascinating. And you have to admit that our nation is so behind the times it's scary. We lock our dementia patients inside hospital wards they don't understand, in places that offer them no quality of life beyond getting the right meds at the correct time. That place in San Luis Obispo is the first in the United States to do it. But it's a start."

Benjamin stood so suddenly that Nora's heart jumped. He looked furious, his mustache jumping.

Or . . . god. He might be crying.

Oh, *come* on. Really?

"Nora." His voice was like the sand on the temblor board at the Exploratorium, the board that demonstrated liquefaction in earthquakes. She could almost see the waves of it threading through the room to her ears.

Whatever it was he was going to say, she didn't want to hear it. "No, thank you," she said.

"You've turned that piece in four times."

Nora felt the shaking in his voice reach her body. So far the earthquake was confined to her shoulders and lungs, but soon it would go deeper, to her belly, and then to her feet, and then she'd collapse to rubble. That wasn't acceptable. Didn't she have insurance for meltdowns in the workplace? "No, I don't think I have."

"The same piece. Different words, differently ordered paragraphs, but the same piece. Every time."

Suddenly it made a sick kind of sense, how familiar the piece felt as she wrote it, how easily she'd come to the conclusions she had. "Why didn't you—I don't think—"

"Nora, you're not fit to work right now. What I need you to do is go get yourself better."

He knew as well as she did that wouldn't happen. A month before, she'd told only Melanie Fine in HR and her officemate Frank about her diagnosis, but the next time she'd gone to work everyone knew. HIPAA was a joke, apparently. Rachel, the intern in Sasha Banks's pocket, the one who tattled to Supply on people who used more than three Splendas per coffee, gave her a soft, "I'm so sorry . . ." the last time they'd passed in front of the vending machine.

Benjamin continued. "HR can help you with the insurance. It's called a medical retirement. It's just a little early, that's all. They'll help with everything."

"I'm confused. *Are* you firing me?"

He teepeed his fingers on top of a pile of paperwork. "No . . ."

"You can't."

"No."

"You're *encouraging* me to take early retirement."

Benjamin looked so damned *relieved*. "Yes."

She didn't have to do it. She could fight. She could write about it, sell it to *The Oprah* magazine. She could do a hell of a job on this one: "How I Lost My Mind but Not My Career." Her readers would love it. She might even get another book deal from it.

If only this were a workmen's comp issue. If only she could blame the fact of her illness on too much newspaper ink in her twenties or on too much lead from absentminded pencil licks.

In twenty seconds, Benjamin would open his eyes again. He'd shake her hand. He'd give her a hug, whisper in her ear how hopeful he was of the future, all the advances science was making, how he wanted her back at her desk as soon as she felt better. If she felt better.

Before he could do any of it, Nora walked out of the room. She didn't want to fight. She didn't want to write an exposé. She didn't want anything but to feel fresh air on her face.

Nora walked to the elevator without stopping at her desk. The elevator took too long to rise, so she took the stairs down to the lobby. She left her desk behind. She left the collection of drawings Ellie had made her over the years and her favorite coffee mug. The computer was theirs—they could wipe the hard drive themselves. When you quit, you only took a box with you if you had a safe place for the contents.

In the bright sunshine outside, Nora stopped, blinking like a mole coming up from underground. A homeless man lurched toward her, muttering, "The end is *nigh*, motherfucker fuck, *end* this bitch." She sidestepped around him, dodging two construction workers sharing a cigarette next to a battered city pickup.

She looked up at the sun and realized a truth (all over again? how could she know if she'd felt this before? did it matter?)—the end *was* nigh, motherfucker. The end was written. Unless she got mowed down in a crosswalk by a Muni bus, unless she suddenly found her body was riddled with previously undiagnosed pancreatic cancer that would take her out in weeks, her ending was pretty much written. As she tucked a twenty into the can of a thin blond woman cradling a fat terrier puppy, she realized that strange feeling in the middle of her chest was relief.

Relief.

Nora would probably never have to have chemo.

She wouldn't break a hip at ninety.

She wouldn't develop debilitating rheumatoid arthritis.

She wouldn't lose her eyesight or her hearing.

Really, she didn't have to worry about *how* she would die, because she wouldn't be there for it. By then, the Nora she'd built—the one she'd thought was the very essence of herself— would be gone. Even her pleasure neurons would degrade from the aggregated amyloid, and she wouldn't take joy anymore from the things she once loved. The person inside her skin who would die wouldn't be *her*.

Who was a person without memory? *What* was a person without memory? Would she be like a dog, happy to wake and eat and sleep, or would she be more like a jellyfish, bobbing gently until she stung without warning?

There was nothing she could do. Nothing to fix.

That, in itself, might be . . .

It might be freedom.

Most likely, she wasn't going to die today, and really, wasn't that all anyone got?

Fuck it.

Isn't that what fearless people said? Fuck it. All of it.

Nora looked up into the sky. The fog had cleared completely, and the sky was azure. The air itself was so beautiful she wanted to push it into her pockets, fill her purse with it. Fall was San Francisco's best season, Nora's favorite. She could walk to Powell and hop a cable car to the water. She could buy flowers at the Ferry Building and ride the early boat home. She could do *anything*.

So she texted Mariana. *What are you doing?*

The answer was so quick her sister must have been looking at her phone. *Working. Why?*

Movie at the Metreon?

Which movie?

Does it matter?

A short pause. Nora imagined Mariana sitting in her office chair. (Her sister had an office. A real one. Her own. It still astonished her.)

I'll be there in fifteen. No butter.

Joy.

Nora wouldn't tell her about the firing. The retirement. Whatever it was that had just happened. Not yet.

Nora would let Mariana think there wasn't any butter on the popcorn even though it wouldn't be true. And even though she didn't like them, Nora would dump Raisinets into the bucket because Mariana loved them melted and salty.

Then they would both lean their heads back and watch the screen, shoulder to shoulder, bumping hands in the popcorn bucket, reveling in the unexpected piece of stolen time.

Chapter Fifty-six

On Halloween, a teacher's workday on which her daughter got out of class at noon, Nora and Ellie drove into the city to have lunch with Mariana, something they hadn't done in a long time. Nora tried to get her to wear a costume. "It'll be fun. Be Glinda. I love that costume on you." Ellie had said something kind like "Okay, maybe," but then she'd come down in a black tank and jeans. She held a cardigan in one hand, her backpack in the other.

"Oh," Nora said, disappointedly.

"But you're not wearing a costume, either," said Ellie.

It was the kid's job to wear the costume, not the mother's.

"Okay, then," said Ellie gamely. "Let's be Rory and Lorelei."

The Gilmore Girls. It had been their favorite show for years, and they'd watched it together over and over, marathoning whole seasons on long Saturdays while tucked up on the couch. Nora's heart rose happily. She looked down at herself. "Should I change? Would Lorelei wear capris?"

Ellie smiled. "Just grab a coffee cup. I'll hold a book. There, we're done."

It was Ellie's first time driving in the city. She was quiet most of the ride, which Nora appreciated. "You're doing great, kid," she said. "You're a natural." It helped that the Prius was an automatic and did well on hills.

Ellie didn't answer.

"Don't you feel like you're doing well?" asked Nora. "Getting past that psycho taxi was no joke."

There was a pause. Then, "Did you make me drive because you can't?"

Of course she had. The week before, Nora had driven into the city to get her final paycheck. She'd gotten lost on Market.

On Market. No one got lost on Market Street. *Tourists* didn't get lost on Market Street.

"Of course not."

"Because you can just tell me that. You don't have to praise my driving. I know I'm not that good."

Nora stomped her invisible brake. "No, *no*! Go left—that's a one-way."

Ellie steered quickly around two bicycles and turned left.

"Good job," said Nora. "Now do you believe I can still drive in the city?"

"Yeah," said Ellie. "I guess."

At the restaurant, one of the new hip places that Mariana always knew about, Nora ordered a Caesar salad. Ellie looked at her funny, but Nora continued, saying to the waiter, "Dressing on the side, please." True, she didn't like anchovies, but it was all she could think of that the restaurant would be sure to have. Every restaurant had some version of a Caesar.

The menu didn't make sense to her.

It had happened once before while she'd been out with Ellie, and that time she'd also been able to cover because that had just been a hamburger joint. Blue cheese with bacon. It didn't matter that the words curled back on themselves, twisted themselves like worms off the page, through her eyes, tunneling into her spongy, recalcitrant, increasingly more amyloid-blocked brain.

But she was able to fake it. That was all she wanted for now.

Nora glanced casually at the wine menu to see if the words had straightened out yet, but they hadn't. She didn't even know if it was the wine menu, actually. It was merely the right size, long and skinny, and the waiter (dressed in a one-piece giraffe costume) had left it on the table. Maybe it advertised desserts. It could be a religious tract for all she knew. The word *cognac* un-kinked at the bottom, dropping with a clink into her mind as she recognized it on the page.

"Oh, I love cognac," Nora said. Her voice was too loud. Too chipper. It used to be Nora could do chipper without even thinking about it. She'd thought it was an innate part of her personality. She'd been proud of it like it was something she'd inherited, like big eyes or perky breasts. She'd thought it would always *be* part of her.

But every day, it got harder. Every day she lost a piece of that chipperness. It dropped off her body—small chunks, one piece at a time—and someday she'd be a small block of bitterness with no memory, a piece of broken agate with no sparkle that someone took off the windowsill and threw out because they thought it was nothing more than trash.

Her sister was looking at her strangely. "It's not even two o'clock. You want cognac?"

"Mom?"

Nora laughed. "Come on, you two. I just said I liked it. I'm not going to order it." She swept her hair off her forehead with the backs of her fingers. When was the last time she'd gotten a haircut? She couldn't remember. "Although if I did, it wouldn't be the end of the world, since Ellie can drive me home."

Mariana broke a breadstick, letting the crumbs fall to her plate. "The biggest plus of a daughter old enough to drive. Cognac at lunch." Her voice was light, and Nora felt an unclenching in her chest, a releasing that came from gratefulness.

If they couldn't fix it, then they could still ignore it. That was a big something. When had she stopping thinking—hoping— they could fix it, fix her? When had that change occurred in her body and her thoughts? Was it outside the *Sentinel* after being fired, when she'd realized she would never die from cancer or break both hips? Was it at home when she'd stared up at the acoustic ceiling in the spare bedroom and realized she could tear it out herself, not worrying about the possible asbestos? Nora didn't know when the knowledge that she wouldn't escape her diagnosis had shifted inside her, but it felt, somehow, okay. It felt all right. Not ideal. But all right.

Nora took a breadstick out of the glass. "I can't believe they still do this. I don't think I've seen breadsticks on a table since *When Harry Met Sally*. Don't they know no one eats bread anymore?"

Ellie said, "They're gluten-free."

"No way."

"It's a gluten-free restaurant." It was said as if Nora won the award for most stupid mother in the universe.

Well, that must have been what it said on the menu. Shit.

"Still. It's weird. I feel like I'm waiting for Tom Hanks. Or was it Billy Crystal?"

"Not Harrison?" said Mariana.

"What?" said Nora as lightly as she could.

"How's it going with him? I haven't seen him since the camping trip."

Didn't her sister get her cues? The wide eyes, the slight shake of her head? She didn't want to talk about Harrison, who still wouldn't let go of the idea of moving in, who wanted to sleep with her every night. He wanted to harness himself to her like a strong ox paired with a weak one, not realizing he was bound to just go in circles that way. "I don't know," she said. "He's fine. Yeah."

"Come on, Mom."

Come on, *what*? Nora desperately wanted to ask what Ellie meant. *Come on, I know you're still fucking Harrison even though you try to hide that part from me? Come on, you're not making sense? Come on, no one in the history of the universe has ever liked a breadstick?*

"I lost my job," Nora said instead.

It was as if she'd set a gerbil on the table. Mariana reached forward—aiming for what?—and knocked the glass of bread-sticks over. Some fell to the tiled floor with a hollow clatter. Ellie stood halfway like she was going to run; then she sat again. She held out her hands, palms up, as if she were waiting for rain. Or praying. Everything on the table gave one solid jump, and Nora realized belatedly it had been her own knees hitting the under-side of the wood.

"What happened?" Mariana finally got the words out.

At the same time, Ellie said, "What did you *do*?"

There weren't words big enough to hold the apology she was looking for. "I'm sorry." She reached to grasp Ellie's still-upturned hands, but she yanked them away. "I'm so sorry." *Look at me.*

Ellie's eyes, though, were on her thick water glass, locked on it as if she were responsible for keeping the water inside it teleki-netically.

Nora turned to Mariana. "I'm sorry."

Mariana sat forward. "Don't be silly. There's absolutely nothing to be sorry for. How could they fire you?"

"It—"

"Don't they know you're going to sue their ass off?"

"What—"

"Americans with Disabilities Act. They haven't heard of it?"

"It was actually early retirement. Not required but strongly encouraged."

Mariana's eyes were wide with disbelief. "And you *took* it?"

"What else was I supposed to do?"

"Sue them. You've worked for the paper for one million years."

Yes, Nora was a dinosaur. "Thanks."

"It was their *job* to take care of you."

It was no one's job but her own.

"It was their job," fumed Mariana. "We should still sue."

"They're my friends."

"They're a corporation. They've never been your friend."

Nora thought again of the way Benjamin had helped her when Paul had left—he'd even once turned in a piece and put her byline on it. They'd been practically rookies then. He'd saved her job. She thought of the way Jerri had been putting banana muffins in her mailbox at work for weeks. They were triple wrapped, first in waxed paper, then foil over that, then tucked into a small ziplock.

"That's not fair to them. They tried." Benjamin had tried. He'd fought to keep her. She knew that he'd hated encouraging her to leave almost as much as she'd hated hearing him do it.

Goddamn, she hoped that was true.

"Does that mean we have to move?" Ellie's face was pale, like she was getting the flu.

"No!" That was exactly why Nora hadn't been going to tell either of them until . . . when? Until they noticed she hadn't visited the office for a month? Until they realized that they didn't hear her fingers clattering at the keyboard every morning until noon? "No, honey, we'll be all right."

"What about college?"

"Smith is still a go. We saved for that. Easy." Nora waved her hand, but Ellie looked even more worried. "You did send it in, right? The essay for early decision? You told me you did."

"Yeah," Ellie muttered. "I said I did, didn't I?"

Mariana's eyes were tight. Pulled. Maybe they both had fevers. "It's bullshit. Fuckers."

"Hey!" Nora gestured weakly toward Ellie.

Mariana didn't even blink. "What? They're fuckers, and that's fucking utter bullshit."

"They did their best."

"What about insurance?"

Ellie's face looked even paler now.

"Stop," said Nora. "We can talk about it later." Not in front of Ellie. She was only thirteen. She shouldn't have to deal with this kind of thing, shouldn't have to think about it.

Wait.

How old was Ellie?

Nora looked at her daughter's white face. "You had walking pneumonia. Remember?"

Ellie bit her bottom lip and said nothing. She shook her head slowly.

"Of course you don't. You were four. They thought it was just croup at first, and then maybe whooping cough. But it was pneumonia, and when your fever spiked, you had a seizure." It had been one of the worst things Nora had ever seen—her child launching backward, her neck at such an unnatural angle she knew she couldn't breathe, only the whites of her eyes showing, spittle frothing at the left corner of her mouth, her fingers splayed so hard they felt like pencils when Nora tried to gather her to her chest. She'd thought Ellie was dying, and even though the phone was in her hand, she couldn't remember the number for 911. She tried 119 first and then 199. The ambulance came when she got the number right, and took Ellie away—they wouldn't let her ride with them. "They said they didn't have the right seat belt for me," said Nora.

"Mama," said Ellie in a voice Nora had never heard before. "You're too pale. Way too pale."

"Nora," said Mariana sharply. "You'll come up with me after lunch"—she gestured vaguely upward as if her office were somehow suspended in the air above them—"and I'll have your office send all your paperwork to me."

Sixteen. That's how old Ellie was. "We don't need to do that."

"Yes, we do. We have to work out your insurance, your severance . . . God, what about your 401(k)?"

"I have long-term disability. It'll be fine." No, Ellie was seventeen. Wasn't she? There had been a birthday. All of them had gotten an extra year to live, an extra year to get closer to dying. Ellie wanting to be tested for the mutation . . . Never. Birthdays were a terrible idea. "How old are we?" she asked Mariana. "We're . . ." They couldn't be forty-five. That was impossible, but if she was doing the math in her head right, if she knew what year it was . . .

"We should go," said Ellie. She stood, scooping her sweater off the back of the chair as a grown-up woman would. "Let's go get her paperwork for you, Aunt Mariana, and then I'm going to take her home."

Her. As if she were the child. "Our food isn't here."

"I've got Kind bars in the office. Don't you worry about a thing, Ellie-belly. We can fix this," said Mariana. She stood, too, leaving only Nora still sitting. When had Mariana become so competent? So efficient and businesslike?

And her Ellie.

Nora barely recognized the young woman standing in front of her, and it had nothing to do with EOAD. Ellie was taller, straighter, her eyes clearer and more sober than they'd ever been. She grew up.

In that moment, because of her, her daughter grew up.

Ellie draped Nora's purse over her shoulder and tucked Nora's cardigan under her arm with her own, the two different woolen greens clashing.

Mariana nodded sharply. "I'll tell the waiter. Where is that damn giraffe?" She peered around the restaurant. "Wait for me out front?"

Ellie nodded. "Will do."

Nora didn't even think she'd ever heard Ellie use that phrase before. Or maybe it was the adult tone of it that was so surprising, the efficiency of it.

Her throat was tight. All of this, all the pain that pulled

between Mariana's and Ellie's eyes, the looks they were shooting each other, the barely held-back tears that swam in their eyes, all of it was because of her.

Will do.

A visceral joy swam through her empty, growling belly.

There sure was a hell of a lot to be said for seeing your daughter grow up in one split second.

She followed Ellie to the front of the restaurant. Her daughter was carrying Nora's sweater for her.

Yep, it sure was something. It was a terrible, dark, awful, wonderful something—a cocoon breaking open, the wet chrysalis wriggling for the first time into its butterfly shape. It was so beautiful Nora wanted to put it in a shadow box it and hang it on her wall at home so she could look at it as long as possible. It was, of course, the only Halloween costume appropriate for her gorgeous daughter, and the best part (and the worst part, too) was that Nora had gotten to see her wearing it.

Chapter Fifty-seven

Clive Wearing, the man who forgot everything but his wife and his music and who could hold on to only a few seconds at a time, wrote all day long. He covered the pages of his notebook with tiny, cramped words, hundreds, thousands, millions of words, most of them stating a version of, "I awoke for the first time, despite my previous claims." He would note the time and underline the statement, scoring it as the only truth he knew. Then he would read the earlier lines written in his own handwriting and scratch them out viciously—those times, the times he'd written that he was awake, those were untrue. Someone else must have written them, even though the words were in his handwriting. The only time he'd ever been awake was *now*, at this exact moment. Nora couldn't stop wondering about semantic versus episodic memory: How did he write? How did he string words together, when he didn't know who he was or how he'd gotten there? How did he think he knew the words to write? How did he remember what a pen was and how to pick it up? How did he remember how to shape a jagged *A* or add the three cross bars to a capital *E*? Was it pleasurable to him? Could he feel happy when he was putting pen to paper? Was it a last grasp at something that he hoped would put everything together again? Or was it a leftover tic, the respiration of ink? One day, using semantic memory, her episodic memory gone, would she remember how to use the coffee maker but not be able to remember what color her own eyes were?

Clive Wearing remembered almost nothing. But he remembered his wife, Deborah, even as she aged. Clive had fallen sick with encephalitis shortly after he married her, and his memory of her was always passionate, his immediate feeling upon seeing her that of new love.

What a glorious, terrible weight for her to bear.

Mariana had come over unexpectedly the night before for dinner. She'd asked for spaghetti, so Nora—surprised—had gotten out a pot to boil water. "No," her sister had said. "The twice-baked kind. Can't we just eat the leftovers from last night?"

Nora couldn't remember eating spaghetti within the last few months. But there in the refrigerator was the red casserole dish she always stored the leftover pasta in, ready to top with Parmesan and rebake until the cheese browned.

Nora hadn't said anything. She'd simply pulled it out and turned on the oven. Mariana texted someone, her lips pulled in as she battered the phone with her thumbs.

"Is that Luke?"

Mariana nodded.

"What are you telling him?" *She's losing it. Only a matter of time now.*

But Mariana had smiled. "Nothing. I just told him when I'd be home." She looked tired, Nora noticed. "I brought over your retirement package. I had my lawyer go over it, and—"

"You have a lawyer?" It had to be Luke's lawyer, didn't it?

"I hired one to set up the corporation and she's come in

handy a few times. Anyway, the package looks good, all but the length of terms. We were talking, and—"

"How's BreathingRoom?" Nora hadn't asked in a while. Had she?

Mariana smiled. "We hit a million."

A million what? Nora tried to think. Dollars? People? Pencils? Puppies?

Her sister clarified, "A million subscribers. For the free version, anyway. But the paid version is already at more than forty thousand. We're making money." A pause. "A lot of money."

"Holy shit." Swearing felt good. Why hadn't Nora used to do it? She couldn't remember.

Mariana's smile turned into laughter. "Right? A million! A freaking million! I hired three more staffers and—get this—a full-time publicist. She got us onto NPR, and next week she's pitching a package to United Airlines. They're thinking about using the relaxation module for one of their channels for nervous fliers. Is that wild?"

Nora hugged Mariana so tightly it hurt. It was wild, yes. And wonderful and amazing. And it was unnerving. In the pit of Nora's stomach, a tiny piece of jealously unspooled, cold and metallic. Her sister was turning into what she was supposed to be, who Nora had always believed Mariana could be. And Nora was flaking apart, iron left to rust in acid rain. "Well, goddamn," Nora heard her inappropriate self say. "Let's celebrate."

After they'd opened a bottle of champagne (Ellie got half a glass), after they'd eaten spaghetti for what was apparently the second time that week (what else had she forgotten?), Nora said, "I want to show you something amazing." She led Mariana and Ellie into her office to show them the YouTube video of Clive Wearing, who by now almost felt like an old friend.

"Look!" she said, turning and pointing at the point at which he greeted his wife with such joy. "Isn't that something?"

Ellie, her eyes wide, her cheeks pale, said, "That's *horrible*."

She turned and ran down the stairs so fast Nora worried she might fall.

"No," was all Mariana said.

"Wait—" Nora stretched out her fingers, but Mariana had already followed Ellie out of the tiny room.

"Wait," she said to no one, alone again. It *was* something.

The week before (the month before? time was getting slipperier, as if it were wet and mossy), she'd gone to an EOAD support group, held in the basement of a church. Only four others had come. Marcia, a woman of about sixty who'd lost her husband at fifty-five to the disease, had been the facilitator. One woman had been driven by her daughter. She'd sat, slack-faced, not appearing to know where or who she was. A fifty-two-year-old man had chattered almost nonstop, as if trying to prove he could still converse. The other man, Dirk, had proclaimed it was his last meeting.

He'd thumped his hands onto his thighs. "You want to know why I'm not coming back? I can't remember where I am half the day. I have to write down every single thing I need to do, and then I forget to look at my list and nothing gets done. My wife can't look me in the eye, says I'm not the person she married. Of course I'm not. None of us are. We thought we were one person, and then it turns out we're just idiots with no memory." He stood. "I came to say I'm done. And thank you, Marcia. You're a sweet woman, and I'm sorry for your loss, but coming to this group has been like being on deathwatch. One person is fine, then they get worse, and their skin sinks in, and their eyes go blank like Jennifer's there"—Jennifer didn't even look at him—"and they stop coming, and then they *die,* and then another person doesn't remember that person at all, then we all go to the funeral and instead of thinking about that person getting slung down into a hole, we're thinking about what they'll sing at our service, what our friends will wear, how often they'll think about us after we're rotting in the dirt. I'm fucking *sick* of this group's funerals."

Nora couldn't breathe. She dropped most of a needle's worth of stitches and didn't look down at them.

Marcia said, "Dirk, I'm—"

"No," he said. "Let me go. At least I'm coherent enough to make an exit, and I'm not going to have a funeral, so this is the last time." Dirk looked down at Nora, her hands still frozen in place. "Have they told you about the loss of impulse control yet?"

She'd read about it. Someday she'd lose her bladder while in the kitchen. She'd argue about nothing for no reason. Nora had spent her whole life reaching for control, loving the feel of clean, tidied surfaces under her fingertips, and to know she'd lose all that . . .

"What they don't tell you is that now you have an excuse to do whatever the fuck you want."

"What?"

Then the man named Dirk leaned over and kissed Nora on the mouth. His lips stayed still, not asking for anything, but they were strong. She smelled coffee, and—faintly—putty, as if he'd been working with wood before the meeting. The kiss was over as fast as it had begun. Nora touched her lower lip. Damn it, she shouldn't be grinning. But she was.

"There," he said. "That's the perk. My gift to you—the knowledge that you have a get-out-of-jail-free card. Use it now before you forget you have it." He tipped an imaginary hat to them and left, bumping open the door with his shoulder, his hands tucked into his sweatshirt pockets. They heard his whistle long after he was out of sight.

Now Nora came back to where she was: in her office, Clive Wearing talking in front of her.

That was the amazing thing. Clive Wearing's brain, so damaged that it held almost *nothing*, still held this: love. Perfect love.

That was everything. It was the thing Nora clung to most of all. In the middle of the night, deep in the throes of the three a.m. terror that made her wonder if she was forgetting how to breathe, that image of Clive Wearing was what got her through. She knew that no matter how the cells in her brain failed, no matter what dropped away from her, she wouldn't forget the way it felt to look into her daughter's eyes, which were the exact color of the piece of green beach glass she'd had in her pocket every day for weeks now. Nora needed to believe, even if she was nothing but a body in a bed, that if Mariana crawled in and wrapped her arms around her, she would know her sister. That she would feel love and warmth. That she would *know*, for that moment, peace.

It was impossible to continue otherwise, without that hope.

So Nora believed. She watched the clip of the video over and over, until she'd memorized every word. "Oh, *look* who's come. Oh, darling."

And again, seven seconds later. "Oh, *look* who's come. Oh, darling." Clive kissed his wife, musically and with great enjoyment. "Can we dance?"

"Oh, *look* who's come. Darling. Can we dance?"

Chapter Fifty-eight

EXCERPT,
**WHEN ELLIE WAS LITTLE:
OUR LIFE IN HOLIDAYS,**
PUBLISHED 2011 BY NORA GLASS

Thanksgiving

When Ellie was little, we had pizza for Thanksgiving.

It was the first Thanksgiving for us to be on our own, and I wasn't thankful for anything. Not one single thing. The Civic had died (again—that time it was a radiator so rusted it looked like a cheese grater). The washing machine had turned toes up, sending a biblical flood across the kitchen floor, and, because I was riding the bus at the time with Ellie, I didn't get the water up in time, and it warped the kitchen linoleum. The clothes dryer was working, but it smoked a little even when it was on low, and I was too scared to use it. That left me washing our clothes in the bathtub and line drying them, heavy from not being spun first. The clothesline itself kept breaking free of the tree I'd tied it to with what I thought was a square knot (but obviously wasn't), so just when I thought I was done with laundry for the day, I'd go out and find our soggy clothing lying in mud puddles. Then all my hand washing in the tub created a clog that I couldn't fix with the cheap plastic snake I'd bought at the hardware store, so when Ellie or I showered, we had to stand in calf-deep water. She didn't like it. I told her to buck up, but she was four. Four-year-olds don't buck up. They smile, they jump like baby goats, they sparkle and rumble and twirl and twinkle, but they do not understand bucking up or why it is sometimes necessary.

Then the stove died, refusing to heat to temperatures of more than two digits, and the toaster went up in a blackened bagel accident.

The refrigerator was the last straw. When I came home to find warm milk and all my carefully planned frozen meals defrosted and gray, I sat on the kitchen floor and sobbed. I had enough money in the bank to pay the mortgage and the utilities, and no more. Alimony and child support were late and often slimmer than they should have been. I couldn't afford to replace a single broken thing.

Really, all I wanted to replace was myself, and I couldn't afford that, either. I wanted the new, shiny version of Nora Glass. I was freelance copyediting as well as working at the paper, and I routinely stayed up past two in the morning to finish a job that would pay for Ellie's day care. Then I got up at six to get us ready for the next round. The woman I saw in the mirror was too skinny, with dark shadows under her eyes. The humor that used to dance there was gone. Ellie had complained that she wanted to live with her aunt, "who always laughs like you used to and has cookies for me."

To this I snapped, "Yeah? Well, those are store-bought." It was my ultimate insult.

I wasn't good at divorce. I wanted to figure out the method to it, the reason behind it. If I could figure out where I'd gone wrong, then I could fix whatever it was and start over. I didn't want Paul back—once my heart started beating again about six months after he left, I was so angry with him I wouldn't have taken him back if he'd showed up covered with hundred-dollar bills. I wanted *myself* back. I'd lost myself, somewhere, along the way. I'd left myself behind like an empty popcorn box, like a sweater forgotten on a train.

No, it was worse than leaving something behind.

I'd failed.

Divorce is, at its very core, the ultimate failure. You can blame many things on circumstances: you lost your condo because of the recession, you lost your job because of downsizing, your album failed because of distribution interruptions. But divorce? You just picked the wrong person. You were wrong, all the way around, about him and, worse, about yourself. You did it all wrong, and there's no absolution. Even if you're both better off being apart, when you say, "I'm divorced," it means, "I failed."

My bread always rose. I got out every stain. My curtains always hung straight. I hated failure more than anything.

One night as I was roughly drying Ellie with a towel I'd have to wash in the tub that took hours to drain, she said with four-year-old honesty, "You used to be fun, Mama. I liked you better then." She wrapped her arms around my neck, smacked a kiss to my cheek, and raced away, bare bottomed and joyful.

The day after she told me I wasn't fun was Thanksgiving. I would *be* fun, by god. I would find where my fun was hiding if it killed me. Hand in hand, we walked to the corner store and bought one turkey breast. I called my twin, even though I knew she had plans with her boyfriend, and left her a message. On our walk home, I pushed Ellie in the swing at the playground until my arms were sore.

At home, I dug through the boxes in the garage until I found what I was looking for: a toaster oven Paul and I had received as a wedding gift and had never used. Ellie was enchanted by the two dials and the high-pitched pings it made. She loved its loud ticking. I cut two potatoes into small pieces and cooked them next to the breast. When they were done, I mashed them, adding salt and the cheap margarine I had started buying. I cut the turkey into two pieces.

The front door burst open. My twin sister, Mariana, tumbled in. She was bleeding from both elbows and both knees, but she was laughing. "I couldn't get a ride from Robby's house, but I borrowed a bike. I kept falling off. I don't think I've ridden one since we were kids. But I'm here! I rode all the way here!"

I boggled at her. "Robby lives in Fremont." A bike ride that length would take four hours, at least.

"Okay, I took BART. And then two buses. I couldn't get the bus bike rack down, though, and two guys had to help me. Then I fell off again and a pizza delivery guy almost ran me over with his car, and he felt so bad about it that he gave me two pizzas because they were made wrong. One's Hawaiian and the other is pepperoni and green onions, which is weird but we can handle that, right? They're bungee-corded to the rack. Ellie-belly, wanna help me carry them in?" Ellie, who was already jumping up and down, squealed in delight.

Together at my big family table, we ate small bites of turkey and potatoes and enormous bites of pizza, using our hands for everything (even the mashed potato!) just because we could. We guzzled sodas I'd found in the garage when I'd been looking for the toaster oven. We let Ellie draw all over the driveway with all the chalk colors, and then we spent an hour playing hopscotch. We played jump rope. After she fell asleep on the couch, my sister and I talked into the late hours over a bottle of cheap wine she'd miraculously managed not to break any of the times she'd fallen off the bike. All three of us slept in my bed that night, together.

And I was thankful again, for everything.

Chapter Fifty-nine

*D*ylan was being a gigantic asshat. Yeah, the Incursers were on the run and the Healers were suddenly on top of the social strata, but they'd talked about that potential universe switch a million times—the game turned on a dime, and by next week the Velocirats could be calling all the shots and they'd all be doomed, Incurser and Healer alike. It didn't matter what plotline Ellie wrote, or how many people chose to play it, if the game's creators hit the override button on the universe.

Don't pick that, Ellie typed as Dyl attempted to grab a flame from a low blue tree.

He ignored her, lifting out the flame and then doing a pain dance as it blackened his arm to his elbow.

I told you so. Only Healers could carry the flame. She had a ball of fire now under her cloak that she hadn't even told him about yet.

Let's go skinny-dipping!

Fine. It was silly, but he loved going there, so she would walk with him through the glade to get to the hot spring. If you walked right at it and at the last minute hit a jump sequence, then your character's clothes would disappear as you cannonballed into the water. Not that you could see junk or anything—the game makers blurred out the genitalia—but it was still kind of funny.

Four other "couples" were already in the springs. How many of them actually knew each other in real life? She wondered if any of them had actually met and actually liked each other. They couldn't possibly be the only two players to ever get together in real life. The game was already huge—there'd been a con dedicated to it in Houston just the month before. There must be other couples in the world who owed their relationship to this purple and green world where Healers couldn't swim but, given the right plants, could fly when necessary.

```
Hey, what's wrong?
```

What? Ellie made Addi tuck a Lopi flower behind her ear.

```
What's up with you?
```

Nothing.

```
Seems like more than that. You want
me to call?
```

No, she didn't.

Ellie hadn't seen Dylan for three weeks, not since she'd met him and his band at a recording studio in Emeryville. He'd been different. Yeah, they were recording a demo and she knew it was important—maybe it was even the equivalent of her applying to colleges—but she still wanted to be . . . looked at. To be seen. He'd practically acted like she wasn't there, just kept fiddling with his guitar, even when they were on breaks. And afterward, when he'd driven her to BART (instead of across the bridge and home), he'd kissed her differently. Like she was . . . something he expected.

They'd had sex three times now. Once at the hotel, which was the best time. Once in his car, which was uncomfortable but okay, and once in his bed while his roommates were chilling in the other room completely baked out of their minds.

Had she done it wrong? Was she bad in bed? Did she not know how to do it right? How would she know if that was true? He was sweet, of course. Dylan was always sweet. And he'd seemed happy; it was pretty obvious he'd been satisfied. (Had she been? She wasn't quite sure. Why was it so confusing? Wasn't it supposed to be a big bang followed by giddiness? Instead, it was kind of awkward and then awesome and then awkward again. God, she really must not be doing it right.)

Dylan had been supposed to come over tomorrow for Thanksgiving—they'd planned it weeks before—but he'd IM'd her that morning and said his brother was coming to town and was taking him out to dinner.

Ellie hadn't even known he had a brother. She knew about his sister, but not a brother.

In the game, Dyl ran up the side of the riverbank (his clothes miraculously reattaching as he went) and kept going. Addi followed him. Dyl ran past the edge of town toward the Hinters. His avatar paused as he juggled two swords.

What are we doing? she typed. Maybe they'd be the first to ever have a "talk" in *Queendom*.

Running.

No. I mean you and me.

Nothing, Ellie. He rarely called her by her real name in the game. *We just ARE.* Dyl ran faster, Addi at his heels. *Tell me a story about where we're going now.*

She could do that. That was, maybe, the only thing she was good at. *Once upon a time,* she started as she hit the command to keep Addi running (she'd pass Dyl eventually; she was just a little bit faster than he was), *at the end of the world, there were two runners on a mission to save the Dragon Queen.* The sky went red over their racing avatars, getting more orange the closer they got to the edge of the game. *Every night, as the sun fell, a great spell would fall on the land . . .*

```
Wanna go back to the springs?
```

Hey. It's my story.

```
Yeah, well, Josh just texted me and
he's going to try to find the
Queen's eggs, too.
```

No! The fewer people looking for the eggs the better. *Did you tell him that's what we were doing out here?*

```
Not really . . .
```

The motion detector went on outside the living room window. Ellie jumped and leaned to look. Her mother wandered past, in the direction of Harrison's house. Shit. She hadn't even heard her leave the kitchen. Ellie didn't type to tell Dylan where she was going—she just raced to the back door. The door was unlocked, the screen door standing open.

Ellie watched while her mother walked across the grass under the moon. She opened her mouth to call her, to say something, but then she saw Harrison's porch light go on. He stepped into its yellow pool and opened his arms.

Her mother folded herself into them.

Ellie's shoulders dropped, and her stomach did, too. She was glad—truly—that her mother had Harrison.

But her mom also had Mariana.

And Mariana had Luke.

Who did that leave her with?

Inside, she typed, *Hey, it's late. I'm going to bed.* She sat at the dining room table and crossed her fingers on both hands. Sometimes he liked to go to sleep at the same time she did. Dyl came into Addi's hut and stood as near to her as his avatar could. Then, with the violins softly playing, they'd sleep as close to each other as two *Queendom* players could.

          K. Night.

That was it. Not even an *XO*. Nothing else.

Ellie's back ached with something that felt dull and heavy. Her knees were stiff as she walked up the stairs. On the landing, she looked at the series of twin pictures hung on the wall. The simply framed pictures showed her mother and Aunt Mariana at various ages, draped over each other, laughing. Always laughing. Sometimes they wore matching clothes ironically, and sometimes they were just themselves. But they were together in every single photo, and they had a story for each one, too. *That was the year we had chickenpox. Remember how itchy those sweaters were?*

In the school pictures of Ellie that hung farther down the hall, chronicling her most awkward ages, she was alone. Just like she was now.

In her room, Ellie set her closed computer on her desk. She tried to rub the muscle in her neck that ached, but she couldn't quite reach it.

Automatically, she brought up the *Queendom* forums page. She could plunge into talk about the game, and that would make her feel better. It always did. She wouldn't be alone if she were in the computer, bouncing Healing recipes off other people, helping newbies figure out how to transform.

Ellie looked down at her hands, the fingertips poised on the enter button.

For the first time in months, she turned the game off. She didn't need the game to take care of her, just like she didn't need her mother to be home or her aunt to watch out for her. She could handle it on her own. She'd sleep with no music tonight, with no soft glow from her Healer's hut to bathe her. Ellie pulled up the covers and shut her eyes resolutely, as if she could will herself to rest. Maybe when she woke in the morning she'd feel different. Stronger. Older.

Maybe she'd feel less alone.

She crossed her fingers again even though they didn't have a good track record and squinched her eyes more tightly closed.

Chapter Sixty

Nora said, "Shit," the word deep and completely heartfelt. The turkey was rotten. The goddamned Thanksgiving turkey was rotten to its core.

"Shit, shit, *shit*." The word was also an apt description of the way the turkey smelled. She'd put the turkey in four hours before and she'd been smelling something bad for two. She'd blamed Ellie's shoes at first. Seventeen-year-old girls normally smelled like many things—Abercrombie perfume and Maybelline Baby Lips—but Ellie had legendarily bad-smelling sneakers. She didn't seem to care, either. When she was Ellie's age, Nora had been horrified by the very idea of any natural smell emanating from her body. She'd fought her underarms with the spray deodorant from the dollar store and, with her babysitting money, she'd bought extra cans that she tucked in her school locker and kept in the bottom of her backpack. Both Nora and Mariana had argued over the baby powder in the mornings before school, tipping it into their plastic flats, hoping that that day would be the day it worked. Instead, they'd only left sweet-and-sour white footprints on the locker room floor as they padded to the gym showers they pretended to take.

Ellie, since she'd gotten old enough to fight body odors, had seemed blithely unconcerned. "Mom! Smell my feet! Aren't they *rank*?" She would take off her shoes when her feet got hot whether she was in the Prius or in the kitchen. Nora knew that Samantha and Vani teased her mercilessly about it, and still Ellie just smiled and shrugged. The Odor-Eaters Nora bought her sat encased in plastic on her desk.

Even on the days Ellie forgot to wear deodorant—which were more days than Nora could honestly understand—she seemed strangely thrilled with her animal scent. "Can you smell me, Mom? I'm *so* foul. I smell like this guy in my seventh period named Jim Wells on a hot day after he's done lacrosse *and* basketball practice."

The Thanksgiving turkey smelled like Ellie's feet and old roadkill and cat shit and, possibly, Jim Wells.

And apparently, a smell that offended her daughter *did* exist. Ellie entered the kitchen with her blue scarf pulled up around her face.

Her voice was muffled. "What *is* that, Mom?"

Nora hadn't been prepared to admit that it was the turkey. It couldn't be. Not this year. "I thought I'd used too much rosemary . . ."

"Rosemary smells nice. Whatever *this* is"—Ellie made a one-handed gesture in the air—"is toxic. I think it might kill me."

Nora snapped, "Then get out of the kitchen." She heaved the turkey out of the oven, appreciating its heft. She'd spent almost forty dollars on this freaking thing. "Maybe the egg in the stuffing is bad. Or maybe it was the bread I used?"

"What did you do?"

Nowadays it was always her. It was always Nora screwing

things up. This time it wasn't her, though. "No, it has to be the stuffing."

"But I helped you make that. It didn't stink."

What Ellie meant by helping was that she had stood near her mother, her cell phone in her hand, texting furiously to Samantha while she snacked on the toasted focaccia Nora used to start the stuffing. Some things didn't change.

Ellie pulled the scarf tighter around her face. "It smells like death."

Nora bit her lip and, with it, the retort she wanted to spit at her daughter. It *was* death—that was the point. Americans celebrated being thankful for life by butchering something, cutting it down in its full-breasted happiest prime. "It can't be the bird," she said. "I won't let it be." Surely she'd be able to pull out whatever the offending thing was and throw it away. "Oh! Maybe I didn't pull out the giblets."

"You did."

"No, I don't think I did."

"Remember? You said you wished we still had Buster so you could give him the heart."

"I did?" Nora felt a spasm of fear low inside her. She set the turkey carefully on the wooden cutting block of the island. "Sure. Right. But maybe I didn't get it all."

"Are you sure you didn't leave this on the doorstep for, like, a week?"

"Don't be silly."

Ellie's voice was softer. "No. Really. Did you . . . maybe . . . buy it last month? Or something?"

Nora held up one oven-mitted hand. "Just stop. Let me figure this out." She *hated* that she couldn't remember when she'd bought the turkey. Or even where she'd bought it, for that matter. She knew how much she'd paid . . . or was that last year's bird that she remembered? *Shit.*

Ellie hopped up on the counter next to the sink, even though Nora had asked her approximately seventy thousand times not to—the tile would get weak eventually—and watched. "I don't know why I'm even staying in here," Ellie said through her scarf. "But it's like I can't turn away. I have to know the disgusting end of this. This is worse than when you hit that mama bird with the car. Remember?"

Of course she remembered. *Not of course. Never of course, not anymore.* "You are *not* helping." Nora took her biggest wooden spoon and jabbed it into the bubbling, noxious cavity. "It's got to be the stuffing."

"If it was the turkey itself, wouldn't you have noticed after you defrosted it? Like, it wouldn't go into the oven and just start stinking."

Nora closed her eyes. She couldn't remember defrosting it. Goddamn it, she was *good* at this part of being a mother. The home-baked cookies and the healthy banana bread with the flax-seed oil snuck in and the caramel apples at Halloween and birthday cakes in any and every shape—Nora was good at doing it and good at helping other people to do the same. Thanksgiving was her high holiday, the most holy of all shined-silver days.

Not this year. The stuffing was in a large yellow bowl, reeking of bloody mayhem, and the stench was only getting worse.

Nora's eyes watered, and from her perch on the counter Ellie choked.

Taking her favorite, sharpest knife from the block, Nora held it over the bird's breast. This was a moment to be savored at a table where your loved ones were gathered around you. Carving was the best part of Thanksgiving—the moment that everyone watched, salivating in appreciation. She should carve into the meat at the long dining table, candles flickering, wine sparkling in her wedding crystal.

Not under the compact fluorescent glare of the kitchen lighting. Not while her daughter gagged.

She held the knife for a moment in the air and then plunged it into the bird.

The turkey fell apart with a wet groan. The breath of it rushing out was enough to make Nora stagger backward.

"Oh, no! Mom!" Ellie's scarf was almost wrapped around her head now and she pulled her knees to her chest.

"Get your feet off the counter!" The demand was automatic.

"Jesus. Do you have a nose? How are you not dying right now? Who *cares* about my feet? My toes smell like roses compared to that nightmare."

"You're right. You're totally right." Nora picked up another oven mitt and picked up the pan, all twenty pounds of bird and metal. She nodded to the kitchen door. Ellie hopped down and opened it for her.

Outside, the afternoon was warm, one of those gifts the Bay Area doled out liberally in the late fall. The big-leaf maple that hung over the backyard had turned a glorious red and orange, seemingly overnight. Through the wooden fence Nora could hear her other neighbors—the not-Harrison neighbors—enjoying their three-o'clock gin and tonic, in which they indulged every day, holiday or not. The familiar clink of ice in their shaker didn't calm her—the sound just rattled her nerves more.

"Get the garbage can lid," she said.

Ellie, still barefoot, danced around her to open it. While she held it open, Nora dumped the whole thing.

"You're not even saving the roasting pan?" Ellie said incredulously.

"We can buy another one."

Then, without a single word, Nora walked back inside the house and slammed the door, leaving Ellie outside alone. She had to get used to it sometime.

Chapter Sixty-one

By four o'clock, when Nora heard Mariana enter, Ellie was on the couch again, playing her game. But that was okay. Ellie had cleaned up the whole turkey mess while Nora had been taking deep breaths in her bedroom, trying to remember—trying so hard to figure out what had happened to the turkey. Ellie had cleaned up the stuffing and washed the spoon that Nora had used on it. A smell of bleach hung in the air with a toxic tang, almost canceling out the scent of freshly baked bread (Nora had gotten up at dawn to set it to rise) and pumpkin spice (ice cream cake, since no one in the family liked pie).

The smell of death was gone.

Mariana swung into the kitchen with a green shopping bag under her arm. "I got three bottles of Martinelli's, two of wine, and one good Scotch, which Harrison and I will enjoy even if you don't."

Nora reached for the list she'd made of things for Mariana to pick up. "Where's Luke?"

Mariana didn't meet her eyes. "Where's Harrison?"

Nora changed the game. "Where are the mashed potatoes?"

Mariana stared. "I don't know. Where are they?"

"No, no, no. We have no turkey, we *have* to have mashed potatoes."

"Okay." Mariana's voice was cautious. "I can make some for you. That's not a problem."

"I don't *have* any. That's the problem. You were supposed to bring them."

"No, honey." Her sister pushed her fingers through her perfectly cut layers. "You asked me to bring drinks."

Nora looked down at the list. "And the potatoes. You make the best ones. Of course I asked you."

Mariana shook her head, as if she were giving up.

That head shake. That was the shake Nora was seeing more and more often, from Ellie, from her sister, from the new doctor at Stanford. As if whatever they were talking about wasn't worth arguing about anymore, as if it were better to give in to her ridiculous beliefs, as if arguing with her would break her.

Potatoes weren't on the list she'd given to Mariana.

Mariana said, "I'll just run to the store."

Nora shook her head. "They'll be out."

"They'll have a potato or two left."

"They'll be closed."

"Safeway's open till five."

"We don't have *time* . . ." Nora's throat closed over the words, sealing shut so that she couldn't say the next ones.

"Nora . . ."

Out. She had to get out. She couldn't be here—she felt like she was dying. Right there. In the kitchen she loved so much, in the jail it had become.

She was already out the door, racing across her yard, before she even knew she was moving. She pounded on Harrison's back door and then, too impatient to wait for him, barreled through it.

He was in the upper bedroom. From the chair he sat in, he'd have been able to see everything: her throwing away the turkey, her pell-mell dash across the lawn.

He kept his eyes on the window. He didn't turn around.

"Why are you here?" she demanded.

"I live here." He sounded tired, as if he hadn't slept.

"Why aren't you at my house?"

"I could ask you the same thing."

No, that wasn't fair. Just because she wouldn't let him move in didn't give him the right . . . "It's Thanksgiving. We always do Thanksgiving together. You bring someone who can't do long division. We make fun of her behind her back. It's tradition." She heard the joke fall flat. This year the only person he was dating was her, and pretty soon, she wouldn't remember how to do any kind of math at all.

Harrison didn't laugh. "Tradition," he echoed. He finally turned, and she could see that he'd been crying. There were no tears on his face, his eyes weren't swollen—it was just there, in the set of his lips. She could tell. No one else in the world would probably be able to.

"I can't do this without you."

"What?" He gripped the arm of the chair. "What can't you do without me?"

Nora's mouth dried.

"Host a turkey dinner?"

She tried to smile. "About that turkey—"

"Or live? You can't live without me?"

The words were stuck behind her gullet, words in eggs that would smash all over the grate of Harrison's truck.

He went on. "What, you can't die without me?"

Fear, frantically electric, zipped through her, leaving a white-hot burn. "Just come over—"

"And then be shuffled away? Across the lawn? Maybe you'll

come get a quickie after dinner, after Ellie's in bed playing her game? You think that's good enough for me?"

"No . . . I know it's—"

"You don't seem to know anything. I thought you'd be better at this."

The words were huge and completely, unutterably unfair. "At *dying*?"

"Fuck, Nora. I thought you'd be better at *living*. You've always been the best one at it. Better than anyone else. You're good at everything, you make everything look easy, but you refuse to look this in the face—"

Bullshit. What did he think she did at four in the morning? When she couldn't sleep, when her eyes fell on the digital clock and wondered how many seconds closer she'd be to death when (if) she finally fell asleep again—did he think she was just lying there thinking about how to perfect an apple pie crust? "I look at it every day. *I* face it. Not you. You have *no* idea what I'm going through."

"I know that!" Harrison stood and coughed. He looked older, suddenly, every year of his fifty-one. When had he become so gaunt? "And whose fault is that? It's not mine, Nora. You shut me out, and that's fine. I can wait for you to let me in, and I can't imagine how hard it is for you. But for you to hide me, to hide what we have together . . ." He held up a hand, his palm creased and so well-known to Nora she could trace the lines on it with her eyes closed. "Ellie knows we're still trying to stay hidden."

Of course Ellie knew. "It's just important that she doesn't feel . . . that I'm not . . ."

"Do you want to go through this with me or without me?"

"With you." The words were reflexive and true.

"Then let me stay with you. Or stay here. I can't be—" Harrison put one hand backward to lean on the chair. "I can't be in this halfway, when it's convenient, when you feel strong enough to be with me."

That was irony for you. When Nora was with Harrison, naked under his sheets, his skin warm against hers, that was the only time she felt free to be weak. Did he really not know that? "I don't want to talk about this on Thanksgiving. My day's been shitty enough."

"That's your decision to make." Harrison sat back down in his chair, his gaze out the window.

"Don't be like this," she said. "Don't do this today."

He didn't turn his head to watch her leave the room.

When she was on the lawn, when she glanced up at the window, he was gone.

Chapter Sixty-two

"*S*pam? *Mom*."

Mariana said, "You're joking." It wasn't a question.

Nora wanted, inappropriately, to laugh. Thirty minutes ago, when she'd plated the Spam (oh, so carefully and thinly sliced, garnished with fresh cranberries and juniper sprigs), she'd sent a picture of it to Twitter with the caption, "Surprisingly and suddenly thankful for canned meat. What are you thankful for today?" Within seconds, the replies were flooding in—jokes and serious answers alike. They weren't, in fact, the only family in America having Spam for Thanksgiving. Two families in Hawaii had replied saying musubi was on their holiday menu, and another woman said she served it with chopped pickles, something Nora couldn't imagine.

"I don't mean to be picky," said Mariana, "but have you lost your mind?"

"Yep," said Nora truthfully. She'd lost quite a lot. Losing her mind was honestly lower on her list right now than losing

Harrison. Why did she feel so cheerful? Like laughing? Was this the inappropriate response the literature said she'd feel? If so, she was in.

"Let's go out," said Mariana. "Restaurants are open. Come on, honey, we shouldn't have to eat meat that cost less than forty-nine cents."

Ellie crossed her arms. "I know you tried, Mom, but we could totally still go out. Or we could get pizza? Like that year you put in the Ellie book?"

"Do you remember that, chipmunk?"

Ellie closed her eyes slowly, and when she opened them, she looked more like Paul than she ever had. Nora remembered why she'd fallen in love with him. Those deep-sea eyes that changed color along with the sky. "Sometimes I think I do," Ellie said.

"Good enough." Nora pulled the white platter closer and helped herself to two pieces. "I don't want to go out and face the rest of the world. Let's just eat the fixings, then." It was just getting funnier. "Minus the mashed potatoes, of course."

Cutting herself a piece of the cold, Jell-O–like meat, Nora was about to put a bite in her mouth when her daughter interrupted her.

"We're not even going to pray?"

Nora's fork stilled in midair. "Pardon?"

"Grace. We always say grace."

"Fine." Prayer. It couldn't hurt. "Would you say it, then?"

Ellie bowed her head and said, "No. You have to."

Heck of a time for her daughter to find religion. Nora closed her eyes and said as quickly as she could, "Lord, thank you for this food, and nourish it to our bodies." Would that be enough for her daughter? Because Nora didn't think she had much more thankfulness left to give.

Mariana, though, continued it for her. "And thank you for this past year, and everything we've been given. Thank you for the love of family and friends, and bless the year to come."

Nora, her eyes open again, saw Ellie nod.

"Amen."

"Amen."

Mariana smiled, her teeth beautiful and even. With her tongue, Nora touched her own upper left incisor. Once upon a time, Mariana's tooth had been equally crooked. When had she gotten that fixed? Was that something that Nora had once known?

Where did the knowledge go, when it left her mind? She held out her hands and looked at the ridges that formed the whorls on her fingertips. Her body knew how to make these. But her brain didn't know how to cook a non-rotten turkey anymore. Apparently.

"Now," said Mariana, leaning forward, putting her elbows on the table. "Tell me why we're eating the only foodstuff lower on the food chain than plastic bags?"

Nora poked the cranberry sauce on her plate. "I'm losing it."

"You just need a bit more sleep. Sleep helps everything."

"I can't remember the date unless I write it on my hand."

"You've been doing that for months, Mom." Ellie's eyes were worried. Ellie's eyes should never look like that. And it was Nora's fault.

"I want to do two things," she said, her throat almost closing again. "And I need help."

Mariana said, "We know. We talked about it, remember? We're here."

"No, you don't know. I didn't tell you what they were." They needed to let her talk. It was her turn. Nora knew what she needed. She'd known for a while. It was time to say it. She put a smile on her face, and the inappropriate giggle that had been hiding in her chest burbled upward. "I want to have fun."

She saw Mariana look at Ellie. Mariana said, "Okay. Of course . . ."

"No, really. *Big* fun. That Thanksgiving we had nothing, the year everything broke? I wasn't fun. I feel like I'm in that same place, and I need to get out of it."

Ellie bounced a little in her chair. "Okay! Like what?"

"Bucket-list stuff. Like, maybe the northern lights."

"Oh!" Ellie clapped and Nora could see her, suddenly, at every age, making that same rapturous face. At three, skinned elbows and happy eyes. At seven, gaps in her teeth but the same overjoyed expression. Now, at—Nora thought very hard—at seventeen. Gorgeous. Luminous in her body, which, please, God (Nora prayed for real this time: *please*, God), wouldn't betray her, ever.

"And Cuba. I've always wanted to go to Cuba," Nora went on.

Mariana leaned forward. "Let me pay."

"No, no . . ." She hadn't gotten that far, hadn't gotten to planning the financial aspect of the trips, but it would work out, wouldn't it? She'd sell another book—did she have time to? She could—

"I have the money." Mariana grinned at Ellie. "I have so much money. It's like someone opened a fire hose in my bank account."

"You have to put that back into your business." Nora refolded the napkin on her lap. She knew how business worked. You spent money to make money.

"I do. I have been. And I've paid Luke back. And I'm *still* making bank. And nothing"—Mariana covered Nora's hand with her own—"would make me happier than taking the three of us around the world."

Would that be okay? Was it allowed? Nora searched her brain for the rule book, but in the jumble she couldn't find it. She tugged the napkin harder.

Ellie said, "Can we go on an Alaskan cruise? I want to see a fjord."

"Yes," said Mariana. "And Antarctica."

"Penguins! I want to see penguins! Oh." Ellie stopped wriggling. "What about school?"

Nora let hope grow inside her. The tendril of it wrapped around the jagged edges inside her chest and grew stronger, taller. "We'll go when you're on break. I would very much love to see penguins myself," she said. Then she added, "Because I'm dying." She said it on purpose, knowing the small green growing thing inside her would fail, knowing she had to do it anyway.

A dark cloud passed over Ellie's face. "Don't."

Mariana said, "Not now."

Nora opened her hands and laid them on the table, face up. "Now is all I've got. We have to be realistic."

"Please don't, Mama."

Oh, Nora hadn't planned for that one. The sneak attack, the child's voice coming from Ellie. That wasn't fair. She felt pain bloom behind her brow. "We have now. Right now. Let's make a list, right here at the table. A happy list of the things we all want to do—" Lists were good. Lists would fix . . . Okay, while she was facing things, Nora could admit they would fix nothing. But they sure helped. Crutches weren't what cured a broken leg, but they made things easier. "I'll start. Penguins. The Great Wall of China. The gondolas in Venice. What do you want to see?" She would live her life not without fear—never without it—but in spite of it. Fear would be the spice, the salt of adventure.

"Mom," said Ellie with patience in her voice. "School?"

"Screw school," Nora went on with a bravado she didn't quite feel. "School can wait."

"No, it can't," said Mariana.

Nora stared at her sister. "What?"

A quick shrug. Mariana reached for another helping of sweet potato hash. "I mean, this year isn't really optional. Not with college coming up."

A prickle of discomfort ran along Nora's forearms. "What do you know about it?"

"Not much. I just know Ellie has to be there."

"She could do independent study." That option would have been over Nora's dead body at this time last year, but this year was different, and her body wasn't dead yet.

"And be satisfied with just a GED?" Mariana shot a quick smile at Ellie. "That doesn't sound like our girl."

Ellie smiled and reached forward, taking a small, unasked-for sip of Mariana's wine. As if they were in cahoots.

Our girl? Ellie was *hers*. All hers. Anger, so quick to start lately, so impossible to let go, flashed up Nora's arms from her fingertips straight to her heart. But she wouldn't argue. Not at the Thanksgiving table. "I need to talk to you in the kitchen, Mariana. Now."

Chapter Sixty-three

Mariana gripped the edge of a barstool at the kitchen island. She'd been listening to Nora's rant long enough, the rant about how Mariana didn't *know* enough to insert her opinion about Ellie. That Mariana had no *right*. "You're seriously thinking that you should pull your daughter out of school less than a year before she goes to college."

"What I'm saying," Nora said, her lips white against her face, "is that you don't have a say in it."

Mariana nodded. "I hear you. I should just butt out."

"Exactly."

"Yeah, well. I can't do that." She straightened her spine, feeling every tiny bit of her half-centimeter height advantage.

Nora laughed, and the sound of it sliced the interior of Mariana's heart. "You think *you* get to say what my daughter does or doesn't do?"

Mariana pulled her lips in.

"Oh, my god," Nora said. "You do think that."

"Now's not the time . . ."

"Now? Now is the only time I have!" Nora hit the top of the cutting board with the flat of her hand, a thump followed by a wooden clatter.

Mariana knew she wasn't handling this right. "Okay, I hear you, we can just—"

"Don't you dare patronize me."

Her temper flared. "So you want me to help you with everything else, but not with Ellie."

There was a long, taut pause. "Yes."

"Why?"

Nora shook her head, refusing to answer.

Mariana heard what she didn't say, though. She already knew the answer. *Not good enough. Fuckup. Never the right one.* "She's my only niece. You're my *sister.*" She bent at the waist, collapsed like a snapped clothesline, and then straightened as if she were being winched back into place.

"One thing." Nora crossed her arms. "I need you to leave me this *one* thing."

"One thing? Fuck, Nora, letting you take care of Ellie isn't like you wanting to pick up the dry cleaning."

"You couldn't even remember the mashed potatoes. Good god, when have I *ever* been able to count on you? And you want to take my daughter away from me?"

"Of course not—"

There was a cough behind them, in the living room.

Ellie stood there, her thin arms long along her sides, her green eyes as wide as a startled cat's. "Mom?"

This was terrible. Mariana didn't know much, but she knew this: she couldn't go back to the table with Nora and pretend everything was fine.

Nothing was fine.

Her sister was dying.

And she'd never be good enough, not even as a fill-in, second-string substitute.

So she said, "Ellie, darlin', I have to leave. I forgot . . ." God, it was hot in here. She had to get out. Go home. Find Luke. Look down. Open her hands. Find her breath.

"She forgot what's important," said Nora. "That's all."

That was too much. "Holy shit. *Excuse me?*" The only important things in the whole world were Nora and Ellie. Mariana never forgot it, not even in her deepest sleep. Never.

Nora went on. "After all the ways I've taken care of you over the years, after all the things I fixed for you, you think you're ready to take over? To just step into my shoes?"

Mariana swiped at her forehead, which was as wet as if she'd just come in from the rain. "The things *you* took care of."

"Do I have to list them?"

"You have a *list?*"

Nora held up a hand. "Feeding you when Mom was too busy or too tired to. Making sure your homework was done while I did my own." With every point, she raised a finger. "Moving out. Finding our apartment. Getting us financial aid, for whatever *that* was worth, since you didn't even stay until graduation. When you came back from India the first time, I put you up again for three years."

"Put me up? I thought we lived together. I didn't know I was considered a charity case."

"Stop it," said Ellie.

"You barely remembered to put money toward rent every month." Nora raised her other hand and with it, more fingers. "Eddie, the goldfish. Timothy, our cat. Antonia, your godchild. Every plant I ever gave you. You're irresponsible. You have no follow-through. You can't be trusted with emotions." She glanced at Ellie, as if she was going to stop, but then she didn't. "You can't be trusted with *her.*"

It felt as though Nora had stabbed her in the gut. It was one thing to wonder. It was another thing altogether to know.

But Nora kept talking, her voice acid. "I don't know why I thought you could take care of my daughter when I was gone. What the hell was I thinking?"

Did she want Mariana to crumble? To be washed away? To be forced into a free fall, through a space so cold she felt she'd never be warm again? "Nora, stop." Mariana looked at Ellie, whose face was white as she held on to the doorframe, neither quite in nor quite out of the kitchen.

Nora said, her hand back on the cutting board as if she might smack it again, "You've never taken care of one thing except your business, and that's brand-new. Congratulations on that, by the way. Good thing you have a million listeners who think you're compassionate. That'll keep you warm at night. Keep up the good work."

Behind them, Ellie started crying.

And Mariana knew it was finally time to tell her sister the truth.

Chapter Sixty-four

"You know nothing. You have no *clue*."

Mariana's face was terrible, and Nora knew her own probably matched. She felt like an inferno inside, a fire that had ice at its core, and Mariana looked the same—her cheeks and eyes red, her lips as white as paper.

Mariana went on. "I never took care of *anything*? You honestly think you've been taking care of *me* this whole time?"

Nora didn't think it; she knew it. Nora had been the one to keep them together, since forever. Since the first moment they slept in the same crib. There was a picture of them somewhere, standing in the rain as toddlers. Nora held the umbrella high over both their heads.

"*Fuck* you." Mariana's voice was so low she was almost inaudible. "I've let you feel that way my whole life. Because that's the one thing you needed."

The taste of Nora's laugh was vinegar in her mouth. "Right."

"You remember that guy Bill? The one you thought got away from me, another one of my failures?"

Bill had been nice. The only truly nice guy her sister had ever dated until Luke.

"He tried to rape me."

Nora gasped. "No. He didn't."

Mariana laughed, a brittle piece of chipped glass. "I couldn't tell you. You would have fallen apart. That was during the time you thought you weren't going to pass your econ class. Remember? You couldn't think of anything else. It was all you thought about and every other night you were on the couch crying, thinking that if you didn't pass, you'd be kicked out of college and you'd wind up living on the streets. You were so upset all the time, hyperventilating when you found mold on the yogurt in the fridge. You could never have handled knowing. You think you're taking care of things, but you've only ever known how to deal with things on the surface. The easy things. If Windex can't clean off the dirt, you're not interested."

"No—"

"I broke his thumb, you know that? Snapped it. You were out in the living room, flirting with some frat guy, and that's all you talked about when we walked home that night. You didn't ask me one thing, and I knew I couldn't tell you."

"His thumb?" Nora's brain felt like sludge. Her sister's words weren't making sense. They were crawling back on themselves, like the words on the menu at the gluten-free restaurant had.

"The reason I came home from India? The reason I left Raúl? I needed an abortion." Mariana spoke through gritted teeth. "The day I had it you got mad at me for not bringing home the half-and-half you wanted me to pick up. I'd taken a cab. I didn't have money for an extra stop on the way home from the clinic."

Nora remembered that day. Mariana had come home with no half-and-half, her face blank. Nora had accused her of being stoned, and her sister had slammed her bedroom door so hard the mirror had fallen off their bathroom wall and shattered. Nora had been furious she'd been the one who had to clean it up. As usual.

The words Nora chose were so distant she almost didn't know how to pronounce them. "No, you would have *told* me that."

"You would have dissolved into nothing."

Ellie was sobbing now, but Nora stayed frozen. Broken. "I would have—"

"If I'd told you, you would have done exactly what you did with everything else. You would tell me it was my fault and then clean it up so it looks tidy from the outside."

It was the worst accusation of all. And the accusation didn't matter, nothing mattered but the fact that Nora hadn't comforted Mariana *then*, when she'd needed it most. Nora hadn't been there for her. "You should have—"

"You think I'm the same person as you, just the weaker version. I'm not. I'm me. I'm only me. Fucked up and forgetful, but fucking real. I'm the Velveteen fucking rabbit, and you're still wearing a goddamned price tag."

"Mariana, no."

Her sister dug her keys out of her purse on the countertop and kept talking while she shook them in front of her. "Let me tell you who I am. For once. Maybe you'll hear it this time if I make it really, really clear to you."

"Mama. Auntie," said Ellie. "Please *stop*." Her voice was a child's. She should go to bed soon, thought Nora, and then realized she had no idea what time it was or how old Ellie was or who she herself was. She glanced at her hands. More lines, her mother's nails . . .

"I'm someone who takes care of *you*, Nora Glass."

"I—"

"Don't interrupt me. You need to know this. When your life fell apart, I came running. I was here every weekend after Paul left. Every single one."

Weakly, Nora managed, "I'm sorry we put you out like that—"

"Oh, *Jesus*, shut up. This is where I wanted to be. I've been taking care of you since before that, though. You think you're the tough one, not because you keep the memories, but because you rewrite them that way. By the time you put something in essay form, you've already changed it in your mind, made yourself into better-than and everyone else into less-than."

The accusation cut like a whip. It was so patently *untrue*. Nothing made sense. Was this the disease? "I don't even—"

"That was fine. I let you think that was okay. That's on me. And it's true, you were the one on track, to get your degree, to find your way in life. Not me. I've always been a fuckup, but that didn't stop me from taking care of you." Mariana's lower lip trembled, and that—just that—was enough to make Nora want to fling herself off the cliff from which she was currently hanging.

And then Mariana delivered the killing blow, the one Nora never saw coming, the one she would never recover from.

Her keys still jingling, Mariana said, "You think you can't die because it would destroy me, but what's actually true is that it destroys you to think about doing this alone. You've never had to struggle through *anything* by yourself. I have. Back then? Starting with Bill trapping me in that room at the party? That's when I knew the truth—that I would have to take care of myself. I knew I could. I'm strong. But you've never seen that. You've been seeing me as a disaster area for so long that you forgot to look at *me*. And it's just going to get worse. I'll be with you when *you* die, taking care of you, but I'll be alone again afterward. As usual. And someday I'll do what you won't have to: die alone." A crystal-shattering pause. "I have to admit, it might be nice not to be judged all the time."

Then her sister was gone.

Her sister was *all* the fucking way gone, leaving nothing behind in the foyer but two Glass women both shaking like they were taking their last breaths, the very last breaths left in the whole world.

Chapter Sixty-five

EXCERPT,
**WHEN ELLIE WAS LITTLE:
OUR LIFE IN HOLIDAYS,**
PUBLISHED 2011 BY NORA GLASS

Christmas

When Ellie was little, she loved for me to tell her stories. Her favorites, of course, were about her or a little girl very much like her, a girl who was brave and fought great battles on horseback or found hidden castles. Her next favorite were stories about me and her father. She liked to think about what Paul was like before she came along. Before he left. She loved our getting-lost-in-the-desert story, and the one about how we once mistook a baby skunk for a kitten in the dark. But the story she asked for most was the one about how we met.

The story always changed. I never told her the real story, which was too prosaic and boring. It was no good for a little girl's bedtime, a little girl who wanted something exciting. So I would make up a story, always changing the elements.

"We met when I was a pirate."

"He was a pirate?"

"No," I would growl, covering my eye with my hand and stomping in a peg-legged circle. "*I* was a pirate. My ship was the *Sea Siren*, and I plundered the oceans, filling the hold with jewels I took from around queens' necks."

She would giggle and fall backward on her bed. "Did you have both your hands?"

I pulled my arm up in my shirt. "Of course not! This was just a hook back then."

"How did they fix it?"

"I was rich. You can buy new arms that work if you're rich."

"Where was Papa?"

"On a kayak."

Ellie gasped. "In the middle of the ocean?"

"Do you think that's very safe? For a tiny kayak to be all the way out there in the big waves?"

Solemnly, she shook her head.

"Me, neither. So I pulled my sailing ship alongside. 'Prepare to be boarded,' I yelled down at him. He looked up, surprised. He'd been napping, you see."

"You woke him up?"

"I did. He was very grumpy about it. Your dad never liked to be woken from a sound sleep."

"Like me!"

"Like you, chipmunk. So he said, 'Don't even think about it!' That made me, as a pirate, very upset. You can imagine."

She nodded solemnly.

"I reached over with my very long arms and put the point of my hook right behind his collar. I hauled him on board and turned him upside down, shaking him to see if any doubloons fell out of his pockets."

"Did some?" Ellie scrambled excitedly to sitting.

I pushed her gently back into her pillows. Story time was about going to sleep, after all. "No money. But lots of jewels."

"What kind?"

"Diameralds. And rupizluli. Do you know what colors those are?"

Her green eyes wide, she shook her head.

"Diameralds are rainbow colored and they come out of rain clouds, and rupizlulis look like sequins but they're actually tiny crystals that fairies dig out of riverbanks after lightning storms."

"Oh . . . ," she breathed.

"So I collected all of them, because they were rolling around the deck of my ship, and you know how I hate dirty floors. And usually, when I turn prisoners upside down and shake them, they start crying. It's to be expected. It's not a very pleasant feeling, as you can imagine. But your dad, he was different."

"How? He didn't cry?"

"Just the opposite. He yelled at me."

"He *did*?"

I nodded. "Well, I deserved it. I was a thief, after all. He said I'd better give him back all his jewels. I said, 'Or what?' And then he said, 'Or I'll sic my pet alligator on you.'"

"Pet alligator?"

"Sure enough, I looked back down in the water, and there was an alligator thrashing his tail so hard he sent water up into the sky for a mile. Maybe a mile and a half."

"What was his name?"

"Alastair."

"That's a funny name for a crocodile."

"It's a funny name for a crocodile, yes. But this was an alligator, and it's a pretty common name among that species."

"Then what?"

"I gave up, obviously. I didn't want to get bitten by Alastair, because he looked like he hadn't brushed his teeth in twenty years."

Ellie touched her freshly clean top teeth. "*Then* what?"

"Then he said he loved me and that he wanted to marry me."

"Alastair did?"

"Your dad did."

"That's silly. Why would a pirate marry a man in a kayak with an alligator?"

Because of his eyes, your eyes. "Because he made me laugh."

"I make you laugh, too."

"All the time." I kissed her and told her to sleep. The next night, the story would be different. I tried to never tell the same one twice.

The actual story was dull. I was twenty-three years old, just a baby. I'd landed my dream job at the *Sentinel*, and I wasn't fully aware yet that really what I'd landed was a glorified gofer position. It was Christmas Day, and there were only ten people in the whole office, all of us rookies. The only place open for lunch was Pho King, but that was okay. I ordered my pho with extra jalapeños and green onions, light on the chicken. The man behind me in line laughed. "I've never heard anyone order it exactly the way I do."

I said without looking around, "Well. We should probably get married."

He laughed again, and I liked the sound of it, round and sweet. "I'm in. How do you feel about roofing materials?"

"Nothing better," I said. Then my eyes met his. I had a

piece of beach glass in my pocket at that very moment that exact shade of green.

We fell in love. He gave me my heart, my Ellie. For that—divorce and failure and alimony and resentment and anger and regret aside—for that, he will always be the best Christmas present I ever got. He gave me my strong, clear Glass girl with his own beautiful matching eyes and my long nose and, of course, a strength that is all her own.

Chapter Sixty-six

Ellie sighed and pressed ctrl-G to holster the knife. Addi jogged behind Dyl.

In-game, Dyl was all man, wide at the shoulder and thigh. He didn't bounce on his toes like he did in real life—the computerized Dyl strode with authority. Ellie watched him jump two creeks in three bounds, his sword flashing at his hip. A thorny Velocirat attacked from under an Islan tree, and in less than a second, before Addi could even unsheathe her knife, he'd cut off its head with an exultant war cry.

If only they could go somewhere and fight things in real life together, instead of hanging out in Oakland bars, talking with his friends about stupid amps and their next unpaid gig.

Over there, she typed. *That's where the smoke came from. I have this idea . . .*

Like a big, manly puppy, Dyl bounded over a ripple of flame that shot out of a hole in the ground. He stopped and swayed back and forth, waiting for Addi to tell him what to do next.

The week before, she'd asked him to meet her at Mills College. The acceptance letter had come and thank god she'd been the one to intercept the mail that day because she still hadn't told her mother that she'd chosen to put in for early decision there and not at Smith. She'd used her own debit card for the application payment, and Mom hadn't even noticed.

She was going to be *pissed*, which, given the fact that she and Aunt Mariana still weren't talking, wasn't good.

But Ellie thought she might have a way around it. She was going to tell her mom about her acceptance as her Christmas present to her. No matter what, her mom couldn't get mad about it if it were a gift, right? *Hey, Mom, I'm staying home. No, not to take care of you. Not at all.*

Mills College was gorgeous, something she hadn't expected it to be. She'd just assumed the brochure had lied. Dylan met her at the front of Mills Hall. "I can't believe this is in the same city I live in," he said.

She felt the same way. Because it was located in a rougher neighborhood in Oakland, she'd expected Mills to be two or three industrial-looking buildings surrounded by razor wire, the students protected by armed guards. Instead, after her two-hour public-transit commute, she'd walked onto campus with no more than a wave to the cheery guard in the shack.

The campus itself was huge, way bigger than she'd thought. Trees were everywhere, so many of them. Wide pathways wound through grass still lush even though it was cold now, and small groups of women weaved their way between Mills Hall and the building her map told her was the tea shop.

"Dude," said Dylan. "This is awesome. You're going to go here?"

"Yeah," she said. It was the first time she'd said it out loud. "I am."

He took her hand, and she felt somehow embarrassed. This was a school full of feminists. Would they look at her and know she was in high school? That she was looking at the campus with her boy-friend, like she was too much of a baby do it herself? She pointed at a fat squirrel, using the opportunity to take her hand back.

Mills Hall was three stories, with a fourth, smaller, cupola-like story on top. She'd read in the brochure that it had once been the only building on campus, back when this was still out in the country, and that in the late 1800s, the hall was where the students lived. Now, a century and a half later, it held classrooms and office space for professors, but looking up at the narrow win-dows, Ellie could imagine girls running up and down the halls in their long dresses, calling out to one another the same way they were doing all around her.

"My brother said only lesbians go here."

Ellie's mouth dropped open. "Excuse me?"

Dylan grinned. "No, that's not a bad thing. You know, the four-year-plan. Isn't that what happens here? No guys, right?"

Two men walked by as he said this, and the taller one gave an exaggerated eye roll.

Ellie hissed, "The international and graduate programs al-low men."

"Still," he said, leaning back and looking up at the windows sparkling in the sun, "you should go for it if you get the chance."

"Seriously?" Ellie wished she'd asked her mother to come with her instead of him. Mom would have loved the long ex-panses of rich, verdant lawn and the way the light blue sky looked almost fake against the dark green of the trees.

Dylan had gotten a little better while they followed a cam-pus guide on the tour, keeping his comments to himself, texting his bandmates as they walked. They'd had lunch at the tea shop. He'd looked over the course brochures with something very close to excitement.

And all Ellie could think was, *What if I was wrong about him?* How could she trust herself if she'd gotten something so essential wrong?

Now, at home, she sat on the couch with her laptop on her knees while her mother banged reassuringly around in the kitchen. Ellie watched Dyl thump a clod of dirt with his battle-ax. *This was where you saw the smoke? Coming out of the ground?*

Yeah. Addi used an earthen spell to move the dirt much more efficiently than Dyl's ax could. *Just give me a sec.*

A reddish glare rose out of the hole she was making, startling her into leaning forward. Two brilliant puffs of gold smoke followed by smaller puffs of purple started belching out of the ground.

What? This couldn't be . . .

Ellie hit the keyboard harder. Could it . . . ? *Holy shit.*

This was it. Excitement stung the back of Ellie's eyes and her breath came faster. Sparkles flew upward into the green-black sky.

This was it. *This* was where Ulra had hidden her cache of eggs. More than a hundred thousand players worldwide, and no one had found this but them. But her.

We did it! he typed.

No.

She'd done it.

Carefully, she tugged a spider's web off a troche bush and made it into a net that she lowered into the hole. Ctrl-K to drop it in, ctrl-J to pull it up, and Addi held a perfect dragon's egg in her hands. Ellie could practically feel its warmth.

```
Can I get the next one?
```

Go, she said. *Away.*

```
What?
```

```
I need you to leave.
```

```
Ha.
```

> **I'm not kidding.**

> Ellie?

> **If you touch one of these eggs, I
> will kill you.**

Dyl took a step backward, and then another one. His sword remained at his side, but Addi kept her left hand on her knife, just in case.

> What's going on? Ellie?

She waited.

> Ellie, what's the problem? Can I
> help?

She didn't have a problem. She had a solution.

Ulra was sick. Only a Healer could fix her, a great healer. If she raised these broodlings herself out here on the edge of the game, if she kept them safe and learned their secrets, she would be—by default—the greatest Healer in *Queendom*. Then she could save Ulra. Ellie had no idea how she hadn't thought of it before, but it was as plain as day before her now.

Pain twisted in Ellie's chest, stabbed behind her eyes. Tears ran down her face, and they weren't about sending Dyl the Incurser away.

Dyl the Incurser was done. And she was, sadly, done with Dylan the man.

Only Ulra mattered. How had she not seen that before?

Ellie could almost hear the incredulity in Dylan's typed words. *You know I'm a fighter. You shouldn't threaten me like that, even if you're kidding.*

It wasn't a threat. It was a promise. If he came between her and the cure for the Queen, he would die, and when he rerolled, she wouldn't accept his offer of Friending. She wasn't a great fighter, but she was better than she used to be. She knew both his moves and his weaknesses.

And now she knew what she was fighting for. It was more—so much more—than a story she'd helped write. Somehow, she was fighting for herself, suddenly, and it fucking *mattered*. She mattered the most. And she was a Glass, goddamn it. She was strong.

Addi cradled the egg more carefully and watched Dyl trudge away. He threw fireballs into the sky, his in-game invention. If you threw them high enough, they exploded above and hung there, drifting down so slowly they looked like a boat's flare. He was doing it on purpose, drawing attention to their hidden world's edge.

It was okay.

She would fight everyone. And she would win.

"Do you think we should have steak for dinner? Have we had that recently?" her mother called from the kitchen. She stuck her head through the arch that led into the living room. "Are you . . . baby, are you crying?"

Instead of closing the computer, instead of lying, instead of making sure her mother didn't see her screen, didn't see what had made her cry, Ellie felt the sobs come harder. Her stomach hurt like she had the flu, and she hoped she wasn't going to throw up.

Mom sat on the couch next to her, folding the afghan around them carefully. She wrapped her arms tight around Ellie. "Is it Dylan?"

"No," Ellie choked. "But I'm going to break up with him." The words made her cry harder, and she hiccuped violently, something she usually did while laughing her ass off, not crying like a baby.

"Why?"

"Because." *Because I got it so wrong. I didn't see what was important.*

"So you're breaking up with him, but that's not why you're crying?" Her mother sounded confused, and Ellie didn't blame her.

"No . . ."

"Is it Smith? Did you hear back?"

Ellie shook her head, feeling tears roll down her cheeks. She gestured toward her laptop.

"Want to show me?"

She did, but she didn't know how to explain it. It was too big, too important. It wasn't just a game.

"It's the game . . . The game."

Her mother waited.

"I found the eggs. The Queen's eggs. I think they're the key to . . ."

Her mother sat next to her, her arm still around Ellie. So warm.

"I think they're the key to healing her."

There was a long pause. "The Queen is sick?"

Ellie buried her face in her hands. It wasn't fair, to cry like this in front of Mom. She'd done so well at *not* doing that, and now she was blowing all of it. Mom needed to be perked up, not brought down by a sobbing daughter who was upset about a dumb *game*.

But her mother didn't seem to mind. Gently, she pulled Ellie's hands away from her face. "You can fix her," she whispered.

Pain shot down Ellie's legs right to her feet and back up again to her heart. This was so *stupid*. Neither Ellie nor Addi could fix a damn thing. Nothing. They were useless. She had no strength, no power.

"You know why I think that?"

Ellie shook her head. She held the afghan so tightly between her fingers that they ached.

"Because you fix me every day. You might not be able to *save* me, or your Queen. But you fix us all the time, my heart. All the time."

She *didn't*. She couldn't. Only one person had that kind of connection with Mom. "You have to make up with Aunt Mariana."

Her mother started to speak, then coughed. She'd been doing more of that lately. "This is about you and me, Ellie."

"But you and her are more important."

Her mother looked surprised. "What?"

"She's your sister."

Frowning, her mother said, "You're my *daughter.*"

Ellie needed her to know it was okay. That she understood. "You two have been together since birth. I get it."

Her mother rocked backward, pushing her hair out of her face. "Do you somehow . . . do you think she's more important to me?"

The tears burned again, and Ellie took a choked breath. "No."

"Is that the truth?"

"Yes. Maybe. I don't know."

"Oh, baby. Oh, no. It's different."

Ellie knew it was different. It was fine. It really was.

"Ellie . . ."

Great, now she'd made her mother cry. *Good work.* "I'm sorry, I didn't mean to—"

"Ellie, you're the reason I'm alive. When I first . . . God, this is so hard to say, but . . . when I was first diagnosed, I thought about killing myself. I thought about it a lot." Her mother's voice cracked, dry. "Mariana would have been okay, with enough time. She would have understood, I think. You, though. I couldn't do that to *you*. And more selfishly, I wanted more of you. More time with my baby. If I didn't have you—honey, if you weren't here? There would be no point. To anything. Ever again."

The words were like water falling on parched earth. Ellie felt herself soak them up and wanted more, but that would be selfish, and it wasn't true anyway. She should be angry that her mother had thought about suicide, and later she probably would be. But at that moment she couldn't help saying, "Really?"

"Really. My sister is part of me. We came into this world as a package deal, and that has pros and cons, just like anything else. But you are *you*. You're totally yourself, standing on your own two feet, totally perfect, and all I want to do is to be near you. Wherever you are. No matter what." She took a deep breath and Ellie echoed it, drawing in the same air. "And no matter where I am, no matter where that is or what happens to me, I'll be near you." Tears slid slowly down her mother's face. "I promise."

Ellie leaned against her mother's shoulder. She didn't fit like she had when she was a child. But she still fit. Her breath felt easier in her lungs. "Make it right. With Aunt Mariana."

"I made her really mad, chipmunk. I thought I knew her and I didn't, and that was my fault. I wasn't looking. I assumed she was just like me, and I was really wrong about a lot of things."

"So *fix* it."

Mom's arms tightened around her. "Sometimes we can't fix everything."

"Yes," said Ellie with every bit of stubbornness she'd ever possessed. "We *can*. We're Glasses. Remember lemon and honey? Use that."

"Tea? I should make her tea?"

"Whatever. Do something that shows you mean it. That you didn't mean to hurt her."

The kiss her mother pressed to her forehead felt like agreement.

Ellie closed her eyes and drank her mother in. At the same time, she thought, *Ctrl-H, ctrl-H, ctrl-H.* Addi was a Healer, but Ellie was the one who gave her those powers. If anyone could heal, she could. Ellie was her mother's. She *belonged* to her. And more—her mother belonged to Ellie.

They were together.

They were each other's.

Chapter Sixty-seven

"Your sister's at the door."

Mariana looked up from her computer. It took her a moment to focus on the words. "No."

"I'm not sending her away."

"You have to."

"Just go to the door."

"That's your job. You're the man of the house. You protect me from people trying to sell me crap."

Luke rolled his eyes. "I put her in the living room." He wandered down the hall, saying over his shoulder, "I'll make coffee."

"She can't have any."

Luke ignored her.

"Thanks for nothing," she yelled at his back.

Mariana sighed.

The living room was the most tasteful room in the house (a long, low, red couch that cost more than any car she'd ever bought herself, a piano that neither of them played), and they never used it. The room didn't match the rest of the rooms in their well-lived-in home. Everywhere else, helmets rested on marble countertops. Bike leathers draped over ottomans in the TV room, and one could as easily find a wrench in a bathroom drawer as a tube of toothpaste. Luke was the one who insisted on keeping the living room nice. Pristine.

It was perfect now. Exactly the right place for someone like Nora.

"Mariana." Nora leaped to standing. At her feet were two Trader Joe's paper bags.

"Is Ellie okay?" It was her first thought. Her very first.

"Yeah. Of course. I came over to . . ."

Mariana folded her arms and waited.

Nora looked at the ground. "It seems stupid now. I should just go. Fuck."

"What's in the bags?"

"Lemons."

Mariana shook her head. "What?"

"I tried to make marmalade. With the lemons from the tree in our backyard. You know how Ellie loves them. I thought it would be nice to make a ton of it for her Christmas present. But I screwed it up. I can't do it by myself. You know, marmalade lasts . . . a long time. Indefinitely."

A long time.

She couldn't just waltz in. Not after the fight they'd had. Mariana had said some harsh things, but they were all true. Nora was the one who hadn't seen any of it coming—Nora was the one whose eyes had been closed for years. For so long.

"How did you get here?"

Nora said, "Uber."

"From Tiburon? How much did that cost?"

"Sixty dollars."

"Wow." Here was where Mariana should say, *You should have called me. I would have come to you.* But she didn't. "That's a lot."

"I need you."

Oh, hell no. She couldn't just pull this, couldn't just turn and do the dance and tell Mariana she was needed and make everything better.

"What do you *want*?"

Nora, her eyes tight like she might cry (god, Mariana would kill her if she did), said, "I want you to make the marmalade with me. With Ellie's lemons. For her."

"Why me? I can't even cook. You're the famous domestic goddess, not me."

"I can't read."

Mariana said, "Excuse me?"

Pulling out a piece of paper from the bag, Nora said, "Some days I can. Some days I can't. Today is one I can't. I can only get through the first few sentences and then the words start to run around. I can almost see them moving on the page. I don't get it. I don't get what it's saying."

"Jesus." What would that be like? Words were Nora's tools. Her superpower.

"Please help me." Nora's eyes met hers and Mariana felt an electric jolt right through to the soles of her feet.

"Damn it." She turned. "You have to do the hard parts. I'm just your narrator."

In the kitchen, they worked in near silence. Several times Mariana considered turning on music, but she didn't know what she'd play. Any love song would be fraught; any happy tune would be difficult to bear.

Instead, she sat on a stool at the counter and read the instructions to Nora. "Wash the lemons well."

No one was better at washing fruit than Nora. Mariana usually rubbed an apple on her shirt before chomping into it, but Nora believed in making sure there were no residual pesticides, no leftover germs from shipping and handling, no toxic wax spray coating. The lemons had come from her very own tree, and still she washed them with a soapy sponge, rinsed them well, and dried them on a tea towel she got out of one of her bags.

As if Mariana didn't have tea towels. She did. (Nora had given them to her. They had T. rexes on them. T. towels. Mariana didn't get them out of their drawer.)

"Cut the lemons in half and juice them, reserving the juice."

She watched Nora handle the knife. Was she careless in her motions yet? Would she stay focused enough not to hurt herself, to slip, to cut her finger off? When would Nora not know how to handle silverware?

What would that time be like?

"Slice the lemon shells crosswise thinly for a smoother marmalade." She looked up. "What the hell is a lemon shell?"

Nora held up a juiced rind. "This."

"How do you know?"

"What else would it be? It's not the juice and it's not the pulp. It has to be the rind."

Mariana scowled at the paper. "You sure this is a good recipe?"

"No. I told you. I couldn't read it very well. It had a lot of stars, so I printed it."

Mariana tasted acid in her mouth, as if she'd sipped the lemon juice out of the bowl.

Luke came in the kitchen. He kissed Nora on the cheek. She looked up at him gratefully. "Hi, big guy."

"Hey, Nora. Glad you're here."

"Luke . . . ," warned Mariana. He wouldn't—couldn't—fix this one.

Fixers.

For the first time, Mariana realized she surrounded herself with them. Had she always done that? Nora, ever, always Nora. Every boyfriend she'd ever had displayed a penchant for taking care of things. Grant, at the office, who read her mind daily. For god's sake, Luke fixed things as a profession. He was a mechanic.

Or, he was, until he'd inherited the dealership and became the boss, but he still came home most days with a black line of grease under his fingernails because he couldn't resist helping, making things better.

Luke said, "Why lemons? Is this lemon jam? Is that a thing?"

"Marmalade," said Mariana. She waved the page at him. "I'll let you know how it goes." Code for *keep moving*.

But Luke poured himself a cup of coffee and leaned on the refrigerator. He would want to help. That's what he did.

Jesus. *She'd been dating Nora.* All these years. Maybe she'd been looking for her sister in every relationship she'd ever had.

Holy shit. It was so obvious. It felt like stubbing her toe on a huge, hard rock made of truth.

"What next?" Nora's face was as open and sweet as a blown tulip.

"Cover the lemon slices with cold water in a big pot." Had Nora done the same thing? Max, Nora's first boyfriend, had been a sweetie but a major pothead. Nora's second boyfriend, Elias, had lost three jobs in the year they'd dated. Jonas had crashed two cars while he was dating Nora, and when he'd borrowed her Civic, he'd worn out the brakes and had never given her a dime to get them fixed. Fuckups. All of them. Even Harrison, when she thought about it. Most of the women he'd brought home over the years weren't smart enough to find their way out of the cul-de-sac to get home. He was smart and good, but emotionally, he'd never had his shit together, which was ironic, since his job as a therapist was to help people figure their own shit out.

The thing he did best was love Nora.

Just like Mariana.

Her sister was staring at her.

The paper shook in Mariana's hands. "Boil. Ten minutes. Then drain and rinse."

Nora smiled. "Just like pasta."

And Paul, of course, was the biggest fuckup of all. He found

things, kept them for a while, and then left, littering them behind him as he went. According to Nora, he'd driven two roofing companies into the ground since he moved into the valley,
each time coming up with new funding, new branding. His new
wife had given him two kids, and Mariana would bet everything
she had that he ignored them completely, too. She'd bet that if he
wasn't out yet, he'd be gone before the kids hit high school.
Though she had no evidence, she wouldn't be surprised if he was
already cheating on Bettina now. Paul had essentially abandoned
the best girl in the world, Ellie, the most wonderful girl, the
special one. Mariana felt her temperature spike and her fingers,
holding the recipe, went sweaty. Over her dead body would that
man have a say in Ellie's future. Not when he'd ignored her past.

Luke said, "Hey, both of you. I've been working on the bedroom upstairs."

What was he talking about? Mariana stared.

"Wanna come look?"

Nora smiled and wiped her hands on her apron. "Okay."

They followed Luke up the staircase. Mariana felt a sense of
heaviness deep in her stomach, as if she'd eaten bricks for breakfast. "What is—"

"It's a surprise." Luke turned and winked at her. "Be surprised."

The bedroom at the end of the hallway was a catchall, a
storage space for his boxes of bike magazines and her bins of
clothes she couldn't quite decide whether or not to donate. It was
a repository for broken things—the outdoor umbrella that had
ripped, old computers that hadn't had their hard drives wiped yet.

He opened the door.

Inside stood . . .

Mariana's throat clenched and she couldn't swallow. Next to
her, Nora gasped and covered her mouth.

Inside stood a white bed. Simple, with a dark wooden frame.
Two brown bedside tables, with lamps made from what looked

like tree branches. The only piece of art on the newly painted blue wall was a glass mosaic of the city skyline.

A white desk was under the window. Next to it perched a red wood chair. The old mirrored closet doors had been changed to white slatted ones, and they stood open. Empty.

Luke said, "I've been doing this when you've been at the office."

Mariana couldn't think of one thing to say. It felt like her brain had been scooped out and replaced with something much more delicate, something that trembled with knowledge she couldn't know yet, knowledge that hovered just over there, just out of her line of sight.

Nora stood frozen on the threshold.

"Go in," urged Luke.

"I can't," Nora said.

"You should."

One step. Then another. Then all three of them were in the space. The clean, welcoming, happy, hopeful space.

"Ellie will like it, I think," said Luke simply. "When she needs it. I'm going to let you both look around."

And he was gone, down the hall, whistling.

Mariana wanted to race after him. When Ellie stayed the night, she always stayed in the guest room. What was *wrong* with that? She wanted to slap Luke. And she wanted to thank him for being the only good man she'd ever found, the only good man she'd ever loved. But instead, she reached out and took Nora's hand.

A guest room wasn't good enough. Ellie deserved her own room, and Luke had known that without asking.

Mariana and Nora sat on the edge of the bed. Mariana could feel a pulse fluttering in her fingertips and didn't know whose it was.

They looked straight forward, out the window that faced the pink and purple Victorian across the street.

"She's always adored that house," said Nora, pointing. Her

voice shook. "She'll love looking at it before she goes to sleep. And seeing it when she wakes."

"Nora, I didn't know."

Her sister dipped her head as if her neck hurt. "I know. I can tell."

"But . . ."

"I know." She gestured to the skyline mosaic. "Look. He used beach glass. For us."

Beach glass. She couldn't believe Luke had . . . *Unbreakable, even broken.*

Mariana had to say it. Just once. "I'll take care of her."

Nora met her eyes. This moment.

This one.

"I know you will," Nora said.

Together, they went downstairs and cooked the lemons till they were sweet and thick. It wasn't enough. Of course it wasn't. But after they'd transferred the hot lemon-sugar mixture to the hot jars using the wide funnel, after they'd boiled the jars again, after they'd subjected them to the heat that would kill every single harmful thing, after they washed most of the dishes, they stuck their spoons into the leftover bit at the bottom of the pan.

It was creamy and sweet, with a sour, perfect bite.

Mariana didn't feel forgiven and she wasn't sure she forgave Nora. Not just yet. *Open hands cling to nothing.* She felt herself breathe, the way she told her subscribers to. From the bottom up, a breath that filled. Next to her at the sink, she heard Nora's steady breathing, too.

There would be lemon marmalade later. And it would last for a long, long time.

Chapter Sixty-eight

*N*ora sat next to the Christmas tree, her legs splayed, her back aching, furious that she kept losing words.

"It's not that hard," she said in abject frustration. "It shouldn't be." She knew she'd lost words when she'd been explaining to them how to make the necklaces—she'd forgotten the word for "pliers," and when she'd tried to laugh it off, Ellie had become unreasonably upset with her, telling her she'd been stuck again. "For ten minutes, Mom. We talked to you for ten minutes, and you just stared at us." Ellie's voice sounded like a child's, plaintive and needful.

This was Christmas. Today should be perfect.

The lemon marmalade had been a bright, sweet start, but only that. Nora needed Christmas to fix the rest. And she had hoped that it would be the day Ellie finally accepted that Nora wasn't going to get better (but that she would never love Ellie less, never, never, never any less, more with every minute that passed).

Instead, they were seated uncomfortably around the coffee

table on the floor, all three of them staring at the bowl of beach glass that usually sat next to Nora's bed, none of them wanting to make necklaces out of the pieces, not even Nora herself.

She was an idiot for thinking this would work. Knowing that didn't make her feel less stubborn, though. "Ellie, you're close. If you use the *pliers*"—she had the word back and she wouldn't let it go—"to wind off that last piece of wire, you'll have it, I think. Look at mine." She held her piece of wire-wrapped green glass. "God, this is ugly."

Mariana snorted. Even though it was a derisive snort, Nora held on to it like it was a kiss. Mariana had barely said a word since she'd arrived. She'd seemed almost . . . shy. She'd sat on her hands and, while she didn't refuse to try making a necklace, she certainly didn't try very hard. Soon it would be dinnertime. (Nora had bought the meal online and had gotten it delivered, a precooked roast and potatoes and the fanciest kind of vegetable dishes Andronico's had. Good enough was good enough now.) Luke would arrive soon, and then Harrison would walk over from his house, and it wouldn't be just the three of them anymore.

What if this was the last Christmas she would have with her sister and her daughter—the last one she would be truly present for?

The wire drew first blood, jamming itself under her thumbnail. "Well, *dang* it."

"Mom, come on. Seriously. Who are we making these for? Do you think we're really going to wear them?"

"Not if it looks like this pile of crap, we're not." On Pinterest, where she'd gotten the idea, Nora had found beautiful images of cloudy green and blue wrapped delicately—ornately—in silver wire, hanging from shining chains. Her beach glass looked like it had been crammed into a temporary steel cage, and it looked bulbously obscene hanging from the leather strap she'd attached it to. She'd made a bully necklace, something destined to hurt the wearer, to attack any friend who dared to go in for a hug.

It was just one more thing to add to the growing list at the back of her Moleskine of things she couldn't do (that was, when she could make out what letters meant). *Drive. Cook at temperatures over 400.* She'd write *Craft with hard objects* at the bottom of the list, but she should probably just write *Craft.* The knitted sock, Ellie had recently pointed out, had gotten so long that it was now an unending tube. Nora had run out of yarn twice. She'd just attached another ball, so the "sock" changed from green to yellow and then to red. She'd laughed and told Ellie she'd changed her mind, that she was making a skinny stoplight scarf, but the truth was she'd forgotten how to bind off. She could look it up on YouTube, of course. But then she was pretty sure she'd forget how to cast on, or even to cast on at all. And her hands needed something to do. She loved her sock-scarf. It was something she could do, something that showed forward progress, even if that progress was technically wrong.

"Screw this," said Nora. She swept all of it—the pliers, the metal snips, and the leather—into the box it had all come in. (Thank god for Amazon. On days she could read, she could still buy whatever she needed, and the mailman brought it to the house, right to her. It was practically like receiving gifts, since every second or third time she had no idea what she'd ordered. A few times she wasn't even sure she *had* ordered what she'd received—an egg spatula, a laser cat toy even though Oscar had died when Ellie was ten—until she went into her order list and confirmed that, yes, the command to send her these things had come from her computer.)

Sometimes it felt like being a blackout drunk. Every time she came to, she had to hope she hadn't done anything embarrassing, that she hadn't danced on a tabletop or stripped off important pieces of clothing while in inappropriate places.

At other times, it felt like nothing at all. Everything was normal, except that now Harrison slept in her bed at night and was usually to be found somewhere inside her house, puttering around in exactly the same way he did in his own house. The morning after he'd stayed all night for the first time, Ellie had asked Harrison, "Are you living here now?" She'd been at the table, eating cereal. There'd been nothing angry in her voice, just curiosity.

Nora had watched Harrison freeze, the glass he was washing hovering in midair. Nora could have jumped in and answered for him (*I gave him a toothbrush, a red one, he forgave me and believed me and got me one for his house, in yellow, we have two homes now*), but Ellie had asked him the question, not her.

"I still live next door, but your mom and I want to spend more time together. Is that okay by you?" Harrison said it like he would have gone back home and stayed there if Ellie had told him that it wasn't all right.

Ellie had nodded without looking up. "Sounds good to me." She hadn't said it with relief or even surprise. It seemed like it might, actually, sound good to her.

Nora had asked Harrison to give them this time before dinner, time for the Glass women to craft together using the beach glass they'd collected over the years. Now she wished he was there. He would make them all laugh. He would use his pliers to make a snowflake out of the wire and tell them the glass deserved to be what it was, just pretty. It didn't need to be something bigger, better.

He'd be right.

"Let's do presents," she said. "No more of this crap."

Ellie got her worried look. "Weren't we just supposed to make one present each for each other? I thought that's what we agreed."

"We did," Nora said.

"Well, you said presents. Plural."

There are three of us, that makes it plural. But she didn't snap it like she wanted to—Nora held her tongue.

Mariana nodded and stood, reaching for her bag. "Let's get it over with before the guys get here."

"Speaking of the guys," Nora tried to say casually, "is Dylan coming?"

"No," was all Ellie said.

That's what she'd thought. Ellie hadn't been playing her game at night; she'd been watching TV with her instead. It had been nice, catching up on Netflix shows, and Nora had tried not to remark on the novelty of it for fear of chasing her away. One weekend they'd binged on a *Gilmore Girls* marathon, something that had made her heart so hopeful it actually hurt. "Do you want to talk about it?"

"No," Ellie said again.

"Are you okay?"

Ellie finally looked up. "Yeah," she said. "I am."

"Good." Nora took a deep breath. "Okay, who's first?"

Mariana, still sitting on her hands, said quickly, "Not me."

"Me, neither," said Ellie.

Nora tamped back irritation. It was *Christmas*. She had Bing Crosby on the stereo and a fake fire snapping on the flat-screen. She'd made mulled cider, but Mariana had refused a cup and Ellie hadn't begged for one (she'd been prepared to say yes). She'd decorated the tree by herself the week before while Ellie did homework, saying she was behind in English.

A rush of grief that made her chest ache was followed just as quickly by the landslide of happiness of being here, with these two. *These* two.

"Okay, I'll go. I kind of have to explain both of them, though." She handed a flat box to each of them. Mariana's was heavier. Both were intricately wrapped, with shiny bows that she'd made herself. She could still remember how to do *that*.

Mariana eyed hers suspiciously, as if it would bite her.

"Go on, open it."

Inside was a photo album. Mariana opened it to a random page in the middle, and there was a picture of the two of them in college, sitting in that crappy little convertible Mariana had bought with the money she'd made at the coffee shop. They were both grinning at whoever was taking the picture of them. They looked identical. Nora herself had to look at their earrings to figure out that she was the one on the left. "You loved that car. That was the first car you ever bought."

Mariana looked up. "It's a photo album of us?" They had those already. Twin books. Nora had made them before.

"Keep looking. It's a photo album of *you*." She reached forward and flipped to one of her favorite pages. "Look. It's all the postcards you sent me from India. And here's the first place you taught yoga. Remember, this was your studio on Fourth, that tiny place you had. And this, this was from the day you came up with the idea of the BreathingRoom app when we were in Dolores Park. Look how big your smile was, like you couldn't fit all your teeth in your head." She turned more pages. "And over here, look. Remember that news show you were on two months ago? I got this still from them. Remember how nervous you were? And here, screenshots of the app. With quotes from users."

Mariana shook her head. "I don't get it."

It was her apology. It was Nora's way of saying, *I see you. I know how amazing you are. You're not a fuckup. I know you've been taking care of me.*

Nora flipped to the front of the book. "Look. You and Mom. I hadn't seen this one in forever. And here's one of you and Ellie . . ."

Mariana stared. "Where are you?"

Fine. If Nora had to say it out loud, she would. "It's to show you how amazing *you* are. In everything you do."

"But where are you?"

"What?"

Mariana flipped the pages rapidly. "Besides that picture of us in my car, you're not in here."

"It's not about me. This is about *you*."

"But I need . . ." Mariana reached forward and touched Nora's wrist. "But I need you."

Nora felt heat hit her cheeks. "Oh." Christ, what a stupid gift. "I'm sorry. I didn't think of that."

Mariana blinked and smiled, though it was weak. "It's okay. It's fine. Okay, moving on. Ellie, how about you open yours?"

Nora turned to Ellie, who was slipping off the bow. God, if she screwed up both of the presents . . . "This is . . . I'm not sure of this one."

"I'm sure it's very nice," said Ellie politely.

Inside the slim box was a simple piece of paper. In a page she'd torn from her journal, Nora had written, "I, Nora Glass, give my permission for my daughter, Ellie Glass, to be tested for the PS1 gene mutation."

Ellie gasped. She put her hand to her stomach.

God, was this wrong, too? Had Nora lost the ability to read emotion as well as keep track of time?

"Mom."

"I know it's what you wanted."

"It is."

"Now you can."

Ellie's eyes were huge. "Now I don't know if I want to."

A tide of relief swelled inside Nora's chest. "Then don't." Goose bumps rose on her arms. "But you can think about it. You can make the decision for yourself. It's not mine to make for you anymore."

"I'm scared."

Nora felt a sob swell in her throat, and she met Mariana's eyes. Her sister raised her chin, as if reminding her to do so. Nora raised hers to match. "Me, too, Ellie."

Ellie hugged her, a brief sharp grasp, and then she let go again. It was enough.

"I want to go next," said Mariana. "Me next."

Chapter Sixty-nine

Mariana's gift to Ellie was simple. It didn't really suit the rules—she hadn't made it, and technically it was more than one gift. But she'd put it together, and it had felt like making something at the time.

Ellie opened the box and then smiled. "Why do people always give me backpacks?" But she looked excited as she peered into it.

"First of all, it's not fugly like that one Harrison gave you last year. Second of all, it's full of stuff for college."

Pulling things out, Ellie started to laugh, which was exactly what Mariana had wanted. "Nerds." A huge box of them, the size of two hands put together.

"Because you'll need so much sugar in college it's ridiculous."

Ellie took out an industrial-sized bottle of aspirin.

"You shouldn't drink when you're underage. *Obviously.* But if you do, take a couple of those before you go to sleep."

Poking deeper into the bag, Ellie laughed again. "Chocolate. Coffee. Windex?"

"Because you can clean everything with Windex. Your mom taught me that. Sinks, mirrors, even the toilet in case of emergencies. There are sponges in there, too, and gloves, because who knows who your roommates will be? You're going to need them." Mariana pointed. "Open that coupon wallet."

Ellie unfolded it. "Gift cards! Wow. Trader Joe's, Starbucks, Amazon, Chili's . . . These are great."

"There's a ton more stuff in there. Sharpies and pencils and erasers and . . ."

"That's wonderful," said Nora softly, leaning to look inside. "I wish I'd thought of that."

Crap, *crap*, her gift to Nora was stupid. So fucking stupid. It wasn't even a gift. It was just . . .

But her sister looked expectantly at her. She smiled. Mariana's heart, which had felt so small and black after their fight, twisted again as if trying to right itself.

Using every bit of courage she had, Mariana handed over the small white box. This could be wrong. This could be so wrong . . .

Nora opened it. She looked curiously into it. "A . . . key?"

Mariana handed the other white box to Ellie. "One for you, too. It's to our house."

Nora nodded. The bedroom. She'd seen. She understood. Ellie didn't, not yet, but she would. Eventually.

"And there's this." Mariana held out her hand. The diamond winked on her ring finger.

"Mariana! What—you said yes? Yes? But why—why did you change your mind?"

Mariana didn't know how to say it, didn't know how to make it not devastating. "I always thought . . ." She'd cried for two days, off and on, after she'd asked Luke if she could still have the ring, laughing through the tears when she had to. It was a dam that had been broken by the weight of the metal Luke had slipped on her finger (the same ring, his grandmother's—he'd gotten it back from the restaurant after all). All the levees she'd thought she had in place had failed, every one. Now, as she saw the pain crease Nora's face, she felt them start again. "Damn it, Nora, I did this for you."

"What?"

She hiccuped around a sob. "I never thought I could pull off marriage if you hadn't managed to get it right."

Nora just stared.

"I never told you this, but I was so glad when he left." She glanced at Ellie, who sat without blinking. "I'm sorry, sugar. But it's true. Him leaving brought your mom back to me."

"But—," started Nora.

"I know," said Mariana, twisting the ring. "It's not fair, but that's what I felt. But . . . I just figured marriage was something the Glass women didn't get right. Like Mom. But now . . . Luke and I will be a family. In case we need to . . ." She looked frantically at Ellie, unable to say it out loud. She couldn't say the worst thing in front of her, she just couldn't.

Ellie moved to a kneeling position. From the back of her pocket she took out a yellow slip of paper. "I think I should give you your present, Aunt Mariana."

With shaking fingers, hating the wetness that slid traitorously down her face, Mariana unfolded it.

"I don't understand." The paper said "BIMMP99."

"It's my password."

"What does it stand for?"

Ellie said, "Boy Is My Mother Pushy and my birth year."

"Why are you giving it to me?"

"For, like, my phone and my computer and stuff."

Next to her, Nora made a choking sound.

"Why . . . ?"

Ellie said, "Because Mom needs my password to make sure I'm not meeting inappropriate men on the Internet or something."

"I've never used it," Nora said.

Ellie gave a strange, sweet smile. "I know."

The password was for her. For Mariana. Ellie was giving it to her for the same reason she would marry Luke—to make a safety net for Ellie, a stronger one, a better one.

Ellie put her hands flat on the coffee table in front of them. "You know the chances are that I'll be eighteen before we need to really worry about any of this. Then I'll be able to take care of myself. And besides, they're coming out with new meds all the time."

"I know," said both Mariana and Nora at the same time. It was a catchphrase they all used. *New meds. Science.* New hope. And after all, who knew what might happen tomorrow?

"I still haven't given Mom my gift." Ellie reached in her back pocket again and pulled out a white envelope that had been folded in half. "Here. Don't be mad."

Chapter Seventy

The envelope was soft, well creased. It said "Mills College" on the outside, and it was addressed to Ellie Glass, and it made absolutely no sense at all.

Congratulations on your Early Decision acceptance to Mills College.

"What is this?"

"That's where I'm going."

"In Oakland? This Mills here?" Nora pointed at the back door as if the college were hiding somewhere in the backyard.

"Yeah."

"You're going to Smith."

"No."

"But you applied to Smith College." Nora was getting used to the feeling of not quite keeping up, but Mariana had the same look on her face, a frowning concentration, as if, if they just listened harder, they could make the words make sense.

"No. I applied ED to Mills instead. That's where I'm going."

Nora slid backward and ran into the couch behind her. She scrambled up it. Good. Now she could look down on her daughter and tell her what was really going to happen. "I haven't saved all that money for Smith for nothing. I know we can talk to the registrar, we can explain what happened—"

"You can do whatever you want," said Ellie evenly. "But I'm going to Mills."

Nora could feel the hot pink of her cheeks had moved to flare over her whole face and neck. "No way. You're going to the school you *want* to go to. I won't allow you to stay here and take care of me."

"You can't really stop me."

"I won't pay for it."

"Then I'll get a loan."

"That would be perfect. Start your grown-up life financially strapped to loans you'll never be able to afford to pay." Nora searched her mind desperately for another argument. "Well, you can't live with me. Not when you're supposed to be in a dorm in Massachusetts."

Her daughter just smiled, as if she'd expected this. "I'll just wait till you forget you said that."

"Jesus!" Nora had a split second of admiration for this creature she and Paul had made. "You ornery little thing. You're a horrible person."

"I know," said Ellie. "I got it from you." She appeared satisfied.

Next to her, Mariana laughed and then gave another sob followed by a hiccup that sounded so much like one of Ellie's.

"You're crying," said Nora in wonder. She couldn't remember when she'd last seen Mariana cry. Maybe after their mother had died, during that twenty-four-hour period they'd stayed in bed before they started organizing the funeral. Even then, though, Nora could remember Mariana turning her face away.

Now she wasn't doing that. Mariana just sat there, letting the teardrops roll off her cheeks to her gray silk shirt, where they darkened as if in emphasis.

"I'm still so *angry* at you," said Mariana.

"I know." And then Nora said, "You're not a fuckup. You've never been one."

Mariana shook her head. "Stop."

"I'm so sorry. I wish I could take it all back, everything I said. I'm so sorry I hurt you. For so long."

"You didn't know me." Mariana's lower lip trembled, slick with tears.

"I've *always* known you." From the first moment she could draw breath, she'd known no one else.

"But you didn't see me."

That part was true. "I'm so sorry." Nora had thought she would cry, too, apologizing, but strangely, with Mariana weeping, she didn't feel like she had to. "I listened to your app last night."

"You did? You always said you couldn't do that."

"I thought it would be too weird to hear your voice, but it was wonderful. You're amazing." Nora had left the earphones in while she lay in the bed next to Harrison, her sister's voice telling her to breathe the last thing she remembered hearing. It had felt like being embraced by light.

The doorbell rang.

All three of them jumped but none of them moved toward the door. It would be Luke, since Harrison always came in through the kitchen. Mariana laughed through her tears, rubbing her face with her hands. "Oh, god. Wait. I need something from you."

Nora bit her bottom lip. Everything depended on this moment. She felt Ellie slide her hand into hers, and she wasn't sure who was consoling whom. She wasn't sure it mattered.

"I need . . . ," Mariana finally said, her voice breaking. "I need help knowing how to turn off the waterworks. Since I started"—she pointed at her cheeks—"they just won't stop. I've been doing this for weeks. Literally."

Nora felt the light from the night before fill her again. It occupied the lining of her lungs, enveloping her soul. She knew the answer to this. She might not know much but she knew this. "You just open your arms."

Another laugh. "That's all?" Mariana held her arms out wide. "I can do that."

Then Nora, with her daughter and her sister, formed a ball, holding one another so tightly that later they'd be bruised. The doorbell rang again, but the outside world could wait. For that moment, there was no one else in the world but the Glass women: occluded, battered, transparent, but beautiful.

Stronger than almost anything else in the world.

Epilogue

**APPLICATION ESSAY,
MILLS COLLEGE
ELLIE GLASS—TIBURON**

My mother is a storyteller. You might know her: Nora Glass. She's famous. Specifically, she's famous for writing about me and her divorce from my father. When I was a kid, I hated it. I absolutely abhorred that the way I lisped my esses was something strangers knew about. People would come up to me at book readings and touch my hair, reminiscing about the time I chopped off my right pigtail, leaving the left one long. I knew nothing about them or their lives, but they knew how I couldn't sleep in the dark after my dad left. It didn't seem fair.

But recently, I've learned what my mother already knew: that power lies in the storytelling itself. If you choose to share the information, you own it. You're in charge of it. If you go through a bad breakup and you tell yourself, "I'm heartbroken," then you'll cry yourself to sleep every night. But if instead you tell yourself, "I'm better off without that loser," then you pat yourself on the back (rubbing in small circles, like my mother does, but you probably already knew that) until you fall peacefully asleep.

The strange thing is: stories with different endings can be true at the very same time. I can be brokenhearted about a boy and also happy to be by myself again. I can be terrified of losing my mother and excited to go to college in the very same second.

I'd always wanted to go to Smith College (you're probably not supposed to say that in a college essay to a rival school, but it takes quite a bit to scare me lately, and this doesn't). When my mother got sick, I still wanted to go. Honestly, I wanted to get as far away from her as possible. Maybe then it wouldn't be true.

But what I learned in my most recent favorite online game, *Queendom*, is that only by protecting yourself can you protect anything that you love. I couldn't take care of my mother until I learned to take care of myself. I had to figure out the answer to: *What do I want the most?* I want so much in this world. I want to play video games and save the Dragon Queen all by myself. I want to write stories like the ones I make up in my games. I want to be successful enough to be able to afford to buy any car I want. I want to be happy. I want to be loved.

Mostly, though, what I want to be is a strong Glass woman who will make the other Glass women proud.

There's a beach near Mendocino where you can lie on your stomach and dig your chin into the sand and watch the ocean through millions of pieces of storm-churned beach glass. The world looks different, fractured but beautiful, and you realize that you're not looking through a kaleidoscope: you *are* the kaleidoscope.

Fractured but beautiful—isn't that a good thing to aim for?

I want to go to Mills so I can be near my mother even though she thinks she would be fine if I left. I want to go to Mills to learn how to be a successful storyteller, and then I want to tell the stories that will break people apart, fracture them into splinters of light and color and sound, and then put them back together again in their own kaleidoscope of beauty.

I want to be a storyteller, like my mother. I want to be a keeper of truth, and when necessary, an inventor of it. That is, after all, how we keep going.

I learned that from my mother.

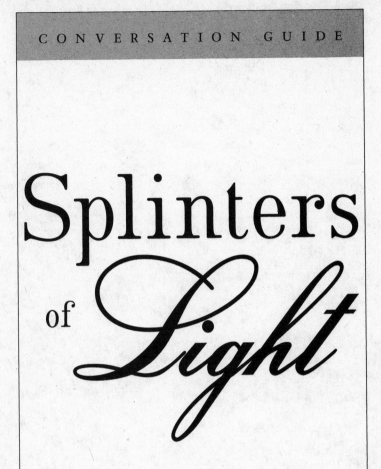

Splinters of Light

Rachael Herron

This Conversation Guide is intended to enrich the

individual reading experience, as well as encourage us

to explore these topics together—because books,

and life, are meant for sharing.

A Conversation with Rachael Herron

Q. How did you get the idea for Splinters of Light?

A. A sensitive, appropriate answer to how I got the idea for this book would be that I had a loved one suffering from early-onset Alzheimer's disease. An understandable answer would be that I'd watched someone struggle through it, that I'd wept at their side, that I'd held their hand as they listened to their prognosis, and that my heart was further broken when the cure wasn't found before they died. If this were something I'd actually experienced, this book would be my way of having closure. But it isn't.

The actual, true answer is more prosaic and much gentler. I was sitting on my couch, my feet up on the coffee table, the cat on my stomach, reading a *People* magazine that featured an article about a teenage boy who was taking care of his forty-six-year-old mother as her EOAD progressed. He managed her medication and his schoolwork. He took care of planning for her safety and for his future.

That boy's story—that glossy page-and-a-half write-up—was something I couldn't let go. I'd flip over in bed in the middle of the night, wondering if he was also awake, worrying about filling out an insurance form. While I was at the grocery store, I imagined the mother getting lost in the aisles she'd been up and down a thousand times, unable to find her son's favorite treat or even to remember what it was.

In addition to being a writer, I'm a 911 dispatcher. Every shift, I hear a dozen stories that are life altering and, very often, tragic. I let go of most of them. Occasionally, an event will shake me up, bringing me to sudden tears over the coffeepot at home, but that happens rarely. I'm able to forget most tragedies I hear. This poor memory is a required feature in dispatchers, as important as the ability to multitask and to drink cold coffee.

I couldn't get that teenage boy and his mom out of my head, though. I began to play with ideas, slipping them around in my mind much the same way Nora does with the sea glass in her pocket. A mother and son . . . no, a daughter. I've always loved writing about the mother-daughter relationship. And who would raise a young woman as her mother slowly slips away? A sister, of course. A close sister. A twin.

After the idea took hold, it seemed as if every other call I took at work was about someone with dementia in some form or another. We get the calls of the wanderers, the ones who left on foot, going somewhere. (I always wondered where they thought they were going. Did they head out the door with a destination in mind, or was it just the desire to move again with long strides, crossing whole city blocks, not just hallways?) One woman with Alzheimer's wandered a hill close to her home for three days in summer heat, only found after a massive grid search. A rescue dog found her wristwatch; then the dog found her. She lived. Another few hours outside, she might not have made it.

She lived. She mattered.

Every day, new advances are made in Alzheimer's treatment. And every day, the disease comes closer to us. To me. To you. Someone you love already has been or will be affected.

As this book took shape in my mind, the characters became real, and the plotline began to twist its way through my imagination like a river twists to the sea. At the same time, I was deeply aware that I had to get it right. I was entering a conversation that I needed to be part of—that we all need to be part of—and I didn't want to do it wrong. The truth is that we are the ones responsible for raising awareness for Alzheimer's disease, and this book is my method of doing that, of opening the dialogue.

How will you answer?

Q. *Are you a twin?*

A. No, I'm not a twin, but I have a younger sister close enough in age to me that there was never a time I didn't remember her being with me. Maybe that's why I've always been fascinated by twins. Or is it a universal fascination? Perhaps we all want that closeness, that ultimate representation of togetherness. We're born alone and we die alone, and honestly, that's an awful lot of aloneness. Coming into the world with someone sounds a lot better. I was always vaguely irritated with my mother that she hadn't pulled that off for me (and slightly annoyed that I hadn't made it happen, either, that I hadn't forced my own wee zygote to split by sheer dint of will).

My mother-in-law is a twin. Jeannie and Janie still like to dress the same, and they sit close together on the sofa. Their words intertwine, their soft Texas drawl the same exact pitch. In the kitchen, they slice carrots, both of them humming tunelessly. I don't think they're aware of the contented noises they murmur to each other. Identical twins, they have the kind of quintessential relationship we all think of when we hear the word.

A friend of mine has a different kind of bond with her sister. While writing the book, I took her out to dinner to pick her brain about it. Over sushi, she told me about the times—long months—she didn't speak to her sister. They were too close and pushed each other away, over and over again. There were misunderstandings, small ones, that blew up disproportionately, and enormous wounds were glossed over and covered up for much too long. My friend loves her sister more than anything else in the world. But sometimes she doesn't like her very much.

This was far more interesting to me than the Bobbsey Twin relationship I'd always thought of when I thought of twins. Twinship didn't only mean a built-in best friend, then (though it could include that); it also meant that you'd always only be considered half of a whole. There existed another part of yourself that you couldn't control, one that you had no say over. You couldn't read your twin's mind, and maybe you wouldn't even want to if you could.

Nora and Mariana started so far apart they couldn't see who the other one really was. Bringing them back together was so difficult, sometimes I thought they wouldn't make it. For the first time in my life, I was grateful not to have a twin. I was thankful my two sisters were well adjusted and strong, completely their own people.

Finally, though, Nora and Mariana made it. Now they stand together, two wholes, facing the same direction, holding hands.

Q. *In your previous novel,* Pack Up the Moon, *you tackled the topic of childhood euthanasia and closed adoption. In* Splinters of Light, *you chose to write about a terrifying disease. What draws you to these darker topics?*

A. There aren't many sure things in life, are there? But I know one thing for sure. In everyone's life, there will be times of pain, and there will be times of joy.

That's it. That's what we get. Placed starkly in a sentence like that, it doesn't sound like much, and it's easy to stick on the terrible part of it. Yeah, you're saying that life sucks, and then we die. Thanks for that.

But that's not what I'm saying. I believe that no matter how low life tugs us, the lifting force of hope is greater. I love the balance of it, how even in the darkest moments, we can be jolted by an unexpected belly laugh rocking through us. We shouldn't laugh, we think. How can we possibly laugh at a time like this? Then we surrender to it and laugh harder.

That's humanity. Human bodies are frail, but the human spirit is amazing in its strength. Oh, god. I think I just said that laughter is the best medicine. That's not what I meant to say (although sometimes I think it's true, as trite as the saying is).

To be quite honest, my editor said *Splinters of Light*—in its first draft—was just too sad. I'd gone so far into studying EOAD I couldn't see a bright spot. Joy? What joy was there in such a tragic disease? What hope could possibly exist?

Then I remembered that I wasn't writing a treatise on dementia. The only medical training I have is my emergency medical dispatcher certificate. I know how to tell people to do CPR, how to staunch a gunshot wound, and how many aspirin to take for chest pain. No one wanted to read my book on early-onset Alzheimer's disease. I was no authority on medicine and never would be, no matter how many books I read.

What I am an authority on is how hard people can love each other.

In my revision, I went back to that. I told the story of Nora and Mariana, twins who had drifted apart but still held the hope of being together again, always. I rewrote Ellie, a girl who loved so frantically she could barely imagine the fact that she was loved equally hard back.

My story wasn't about a disease; it was about them.

Multicolored light started to gleam at me as I revised, the beach glass I put in their pockets winking back at me.

Hope, in my books (and in my heart), always has the last word.

QUESTIONS
FOR DISCUSSION

1. How are Nora and Mariana similar as the book opens? How are they different? How do their arcs change as the story unfolds?

2. Nora sleeps with Harrison for the first time before she's diagnosed. Why do you think it took so long for them to get together, and what changes after her diagnosis?

3. What is the relationship between Mariana and Ellie like at the beginning of the book? By the last page, how has this changed?

4. This is a book about the relationships between female family members. What is the role of men in *Splinters of Light*?

5. Nora spends time writing lessons to her daughter (about lipstick, flirting, responsibility). What did she leave out? What would you want your own daughter to know?

6. What do you think Mariana believes most about motherhood?

7. Ellie wants to, and does, have sex during the course of the book. How is this part of growing up for her? How much does it mean to her?

8. At Nora's darkest moment, she almost loses her sister. What does Mariana's revelation to her about their relationship mean to how the sisters will work together in the future?

9. Do you think Ellie should be tested for the disease her mother has?

10. Beach glass is a central metaphor in *Splinters of Light*. Is there something in your own house that you could consider a similar metaphor?

Courtesy of Bethany Herron, 2014

Rachael Herron received her MFA in English and creative writing from Mills College, and when she's not busy writing, she's a 911 medical/fire dispatcher for a Bay Area fire department. She is the author of *Pack Up the Moon*, the Cypress Hollow romance series, and the memoir *A Life in Stitches*. She is an accomplished knitter and lives in Oakland with her wife, Lala, and their menagerie of cats and dogs.

CONNECT ONLINE

RachaelHerron.com
twitter.com/RachaelHerron
facebook.com/Rachael.Herron.Author

CONNECT VIA MAIL

Rachael loves snail mail.
Feel free to write to her:
3542 Fruitvale Ave: #135,
Oakland, CA 94605